Praise for The Danish Girl

'David Ebershoff's extraordinary debut novel is actually based on a true story . . . beautifully written. It is absolutely engrossing. A seasoned author would have been proud of producing this elegant, assured and intelligent tale; as a first novel, it is astonishing'   *Sunday Express*

'Intriguing and captivating . . . a resonant fable about metamorphosis and the construction of identity. This admirable book deserves to find a wide readership'   *Daily Telegraph*

'[An] affecting and graceful debut . . . The bending of gender in fiction is long established, going back to ancient Greek mythology . . . He conveys an impressive sense of place and period – the Copenhagen, Paris and Dresden of the time are stylishly recreated. He is sensitivie without being sentimental; his prose is clean and elegant. What Ebershoff exudes, above all, is the sense of a writer who is at one with his writing'   *New Statesman*

'Be enchanted by *The Danish Girl* . . . elegant and sensitive writing'   *Elle*

'The book is a sensuous treat, its symbolic visual imagery combining with mesmeric recreations of period and place . . . Einar and his wife are treated with sympathy, and a potentially sensational or bizarre subject is treated with dignity'   *Art Newspaper*

'This is a curiously touching tale, told in a lucid and sensitive style that shows great insight into an extraordinary predicament. David Ebershoff manages to avoid any hit of prurience or pornography. Instead he has written an engrossing story of true love, suffering and sacrifice'   *Sunday Telegraph*

David Ebershoff's debut novel, *The Danish Girl*, won the 2000 Lambda Literary Award for transgender fiction and has been adapted into a major motion picture starring Academy Award-winner Eddie Redmayne. His most recent novel is the #1 bestseller *The 19th Wife*, which was made into a television movie that has aired around the globe. He is also the author of the novel *Pasadena* and the collection of short stories, *The Rose City*. His books have been translated into twenty languages to critical acclaim. Ebershoff has appeared twice on *Out Magazine*'s annual Out 100 list of influential LGBT people. He teaches in the graduate writing program at Columbia University and has worked for many years as an editor at Random House. Originally from California, he lives in New York City.

THE
DANISH GIRL

DAVID EBERSHOFF

WEIDENFELD & NICOLSON

For Mark Nelson

A W&N PAPERBACK

First published in Great Britain in 2000
by Weidenfeld & Nicolson
This paperback edition published in 2015
by Weidenfeld & Nicolson,
an imprint of the Orion Publishing Group,
Carmelite House, 50 Victoria Embankment,
London EC4Y 0DZ

An Hachette UK company

7 9 10 8 6

This edition published by arrangement with Viking,
an imprint of Penguin Publishing Group,
a division of Random House LLC.

Copyright © David Ebershoff 2000

The right of David Ebershoff to be identified as the author
of this work has been asserted by him in accordance
with the Copyright, Designs and Patents Act 1988.

A CIP catalogue record for this book
is available from the British Library.

ISBN 978-1-4746-0157-3

Printed and bound in Great Britain by Clays Ltd, St Ives plc

The Orion Publishing Group's policy is to use papers that
are natural, renewable and recyclable products and
made from wood grown in sustainable forests. The logging
and manufacturing processes are expected to conform to
the environmental regulations of the country of origin.

www.orionbooks.co.uk

Part One

Copenhagen
1925

One

૮ৡৡৡ৴৶

His wife knew first. 'Do me a small favour?' Greta called from the bedroom that first afternoon. 'Just help me with something for a little bit?'

'Of course,' Einar said, his eyes on the canvas. 'Anything at all.'

The day was cool, the chill blowing in from the Baltic. They were in their apartment in the Widow House, Einar, small and not yet thirty-five, painting from memory a winter scene of the Kattegat Sea. The black water was white-capped and cruel, the grave of hundreds of fishermen returning to Copenhagen with their salted catch. The neighbour below was a sailor, a man with a bullet-shaped head who cursed his wife. When Einar painted the grey curl of each wave, he imagined the sailor drowning, a desperate hand raised, his potato-vodka voice still calling his wife a port whore. It was how Einar knew just how dark to mix his paints: grey enough to swallow a man like that, to fold over like batter his sinking growl.

'I'll be out in a minute,' said Greta, younger than her husband and handsome with a wide flat face. 'Then we can start.'

In this way as well Einar was different from his wife. He painted the land and the sea – small rectangles lit by June's angled light, or dimmed by the dull January sun. Greta painted portraits, often to full scale, of mildly important people with pink lips and shine in the grain of their hair. Herr I. Glückstadt, the financier behind the Copenhagen Free Harbour. Christian Dahlgaard, furrier to the King. Ivar Knudsen,

member of the ship-building firm Burmeister and Wain.
Today was to have been Anna Fonsmark, mezzo-soprano from
the Royal Danish Opera. Managing directors and industry
titans commissioned Greta to paint portraits that hung in
offices, above a filing cabinet, or along a corridor nicked by a
worker's trolley.

Greta appeared in the door frame. 'You sure you won't
mind stopping for a bit to help me out?' she said, her hair
pulled back. 'I wouldn't have asked if it weren't important. It's
just that Anna's cancelled again. So would you mind trying on
her stockings?' Greta asked. 'And her shoes?'

The April sun was behind Greta, filtering through the silk
hanging limply in her hand. Through the window, Einar could
see the tower of Rundetårn, like an enormous brick chimney,
and above it the Deutscher Aero-Lloyd puttering out on its
daily return to Berlin.

'Greta?' Einar said. 'What do you mean?' An oily bead of
paint dropped from his brush to his boot. Edvard IV began to
bark, his white head turning from Einar to Greta and back.

'Anna's cancelled again,' Greta said. 'She has an extra
rehearsal of *Carmen*. I need a pair of legs to finish her portrait,
or I'll never get it done. And then I thought to myself, yours
might do.'

Greta moved towards him, the shoes in her other hand
sennep-yellow with pewter buckles. She was wearing her
button-front smock with the patch pockets where she tucked
things she didn't want Einar to see.

'But I can't wear Anna's shoes,' Einar said. Looking at them,
Einar imagined that the shoes might in fact fit his feet, which
were small and arched and padded softly on the heel. His toes
were slender, with a few fine black hairs. He imagined the
wrinkled roll of the stocking gliding over the white bone of his
ankle. Over the small cushion of his calf. Clicking into the
hook of a garter. Einar had to shut his eyes.

The shoes were like the ones they had seen the previous
week in the window of Fonnesbech's department store,
displayed on a mannequin in a midnight-blue dress. Einar and

Greta had stopped to admire the window, which was trimmed with a garland of jonquils. Greta said, 'Pretty, yes?' When he didn't respond, his reflection wide-eyed in the plate glass, Greta had to pull him away from Fonnesbech's window. She tugged him down the street, past the pipe shop, saying, 'Einar, are you all right?'

The front room of the apartment served as their studio. Its ceiling was ribbed with thin beams and vaulted like an upside-down dory. Sea mist had warped the dormer windows, and the floor tilted imperceptibly to the west. In the afternoon, when the sun beat against the Widow House, a faint smell of herring would seep from its walls. In winter the skylights would leak, a cold drizzle bubbling the paint on the wall. Einar and Greta stood their easels beneath the twin skylights, next to the boxes of oil paint ordered from Herr Salathoff in Munich, and the racks of blank canvases. When Einar and Greta weren't painting, they protected everything beneath green tarps the sailor below had abandoned on the landing.

'Why do you want me to wear her shoes?' Einar asked. He sat in the rope-bottom chair that had come from the back shed of his grandmother's farm. Edvard IV jumped into his lap; the dog was trembling from the yelling of the sailor below.

'For my painting of Anna,' Greta said. And then, 'I'd do it for you.' On the point of her cheek was a single shallow chickenpox scar. Her finger was brushing it gently, something she did, Einar knew, when she was anxious.

Greta knelt to unlace Einar's boots. Her hair was long and yellow, more Danish in colour than his; she would push it behind her ears whenever she wanted to get busy on something new. Now it was slipping over her face as she picked at the knot in Einar's laces. She smelled of orange oil, which her mother shipped over once a year in a case of brown bottles labelled PURE PASADENA EXTRACT. Her mother thought Greta was baking tea cakes with the oil, but instead Greta used it to dab behind her ears.

Greta began to wash Einar's feet in the basin. She was gentle but efficient, quickly pulling the sea sponge between his toes.

Einar rolled up his trousers even further. His calves looked, he suddenly thought, shapely. He delicately pointed his foot, and Edvard IV moved to lick the water from his little toe, the one that was hammer-headed and born without a nail.

'We'll keep this our secret, Greta?' Einar whispered. 'You won't tell anyone, will you?' He was both frightened and excited, and the child's fist of his heart was beating in his throat.

'Who would I tell?'

'Anna.'

'Anna doesn't need to know,' Greta said. Even so, Anna was an opera singer, Einar thought. She was used to men dressing in women's clothes. And women in men's, the *Hosenrolle*. It was the oldest deceit in the world. And on the opera stage it meant nothing at all – nothing but confusion. A confusion that was always resolved in the final act.

'Nobody needs to know anything,' Greta said, and Einar, who felt as if a white stage light were on him, began to relax and work the stocking up his calf.

'You're putting it on backwards,' Greta said, righting the seam. 'Pull gently.'

The second stocking ripped. 'Do you have another?' Einar asked.

Greta's face froze, as if she were just realizing something; then she went to a drawer in the pickled-ash wardrobe. The wardrobe had a closet on top with an oval mirror in its door, and three drawers with brass-hoop handles; the top one Greta locked with a little key.

'These are heavier,' Greta said, handing Einar a second pair. Folded neatly into a square, the stockings looked to Einar like a patch of flesh – a patch of Greta's skin, brown from a summer holiday in Menton. 'Please be careful,' she said. 'I was going to wear them tomorrow.'

The parting in Greta's hair revealed a strip of silvery-white flesh, and Einar began to wonder what she was thinking beneath it. With her eyes slanted up and her mouth pinched, she seemed intent on something. Einar felt incapable of asking;

he nearly felt bound, with an old paint rag tied across his mouth. And so he wondered about his wife silently, with a touch of resentment ripening beneath his face, which was pale and smooth and quite like the skin of a white peach. 'Aren't you a pretty man,' she had said, years ago, when they were first alone.

Greta must have noticed his discomfort, because she reached out and held Einar's cheeks and said, 'It means nothing.' And then, 'When will you stop worrying about what other people think?'

Einar loved it when Greta made such declarations – the way she'd swat her hands through the air and claim her beliefs as the faith of the rest of the world. He thought it her most American trait, that and her taste for silver jewellery.

'It's a good thing you don't have much hair on your legs,' Greta said, as if noticing it for the first time. She was mixing her oil paints in the little ceramic Knabstrup bowls. Greta had finished the upper half of Anna's body, which years of digesting buttered salmon had buried in a fine layer of fat. Einar was impressed with the way Greta had painted Anna's hands holding a bouquet of day lilies. The fingers were carefully rendered, the knuckles puckered, the nails clear but opaque. The lilies were a pretty moon-white, stained with rusty pollen. Greta was an inconsistent painter, but Einar never told her so. Instead, he praised as much as he could, perhaps too much. But he helped her wherever possible, and would try to teach her techniques he thought she didn't know, especially about light and distance. If Greta ever found the right subject, Einar had no doubt, she would become a fine painter. Outside the Widow House a cloud shifted, and sunlight fell on the half-portrait of Anna.

The model's platform Greta used was a lacquer trunk bought from the Cantonese laundress who would make a pick-up every other day, announcing herself not with a call from the street but with the *ping!* of the gold cymbals strapped to her fingers.

Standing on the trunk, Einar began to feel dizzy and warm.

He looked down at his shins, the silk smooth except for a few hairs bursting through like the tiny hard fuzz on a bean. The yellow shoes looked too dainty to support him, but his feet felt natural arched up, as if he was stretching a long-unused muscle. Something began to run through Einar's head, and it made him think of a fox chasing a fieldmouse: the thin red nose of the fox digging for the mouse through the folds of a pulse field.

'Stand still,' Greta said. Einar looked out of the window and saw the fluted dome of the Royal Theatre, where he sometimes painted sets for the opera company. Right now, inside, Anna was rehearsing *Carmen*, her soft arms raised defiantly in front of the backdrop he'd painted of the Seville bullring. Sometimes when Einar was at the theatre painting, Anna's voice would rise in the hall like a chute of copper. It would make him tremble so much that his brush would smudge the backdrop, and he would rub his fists against his eyes. Anna's wasn't a beautiful voice − rough-edged and sorrowful, a bit used, somehow male and female at once. Yet it had more vibrancy than most Danish voices, which were often thin and white and too pretty to trigger a shiver. Anna's voice had the heat of the south; it warmed Einar, as if her throat were red with coals. He would climb down from his ladder backstage and move to the theatre's wings: he'd watch Anna, in her white lamb's-wool tunic, open her square mouth as she rehearsed with Conductor Dyvik. She would lean forward when she sang; Anna always said there was a musical gravity pulling her chin towards the orchestra pit. 'I think of a thin silver chain connected to the tip of the conductor's baton and fastened right here,' she would say, pointing to the mole that sat on her chin like a crumb. 'Without that little chain, I almost feel I wouldn't know what to do. I wouldn't know how to be me.'

When Greta painted, she'd pull her hair back with a tortoiseshell comb; it made her face look larger, as if Einar were looking at it through a bowl of water. Greta was probably the tallest woman he'd ever known, her head high enough to glance over the half-lace curtains ground-floor

residents hung in their street windows. Next to her Einar felt
small, as if he were her son, looking up beyond her chin to her
eyes, reaching for a hanging hand. Her patch-pocket smock
was a special order from the white-bunned seamstress around
the corner, who measured Greta's chest and arms with a
yellow tape and with admiration and disbelief that such a large,
healthy woman wasn't a Dane.

Greta painted with a flexible concentration that Einar
admired. She was able to dab at the gleam in a left eye and then
answer the door and accept the delivery from the Busk Milk
Supply Company and return effortlessly to the slightly duller
glare in the right. She'd sing what she called campfire songs
while she painted. She'd tell the person she was painting about
her girlhood in California, where peacocks nested in her
father's orange groves; she'd tell her female subjects – as Einar
once overheard upon returning to the apartment's door at the
top of the dark stairs – about their longer and longer intervals
between intimacy: 'He takes it so very personally. But I never
blame him,' she'd say, and Einar would imagine her pushing
her hair behind her ears.

'They're drooping,' Greta said, pointing her paintbrush at
his stockings. 'Pull them up.'

'Is this really necessary?'

The sailor below slammed a door, and then it was silent
except for his giggling wife.

'Oh, Einar,' Greta said. 'Will you ever relax?' Her smile
sank and disappeared into her face. Edvard IV trotted into the
bedroom, and began to dig through the bedclothes; then came
a fed baby's sigh. He was an old dog, from the farm in Jutland,
born in a bog; his mother and the rest of the litter had
drowned in the damp peat.

The apartment was in the attic of a building the government
opened in the previous century for the widows of fishermen. It
had windows facing north, south and west and, unlike most of
the townhouses in Copenhagen, could give Einar and Greta
enough room and light to paint. They had almost moved into
one of the burgher houses in Christianshavn on the other side

of the Inderhavnn, where artists were settling in with the
prostitutes and the gambling drunks, alongside the cement-
mixing firms and the importers. Greta said she could live
anywhere, that nothing was too seedy for her; but Einar, who
had slept under a thatch roof for the first fifteen years of his life,
decided against it, and found the space in the Widow House.

The façade was painted red and the house sat one block
from Nyhavns Kanal. The dormer windows stuck out of the
steep, clay-tile roof, which was black with moss, and the
skylights were cut high in the pitch. The other buildings on
the street were whitewashed, with eight-panelled doors
painted the colour of kelp. Across the way lived a doctor
named Møller who received emergency calls from women
giving birth in the night. But few motor cars sputtered down
the street, which dead-ended at the Inderhavnen, making it
quiet enough to hear the echo of a shy girl's cry.

'I need to get back to my own work,' Einar finally said, tired
of standing in the shoes, the pewter buckles pressing sharply.

'Does that mean you don't want to try on her dress?'

When she said the word 'dress' his stomach filled with heat,
followed by a clot of shame rising in his chest. 'No, I don't
think so,' Einar said.

'Not even for a few minutes?' she asked. 'I need to paint the
hem against her knees.' Greta was sitting on the rope-bottom
chair beside him, stroking Einar's calf through the silk. Her
hand was hypnotic, its touch telling him to close his eyes. He
could hear nothing but the little rough scratch of her fingernail
against the silk.

But then Greta stopped. 'No, I'm sorry,' she said. 'I
shouldn't have asked.'

Now Einar saw that the door to the pickled-ash wardrobe
was open, and hanging inside was Anna's dress. It was white,
with drop beads along the knee-hem and the cuff. A window
was cracked, and the dress was swaying gently on the hanger.
There was something about the dress – about the dull sheen of
its silk, about the bib of lace in the bodice, about the hook-

buttons on the cuffs, unlatched and split apart like little mouths
– that made Einar want to touch it.

'Do you like it?' Greta asked.

He thought about saying no, but that would have been a lie.
He liked the dress, and he could nearly feel the flesh beneath
his skin ripening.

'Then just slip it on for a few minutes.' Greta brought it to
Einar and held it to his chest.

'Greta,' he said, 'What if I—'

'Just take off your shirt,' she said.

And he did.

'What if I—'

'Just close your eyes,' she said.

And he did.

Even with his eyes closed, standing shirtless in front of his
wife felt obscene. It felt as if she'd caught him doing something
he had promised he would avoid – not like adultery, but more
like resuming a bad habit he'd given his word he would quit,
like drinking aquavit in the canal bars of Christianshavn or
eating *frikadeller* in bed or shuffling through the deck of suede-
backed girlie cards he once bought on a lonely afternoon.

'And your trousers,' Greta said. Her hand reached out, and
she politely turned her head. The bedroom window was open,
and the brisk fishy air was pimpling his skin.

Einar quickly pulled the dress over his head, adjusting the
lap. He was sweating in the pits of his arms, in the small of his
back. The heat was making him wish he could close his eyes
and return to the days when he was a boy and what dangled
between his legs was as small and useless as a white radish.

Greta only said, 'Good.' Then she lifted her brush to the
canvas. Her blue eyes narrowed, as if examining something on
the point of her nose.

A strange watery feeling was filling Einar as he stood on the
lacquer trunk, the sunlight moving across him, the scent of
herring in the air. The dress was loose everywhere except in
the sleeves, and he felt warm and submerged, as if dipping into

a summer sea. The fox was chasing the mouse, and there was a distant voice in his head: the soft cry of a scared little girl.

It became difficult for Einar to keep his eyes open, to continue watching Greta's fast, fish-like movements as her hand darted at the canvas, then pulled away, her silver bracelets and rings turning like a school of chub. It became difficult for him to continue thinking about Anna singing over at the Royal Theatre, her chin leaning towards the conductor's baton. Einar could concentrate only on the silk dressing his skin, as if it were a bandage. Yes, that was how it felt the first time: the silk was so fine and airy that it felt like a gauze – a balm-soaked gauze lying delicately on healing skin. Even the embarrassment of standing before his wife began to no longer matter, for she was busy painting with a foreign intensity in her face. Einar was beginning to enter a shadowy world of dreams where Anna's dress could belong to anyone, even to him.

And just as his eyelids were becoming heavy and the studio was beginning to dim, just as he sighed and let his shoulders fall, and Edvard IV was snoring in the bedroom, just at this moment Anna's coppery voice sang out, 'Take a look at Einar!'

His eyes opened. Greta and Anna were pointing, their faces bright, their lips peeled apart. Edvard IV began to bark in front of Einar. And Einar Wegener couldn't move.

Greta took from Anna her bouquet of day lilies, a gift from a stage-door fan, and pressed them into Einar's arms. With his head lifted like a little trumpet player, Edvard IV began to run protective circles around Einar. While the two women laughed some more, Einar's eyes began to roll back into his head, filling with tears. He was stung by their laughter, along with the perfume of the white lilies, whose rusty pistils were leaving dusty prints in the lap of the dress, against the garish lump in his groin, on the stockings, all over his open wet hands.

'You're a whore,' the sailor below called tenderly. 'You're one hell of a beautiful whore.'

From downstairs, the silence implied a forgiving kiss. Then there was even louder laughter from Greta and Anna, and just as Einar was about to beg them to leave the studio, to let him change out of the dress in peace, Greta said, her voice soft and careful and unfamiliar, 'Why don't we call you Lili?'

Greta Wegener was twenty-nine, a painter. She was a Californian. She was a Waud, her grandfather, Apsley Haven Waud, rich from land grants, her father, Apsley Jr, richer from orange groves. Before she moved to Denmark when she was ten, the furthest she had ever ventured from Pasadena was San Francisco, where one day she was playing roller hoop in front of her Aunt Lizzie's house on Nob Hill when she accidentally nudged her twin brother into the path of a carriage. Carlisle survived, a long shiny dent permanently sunk into his shin; some people said he was never the same. When she was older, Greta would say that Carlisle had never had what she called a western spine. 'Some Wauds are born with it,' she observed when she was ten and tall and practising Danish phrases on the teak deck on the voyage over, 'and some are not.' The Danes certainly didn't have western spines; and yet why should they? So Greta forgave them – at least most of the time. She especially forgave Einar, her first art professor and her second husband. By the spring of 1925 they had been married for more than six years: on certain mornings it felt to Greta like six weeks; on others, six well-lived lives.

Einar and Greta first met at the Royal Academy of Fine Arts on 1 September 1914, only weeks after the Kaiser rumbled across the hillocks of Luxembourg and Belgium. Greta was seventeen. Einar was in his twenties, already a lecturer in painting, already shy and easily embarrassed around teenagers, a bachelor. Even then she was broad-shouldered, with the posture of an early childhood spent on horseback. She let her hair grow to the small of her back, which seemed a bit provocative on Copenhagen's few remaining gas-flickering streets. The Danes excused her because she was from California, a place nearly none of them had seen but where they imagined people like Greta lived in open houses shaded by date palms, where stones of gold pushed their way through the black soil in the garden.

One day Greta plucked her eyebrows, and they never grew back, which she saw as more of a convenience than anything else. Each morning she drew them in place with the waxy pencils she bought in the windowless room on the third floor of Magasin du Nord, where women with *situations de beauté* discreetly shopped. Greta had an irrepressible habit of picking at the pores in her nose anytime she opened a book, and this had already left a few pencil-tip scars in her skin, about which she remained concerned. She thought of herself as the tallest girl in Copenhagen, which probably wasn't true, what with Grethe Janssen, a lithe beauty and also the Mayor's mistress, dashing in and out of the shops in the lobby of the Hôtel d'Angleterre in crystal-beaded gowns, even in the middle of the day.

In any case, Greta also thought of herself as the least likely to marry. When a young man – a pan-faced Dane of a declining aristocratic clan or the son of an American steel magnate touring Europe for the year – asked her to the ballet or for a sail through the canals of Christianshavn, her first thought was always: You won't catch me. All she wanted to be was a bluestocking: a perpetually young woman who was free to paint daily in the light of the window and whose only social company occurred at midnight when a group of eight would meet in Sebastian's, her favourite pub, for two quick snifters of cherry-flavoured Peter Heering before the long-faced police would turn up at one o'clock to shut down the house for the night.

But even Greta knew that not only was this silly, it was also impossible. Why, young Miss Greta Waud would never be permitted to live like that at all.

When she was a little girl, she used to write over and over in her penmanship notebook, 'Greta Greta Greta,' deliberately leaving off the 'Waud' as if to test what it would be like to be plain old Greta – something no one ever called her. She didn't want anyone to know who her family was. Even as an adolescent, she never wanted to coast on any sort of connections. She despised anyone who relied excessively on antecedents. What was the point?

She had come to Denmark as a girl when her father, a long-armed man with a lamb-chop beard, took his post at the embassy. 'Why would you want to do that?' Greta had said when he first told her of his new assignment. 'Now, Greta,' her mother replied, 'be nice. He's your father.' What Greta was forgetting was that his mother, her very own grandmother, Gerda Carlsen, for whom Greta had been named, was a Dane, with blond hair the colour of beechwood. Raised on Bornholm, Gerda was known for the blood-red poppies she wore behind her ears – and for being the first girl in the family to leave the Baltic island, sailing not for Copenhagen, like most curious youngsters intent on leaving their family behind, but for southern California, which in those days was like telling your family you were emigrating to the moon. A few years of horsework on the right ranch brought her to the attention of Apsley Waud Sr, and soon enough the tall girl from Bornholm who wore her hair to her hips and pinned with poppies was a California matriarch. When Greta's father told her he was taking the family back to Denmark, it was a bit insensitive of her – even Greta had to admit – to fail to make the connection, to not realize that this was her father's way of making restitution to his mother, to blue-eyed Gerda Carlsen Waud, who lost her life when her son, Apsley Jr, then just a young man, led her to the lip of Pasadena's Arroyo Seco to take her photograph in front of the vista and then watched in horror as the ant-gnawed soil crumbled away and flung his mother into the canyon below, down into the deadly Y-branch of a knotty sycamore.

At the Royal Academy in the autumn of 1914, Greta

assumed that most people, particularly the administrators, gossiped about two things: the war and her. She always caused a stir, no matter where she went, what with her train of blond hair like a wake behind her. Especially in southern California. Why, it was only last year, when she returned to Pasadena for a summer of tennis and riding lessons, when one day the boy who drove the butcher wagon caught her eye. His hair was black and curly and his hot hand pulled her up to the front plank-seat and together they rode down to Wilshire Boulevard and back. She watched him manipulate the iron tongs as he unloaded the rib roasts and the racks of lamb at the houses in Hancock Park. On the ride home, not once did the boy try to kiss her, which disappointed Greta, who for the first time had doubts about the length of her yellow hair. At the end of the ride, the boy said only, 'So long.' And so Greta shrugged and went to her room. But the next morning, at the breakfast table, her mother, who was thin in the lip, said, 'Greta, my dear. Would you please explain this?' Her mother unfolded a piece of stationery from the *American Weekly*. On it was a cryptic note that simply said, 'Does young Miss Greta Waud plan a career in butchery?' For weeks the threat of a society-page exposure shadowed the mansion. Each morning the fingers-in-mouth whistle of the newspaper boy caused the household to freeze in its step. The story never ran, but of course the gossip eventually leaked. For two days the telephone in the upstairs hall rang and rang and rang. Greta's father could no longer take his lunch at the California Club downtown, and her mother had a devil of a time securing a second source of meat. Soon her parents cancelled the summer in California, and Greta returned to Copenhagen in time for the August aurora borealis and the fireworks bursting over Tivoli.

That September at the end of her youth, when war could be heard in the thunderclouds, Greta enrolled at the Royal Academy. On the first day of classes, it surprised Greta when Einar, standing in front of a blackboard dusty with the ghost of a previous lesson, asked her, 'And Miss? Your name?'

When Greta answered the question, Einar — or Professor

Wegener, as she thought of him then – marked his class log
and moved on. His eyes, which were as brown and wide as a
doll's, returned to her and then jumped away. Judging by his
skittishness, Greta began to think he'd never met an American
in his life. She flipped the panel of her hair over her shoulder,
as if waving a flag.

Then, early in the school year, someone must have
whispered to Einar about her father and the embassy and
maybe even the butcher-wagon story – yes, gossip hopped the
Atlantic, even then – because Einar became even more
awkward around her. It disappointed her that he was proving
to be one of those men who found it impossible to be
comfortable around a rich girl. This nearly burned her up
alive, because she'd never asked to be rich; not that she minded
it all the time, but even so. Einar was unable to recommend
which paintings to view in Kunstudstillingen, and incapable of
describing the best route to the art supply shop near
Kommunehospitalet. She invited him to a reception at the
American embassy for a shipbuilder visiting from Connecticut,
but he refused. He declined her request for an escort to the
opera. He would hardly look at her when they spoke. But she
looked at him, both when they met and from far away,
through a window as he crossed the academy's courtyard, his
steps short and fast. He was small in the chest, with a round
face, skin pale and eyes so dark that Greta had no idea what lay
behind them. Simply by speaking to him, Greta could force a
flush through Einar's face from throat to temple. He was
childlike, and this fascinated Greta, in part because she had
always been so overgrown and outspoken that people had
treated her, even when she was little, more or less like an adult.
She once asked him, 'Are you married, Professor?' and this
caused his eyelids to flutter uncontrollably. His lips pushed
together as he attempted to say the seemingly unfamiliar word
'No.'

The other students whispered about Professor Wegener.
'From a family of gnomes,' one girl said. 'Was blind until he
was fifteen,' said another girl. 'Born in a bog,' said a boy who

was trying to get Greta's attention. The boy painted pictures of Greek statues, and Greta couldn't think of anything more boring, or anyone. When he asked to take her to ride the Ferris wheel in Tivoli she simply rolled her eyes. 'Well, Professor Wegener isn't going to take you, if that's what you're waiting for,' the boy replied, kicking his boot against the trunk of an elm.

At home, her mother, ever mindful of the butcher-wagon incident, studied Greta cautiously whenever she returned for the evening, the light of the fireplace revealing nothing in Greta's eyes. One evening her mother said, 'Greta, my dear, if you don't arrange an escort for your birthday party, then I'm going to have to ask someone for you.' She was needlepointing at the parlour's hearth, and Greta could hear Carlisle upstairs in his room bouncing a tennis ball. 'I'm sure Countess von der Recke's son would like to go with you,' Mrs Waud was saying. 'Of course he doesn't dance, but he's a handsome enough boy, as long as you ignore that awful hump, wouldn't you agree? Greta?' Greta's mother lifted her pointy face. The fire in the hearth was weak and red, and the *tap-tap-tap* of Carlisle's ball filled the room, causing the chandelier to tremble. 'When will he stop that?' Mrs Waud snapped. 'Silly tennis ball.' She folded up her needlepoint and stood, her body taking a rigid stance, as if she were an accusatory arrow pointed in the direction of Carlisle's room. 'I suppose there's always Carlisle,' she said with a sigh. And then, as if the flames in the fireplace had suddenly leaped higher and brightened the parlour, Mrs Waud said, 'Well, yes, that's right. There's always Carlisle. Why not go with Carlisle? He hasn't found a girl to take, either. You two could go together, the birthday couple.' But Greta, who remained in the parlour's door frame, protested with her hands and said, 'Carlisle? I can't go with Carlisle! That wouldn't be any fun. Besides, I'm quite capable of finding my own escort.' Her mother's eyebrows, which were grey as pigeon feathers, arched up. She said, 'Oh really? Who?'

Greta could feel her nails pressing into the palms of her

hands as she said, 'You just wait and see. I'll bring who I want. I'm not going to go with my own brother.' She was playing with her hair, and staring at her mother, and upstairs was the *tap-tap-tap* of the tennis ball. 'Just wait and see,' Greta said. 'After all, I'm going to be eighteen.'

The next week Greta caught Einar on the stairs in the Royal Academy. He was holding the white balustrade when she placed her hand on his wrist and said, 'May I talk to you?'

It was late and no one else was around and the stairwell was quiet. Professor Wegener was wearing a brown suit with a white collar tinged brown. He was carrying a small blank canvas the size of a book. 'We're having a supper to celebrate my birthday,' Greta said. 'I'm going to be eighteen. My twin brother and me.' And then, 'I was wondering if you'd want to come along?'

Einar looked as if he'd eaten something rotten, the colour seeping from his face. 'Miss, please,' he finally said. 'Maybe you ought to enrol in another seminar? It might be best.' He touched his throat, as if something delicate and cherished were dangling there.

It was then that Greta realized that Professor Wegener was in some ways even younger than she. His face was a boy's, with a small mouth and perpetually red ears. His pale brown hair was hanging impishly over his forehead. Just then something told Greta to cup Einar's face in her hands. He jumped slightly as her fingers fell on his cheeks, but then he was still. She held her professor's narrow head, his warm temples between her palms. Greta continued to hold Einar, and he let her. Then she kissed him, the small canvas tucked between them. It was then that Greta knew Einar Wegener was not only the man she wanted to escort her to her eighteenth birthday party but also the man she would marry. 'Aren't you a pretty man,' she said.

'May I go?' Einar asked.

'You mean to the party?'

'Well, that's not—'

'Of course you can go to the party. That's why I asked you.'

Then, to both their surprise, Einar turned his face to Greta's for a second kiss.

But before the party, before Greta turned eighteen, Greta's father decided Europe was no longer safe. Not long after Germany struck out for France, Greta's father sent his family home from Denmark. 'If the Kaiser will roll through Belgium, what's to stop him from detouring up here?' he asked at the blond-wood table in the dining room. 'Good point,' Greta's mother replied, floating around the room with bundles of shipping straw. Greta, who felt like a fleeing refugee, boarded the *Princess Dagmar* with nothing in her pocket but a short note from Einar that said only: 'Please forget me. It's probably for the best.'

Now, more than ten years later, in the damp spring of 1925, Greta felt as if she were holding a secret about her husband. The first few weeks after the session with Anna's dress, Greta and Einar said nothing about it. They stayed busy at their easels, carefully stepping out of each other's way. The portrait of Anna was complete, and now Greta was looking for another commission. On one or two occasions, at dinner or while they were both reading late at night, something would make Greta think of the dress, and she would nearly call him Lili. But she managed to stop herself. Only once did she respond to a question of his by saying, 'What was that, Lili?' Immediately she apologized. They both laughed and she kissed his forehead. She didn't think of it again, and it was as if Lili were nothing more than a character in a play they had seen at the Folketeatret.

Then, one evening, Greta was reading about the Social Liberals in *Politiken*, the lamp shedding a cone of light around her chair. Einar moved towards her and sat at her feet, placing his head in her lap. Its warm heaviness rested against her thighs as she read the newspaper. She stroked his hair, her hand lifting every minute or so to turn the page. When she finished, she folded it up to begin the crossword puzzle, pulling a pencil from the patch pocket of her smock.

'I've been thinking about her,' Einar said.

'Who's that?'

'Little Lili.'

'Then why don't we see her again?' Greta said, her face barely lifting from the puzzle, her finger, smudged with newsprint, brushing at the chickenpox scar.

Greta could say things without really meaning them, her urge to contradict, to be radical, perpetually bubbling up inside. Throughout their marriage she had made equally absurd proposals: Why don't we move back to Pasadena to harvest oranges? Why don't we start a little clinic in our apartment for the prostitutes of Istedgade? Why don't we move somewhere neutral, like Nevada, where no one will ever know who we are? Things are said in the great cave of wedlock, and thankfully most just hover, small and black and harmlessly upside-down like a sleeping bat. At least that's how Greta thought of it; what Einar thought, she couldn't say.

She once tried to paint a sleeping bat – the black double membrane of skin draped over the mouse body – but she failed. She lacked the technical skill for the elongated fingers and the small, clawed thumb; for the grey translucence in the stretched wings. She had not trained to paint the haunch of animals. Over the years Einar, who occasionally painted a sow or a sparrow or even Edvard IV into his landscapes, had promised he would teach her. But whenever they sat down to a lesson, something would happen: a cable would arrive from California, the laundress would *ping!* her finger cymbals from the street, the telephone would ring with a call from one of Einar's patrons, who were often silver-haired and titled and lived behind narrow green shutters that remained latched with a little hook.

A few days later, Greta was returning to the Widow House from a meeting with a gallery owner who would eventually reject her paintings. The dealer, a handsome man with a freckle like a chocolate stain on his throat, hadn't actually turned Greta away; but the way he tapped his fingers against his chin told Greta he wasn't impressed. 'All portraits?' he had

asked. The man knew, as did all of Copenhagen, that she was
married to Einar Wegener. Greta felt because of this that the
dealer expected quaint landscapes from her. 'Do you ever
think your pictures are perhaps too' – he struggled for the right
word – 'rapturous?' This just about boiled Greta up, and she
felt the heat catching inside her dress, the one with the tuxedo
lapels. Too rapturous? How could anything be too rapturous?
She snatched her portfolio from the dealer's hand and turned
on her heel. She was still warm and damp in the face by the
time she arrived at the top of the stairs of the Widow House.

When she opened the door, she found a girl sitting in the
rope-bottom chair, and at first Greta couldn't think who she
was. The girl was facing the window, a book in her hands and
Edvard IV in her lap. She was wearing a blue dress with a
detachable white collar, and lying across the bone at the top of
her spine was one of Greta's gold chains. The girl – did Greta
know her? – smelled of mint and milk.

The sailor below was yelling at his wife, and each time the
word 'whore' came through the floorboards, the girl's neck
would blush. And then it would fade. '*Luder*,' the man yelled
over and over, and so rose and fell the flush in the girl's throat.

'Lili?' Greta finally said.

'It's a wonderful book.' Lili lifted the history of California
that Greta's father had shipped over in a crate with tins of
sugared lemons, the supply of Pure Pasadena Extract, and a
gunnysack of eucalyptus bells for steaming her face.

'I don't want to disturb you,' Greta said.

Lili made a feathery murmur. Edvard IV growled lazily, his
ears lifting. The door to the apartment was still open, and
Greta hadn't removed her coat. Lili returned to her book, and
Greta looked at Lili's pale neck rising out of the petals of her
collar. Greta wasn't sure what her husband wanted her to do
next. She told herself that this was important to Einar, that she
should follow his lead – not a natural impulse for Greta. She
stood in the entry of the apartment, one hand behind her
holding the knob of the door, while Lili sat quietly in the
chair, in a pane of sunlight. She ignored Greta, who was

hoping Lili would rise and take Greta's hands in hers. But that
didn't happen, and eventually Greta realized she should leave
Lili alone, and so she closed the door to the apartment behind
her and headed down the dark stairs and into the street, where
she met the Cantonese laundress and sent her away.

Later, when Greta returned to the Widow House, Einar was
painting. He was wearing his checked-tweed trousers and
waistcoat, his shirtsleeves rolled to the elbow. His head looked
small in his collar and above the lumpy knot of his tie. His face
was full and pink in the cheek, his little pouty mouth sucking
on the end of his filbert brush. 'It's coming along,' he said
cheerfully. 'I finally mixed the right colours for the snow on
the heath. Have a look?'

Einar painted scenes so small you could balance the canvases
in your hands. This particular painting was dark, a bog in a
winter dusk; a thin line of dingy snow was the only distinction
between the spongy soil and the sky. 'It's the bog in
Bluetooth?' Greta said. Recently she had tired of Einar's
landscapes. She never understood how he could paint them
over and over. He would finish off this heath tonight and
begin another in the morning.

On the table was a loaf of rye bread. Einar had done the
shopping, which wasn't like him. There was also a tub of
shrimp on ice, and a dish of shredded beef. And a bowl of
pickled pearl onions, which reminded Greta of the beads she
and Carlisle had strung when they were little and he was still
too lame to play outside. 'Was Lili here?' She felt the need to
mention it, for Greta knew that Einar would leave it unsaid.

'For an hour. Maybe less. Can't you smell her? Her
perfume?' He was rinsing his brushes in a jar, the water a pale
white like the thin milk Greta had had to buy when she first
returned to Denmark after the war.

Greta didn't know what to say; she didn't know what her
husband wanted her to say. 'Is she coming back?'

'Only if you want her to,' Einar said, his back to her.

His shoulders were no wider than a boy's. So slight a man
was he that Greta sometimes felt she could wrap her arms

twice around him. She watched his right shoulder shake as he
rinsed the brushes, and something in her told her to stand
behind him and take hold of his arms, to whisper to him to
stand still. All she wanted to do was to allow him his desires,
but at the same time she had the irrepressible urge to hold him
in her arms and tell him what to do about Lili. And there they
were, in the apartment in the attic of the Widow House, with
dusk filling the windows, and Greta holding Einar tightly, his
arms stiff at his side. Eventually she said – but only as it
occurred to her – 'It's up to Lili. It's whatever she wants to do.'

In June the city was throwing the Artists Ball at Rådhuset. For
a week Greta kept the invitation in her pocket, wondering
what to do about it. Einar had recently said he didn't want to
go to any more balls. But Greta had another idea; she had
come to see in Einar's eyes a longing he wasn't prepared to
admit.

One night at the theatre, she gently asked, 'Would you like
to go as Lili?' She asked because she guessed it was what Einar
wanted. He would never confess such a desire; he rarely
confessed anything to her, unless she prodded, in which case
his true feelings would pour out, and she would listen
patiently, sinking her chin into her fist.

They were at the Royal Theatre, up in the gallery. The red
velvet on the armrests was worn bald, and over the proscenium
was inscribed the legend EJ BLOT TIL LYST. The black oak floors
had been waxed that afternoon, and a sweet medicinal odour
hung in the air, making Greta think of the smell of the
apartment after Einar had cleaned and mopped.

Einar's hands were trembling, his throat turning pink. Greta
and Einar were nearly as high up as the electric chandelier,
with its great smoked-glass balls. The light was revealing the
down on Einar's cheek just beneath his ears, where most men
wore sideburns. His beard was so light that he shaved just once
a week; there were so few whiskers on his upper lip that Greta
could count them if she liked. In his cheek there was a colour,

like a tea rose, which Greta sometimes envied out of the corner of her eye.

The orchestra was tuning up, preparing for its long descent into *Tristan und Isolde*. The couple next to Einar and Greta were discreetly removing their evening slippers. 'I thought we said we weren't going to the ball this year,' Einar finally said.

'We don't have to go. I just thought—'

The lights dimmed, and the conductor made his way to the head of the pit. For the next five hours Einar sat rigid, his legs pressed together, his programme tight in his fist. Greta knew he was thinking of Lili, as if she were a younger sister away for a very long time but now due home. Tonight Anna was singing Brangäne, Isolde's maidservant. Her voice made Greta think of coals in a stove, and although it wasn't pretty like a soprano's, it was warm at the edges and correct; how else should a maidservant sound? 'Some of the most interesting women I know aren't especially beautiful,' she would later comment to Einar, when they were in bed, when Greta's hand was beneath the heat of his hip, when she was on the steep cliff of sleep and she couldn't properly think of where she was, Copenhagen or California.

The next day, when Greta returned from a meeting with another gallery owner, a man who was too mousy and insignificant even to pique Greta with his rejection, she went to kiss Einar. There, on his cheek and in his hair, was the ghost of Lili, the lingering scent of mint and milk.

'Was Lili here again?'

'The whole afternoon.'

'What did she do?'

'She went over to Fonnesbech's and bought herself a few things.'

'All alone?' Greta said.

Einar nodded. He had finished painting for the day and was in the walnut-armed reading chair, *Politiken* spread in his hands and Edvard IV curled at his feet. 'She said to tell you she wants to go to the ball.'

Greta didn't say anything. She felt as if someone were

explaining the rules of a new parlour game: she was listening and nodding but actually thinking to herself, I hope I understand this better once the game begins.

'You want her to go, don't you?' Einar asked. 'It's OK with you if she goes instead of me?'

Greta, who was twisting the tips of her hair into a knot that would later snarl, said, 'I don't mind at all.'

At night Greta would lie in bed, her arm over Einar's chest. When they married, Einar's grandmother had given them a beechwood sleigh bed. It was a bit small, like everyone in the Wegener family except Einar's father. Over the years Greta grew used to sleeping at a diagonal, her legs stacked across Einar's. Sometimes, when she doubted this life she had created for herself in Denmark, she would feel as if she were a little girl, and Einar, with his china-doll face and his pretty feet, her most beloved toy. When he slept, his lips would pout and glisten. His hair would hang like a wreath around his face. Greta couldn't count the nights she had stayed up watching his long lashes fluttering while he was dreaming.

Deep in the night their bedroom was silent except for the horn of the ferry leaving for Bornholm, the Baltic island where her grandmother had first come from. More and more, Greta would lie awake thinking about Lili, about her rural face with the tremblingly bold upper lip and her eyes so brown and watery that Greta couldn't tell whether or not they were on the verge of tears. About Lili's fleshy little nose, which somehow made her look like a girl still growing into a woman's body.

Lili turned out to be even shyer than Einar. Or at least at first. Her head would dip when she spoke, and sometimes she would become too nervous to say anything at all. When asked a question as simple as 'Did you hear about the terrible fire on the Royal Greenland Trading Company's docks?' she would stare at Greta or Anna and then turn away. Lili preferred to write notes and prop them around the apartment, leaving postcards bought from the blind woman outside Tivoli's iron gates on the pickled-ash wardrobe or on the little ledge of Greta's easel.

But I won't know anyone at the ball. Do you really think I should go?

Is it fair to leave Einar behind? Won't he mind?

And once:

I don't think I'm pretty enough. Please advise.

Greta returned the notes, standing them against a bowl of pears just before leaving the apartment:

It's too late. I've already told everyone you're coming. Please don't worry, everyone thinks Lili is Einar's cousin from Bluetooth. A few have asked if you would need an escort, but I said it wasn't necessary. You don't mind, do you? I didn't think you were — is this the right word? — ready.

In the evenings Einar and Greta would dine with friends at their favourite café along Nyhavns Kanal. Sometimes he'd become a little drunk on aquavit and boast childishly of the success of one of his exhibitions. 'All the paintings sold!' he'd say, reminding Greta of Carlisle, who would endlessly boast of a good grade in geometry, or a handsome new friend.

But Einar's talk would embarrass Greta, who tried not to listen whenever money was discussed; after all, what was there to say? Couldn't they pretend it didn't matter to either of them? She would glare at Einar across the table, salmon bones bare and oily on the platter. She'd never told Einar about the trust her father had sent her off to Denmark with, to say nothing of the income wired into an account at Landmands-banken at the end of each orange season — not out of selfishness, but because she was too concerned that all that money would transform her into someone else, someone whose company she herself wouldn't enjoy. One regrettable day she bought the whole apartment building, the Widow House, but she could never bring herself to tell Einar, who each month delivered the rent cheque to a clerk at Land-mandsbanken with a bit of a grudge in his step. Even Greta knew this had been a mistake, but how could she fix it now?

When Einar became excited he'd knock his fists against the table, his hair falling around his face; the collar of his shirt would split open, revealing his smooth pink chest. He was without any fat on his body, except for his soft breasts, which were as small as dumplings. Greta would pat his wrist, trying to urge him to slow down on the aquavit — the way her mother had done when Greta was a girl drinking Tennis Specials at the Valley Hunt Club. But Einar never seemed to understand her signals, and instead he'd bring the slim glass to his lips and smile around the table, as if seeking approval.

Physically, Einar was an unusual man; this Greta knew. She would think this when his shirt would split open further, and everyone at the table could get a peek of his chest, which was as obscene as the breast of a girl a few days into puberty. With his pretty hair and his chin smooth as a teacup, he could be a confusing sight. He was so beautiful that sometimes old women in Kongens Have would break the law and offer him tulips picked from a public bed. His lips were pinker than any of the sticks of colour Greta could buy on the third floor of Magasin du Nord.

'Tell them why you won't be at the ball,' Greta said one night at dinner. It was warm, and they were eating at a table outside in the light of a torch. Earlier, two boats in the canal had collided, and the night smelled of kerosene and split wood.

'The ball?' Einar asked, tilting his head.

'Greta says your cousin is coming from Jutland,' said Helene Albeck, a secretary at the Royal Greenland Trading Company. She was compact in her little green dress with the low-hanging waist; once, when she was drunk, she took Einar's hand and pressed it against her lap. Einar resisted instantly, which pleased

Greta, who had witnessed the incident through a slat in the kitchen door.

'My cousin?' Einar said, sounding confused. His upper lip became dewy, and he said nothing, as if he'd forgotten how to speak.

This happened more than once. Greta would mention Lili to a friend, even to Anna, and Einar's face would pinch up, as if he had no idea who Lili was. He and Greta never spoke about it afterwards, about his childlike miscomprehension: Lili who? Oh, yes, Lili. My cousin? Yes, my cousin, Lili. The next day the same thing would occur again. It was as if their little secret were really just Greta's little secret, as if she were plotting behind Einar's back. She considered discussing it with him directly but decided against it. Perhaps she feared she would crush him. Or that he would resent her intrusion. Or maybe her greatest fear was that Lili would disappear for ever, the detachable white collar fluttering as she fled, leaving Greta alone in the Widow House.

Three

❧

Einar's father was a failed cereal farmer, an expelled member of the Society for Cultivating the Heath. The first night he ever left his mother's farmhouse in Bluetooth was when he rode up to Skagen, the fingertip of Denmark, to fetch his bride from a shop that sewed fishing nets. He slept in a seaside inn with a seaweed roof and woke at dawn to marry. The second and last night away from Bluetooth he returned to Skagen with his wife's body and baby Einar wrapped in a plaid blanket. Because the ground around Skagen was too hard with hoarfrost for grave-digging, they wrapped Einar's mother in a fishing net picked clean of gills and laid her like an anchor into the icy sea. The week before, a grey wave had washed the inn with the seawood roof into the Kattegat, and so this time Einar's father slept in the net shop, among the rusted hook-needles and the cord and the faint smell of primrose for which Einar's mother was known.

His father was tall and weak, a victim of delicate bones. He walked with a knotwood staff, holding on to furniture. When Einar was little, his father was bedridden with maladies the doctor simply called rare. During the day Einar would sneak into his father's room while he was asleep. Einar would find foam collected on his father's lips, bubbled with breath. Einar would tiptoe forward, reaching to touch his father's golden curls. Einar had always wanted hair like that, so thick a silver comb could sit in it as prettily as tinsel on a Christmas tree. But even more lovely than his hair was his illness, the mysterious malady that bled away his energy and caused his egg-shaped eyes to turn milky and soft, his fingers yellow and frail. Einar found his father beautiful – a man lost in a useless, wheezing, slightly rank shell of a body. A man confounded by a body that no longer worked for him.

On some days Einar would climb into the small beechwood bed and slip beneath the eiderdown. His grandmother had patched the holes in the comforter with tiny pellets of peppermint gum, and now the bed smelled fresh and green. Einar would lie with his head sunk into the pillow, and little Edvard II would curl between him and his father, his white tail flicking against the bedclothes. The dog would groan and sigh, and then sneeze. Einar would do the same. He did this because he knew how much his father loved Edvard, and Einar wanted his father to love him just the same.

Einar would rest there and feel the weak heat from his father's bones, his ribs showing through his nightshirt. The green veins in his throat would pulse with exhaustion. Einar would take his father's hand and hold it until his grandmother, her body small and rectangular, came to the door and shooed Einar away. 'You'll only make him worse,' she'd say, too busy with the fields and the neighbours calling with sympathy to tend to Einar.

Yet, despite his admiration, Einar also resented his father, sometimes cursing him as he dug in the bog, his spade cutting through the peat. On the table next to his father's sickbed was an oval daguerreotype of Einar's mother, her hair twisted into a wreath around her head, her eyes silvery. Whenever Einar picked it up, his father would take it away and say, 'You're disturbing her.' Opposite the bed was the pickled-ash wardrobe where her clothes waited, exactly as she'd left them the day she gave birth to Einar. A drawer of felt skirts with pebbles sewn into the hem to hold them against the wind; a drawer of wool underclothes, grey as sky; on hangers a few gabardine dresses with muttonchop sleeves; her wedding dress, now yellow, packed in tissue that would break apart at the touch. There was a drawstring bag that rattled with amber beads and a black cameo brooch and a small diamond set in prongs.

Every now and then, in a burst of health, his father would leave the farmhouse. One day when he returned from an hour of chat at the neighbour's kitchen table, he found Einar, small at age seven, in the drawers, the amber beads twisted around his throat, a yellow deck-scarf on his head like long, beautiful hair.

His father's face turned red, and his eyes seemed to sink into his skull. Einar could hear the angry rattle of his father's breath in his throat. 'You can't do that!' his father said. 'Little boys can't do that!' And little Einar replied, 'But why not?'

His father died when Einar was fourteen. The grave diggers charged an extra ten kroner to shovel out a hole long enough to hold his coffin. In the churchyard his grandmother, who had now buried all her children, gave Einar a small notebook with a pewter cover. 'Write your private thoughts in it,' she instructed, her face as flat and round as a saucer; that flat face showed her relief that her queer, unproductive son had at last moved on. The notebook was the size of a playing card, with a lapis lazuli pencil held to the spine by ostrich-leather loops. She had plucked it from a sleeping Prussian soldier when the German Confederation occupied Jutland during the war of 1864. 'Took his notebook and then shot him,' she sometimes said, churning her cheese.

Bluetooth was named for Denmark's first king. No one really knew when it was founded, or where its people came from, although there were myths about the Greenland settlers giving up on that rocky land and releasing their sheep to graze here. It was not much more than a village surrounded by bogs. Everything in Bluetooth was always wet: feet, dogs and, sometimes in the spring, carpets and the walls of halls. There was a plank walkway that crossed the spongy ground leading to the main road and then the grain fields beyond. Every year the walkway would sink the length of a girl's arm, and in May, when the hoarfrost melted to bits no bigger than fish scales, the men of Bluetooth would rehammer the warping planks into the few yellow heaps of solid ground.

As a boy Einar had a friend named Hans who lived on the edge of the village in a brick villa that had the town's first telephone. One day, before they were close friends, Hans charged Einar an *øre* to pick up the receiver. He heard nothing, only the staticky hollow silence. 'If there was anyone to call, you know I'd let you,' Hans said, throwing his arm around Einar's shoulder and rocking him gently.

Hans's father was a baron. His mother, whose grey hair was twisted tightly, spoke to him only in French. Hans had freckles on the lower half of his face and was, like Einar, smaller than most other boys. But unlike Einar's, Hans had a voice that was fast and raspy, that of a good, always excited boy who spoke with equal enthusiasm and confidence to his best friend, his Corsican governess and the red-nosed deacon. He was the type of boy who at night would fall asleep instantly, exhausted and happy, suddenly quieter than the bog. Einar knew this because whenever he slept at the villa he would lie awake till dawn, too excited ever to seal his eyes.

Hans was two years older than Einar, but that didn't seem to matter. At fourteen, Hans was small for his age yet taller than Einar. With his head handsomely larger in proportion to his body, Hans seemed when Einar was twelve, more like an adult than any other boy he knew. Hans understood the grown-ups who ran the world: he knew they didn't appreciate their inconsistencies being called out. 'No, no – say nothing,' he'd advise when Einar's father, nearly always bemoaning his bedridden state, would throw back the eiderdown and fly to the teapot whenever Mrs Bohr or Mrs Lange stopped by for gossip. Or Hans would suggest – the way he did, with his fingers pressed together into a small fin-like paddle – not to tell Einar's father that he wanted to be a painter. 'You'll change your mind again and again. Why worry him now?' Hans would say, his pressed-together fingers touching Einar's arm, causing the little black hairs to stand alert, their bases pimpled and hard. Because Hans knew so much, Einar thought certainly he must be right. 'Dreams shouldn't be shared,' Hans told Einar one day when teaching him to climb the ancient oak that grew on the edge of the bog. Its roots wrapped mysteriously around a boulder so white and speckled with mica that you couldn't look directly at it on a sunny day. 'I want to run away to Paris, but I'm not going to tell anyone about it. I'm going to keep it to myself. One day I'll be gone. *That's* when people will know,' Hans said, swinging upside-down from a branch, his shirt creeping down to expose the hairs sprouting in the bowl of his sternum. Were he to let loose and fall, he'd slip neatly away into the open, bubbling mud.

But Hans never disappeared into the bog. By the time Einar was thirteen, he and Hans had become best friends. This surprised Einar, who expected nothing less than scorn from a boy like Hans. Yet instead Hans would ask Einar to play tennis on the rye-grass court marked out with powdered sugar next to the villa. When he discovered Einar couldn't swing a racquet with any precision, Hans instructed him on the rules of umpiring, claiming it was more important anyway. One afternoon Hans and one of his brothers – there were four in all – decided, in an effort to rankle their mother, to play tennis naked. Einar sat in a sweater on a lichened rock, a pink paper parasol set up by Hans protecting him from the sun. Einar tried to call the match objectively, although he felt unprepared to do anything but help Hans win. And so Einar sat on the rock calling the points – 'Forty–love for Hans . . . An ace for Hans' – as Hans and his brother glided over the rye grass chasing the ball, their cheerfully pink penises flopping around like schnauzer tails, causing Einar to heat up under the parasol until Hans's match point. Then the three boys towelled off, and Hans's bare warm arm fell across Einar's back.

Hans had a paper-and-balsa kite, brought back from Berlin by the baroness. It was shaped like a submarine, and Hans loved to set it sailing up into the sky. He'd lie in the lucerne grass and watch the kite floating above the bog, the spool of string clamped between his knees. 'The Kaiser has a kite just like this one,' he'd say, blades of grass between his lips. He tried to teach Einar to get it aloft, but Einar was never capable of finding the right current of air. Over and over the rice-paper kite would rush up in a column of breeze, and then crash to the ground; and each time Einar would watch Hans wince

as the kite returned to earth. The boys would rush over to the
kite, which would be lying upside-down. Einar would say, 'I
don't know what happened, Hans. I'm so sorry, Hans.' Hans
would pick up the kite and shake off the dandelions and say,
'Good as new.' But Einar could never learn to fly the kite; and
so one day, when the boys were sprawled on their backs in the
lucerne grass, Hans said, 'Here. You steer.' He set the spool of
string between Einar's knees and then resettled himself in the
field. Einar could feel the foxholes beneath him. Each time the
kite pulled on the string the spool would rotate, and Einar's
back would arch up. 'That's right,' Hans said. 'Guide her with
your knees.' And Einar got more and more used to the
spinning spool, and the kite dipping and rising with the wrens.
The boys were laughing, their noses burning in the sun. Hans
was tickling Einar's stomach with a reed. His face was so close
to Hans's that he could feel, through the grass, his breath. Einar
wanted to lie so close to Hans that their knees would touch,
and at that moment Hans seemed open to anything at all. Einar
scooted towards his best friend, and the only strip of cloud in
the sky peeled itself away, and the sun fell on the boys' faces.
And just then, as Einar moved his bony knee towards Hans's,
an angry gust of wind yanked on the kite, and the spool lifted
from the clamp of Einar's knees. The boys watched the
submarine of the kite sail above the elm trees, rising at first but
then crashing into the black centre of the bog, which
swallowed it as if it were as heavy as a stone.

'Hans,' Einar said.

'It's OK,' Hans said, his voice a stunned whisper. 'Just don't
tell my mother.'

The summer before Einar's father died, Hans and Einar
were playing in Einar's grandmother's sphagnum fields, the
mud swishing through their boots. It was warm, and they had
been in the fields most of the morning, and suddenly Hans
touched Einar's wrist and said, 'Einar, dear, what's for dinner?'
It was about noon, and Hans knew no one was in the
farmhouse except Einar's father, who was asleep upright in his
bed.

Hans had begun to grow by then. He was fifteen, and his body was filling out to match the size of his head. A fin of an Adam's apple had appeared in his throat, and he was now much taller than Einar, who at thirteen still hadn't budged in height. Hans nudged Einar towards the farmhouse. In the kitchen Hans sat at the head of the table and tucked a napkin into his collar. Einar had never before cooked a meal, and he stood blankly at the stove. Hans quietly said, 'Light a fire. Boil some water. Drop in a few potatoes and a mutton joint.' Then, more vaguely, his gravelly voice suddenly smooth: 'Einar. Let's pretend.'

Hans found Einar's grandmother's apron with the cotton-grass strings hanging limply next to the stovepipe. He brought it to Einar and cautiously tied it around his waist. Hans touched the nape of Einar's neck, as if there were a panel of hair he needed to lift aside. 'You never played this game?' Hans whispered, his voice hot and creamy on Einar's ear, his fingers with their gnawed-down nails on Einar's neck. Hans pulled the apron tighter until Einar had to lift his ribs with an astonished, grateful breath, his lungs filling just as Einar's father padded into the kitchen, his eyes wide and his mouth puckered into a large O.

Einar felt the apron drop to his feet.

'Leave the boy alone!' His father's walking stick was raised at Hans.

The door slammed, and the kitchen became shadowy and small. Einar could hear Hans's boots squish through the mud, heading towards the bog. Einar could hear the wheeze of his father's breath and then the flat punch of his fist landing on Einar's cheek. Then, across the bog and the tadpole pools, over the sphagnum field, trailing into the afternoon, came Hans's voice in a little song:

> There once was an old man who lived on a bog
> And his pretty little son, and their lazy little dog.

Four

❧

Greta spent her eighteenth birthday on the *Princess Dagmar*, sulking at its rail. She hadn't returned to California since the summer of the butcher-wagon incident. The thought of the whitewashed brick house on the hill, with its view of the eagle-nested Arroyo Seco, the thought of the San Gabriel Mountains purpling at sunset, filled her with regret. She knew her mother would want her to take up with the daughters of her friend – with Henrietta, whose family owned the oceanside oilfields down in El Segundo; with Margaret, whose family owned the newspaper; with Dottie Anne, whose family owned the largest ranch in California, a parcel of land south of Los Angeles not much smaller than all of Denmark. Greta's parents expected her to proceed as if she were one of them, as if she'd never left, as if she should become the young Californian woman she was born to be: smart, schooled, horse-trained and silent. There was the Christmas debutante ball at the Valley Hunt Club, where the girls would descend the staircase in white organdy dresses, albino.poinsettia leaves pinned to their hair. 'How appropriate that we'd return to Pasadena in time for your coming-out,' Greta's mother clucked nearly every day on the *Princess Dagmar* on the return voyage. 'Thank God for the Germans!'

Greta's room in the house on the hill had an arched window that overlooked the rear lawn and the roses, their petals fringed brown in the autumn heat. Despite the good light, the room was too small to paint in. After only two days she felt cramped, as if the house, with its three floors of bedrooms and the Japanese maids whose geta sandals clacked up and down the back staircase, were choking her imagination. 'Mother, I just have to return to Denmark right away – tomorrow even! It's too confining for me here,' she complained. 'Maybe it's fine for you and Carlisle, but I feel as if I can't get anything done. I feel as if I've forgotten how to paint.'

'But Greta, dear, that's impossible,' said her mother, who was busy converting the stable into a garage. 'How could California cramp anyone? And compared to little Denmark!' Greta agreed that it didn't make sense, but this was how she felt.

Her father sent over a statistical survey of Denmark published by the Royal Scientific Control Societies. Greta spent a week with it, studying its charts with both self-pity and longing: last year there were 1,467,000 pigs in Denmark, and 726,000 sheep. The total number of hens: 12,000,000. She would read the figures and then turn her head to the arched window. She memorized them, certain she would need them shortly, although for what, she couldn't say. Again she'd 'try her mother: 'Can't I go back? I don't give a hoot about the Germans!'

Lonely, Greta would walk down to the Arroyo Seco, along the dry riverbed where the killdeer birds hunted for water. The *arroyo* was burned out in autumn, the sage grass and the mustard shrubs, the desert lavender and the stink lilies all brown brittle bones of plants; the toyon, the coffeeberry, the elderberry, the lemonade sumac all dry in the branch. The air in California was so parched that Greta's skin was cracking; as she walked along the sandy riverbed she could nearly feel the inner panel of her nose crack and bleed. A gopher hurried in front of her, sensing a hawk circling above. The oak leaves shook crisply in a breeze. She thought about the narrow streets of Copenhagen, where slouching buildings hung to the kerb like an old man afraid to step into traffic. She thought about Einar Wegener, who seemed as vague as a dream.

In Copenhagen, everyone had known her but no one ever expected anything from her; she was more exotic than the black-haired laundresses who had wandered across the earth from Canton and now worked in the little shops on Istedgade. In Copenhagen she was given respect no matter how she behaved, the same way the Danes tolerated the dozens of eccentric countesses who needlepointed in their mossy manors. In California, she was once again Miss Greta Waud, twin sister of Carlisle, orange heiress. Eyes continually turned her way. There were fewer than ten men in Los Angeles County suitable for her to marry. There was an Italianate house on the other side of the Arroyo Seco everyone knew she would move into. Its nurseries and screened playrooms she would fill with children. 'There's no need to wait now,' her mother said the first week back. 'Let's not forget you've turned eighteen.' And of course no one had forgotten about the butcher wagon. There was a different boy on the delivery route, but whenever the truck rattled up the drive a brief moment of embarrassment would fall over the whitewashed house.

Lame Carlisle, whose leg had always ached in the Danish chill, was preparing to enter Stanford; it was the first time she became jealous of him – the fact that he was allowed to hobble across the sandy courtyard to class under the clear blank Palo Alto sun while she would have to sit in the sunroom with a sketchbook in her lap.

She started wearing a painter's smock, and in the front pocket she kept Einar's note. She sat in the sunroom and wrote him letters, although it was difficult to think of anything she wanted to report to him. She didn't want to tell him that she hadn't painted since she left Denmark. She didn't want to write about the weather; that was something her mother would do. Instead she wrote letters about what she would do when she returned to Copenhagen: re-enrol in the Royal Academy; try to arrange a little exhibit of her paintings at Den Frie Udstilling; persuade Einar to escort her to her nineteenth birthday party. During her first month in California she would walk to the post office on Colorado Street to mail the letters. 'Could be slow,' the clerk would say through the brass slats in the window. And Greta would reply, 'Don't tell me the Germans have now ruined the mail too!'

She couldn't live like this, she told one of the Japanese maids, Akiko, a girl with a runny nose. The maid bowed and brought Greta a camellia floating in a silver bowl. Something is going to have to change, Greta told herself, as she burned up with anger, although she was mad at no one in particular, except the Kaiser. There she was, the freest girl in Copenhagen, if not the whole world, and now that dirty German had just about ruined her life! An exile – that's what she'd become. Banished to California, where the rose bushes grew to ten feet and the coyotes in the canyon cried at night. She could hardly believe that she had become the type of girl who looked forward to nothing more in the day than when the mail arrived, a bundle of envelopes, none of them from Einar.

She cabled her father, begging for his permission to return to Denmark. 'The sea lanes are no longer safe,' was his answer. She demanded that her mother let her go up to Stanford with Carlisle, but her mother said the only schools appropriate for Greta were the Seven Sisters back in the snowy east.

'I feel like I'm being crushed,' she told her mother.

'Don't be so dramatic,' Mrs Waud replied, busy managing the reseeding of the winter lawns and the poppy beds.

One day Akiko tapped delicately on Greta's door and, with her head bowed, brought Greta a pamphlet. 'I am sorry,' Akiko said. Then she rushed out, her getas clacking. The pamphlet announced the next meeting of the Pasadena Arts & Crafts Society. Greta thought about the society's amateurs with their Paris-style palettes and threw away the pamphlet. She turned to her sketchpad but could think of nothing to draw.

A week later, Akiko returned to her door. She handed Greta a second pamphlet. 'I am sorry,' Akiko said, her hand covering her mouth. 'But I think you like.'

It was only after Akiko delivered a third pamphlet that Greta decided to attend a meeting. The society owned a bungalow above Pasadena in the foothills. The previous week, a mountain lion, as yellow as a sunflower, had pounced down from the scrub pine at the end of the road and snatched a neighbour's baby. The society's members could talk of nothing

else. The agenda was abandoned, and there was a discussion of
a mural depicting the scene. 'It'll be called *Lion Descending!*'
someone said. 'Why not a mosaic?' another member proposed.
The society was made up mostly of women, but there were a
few men, many of whom wore felt berets. As the meeting
moved closer to agreeing upon a collective painting to be
presented to the city library on New Year's Day, Greta slipped
to the back of the room. She had been right.

'You're not volunteering?' a man said.

It was Teddy Cross, with his white forehead and long neck
that tilted to the left. Teddy Cross, who suggested they leave
the meeting and visit his ceramics studio on Colorado Street
where his kiln burned walnut logs night and day; whose right
ankle was meaty with muscle from pumping the foot pedal of
his potter's wheel. Teddy Cross, who would become Greta's
husband as a result of the Christmas debutante hall at the
Valley Hunt Club; who, before the end of the Great War,
would die beneath Greta's gaze.

He was the second man Greta loved. She loved Teddy for
the slender-necked vases he shaped out of white clay and
ground glass. She loved his quiet, stubbly face and the way his
mouth would hang open as he dipped his pottery into tubs of
glaze. He was from Bakersfield, the son of strawberry farmers;
a childhood of squinting had permanently creased the skin
around his eyes. He would ask Greta about Copenhagen,
about its canals and its king, but would never comment on
anything she told him, his eyelids the only thing moving in his
face. She told him there was a great landscape painter there
who was in love with her, but Teddy only stared. He'd never
been east of the Mojave, and the only time he was in one of
the mansions along Orange Grove Boulevard was when he
was hired to create tiles for hearths and sleeping-porch floors.

Greta loved the idea of dating him; of taking him around to
the tennis-court pavilions where Pasadena's dinner dances
were held that autumn; of showing him off to the girls from
the Valley Hunt Club, as if to say she wasn't one of them, not
any more – she'd lived in Europe, after all. She would climb

up in the butcher wagon if she wanted, or she would have a ceramicist as an escort.

As expected, Greta's mother refused to allow Teddy Cross in the house. But that didn't stop Greta from touring him around Pasadena, visiting boring Henrietta and Margaret and Dottie Anne in their shade gardens. Those girls didn't seem to mind Teddy, which Greta took to mean they were actually ignoring him. His ceramics were in such demand that, Greta discovered, there was a respectable charm in the way he arrived at parties with bits of clay jammed beneath his fingernails. Greta's mother, who would often say at the dinner dances that she'd take California's *terra infirma* any day over 'old, old Europe', would pat Teddy's hand whenever they met in public, a gesture that infuriated Greta. Her mother knew that, were she publicly to dismiss Teddy Cross, the dispute would end up in the *American Weekly*.

'They look down at you,' Greta said to Teddy during one of the parties.

'Only some of them,' he replied, seemingly happy to sit with Greta on the wicker couch out by the swimming pool as the Santa Anas blew palm fronds to the ground and the party burned on in the mansion's windows. If he only knew! Greta would think, ready to fight – whom or what, she didn't know, but she was ready.

Then one day the mail arrived in its twine-bound bundle, and Akiko delivered a blue envelope to Greta's door. She looked at it for a long time, balancing its delicate weight in her palm. She could hardly believe Einar had written, and her mind began to race with what he might have to say to her: *It seems as if the war is nearly over and we should be together again by Christmas.* Or: *I'm coming to California on the next crossing.* Or maybe even: *Your letters mean more to me than I can say.*

It was possible, Greta told herself, the envelope in her lap. He could have changed his mind. Anything was possible.

Then Greta ripped through the seal.

The letter was addressed 'Dear Miss Waud,' and said only: 'Given the course of events, worldly and otherwise, I expect we will never see each other again, which is probably for the best.'

Greta folded the paper and tucked it into her pocket. Why did Einar think like that? she asked herself, wiping her eyes with the hem of her smock. Why didn't he have any sense of hope at all? Regretfully, she had no idea what she could do.

Then Akiko returned to Greta's door and said, 'It's Mr Cross. On the telephone.'

And so on the telephone in the upstairs hall, within earshot of her mother, Greta asked Teddy to escort her to the debutante ball. He agreed on one condition – that Greta stop worrying about how he'd get along with her mother. 'I'm going to ask her to dance with me and then you'll see,' he said. But Greta rolled her eyes, thinking Teddy didn't know what he was getting himself into. When she hung up, her mother said, 'Well, now that it's done, just be sure to help him with his tails.'

There were seven girls in her debutante class. Their escorts were young men home for the holidays from Harvard and Princeton or from army bases in Tennessee and San Francisco. A girl with asthma asked Carlisle, her lungs too weak to need a reliable dancing partner. And Greta, who was for the first time beginning to think that she would have to forget all about Einar Wegener, prepared by practising her curtsy.

The white dress with the empire waist never fitted Greta right. It was flouncy in the shoulders and a fraction too short, revealing her feet. Or at least that's how Greta felt about it; she could think only of her long, blocky feet showing when she descended the staircase in the Valley Hunt Club's front hall. The staircase's banister was wrapped in a garland twisted with evergreens, apples and red lilies. Guests in white tie were scattered around the club sipping spiked Tennis Specials, politely watching the seven debutantes descend. There were four Christmas trees up for decoration, and in the fireplaces dark flames were gnawing on the redwood logs.

One of the girls brought a silver flask of whisky, its cap made of mother-of-pearl. She and the other debs passed it around while they dressed and pinned the poinsettia leaves into their hair. The flask made the evening brighter, as if the club manager had turned up the wall sconces to their highest voltage. It made the black fires in the fireplaces seem almost like beasts about to jump the screens.

When Greta reached the foot of the stairs, she curtsied deeply, bringing her chin to the Oriental carpet. The club members applauded, balancing their punch cups. Then she entered the ballroom, and there, waiting, was Teddy Cross. In his white tie he looked taller than usual. His hair was shiny with tonic, and there was something unfamiliar about him: he looked almost Danish, with his dark blond hair and his wrinkled eyes and his good brown tan; with his sharp Adam's apple rising and falling nervously.

Later that night, after the waltzes and the roast beef and the strawberries served in Oregon champagne, Greta and Teddy slipped out of the clubhouse and walked towards the tennis courts. The night was clear and cold, and Greta had to lift her dress from the dew collecting on the baselines. She was a little drunk, she knew, because earlier she had made an unfortunate joke about the strawberries and Teddy's parents. She apologized to him immediately but, from the way he folded his napkin on the table, he seemed a little hurt.

The walk on the tennis courts was her idea, as if to try to make it up to Teddy, all of this, her strange Pasadena life that she had hurled upon him. But she didn't have a plan, hadn't thought of what she would offer him. They reached the pavilion on the far court, where there was a water cooler and a wicker settee painted green. On the sofa, which smelled like dry, termite-eaten wood, they began to kiss.

She couldn't help thinking how different Teddy's kiss was from Einar's. On the *Princess Dagmar* she had stood at the mirror in her stateroom and kissed herself. The flat cold surface had somehow reminded her of kissing Einar, and she began to think of that kiss on the stairs of the Royal Academy as something similar to kissing herself. But Teddy's kiss was not like that at all. His lips were rough and firm and the whiskers on his upper lip scratched at her mouth. His neck, nuzzling into her own, was strong and hard.

With the ball playing on in the clubhouse, Greta thought she had better speed things up. She knew what she should do next, but it took her a few minutes of coaching herself. Lift your hand over to his . . . Oh, it was hard enough thinking about it, let alone actually instigating it! But she wanted to do it, or at least she thought she wanted to, and she was sure it was what Teddy wanted too, what with his neck with its wire-brush whiskers turning and shaking strongly. Greta counted to three and held her breath and reached for Teddy's flies.

His hand stopped her. 'No, no,' he said, holding her wrist.

Greta had never thought he would say no. She knew the moonlight was bright enough that were she to look up into his face she would see the coiled concern for propriety that would embarrass her deeply. Greta thought of the last time she had let a man try to say no to her: and now she and Einar were separated by a continent and a sea, to say nothing of a pyrotechnic war.

On the wicker settee of the Valley Hunt Club's outermost court, there Greta Waud and Teddy Cross sat for a minute, her wrist still cuffed by his callused hand.

Again she asked herself what to do next, but now, as if propelled by an urge she had never before known, she pushed her face into Teddy's lap. Greta began to use every trick she had read about in the novels she bought on the naughty side of Copenhagen's Central Station, and from the chatty, slutty Lithuanian maids who had run her mother's house. Teddy tried to protest again, but each 'no' passed his lips less and less forcefully. Eventually he released her hand.

By the time they were finished her dress was wrinkled and bunched up on the empire waist. His tails had somehow ripped. And Greta, who had never gone this fast or this far, was lying under the thin long heap of Teddy, feeling his heart knock, knock, knock on her breast, and smelling his bitter salty scent damp between her legs. Already she knew what would come next, and Greta wrapped her arms around Teddy's back in resignation and thought to herself, It's OK with me as long as he takes me away from here.

They were married on the last day of February in the garden of the house on Orange Grove Boulevard. The Japanese maids sprinkled the lawn with camellia petals, and Teddy wore a new pair of tails. It was a small wedding, only cousins from San Marino and Hancock Park and Newport Beach. Their neighbour, a chewing-gum heiress from Chicago, attended as well, because, as Mrs Waud put it through her teeth, she had gone through this with her daughter too. Teddy's parents were invited, although no one expected them to come; crossing Ridge Route from Bakersfield in February wasn't always possible.

Immediately after the wedding and a short honeymoon in a garden suite at the Hotel del Coronado in San Diego, where Greta cried every day – not because she was married to Teddy Cross but because she was now even further from her beloved Denmark and the life she wanted to lead – Greta's parents sent them to live in Bakersfield. Mr Waud bought Greta and Teddy a small Spanish house with a red tile roof and Seville grating on the windows and a little garage covered by bougainvillaea. Mrs Waud sent Akiko to live with them. The banister of the Bakersfield house was wrought iron, and the doorways between the rooms were arched. There was a kidney-shaped swimming pool and a small step-down living room with bookshelves. The house was in a grove of date palms, and inside it was always shadowy and cool.

Teddy's parents came to visit once; they were stooped and their hands were faintly pink from the strawberries. They lived out in the fields, on a few acres of loam, in a two-roomer built from eucalyptus plank. Their eyes were sealed beneath skin folded by the sun, and they were nearly silent in Greta's step-down living room, holding each other nervously, jointly examining the wealth that lay before them: the Spanish house, the plein-air painting above the fireplace, Akiko's thick geta sandals clacking as she delivered a tray. Greta poured Mr and

Mrs Cross iced hibiscus tea, and together they all sat on the white sofas Mrs Waud had ordered from Gump's. Everyone was uncomfortable and regretful that things had come to this. Greta drove the senior Crosses back to their house in her Mercer Raceabout, the two-seater forcing Mrs Cross to curl into Mr Cross's lap. Night was falling quickly as the car sped along the road, and the early spring chill was creeping across the fields. A wind was whistling through the furrows, throwing dirt into the air. Greta had to use her wipers to clear the sandy loam from the windscreen. In the distance a gold light burned in the Crosses' plank house. The soil was blowing so strongly that Greta could see nothing but the light of the house, and it was as if she and Mr and Mrs Cross were thinking of the same thing, because just then Mrs Cross said, 'Where Teddy was born.' And Mr Cross, his hands wrapped around his wife, said, 'Always said he'd be coming back.'

For the rest of the spring Greta napped on one of the white sofas in the step-down living room. She hated Bakersfield, she hated the Spanish house, she even sometimes hated the baby growing inside her. Not once, however, did she hate Teddy Cross. In the afternoons, she would read while he brought a steady supply of warm flannels for her forehead. Greta was swelling quickly, and she felt sicker with each day. Before May she was spending nights in the living room as well, too sick and heavy to climb the stairs. Teddy took to sleeping on a camp-bed at her side.

By early June, Bakersfield had settled into its summer heat; it would reach a hundred degrees before nine in the morning. Akiko would fold paper fans for Greta; Teddy brought cold compresses instead of hot. And when Greta became really sick, Akiko served her cold green tea from a lacquered cup while Teddy read poetry aloud.

But then one day, while Teddy was down in Pasadena collecting a wheel from his old studio, which he had never closed, the heat and the sickness came to an end. Together, Greta and Akiko, whose hair was as black as a raven's wing, delivered a blue baby boy, the umbilical cord around his neck

like a little tie. Greta baptized him Carlisle. A day later, she and
Teddy buried him in the yard of the senior Crosses' eucalyptus
house, in the blowing loam, at the rim of the whispering
strawberry fields.

Five

❧❦❧

The little cobblestone street that stitched across Copenhagen was dark and safe enough, Lili thought, for the privacy of a secret transaction. The street was too narrow for lamps, a window on one side nearly opening into the window on the opposite. The people who lived there were stingy about the light in their front rooms, and all was now dark except for the few businesses still open. There was a Turkish coffee house where customers sat on velvet pillows in the window. Further down was a bordello, discreet behind its shutters, its brass doorbell shaped like a nipple. Further was a basement bar, where, as Greta and Lili passed, a skinny man with a waxed moustache quickly disappeared down the steps to a place where he could meet others like himself.

Lili was in a chiffon dress with a linen sailor's collar and cuffs. The dress was making a soft noise as she walked, and she kept her mind on the *swish-swish*, nervously trying not to think of what lay ahead. Greta had lent her the rope of pearls that was twisted three times around her throat, hiding most of it. Lili was also wearing a velvet cap, bought only that morning at Fonnesbech's, and she had sunk into it the pin of Greta's yellow-diamond and onyx brooch shaped like a monarch butterfly.

'You're so beautiful I want to kiss you,' Greta had said when Lili was dressing. Greta was so excited that she took Lili in her arms and waltzed her around the apartment while Edvard IV barked and barked. Lili closed her eyes – so stiff and heavy beneath the caking of powder! – and imagined that Copenhagen was a city where both Lili and Einar could live as one.

The street ended on Rådhuspladsen, the great square across from Tivoli. The fountain with spouting dragons was tinkling, and across from the Palace Hotel was a column capped with a pair of bronze Vikings blowing their *lure*. The square was active, with people entering the midnight ball, and Norwegian tourists excited about tomorrow's bicycle race from Copenhagen to Oslo.

Greta didn't push Lili. She let her stand at the edge of Rådhuspladsen and wait until little Lili had filled up inside Einar, like a hand filling a puppet.

Beneath the Rådhuset's copper-sheathed spire, the four-dialled clock rising more than three hundred feet above her, Lili felt as if she were carrying the greatest secret in the world – she was about to fool all of Copenhagen. At the same time, another part of her knew that this was the most difficult game she would ever play. It made her think of the summer in Bluetooth, and the crashing submarine kite. Einar Wegener, with his small round face, seemed to be slipping down a tunnel. Lili looked at Greta, in her black dress, and felt grateful for all that lay ahead of her. Out of nowhere had come Lili. Yes, thanks were due to Greta.

The people entering the city hall looked smart and happy, *lagerøl* lifting the colour in their cheeks. There were young ladies in candy-coloured dresses fanning their chests, asking one another where all the famous painters were. 'Which one is Ejnar Nielsen?' one woman said. 'Is that Erik Henningsen?' There were young men with wax-tipped moustaches and Sumatran cigars. There were the young industrialists, who, with their money made fast from mass-produced crockery and cooking pans moulded by hissing machinery, came to move themselves up through society.

'You won't leave me?' Lili asked Greta.

'Never.'

Yet already Lili was stirring.

Inside the Rådhuset there was a covered courtyard decorated in the style of the Italian Renaissance. On three sides were open galleries supported by pillars. Above, a canopy of crossing timber beams. On the stage was an orchestra, and there was a long table with trays of oysters. Hundreds of people were dancing, hands of handsome men on the slender waists of women whose eyelids were painted blue. Two girls on a bench were writing a note to someone, giggling over it. There was a circle of men in tuxedos with their hands in their pockets, their eyes roaming. Lili was stirring. She could hardly take it all in. She felt the wingbeat of panic in her chest, knowing she didn't belong. She thought about leaving, but it was too late. Lili was at the ball, its smoke and its music already weaving their way through her eyes and ears. If she said she was going to leave, Greta would only tell her to settle down; Greta would tell her not to worry, there was nothing in the world to worry about at all. She'd swat her hands through the air and laugh.

Next to Lili was a tall girl in a strappy dress who was smoking a silver cigarette as she talked to a man whose face was so dark he must have been from the south. The woman was slender, her back quilted prettily with muscle, and the man seemed so in love with her that he could only nod and agree and, then, stop her from talking with a long kiss.

'There's Helene,' Greta said. Across the room was Helene Albeck, her short black hair cut sharply in a way Greta explained was now fashionable in Paris.

'You go and talk to her,' Lili said.

'And leave you?'

'I'm not sure I want to talk to anyone just yet.'

Greta crossed through the dancers, her hair down her back. She kissed Helene, who seemed anxious to tell Greta something. At the Royal Greenland Trading Company, Helene managed the paintings, gramophones, gold-rimmed dinner plates and other luxuries that were included in the summer shipments that set sail each Tuesday from Copenhagen. For two years Helene had arranged for Einar's paintings to be crated up and shipped to Godthåb, where an agent would auction them off. The money was slow to return across the north Atlantic, but when it did Einar would proudly present it to Greta in a leather accordion file.

The dancers shifted, and then Greta and Helene were out of sight. Lili was sitting on a mahogany bench carved with mermaids. It was warm in the covered courtyard, and she peeled back her shawl. As she was folding it, a young man came to the bench and said, 'May I?' He was tall, and his hair was a yellowy brown with thick corkscrew curls that twirled past his jaw. Out of the corner of her eye Lili watched him check his pocket watch, watched him cross and uncross his legs. He had a faint grainy smell, and his ears were pink with either warmth or nerves.

From her clutch-bag, Lili pulled out the pewter notebook given to Einar by his grandmother, and she started to write notes to herself about the man. He looks like Einar's father as a young man, she wrote. His father when he was healthy and still working the sphagnum fields. This must be why I'm staring, Lili put down in the little notebook. Why else can't I stop looking at him? Why can't I stop looking at his long feet, at the wiry whiskers growing down his cheeks in a half-beard? At the aquiline nose and the full lips. At the thick curly hair.

The man leaned over. 'Are you a reporter?'

Lili looked up from her lap.

'A poetess, then?'

'Neither.'

'Then what are you writing?'

'Oh, this?' she said, startled that he had spoken to her. 'It's nothing at all.' Even though she was sitting next to the man, she couldn't believe he had noticed her. It felt to her as if no one could see her. She hardly felt real.

'Are you an artist?' the man asked.

But Lili gathered her shawl and her clutch-bag and said, 'I'm sorry.'

She was too surprised to find herself here to continue speaking with him. By now she was even warmer, and she had a sudden urge to remove her clothes and swim out to sea. She exited the hall through a portal that led to a back-park.

Outside there was a breeze. An old oak canopied the little park, as if protecting it from someone who had climbed the Rådhuset's spire to spy. There was a smell of roses and turned soil. The patch of lawn was silvery, the colour of the wing of a flying fish. Lili took a few steps and then saw the couple from before, the girl in the strappy dress and her admirer, kissing behind an oak scrub. The man was holding the woman's thigh, her dress pushed up to her hip, the clasp of her garter bright in the night.

Startled, Lili turned away and walked right into the man from the bench.

'Do you know what they say about this old oak?' he said.

'No.'

'They say if you eat its acorns you can make a wish and become anyone you want for a day.'

'Why would they say that?'

'Because it's true.' He took her hand and led her to a bench.

He turned out to be a painter named Henrik Sandahl. Recently he'd exhibited a series of paintings of North Sea fish: square canvases of plaice, dab, turbot, the elusive, sharp-faced witch. Greta had seen the paintings. One day she returned to the apartment, immediately dropping her bag and her keys, her eyes wide. 'I've never seen anything like it,' she told Einar. 'You have to go and see them for yourself. Who ever thought you could fall in love with the face of a cod?'

'Are you here with someone?' Henrik asked.

'My cousin's wife.'

'Who's that?'

Lili told him.

'Einar Wegener?' Henrik said. 'I see.'

'Do you know him?' Lili asked.

'No, but he's a good painter. Better than most people think.' He paused. 'I'm sure you know, but many people these days say he's old-fashioned.'

It was the first time that Einar sensed how he was turning

the world on its head by dressing as Lili. He could eliminate himself by pulling the camisole with the scallop-lace hem over his head. Einar could duck out of society by lifting his elbows and clasping the triple strand of Spanish pearls around his neck. He could comb his long soft hair around his face, and then tilt his head like an eager adolescent girl.

Then Henrik took Lili's hand. The wiry hairs on his wrist startled her, because the only hand she had ever held was Greta's.

'Tell me about yourself, Lili,' Henrik said.

'I was named after the flower.'

'Why do girls say silly things like that?'

'Because it's true.'

'I don't believe girls when they say they're like a flower.'

'I'm not sure what else I can tell you.'

'Start with where you come from.'

'Jutland. A little village called Bluetooth, on a bog.' She told Henrik about the lucerne-grass fields, about the icy rain that could punch holes in the side of the farmhouse.

'If I were to give you an acorn to eat,' Henrik said, 'who would you want to be?'

'I have no idea,' she said.

'But make a wish.'

'I can't.'

'OK then, don't make a wish.' And then Henrik began to tell the story of a Polish prince who freed every woman in his country from another day's labour; that was who Henrik wanted to be.

Before she knew it, it was late, the very middle of the night. The wind had picked up, and the oak tree, with its ear-shaped leaves, was bending as if to overhear Henrik and Lili. The moon had slipped away, and all was dark except the gold light coming through the portals of the Rådhuset. Henrik had taken Lili's hand, kneading the fleshy base of the thumb, but it felt to Lili as if the hand and thumb belonged to someone else. It was as if someone else were coming to claim her.

'Shouldn't we have met sooner than tonight?' Henrik said,

his fingers trembling, fidgeting with a loose thread on the cuff
of his coat.

Lili heard Einar laugh, a bubbly air pocket of a giggle; inside
the air pocket was the distantly sour breath of Einar. Einar was
chuckling about the clumsiness of another man courting and
carrying on. Had he ever said something so ridiculous to
Greta? Not likely; Greta would have told him to cut the
nonsense. She would have shaken her silver bracelets and
said, 'Oh, for Pete's sake,' her eyes rolling in her head. She
would have said she'd leave the restaurant if Einar didn't stop
treating her like a child. Greta would have abruptly turned to
the haddock on her plate and not spoken again until there
was nothing left but the hollow head resting in a bed of
vinegar. Then she would have kissed Einar and walked him
home.

'I need to go and look for Greta,' Lili said.

A fog had rolled in from the harbour, and now she was cold.
The thought came this way: Lili, with her bare forearms, was
feeling the wind, not Einar; she felt the quick damp air run
through the nearly invisible vine of hair that grew up the nape
of her neck. Deeper, beneath the chiffon and the camisole and
finally the woollen drawstring underpants, Einar was becoming
cold, too – but only as you become cold by watching a coatless
person struggle against the chill. He realized that Lili and he
shared something: a pair of oyster-blue lungs; a chugging heart;
their eyes, often rimmed pink with fatigue. But in the skull it
was almost as if there were two brains, a walnut halved: his and
hers.

'Tell Greta I'll walk you home,' Henrik said.

Lili said, 'Only if you promise to leave me around the
corner from the Widow House. Einar might be waiting up,
and he wouldn't want to see me alone with a stranger. Then
he and Greta would worry whether or not I'm old enough to
live in Copenhagen. They're like that, always wondering what
to do with me, wondering if I'm about to stumble across
trouble.'

Henrik, whose lips were flat and purple and cracked just down the middle, kissed Lili. His head swooped in, his mouth landed on hers and then pulled away. He did it again, and again, while his hand kneaded the flesh above her elbow, and then the small of her back.

What surprised her most about a man's kiss was the scratch of the whiskers, and the dense hot weight of a young man's arm. The tip of his tongue was strangely smooth, as if a scalding tea had burned off the bumpy buds. Lili wanted to push him away and say she couldn't do this, but it suddenly seemed like an impossible task. As if her hand could never shove away Henrik, whose corkscrew hair was twisting like rope around her throat.

Henrik pulled her from the iron bench. She was worried that he might embrace her and feel through the dress her oddly shaped body, bony and breastless, with a painful, swollen ache tucked between her thighs. He led Lili down a side corridor in the Rådhuset, his hand offered as a tow. His head seemed like a puppet's, bobbing happily; it was round and cranial, with a touch of Mongol in the forehead. And this was why, perhaps, Einar felt free to grip Henrik's moist fist and follow: it was a game, part of the game of Lili, and games counted for nearly nothing. Games weren't art, they weren't painting; and they certainly weren't life. Not once before – and not even tonight with Henrik's hand sweating in his palm – did Einar ever consider himself abnormal, or off the mark. His doctor, when he'd gone to him last year with a question about their inability to produce children, had asked, 'Do you ever long for someone other than your wife, Einar? For another man, perhaps?' 'No, never. Not at all,' he replied. 'Your inkling is wrong.' Einar told the doctor that he, too, became disturbed when he saw the men with the quick, frightened eyes and the excessively pink skin loitering near the toilets in Ørsted-sparken. Homosexual! How far from the truth!

And, again, this was why Einar held Henrik's hand and ran down the back passageway with the Danish flags hanging from the burnished beams. Why he tripped in the *sennep*-yellow

shoes Greta had first given him that April afternoon when she
needed a pair of legs to paint. Why he allowed the narrow
camisole to bind his stride: Einar was playing a game. He knew
it. Greta knew it. But he also knew nothing, nothing about
himself.

Outside in Rådhuspladsen, a tram clanged by, its bell
friendly and sad. Three Norwegians were sitting on the rim of
the fountain, laughing and drunk.

'Which way?' Henrik asked. He seemed shorter on the
street, out on the open *plads* that smelled of the nearby cart
selling coffee and spice biscuits. There was something hot in
the secret pit of Einar's stomach, and all he could do was look
around at the fountain and the bronze lurblowers and the steep
pitch of the roofs of the buildings surrounding the square.

'Where to?' Henrik asked again. He looked to the sky, his
nostrils trembling.

Then Einar had an idea; Lili had an idea. And as strange as it
might seem, it was like that: floating somewhere above
Rådhuspladsen Einar watched Lili, with her determined upper
lip, whisper to Henrik, 'Come.' He heard her think: Greta will
never know. What Lili was referring to – Greta will never
know what? – Einar didn't find out. When he, Einar, the
remote owner of the borrowed body, was about to ask Lili
what she was referring to; when he, Einar, floating above like a
circling ghost, was about to lean in and ask – not exactly the
way a driver at a fork asks himself which road to take, but
almost – *What won't Greta know?*, just then Lili, with her
forearms flushed with heat, with chiffon in her fists, her half of
the walnut brain electric with the current of thought, felt a
warm trickle run from her nose to her lips.

'My God, you're bleeding!' Henrik cried.

She brought her hand to her nose. The blood was thick,
running over her mouth. The music from the Rådhuset was
ringing in her nose. With each drop she felt more cleansed,
empty but cleansed.

'What happened?' Henrik asked. 'How did this happen?' He
was yelling, and the blood seemed to run a little heavier in

gratitude for his concern. 'Let me get you some help.' Before
she could stop him, he was running across Rådhuspladsen to
some people getting into a car. He was about to tap the
shoulder of a woman holding open the door. Lili watched
Henrik's finger slowly unfurl. Then she realized.

Lili tried to call 'No!' – but she couldn't speak at all. Henrik
was tapping the black sturdy back of Greta, who was on the
street putting Helene into the Royal Greenland Trading
Company's official car.

It was as if Greta never saw Henrik. She only saw Lili, her
blood bright across Rådhuspladsen. Greta's face tightened, and
Lili thought she heard Greta whisper, 'Oh no. For God's sake,
no.' The next thing Lili knew, Greta's blue scarf, the Lili she
had been secretly borrowing, was pressed to Lili's nose, and she
was collapsing into Greta's arms, hearing softly, like a lullaby,
'Lili, are you all right? Oh, Lili, please be all right.' And then,
'Did he hurt you?'

Lili shook her head.

'How did this happen?' Greta asked, her thumbs rubbing
circles into Lili's temples. Lili couldn't say anything, could only
watch Henrik, frightened of Greta, run across Rådhuspladsen,
his legs long and swift, his spiralled hair swaying at the tips, the
handsome slap of his foot on the cobble eerily similar to the flat
punch of Einar's father's hand to his cheek when he discovered
Einar in his grandmother's apron as Hans's lips pressed towards
his neck.

Six

That summer, the dealer who sold Einar's work agreed to display ten of Greta's paintings for two weeks. Einar arranged it, requesting the favour – *My wife is becoming frustrated*, he began in a letter to Herr Rasmussen – on a sheet of letterhead, though Greta wasn't supposed to know about that. Regretfully, she unsealed the letter Einar asked her to post, using a kettle and a fingernail – for no good reason, really, except that sometimes Greta became overwhelmed with a curiosity about her husband and what he did when he was away from her: what he was reading, where he ate his lunch, whom he spoke to, and about what. It's not because I'm jealous, Greta told herself, delicately resealing the envelope. No, it's simply because I'm in love.

Rasmussen was bald, with Chinese-shaped eyes, a widower. He lived with his two children in an apartment near Amalienborg. When he said he'd hang her most recent paintings, Greta was tempted to say she didn't want his help. Then she thought about it and realized she did. To Einar she coyly said, 'I'm not sure whether you spoke to Rasmussen or not. But thankfully he's come around.'

At a furniture store on Ravnsborggade she bought ten chairs and retacked their cushions in red damask. The chairs she placed in front of each painting at the gallery. 'For reflection,' she suggested to Rasmussen, arranging them just so. Then she wrote to every European newspaper editor on the list Einar had put together over the years. The invitation announced an important debut – words Greta had trouble putting down, so boastful they seemed, so transactional, but she went ahead, at Einar's urging. 'If that's what it takes,' she said. She hand-delivered the invitations to the offices of *Berlingske Tidende*, *Nationaltidende* and *Politiken*, where a clerk in a little grey cap turned her away with a sneer.

Greta's paintings were oversized and glossy with a shellacking process she created from varnish. They were so shiny and hard you could clean them like windows. The few critics who came to the gallery picked their way around the red damask chairs and ate the honey crackers Greta had set out in a silver dish. She escorted the critics, whose little notepads remained open and disturbingly blank. 'This one is Anna Fonsmark. You know, the mezzo-soprano,' Greta would say. 'The trouble I had getting her to pose!' Or, 'He's the furrier to the King. Did you notice the circle of minks in the corner, symbolizing his trade?' When she said things like that she regretted them immediately; the crassness of her comments would ring in the air as if it were echoing off the shellacked paintings. She would think of her mother, and Greta would blush. But sometimes Greta was filled with too much immediate energy to stop and think and plan and plot. The energy was the fluid running up and down her western spine.

She had to admit to herself that some of the critics had come only because she was Einar Wegener's wife. 'How's Einar's work coming along?' a few would ask. 'When can we expect his next show?' One critic came because she was a Californian and he wanted to hear about the plein-air painters working there – as if Greta might know anything at all about the bearded men mixing their paints in the startling sunlight of Laguna Niguel.

The gallery on Krystalgade was cramped and, in the heatwave that coincided with her exhibition, smelled of the cheese shop next door. Greta worried that the odour of fontina would settle into her canvases, but Einar told her it was impossible, not with the shellac. 'They're impenetrable,' he remarked of her paintings, which sounded – once it was said, hovering between the two of them like a bat – unkind.

The next day, when Greta returned to the apartment, she found Lili crocheting a hairnet, the needles clicking in her lap. Neither Einar nor Greta ever figured out the origins of Lili's bloody nose at the Artists Ball. But about a month after, her nose began to bleed again, a couple of warm red bursts over the course of three days in July. Einar said it was nothing, but Greta worried, like a mother watching a son's early cough. Recently, in the middle of the night, Greta had begun to climb out of bed and go to her easel to paint an ashen Lili collapsing in Henrik's arms. The painting was large, nearly life-size, and more real, with its bright colours and flat shapes, than Greta's memory of Lili bleeding outside the Artists Ball. In the slanting background was the fountain with the spewing dragons, and the bronze Viking *lurblowers*. A frail Lili filled the painting, a man's arms around her, his hair falling into her face. She would never forget the sight of it, Greta told herself as she painted, the climbing mix of horror and confusion and outrage still palpable on the knuckles of her spine. She knew something had changed.

'Have you been here long?' Greta now asked Lili.

'Less than an hour.' The needles continued to click in her lap. 'I went out. I walked through Kongens Have and crocheted on a bench. Have you seen the roses yet?'

'Do you think it's a good idea? For you to be outside? All alone?'

'I wasn't alone,' Lili said. 'Henrik met me. He met me on the bench.'

'Henrik,' Greta said. 'I see.' Through the corner of her eye, Greta studied her husband. She had no idea what he wanted from this, from Lili, and yet there he was, dressed in a brown skirt and a white blouse with capped sleeves and the old-fashioned shoes with the pewter buckles she had given him that first day. Yes, there he was. A vague regret filled Greta's throat: she wished she were both more and less involved in the comings and goings of Lili. Greta realized she would never know exactly what was the right thing for her to do.

'How is the fish painter?' Greta asked.

Lili sat forward in her chair and began to tell the story of
Henrik's recent trip to New York, where he dined with Mrs
Rockefeller. 'He's becoming an important painter,' Lili went
on, describing the people in the art world who were talking
about Henrik. 'Did you know he's an orphan?' Lili said,
describing his youth as a sailor's apprentice on a schooner that
fished the North Sea. Lili then reported that Henrik had
declared, on the bench in Kongens Have in front of the box
hedge, that he'd never met a girl like Lili.

'It's clear he's taken with you.' Greta could see the heat in
Lili's face. Greta had just returned from an uneventful day at
the gallery, her ten paintings all on the wall and unsold. Now
all of this – the sight of her husband in the plain brown skirt;
the story of Henrik receiving an invitation to dine with Mrs
Rockefeller at the National Arts Club on Gramercy Park; the
strange thought of Lili and Henrik on a public bench in the
shadow of Rosenborg Slot's turrets – caught up with her.
Greta suddenly asked, 'Tell me, Lili. Have you ever kissed a
man?'

Lili stopped, her lace limp in her lap.

It was almost as if the question had tumbled with its own
will out of Greta's mouth. She had never wondered about this
before, because Einar had always been sexually awkward and
without initiative. It seemed impossible to Greta that he would
have ever pursued such a foreign longing. Why, without her,
Einar would never have found Lili. 'Would Henrik be the
first?' Greta said. 'The first to kiss you?'

Lili thought about this, her brow bunching up. Through the
floorboards came the potato-vodka voice of the sailor. 'Don't
lie to me!' he was yelling. 'I can tell when you're lying to me.'

'In Bluetooth,' Lili began, 'there was a boy named Hans.' It
was the first Greta heard of Hans. Lili spoke of him ecstatically,
with her fingers pressed together and held up in the air. It was
as if she were in a trance as she told Greta of Hans's climbing
tricks on the ancient oak, of his pebbly little voice, of his
submarine-shaped kite sinking into the bog.

'And you haven't heard from him since?' Greta asked.

'I understand he's moved to Paris,' Lili said, resuming her crocheting. 'He's an art dealer, but that's all I know. Deals in art for Americans.' Then she rose and went into the bedroom, where Edvard IV was growling in his sleep, and shut the door. An hour later, when Einar emerged, it was as if Lili had never been there. Except for the scent of mint and milk, it was as if she didn't really exist at all.

By the end of the two weeks none of Greta's paintings had sold. She could no longer blame her lack of success on the economy, what with the Great War seven years in the past and the Danish economy chugging and panting with growth and speculation. But the failed show didn't surprise her. Since they had married, Einar's reputation had overshadowed hers. His little dark paintings of moors and storms – really, some were no more than grey paint on black – earned more and more kroner each year. Meanwhile Greta sold nothing but the drab commissions of corporate directors who refused to crack a smile. The more personal portraits she painted – of Anna, of the blind woman at the gate of Tivoli, and now of Lili – went unnoticed. After all, who would buy Greta's work over Einar's, the bright, bold American's over the subtle, cosy Dane's? What critic in all of Denmark, where artistic styles from the nineteenth century were still considered new and questionable, would dare praise her style over his? This was how Greta felt; even Einar, when prodded, admitted it might be true. 'I hate feeling like this,' she would sometimes say, her cheeks mumpy with an envy that could not be dismissed as petty.

One painting, however, drew some interest. It was a triptych, painted on hinged boards. Greta had started it the day after the ball at Rådhuset. It was three views of a girl's head at full scale: a girl removed in thought, her eyelids tired and red; a girl white with fear, her cheeks hollow; a girl over-excited, her hair slipping from its clip, her lip dewy. Greta had used a fine rabbit's-hair brush and egg tempera, which gave the girl's skin a translucence, a nightworm's glow. On this one painting, she decided not to apply the shellac. Standing in front of it, one or two critics withdrew their pencils from their breast pockets. Greta's heart began to beat against her ribs as she heard the lead tips scraping against the notepads. One critic cleared his throat; a second, a Frenchman with a little grey wart on the rim of his eye, said to Greta, 'This one yours as well?'

But the painting, called *Lili Thrice*, could not rescue the show. Rasmussen, a short man who had recently sailed to New York to swap paintings by Hammershøi and Krøyer for shares in the steel companies of Pennsylvania, crated up Greta's portraits for return. 'I'll keep the one of the girl for consignment,' he said, logging it into his books.

It was several weeks later that the clipping from a Parisian art journal arrived in the mail, care of Rasmussen's gallery. The article was a summary of Scandinavian modern art; buried in the paragraphs on Denmark's most talented was a brief mention – most people probably never even saw it – of Greta. 'A wild and rhapsodic imagination,' it said of Greta. 'Her painting of a young girl named Lili would be frightening if it wasn't so beautiful.' The review said nothing else. It was as cursory as surveys tend to be. Rasmussen had forwarded the clipping to Greta, who read it with a mixture of feeling she couldn't articulate to anyone: to her, even more startling than the praise was the absence of Einar's name. Danish art was summed up, and Einar hovered nowhere. She tucked the clipping into a drawer in the pickled-ash wardrobe. It went beneath the sepia prints of Teddy and the letters from her father in Pasadena describing the orange harvest, the coyote hunts and the society of lady painters in Santa Monica she could join if she ever decided to leave Denmark for good. Greta would never hand the article to Einar. It was hers; the words of praise were hers. Again, she didn't feel the need to share.

But Greta couldn't just read the review and then fold it away in a drawer. No, she had to react, and so she immediately wrote to the critic with an idea.

'Thank you for your thoughtful review,' she began.

It will have a special place in my clippings file. Your words were just too kind. I hope you'll look me up the next time you're in Copenhagen. Ours is a small city, but refined. Something tells me you haven't seen it properly. In the mean time, there's one more thing I'd like to ask you. My husband, Einar Wegener, the landscapist, has lost track of a close childhood friend. The only thing my husband knows of him is that he lives in Paris and is, perhaps, an art dealer. Would you happen to know him, Hans Axgil, the baron? He's from Bluetooth, on Jutland. My husband would like to find him. Apparently they were uncommonly close as boys. My husband becomes quite nostalgic – as men do when they recall their youth – when he speaks of Hans and their childhood together in Bluetooth, which is really only a bog. But I thought you might at least know of Hans, since the world of the Arts is smaller than we all think. If you have an address, that would be, again, too kind. Please send it to me, and I'll be sure to pass it to Einar. He would be grateful.

Seven

࿇

A week after the Artists Ball, Lili met Henrik in Kongens Have three evenings in a row. Still unsure of herself, she agreed to see him only at dusk, which at the end of June came late after supper. Each night as she dressed, pulling a skirt from the wardrobe, preparing for her assignation, she would become heavy with guilt. Greta would be reading the newspaper in the front room, and Lili could nearly feel Greta's eye on her as she applied the powder and the lipstick and filled her camisole with rolled socks. Lili would tiptoe around Edvard IV, who was sprawled on the little oval carpet in front of the mirror. Lili would study her profile in the mirror, first from the left, then from the right. She felt sorry about leaving Greta to her newspaper and the cone of light from her reading lamp – but not sorry enough to fail to meet Henrik at the proposed iron streetlamp.

'Are you going out?' Greta asked the first night Lili headed towards the front door, just as the horn of the Bornholm ferry was calling.

'For a walk,' Lili said. 'For some fresh air. It's too nice to be inside.'

'At this hour?'

'As long as you don't mind.'

'I don't mind,' Greta said, pointing to the pile of newspapers at her feet that she still wanted to read before going to bed. 'But all alone?'

'I won't be exactly alone.' Lili couldn't look at Greta when she said this, her eyes averted to the floor. 'I'm meeting Henrik.' And then, 'But only for a stroll.'

Lili watched Greta's face. Her cheeks were twitching and it seemed as if she was grinding her teeth. Greta sat up in her reading chair. She creased the newspaper sharply in her lap. 'Don't stay out too late,' She finally said.

Henrik kept Lili waiting nearly twenty minutes beneath the streetlamp. She began to worry that maybe he had changed his mind, that perhaps he had realized something about her. It frightened her, to be alone on the street. But she was also thrilled by the sense of freedom, the rapid pulse in her throat telling her she could do almost anything she pleased.

When Henrik finally arrived, he was out of breath, sweat on his upper lip. He apologized. 'I was painting and lost track of time. Does that ever happen to you, Lili? When you nearly forget who or where you are?'

They walked for a half-hour, in the warm night. They didn't say much, and it felt to Lili as if there was nothing to say. Henrik took her hand. When they were on a street empty but for a stray dog, he kissed her.

They met again the next two nights, each time Lili slipping out of the apartment under Greta's gaze rising above the edge of the newspaper. Each time Henrik arriving late, running, paint beneath his fingernails, splattered in his curls.

'I'd like to meet Greta some day,' Henrik said. 'To prove to her I'm not really the type of man who runs away from a fainting woman.'

They stayed out late that third night, past the call of the last tram, past one o'clock when the pubs closed. Lili kept her hand in Henrik's as they walked through the city, looking in the flat black reflection of shop windows, kissing in the dark provided by doorways. She knew she should return to the Widow House, but something in her wanted to stay out for ever.

Lili was sure Greta would be up waiting for her, her eye never having left the front door. But the apartment was dark when Lili got home, and she washed her face and removed her clothes and climbed into bed as Einar.

The next day Greta told Lili she should stop seeing Henrik. 'Do you think it's fair to him?' she asked. 'To deceive him like this? What do you think he would think?'

But Lili didn't quite understand what Greta meant. What would Henrik think about what? Unless Greta plainly told her, often Lili forgot who she was.

'I don't want to stop seeing him,' she said.

'Then please, stop seeing him for me.'

Lili said she'd try, but even as she said it she knew it would be impossible. As she stood in the front room, by Einar's empty easel, she knew she was lying to Greta. But Lili couldn't help it. She could hardly help herself.

And so Lili and Henrik began to meet secretly, at the end of the afternoon, before it was time for Lili to return home for supper. At first it was difficult for Lili to see Henrik in the daylight, with the sun harsh in her face. She feared he would discover that she wasn't really beautiful, or worse. She would tie a scarf around her head, the knot beneath her chin. She felt comfortable sitting with him only in the darkened Rialto movie house, her hand in his; or in the hushed library of the Royal Academy, the reading room dimmed by green canvas roller shades.

One night Lili told Henrik to meet her by the lake in Ørstedsparken at nine o'clock. There were two swans gliding in the water, and a willow leaning towards the grass. Henrik was late, and when he arrived he kissed her forehead. 'I know we only have a few minutes,' he said, his hair brushing her throat.

But Greta was at a reception at the American Embassy that night. She would be gone for another few hours, and Lili was about to tell Henrik they could dine freely together at the restaurant with the wainscot walls on Gråbrødre Torv. They could stroll down Langelinie like any other Danish couple out on a fine summer night. She could hardly believe the good news she was about to break to Henrik, who had become used to meeting Lili for twenty minutes at a time. 'I have something to tell you,' she said.

Henrik took her hand and kissed it and then held it against his chest. 'Oh, Lili – don't say any more,' he said. 'I already know. Don't worry about anything, but I already know.' His face was open, his eyebrows lifted.

Lili pulled her hand from Henrik's. It was quiet in the park, the workers who cross it on their way home already at their dinner tables, and a man was loitering near the toilets, lighting a book of matches one by one. A second man walked by and then looked over his shoulder.

What does Henrik know? Lili was asking herself, but soon she came to understand.

Henrik's eyebrows were still lifted, and a terrible shudder rose through Lili, and it suddenly was as if Einar were a third person there – as if he were one step removed from Lili and Henrik's intimate circle of confession, witnessing it all. There he was, Einar in the young girl's dress, flirting with a younger man. It was an awful sight.

Lili shuddered again. The man in front of the toilet entered, and then there was a loud crash, a dustbin knocked over.

'I'm afraid I can't see you any more,' Lili finally said. 'I'm going to have to say goodbye to you tonight.'

'What are you talking about?' Henrik said. 'Why are you saying this?'

'I just can't see you any more. Not right now,' she said.

He reached for Lili's hand but she refused. 'But it doesn't make any difference to me. Is that what this is about? That's what I'm trying to tell you. Is this because you think that I won't—'

'Not right now,' she said again, and Lili left him. She crossed the grass, which was dry in summer, nearly snapping beneath her feet, and climbed the path out of the park. 'Lili,' he cried from beneath the willow. There would be a few hours to rehang Lili's dress and to bathe and to begin another painting. Einar would wait for Greta, who would come home and unfasten her hat and ask, 'Did you have a nice evening?'

and who would kiss his forehead in a way that would show them both that Greta had been right.

Eight

For their August holiday, Greta and Einar returned, as they did every summer, to Menton, a French harbour town on the border of Italy. After the long summer Greta said goodbye to Copenhagen with a sense of relief. As their train rattled south and over the Maritime Alps, she felt as if she was leaving something behind.

This year, on a tip from Anna, who had sung at the opera in Monte Carlo in May, Greta and Einar rented an apartment on the avenue Boyer, across the street from Menton's municipal casino. The apartment's owner was an American who had hurried to France after the war to buy up the shuttered garment factories of Provence. He became rich and now lived in New York, his mail full of profits from the simple, unlined housedresses he sold to every housewife south of Lyons.

The apartment had a cold orange marble floor and a second bedroom painted red and, in the living room, a Chinese screen inlaid with abalone shell. The front windows opened on to little terraces wide enough for a row of geranium pots and two wire chairs. There Einar and Greta would sit in the hot nights, Greta's feet on the rail, a rare breeze blowing up from the lemon and orange trees in the park below. Greta was tired, and she and Einar could pass an evening saying no more than 'Good-night.'

On the fifth day of their holiday, the weather turned. Sirocco winds from North Africa hurtled across the dimpled Mediterranean, up the rocky beach and through the open terrace doors, knocking over the Chinese screen.

Greta and Einar were napping in the red bedroom when they heard the crash. They found the screen flat against the camelback sofa. The screen had been hiding a rack of sample housedresses manufactured by the apartment's owner in his factories. The dresses, white with floral prints, were fluttering on the rack, as if a child were tugging on their hems.

They were rather plain, Greta thought, with their ugly cuffed sleeves and button fronts convenient for breastfeeding — so plain and practical she began to feel a remote sense of dislike for the women who wore them. She moved to set right the Chinese screen. 'Give me a hand?' she said.

Einar was standing next to the sample rack, the dress hems blowing against his leg. His face was still. Greta could see the veins in his temples pulsing. She could see his fingers, which she always thought of as the fingers of a pianist, not a painter, trembling. 'I was thinking of asking Lili to visit us,' he said. 'She's never been to France.'

Greta had never turned Lili away. There were times, over the course of the summer, when Einar would announce that Lili would be coming to dinner and Greta, drained from a day attending her failed exhibition, would think, Oh, Lord, the last thing I want to do right now is dine with my husband dressed up as a girl. But Greta would keep such a thought to herself, biting her lip until she could taste her own blood. She knew she couldn't stop Einar. She knew, from what had happened with Henrik, that Lili had a will of her own.

In the weeks before they left for Menton, Lili had begun to appear unannounced in the afternoons. Greta would leave the Widow House for an appointment. When she returned she'd find Lili at the window in a loose dress, the back buttons unfastened. Greta would help her finish dressing, clasping a string of amber beads around her throat. It never ceased to startle Greta, finding her husband like that, waiting with the neckline of a dress open across his pale shoulders. She never once said anything to Einar, or to Lili. Instead, she would always welcome Lili as if she were an amusing foreign friend. She'd hum and gossip as she helped Lili into her shoes. Greta would tip a bottle of perfume against her forefinger and then run her sweet fingertip down Lili's throat and up the inside of her arm. She would stand Lili in front of the mirror and whisper, her voice the soft intimate voice of wedlock, 'There now . . . so very pretty.'

All of this Greta did with a sense of devotion, for she always believed she could defy anyone in the world except her husband. It had been the same with Teddy. She could cross her mother and argue with her father and snub all of Pasadena and Copenhagen alike, but in her chest was a bottomless well of tolerance for the man she loved. She never questioned it, why she allowed Lili to come into their lives. Anything to make Einar happy, she would tell herself. Anything at all.

And yet, Greta being Greta, this open devotion sometimes chafed her. After Lili's assignations with Henrik, Greta began to escort her on her trips into the Copenhagen streets. Lili had told her that she would never see Henrik again, that they'd had a falling-out, but even so, Greta knew there were dozens of other young men who could flatter Lili until she blushed and fell into their arms. And so Greta and Lili would stroll with their arms linked at the elbow through the box hedges of the park. Greta's eyes would patrol the gravel paths for potential suitors, knowing what Lili, with her moist brown eyes, could stir in young Danish men. One day Greta took a photograph of Lili at the gate of Rosenborg Slot, the slim brick castle behind Lili blurry and vaguely menacing. Another day Lili stopped Greta at the marionette theatre and sat with the children, her face as tentative, her legs as coltish, as theirs.

'Greta?' Einar said again. He was leaning against the rack of sample dresses. The Chinese screen was still lying against the sofa. 'You won't mind if Lili visits us here?'

Greta began to stand the screen upright. Since they arrived in France she hadn't painted. She hadn't met anyone interesting enough to ask to sit for a portrait. The weather had been heavy and humid, making it difficult for paint to dry on the canvas. Over the summer she had begun to change her style, using brighter colours, especially pinks and yellows and golds, and flatter lines and an even larger scale. It was a new way of painting for Greta, and it took her a longer time to start again at a blank canvas. She hardly felt confident about the paintings. With their oversized, pastel tone of joy, her recent paintings required, on Greta's part, an inner sense of rapture. Nothing made her happier than painting Lili.

Greta thought about starting a full-scale portrait of her on the terrace, a breeze lifting her hair and the hem of her housedress, the little brown roses on the dress a pretty blur, the expression on Lili's face just like the one on her husband's at this very moment – hot, anxious, his skin tight and red and about to burst.

Greta and Lili were walking to L'Orchidée on quai Bonaparte. The restaurant was known for its ink-boiled squid, or so Hans had written, proposing an evening to meet. On the street the shops were closed for the night. Little sacks of yesterday's rubbish were resting on the kerb. The cobblestones were loose in the road, rutted from the pneumatics of motor cars.

Hans's letter was in Greta's pocket, and she was rubbing its corner against her wedding ring as she and Lili walked along rue St Michel towards the harbour. To Greta, one of the nicer Danish customs was that the wedding band was worn on the right hand. When she'd returned to Denmark a widow, she'd swore to herself she would never remove the brushed-gold band Teddy had given her. But then Einar offered her his own band, a simple loop of gold. She didn't know how she could remove Teddy's ring; she thought of him giving it to her, clumsily searching his pockets for the little black velvet box. But then Greta realized she wouldn't have to take Teddy's off, and now she wore both. She played with the rings equally, turning them on her fingers absent-mindedly.

Greta never told Einar much about Teddy Cross. She had returned to Denmark on Armistice Day, a widow for six months, her name again Greta Waud. He died for no good reason at all, she would say when friends asked about her first husband. After all, Greta would think, dying when you're

twenty-four and live in California's clean dry heat is the result
of just that: the cruelty of the world. It made no sense, really.
Certainly Teddy didn't have a western spine, another unjust
fate. Sometimes she'd also think, with her eyes sealed to stem
the regret: perhaps she and Teddy were never meant to be
married. Perhaps his love for her was never as great as hers for
him.

Greta and Lili were almost at the restaurant when she
stopped Lili and said, 'Don't be angry with me, but I have a
little surprise for you.' She pushed Lili's fringe out of her eyes.
'I'm sorry for not telling you earlier, but I thought it'd be
easier for you to hear about it just before.'

'Hear about what?'

'That we're having dinner with Hans.'

Lili's face went white, and it was clear that she understood.
She pressed her forehead against the window of a closed
charcuterie. Inside, skinned piglets were hanging from a rope
like pink pennants. Even so, Lili asked. 'Hans who?'

'Come on now. No panicking. It's Hans. He wants to see
you.'

The Parisian critic with the wart on the rim of his eye had
quickly answered Greta's letter, sending Hans's address and a
further enquiry about Greta's painting. The attention from the
critic nearly threw Greta into a reverie. Paris was asking after
her art! she told herself, opening her box of stationery from
Århus and filling her pen with ink. First she wrote to the critic:
Is there a life for me in Paris? she asked. Should my husband
and I consider leaving Denmark, where no one knows what to
think of me? Would our lives be freer in Paris?

Then Greta wrote to Hans: My husband seems never to
have forgotten you, she began. When he is dreaming at his
easel, I know he is thinking of you hanging from the oak
above the bog. His face softens and nearly shrinks. It is as if he
is becoming thirteen again, with shiny eyes and a smooth chin.

Now in his mid-thirties, Hans Axgil had a thin nose and
wrists covered with a dense blond hair. He had become a
large, sturdy man, his neck rising thick out of his chest; it made

Greta think of the old sycamore stump at the rear of her California garden. Einar had described Hans as small, the runt of the bog. His nickname had been Valnød, or Walnut; some said it was because in the summer his skin turned pale brown, as if dimly soiled from Bluetooth's perpetual mud, a pool of which had served as his birth bed when his mother's coach, overturned in a hailstorm, stranded her and her two maids on a heath with nothing but matchlight and the driver's canvas coat offered as a nativity tarp.

Now of course Hans was a man, large in a Germanic way. He shook other people's hands with both of his; those same hands often hooked together at the nape of his neck when he was telling a story. He drank nothing but champagne or carbonated water. He dined only on fish, having once eaten a venison chop and then lost his appetite for a month. He was an art dealer, shepherding Dutch masters to rich Americans who collected for the sake of amassing. It was a business, he described, with a smile revealing two incisors like drills, as often immoral. 'Not always, but often enough,' he said. Hans's favourite sport was still tennis. 'The best part of France is its *terre battue*. The red clay. The white tennis balls with the gummy seams. The umpire sitting up in his chair.'

The restaurant was across the road from the harbour. There were eight tables on the pavement, beneath striped parasols anchored in tins of rocks. In the harbour sailing boats were arriving home. Holidaymakers stood on the docks, holding hands, the backs of their knees sunburned. On the restaurant's tables were vases of marigolds, and sheets of white paper protecting the cloth.

Not until they were about to sit at the table, where Hans was waiting with his hands behind his neck, did Greta become anxious about her plan. Not until now did she worry that Hans might see the resemblance to Einar in Lili's face. What would Greta do if Hans were to lean across the table and say, 'Is this pretty little creature my old friend Einar?' It seemed unimaginable; but even so, what would Greta do if Hans were to ask such a question? And what would Lili do? Then Greta looked at Lili, pretty in one of the housedresses and tanned from lying on the bathing raft that floated in the sea. Greta shook her head. No, there was no one there but Lili. Even Greta saw only Lili. And besides, Greta thought as the waiter pulled out the chairs at the table and Hans moved to kiss first Greta and then Lili, Hans no longer resembled the boy Einar had described from his youth.

'Yes, now, tell me about Einar,' Hans said as the ink-boiled squid was served in a tureen.

'Alone in Copenhagen tonight, I'm afraid,' Greta answered. 'Too busy with his work even for a holiday.'

Lili nodded, bringing the corner of her napkin to her mouth. Hans leaned back in his chair, his fork spearing the squid. He said, 'Sounds like Einar.' Hans then told them how Einar used to carry his box of pastels to the side of the road to draw scenes of the bog on the boulders. At night the drawings would wash off in the rain, and the next day he'd haul the box back and sketch again.

'Sometimes he'd draw pictures of you,' Lili said.

'Oh, yes, for hours. I would sit at the edge of the road so he could sketch my face on to a rock.'

Lili, Greta noticed, pushed her shoulders back just a bit, her breasts lifting like the papery, puckered mimosas that grew in the mountains above Menton. Greta forgot, or almost forgot, that they weren't breasts; they were avocado stones wrapped in silk handkerchiefs, tucked into the summer camisole Greta had bought that morning at the department store by the station.

Greta also noticed the way Lili – with Einar's dark eyes alive beneath the powder on the lids – spoke with Hans about Jutland. There was a longing in the way she bit her lip before she answered one of Hans's questions. The way she turned up her chin.

'I know Einar would like to see you sometime,' Lili said. 'He told me the day you ran away from Bluetooth was the worst day of his life. He says you were the only one who let him paint in peace, who told him that, no matter what, it was OK for him to become a painter.' Her hand, which under the candle lamp looked too bony and fine to be a man's, uncurled and arced towards Hans's shoulder.

Later that night she and Greta were taking the cage lift to the rented apartment. Greta was tired, and she wanted Einar to pull off his dress and wipe his lips. 'Hans didn't work it out, did he?' she said, her arms folded across her breasts, which, the way things were, hung more flatly than Lili's. There were two bare bulbs in the socket in the lift ceiling; the light showed the lines in Einar's forehead and around his mouth where the orangish foundation was collecting into clots. The little fin in Einar's throat suddenly appeared above his amber beads. His odour was male: the wet-leaf smell that came from the dark coves where his arm met his shoulder, his left leg his right.

Greta fell asleep before Einar came to bed. When she woke, she discovered Lili lying in her camisole beneath the summer sheet. Her hair was matted, her face, in the weak light, clean and beginning to whisker on the cheek. Lili was on her back, the tiny weight of the sheet falling around the pear-shaped bumps of her breasts, and then, lower, around the lump that grew between the legs. Never before had Lili slept with Greta; they had eaten breakfast together in silk kimonos patterned with cranes, and shopped for stockings together, Greta always paying, like a mother or an odd, barren aunt. But Einar had never come to bed dressed as Lili. Greta's heart, knocking against her chest, felt as hard as the stone of a fruit. Was this to be part of the game, too? Should she kiss Lili as she might kiss her husband?

They were intimate infrequently. Typically Greta blamed herself. She'd stay up late painting, or reading, and by the time she pulled back the bedclothes and slipped underneath, Einar would be asleep. Sometimes she would nudge him, hoping to wake him. But Einar was a sound sleeper, and soon she too would fall asleep. She would hold him through the night, waking up like that, with her arm over his chest. Their eyes would meet in the quiet of morning. Often she would long to touch him, and as her hand began to stroke first his chest and then his thigh, Einar would rub his fists in his eyes and leap out of bed. 'Is there anything wrong?' Greta would call, still wrapped in the bedclothes. 'Not a thing,' he'd reply, running the water in the bath. 'Nothing at all.'

The times they did make love, usually instigated by Greta but not always, Greta would end up feeling as if something inappropriate had occurred. As if she should no longer want to touch him. As if he were no longer her husband.

Now Lili shifted. Her body, which reminded Greta of a long coil, was on its side, the freckles on her back staring out at Greta, the single raised mole in the shape of Zealand as horrible and black as a leech. Lili's hip, beneath the pilled summer sheet, raised up like the camelback sofa in the living room of the rented apartment. Where had this curved hip come from? – curved like the corniche that snaked up the Côte from the Italian border to Nice; curved like the bulbous vases with the slender necks Teddy had thrown on to his foot-powered wheel. It seemed like the hip of a woman, not her husband's. It felt as if someone she didn't know was in her bed. Greta thought about the hip until dawn arrived on the apartment's narrow terraces, and a rain cooled the room off so that Lili had to snap the summer sheet to her chin for warmth, the mound of the hip disappearing beneath the taut tent of the sheet. They fell asleep again, and when Greta woke she found Lili holding two cups of coffee. Lili was smiling, and then she tried to slip back beneath the sheet, but the coffee cups tipped. Greta watched the coffee spill across the bed, towards her hand, and Lili began to cry.

Later, in the afternoon, when Einar was behind the spare bedroom's door transforming himself into Lili, Greta stripped the bed. She took the sheet, musty and milky with the mixed smell of Einar and Lili and the coffee, and held it over the terrace rail, bringing a match to its corner. Something in her wanted to see it burn away. Soon the sheet was billowing with fire, and Greta watched the flame-edged bits break away as she thought about Teddy and Einar. Scraps of sheet, trailing thin black smoke, were fluttering from the terrace, delicately rising and dipping in the summer breeze and eventually landing in the waxy leaves of the lemon and orange trees in the park below. A woman from the street called to Greta, but she ignored her, and Greta shut her eyes.

She never told Einar about the fire in Teddy's pottery studio on Colorado Street. In the front office there was a shallow fireplace decorated with Teddy's orange mission-style tiles. One day in January, in a fit of tidying, Greta crammed the Christmas garlands into the hearth, where a low fire was already smouldering. A white, thick smoke began to rise from the brittle greens. Then there was a crackling that popped with such a buckshot piercing that it brought Teddy from his workshop in the rear. He stood in the double door. In his face Greta could read the question: *What are you doing?* Then, together, they watched a flame lift out of the smoking garland; then a second reached out like an arm and lit the wicker rocking chair.

Almost instantly the room was on fire. Teddy pulled Greta out to Colorado Street. They weren't on the pavement more than a few seconds before the fists of the flames punched through the twin plate-glass windows. Greta and Teddy stepped into the street, into the traffic, drivers slowing with O-mouthed leers and the horses bucking violently away from the burning building and the cars careening away.

Everything Greta thought of saying just then sounded despicable. An apology would sound empty, she told herself over and over, as the flames rose higher than the streetlamps and the telephone lines which normally sagged under the weight of blue jays. What a sight it was, and yet there was nothing for Greta to say, except 'What have I done?'

'I can always start over,' Teddy said. Inside, cracking and exploding and shattering into black bits of nothing, were hundreds of vases and tiles, his two kilns, his filing cabinet stuffed with orders, his self-made potter's life. Still stuck in Greta's mouth was that empty apology. It felt glued to her tongue, like a cube of ice that wouldn't melt. For several minutes, she couldn't say anything else, not until the building's roof fell in on itself, as lightly as a burning, billowing sheet.

'I didn't mean to.' She wondered if Teddy would believe her. As a reporter from the *American Weekly* showed up at the scene, his pencils tucked into the band that held up his shirtsleeves, Greta wondered if anyone in Pasadena would believe her.

'I know,' Teddy said, over and over. He took Greta's hand in his own and stopped her from saying another thing. They watched the flames pull down the front wall. They watched the firemen unroll their flat, limp hose. Greta and Teddy watched, standing silently, until a damp gurgle rose up in his throat and emerged from his lips as an ominous cough.

Nine

When Einar asked her about it, Greta told him things he couldn't remember.

'You mean you've forgotten?' she said the next morning. 'That you asked him to meet you again?'

Einar could recall only part of the previous night. When Greta told him that Lili had stood on her toes to kiss Hans good-night, he became so embarrassed that he pulled a wire chair to the terrace and, for nearly an hour, stared out over the lemon trees in the park. It didn't seem possible. It was as if he hadn't been there.

'He was happy to meet Lili. And he spoke so fondly of Einar. He can't wait to see you again. Do you remember that?' Greta asked. She hadn't slept well. Her eyes were nearly lost in their sockets. 'You promised him that he could see Lili again today.'

'It wasn't me,' Einar said. 'It was Lili.'

'Yes,' Greta said. 'It was Lili. I keep forgetting.'

'If you didn't want her to visit us here, then why didn't you say so?'

'Of course I wanted Lili to visit. It's just that . . .' and Greta paused. 'It's just that I'm not sure what you want me to do about her.' She turned in the camelback sofa and began to pick at the abalone in the Chinese screen.

'There's nothing for you to do,' Einar said. 'Don't you see?'

He wondered why Greta couldn't let Lili come and go without worrying so much. If it didn't upset him, then why should Greta become concerned? If only she would quietly welcome Lili when it was time to paint her portrait. If only Greta wouldn't pry with her questions – to say nothing about her eyes – when Lili slipped in and out of the apartment. Sometimes just knowing Greta was on the other side of the door, waiting for Lili to return, was enough to fill her with a moist little fury that collected in the pits of her arms.

And yet Einar knew that he and yes, Lili too, needed Greta.

Hans was expecting Lili at four o'clock. They had agreed to meet in front of the municipal casino, which sat on the promenade du Midi behind the rocky beach. Greta was painting in the living room that morning. Einar was trying to paint in the hall, which had a view of the backside of St-Michel Church, its stone dark and red with morning shadow. Every fifteen minutes or so Greta would mutter, 'Goddamm it,' like the soft quarter gong of a mantel clock.

When he checked on her, Greta was leaning against a stool. She had several shades of blue along the rim of her canvas. In her lap was her sketch pad, sooty and smudged. Edvard IV was curled at her feet. Greta looked up, her face nearly as white as Edvard's coat. 'I want to paint Lili,' she said.

'She won't be here until later,' Einar said. 'She doesn't have to meet Hans until four. Maybe after that?'

'Please get her.' Greta wouldn't look at him, her voice quieter than usual.

For a moment, Einar felt like defying his wife. He had his own painting to finish. He had told himself that he would call up Lili in the afternoon, that he'd spend the morning painting, which he'd been ignoring so much lately, and buying the groceries at the market. But now Greta wanted him to choose Lili over himself. Greta wanted him to give up his own painting for hers. He didn't want to. He didn't long for Lili just then. He felt as if Greta was forcing him to choose. 'Maybe you can spend an hour with her before Hans comes over?'

'Einar,' Greta said. 'Please.'

Several of the housedresses were now hanging in the bedroom closet. Greta had said they were ugly, their styles

suited for nursemaids, but Einar found their plainness pretty, as
if the most ordinary woman in the world might wear one. He
thumbed through the hangers on the lead pipe, fingering the
little starched collars. The one printed with peonies was a bit
sheer; the one printed with frogs was big in the bust, and
stained. The morning was warm, and Einar wiped his lip on
his sleeve. Something made him feel as if his soul were trapped
in a wrought-iron cage: his heart nudging its nose against his
ribs, Lili stirring from within, shaking herself awake, rubbing
her side against the bars of Einar's body.

He chose a dress. It was white, printed with pink conch
shells. Its hem hung to his calf. The white and pink looked
pretty against his leg, which had taken colour from the French
sun.

The key in the door lock was loose in its hole. He thought
about locking it, but he knew Greta would never come in
without knocking. Once, early in their marriage, Greta walked
in on Einar while he was in the bath singing a folksong: *There
once was an old man who lived on a bog* . . . It should have been
innocent enough, Einar knew, a young wife finding her
husband bathing, happily singing to himself. From the tub,
Einar could see the arousal filling Greta's face. 'Don't stop,' she
said, moving closer. But Einar could hardly find the strength to
breathe, so exposed he felt, so ashamed, his bony arms crossed
over his torso, hands like fig leaves. Greta finally realized what
she had done, because she said, leaving the bathroom, 'I'm so
sorry. I should have knocked.'

Now Einar removed his clothes, turning his back to the
mirror. In the drawer of the bedstand was a roll of white
medical tape and scissors. The tape was gooey and textured like
a canvas, and Einar pulled out a length and cut it into five
pieces. Each piece he stuck to the edge of the bedpost. Then,
shutting his eyes and feeling himself slide down through the
tunnel of his soul, Einar pulled his penis back and taped it up in
the blank space just beneath his groin.

The undergarments were made from a blend of something
stretchy Einar was sure the Americans had invented. 'There's

no use in spending good money on silk for things you'll only wear once or twice,' Greta had said, handing him the package, and Einar had been too shy to disagree.

The panties were cut in a square shape and were silvery like the abalone inlaid in the screen. The garter belt was cotton, fringed with papery lace. It had eight small brass hooks to support the stockings, a mechanism Einar still found thrillingly complicated. When the avocado seeds had begun to rot in their silk handkerchiefs, he had inserted two Mediterranean sea sponges into the shallow cups of his camisole.

Then he pulled the dress over his head.

He'd begun to think of his make-up box as his palette. Brush-strokes to the brow. Light dabs to the lids. Lines on the lips. Blended streaks on the cheek. It was just like painting – like his brush turning a blank canvas into the winter Kattegat.

The clothes and the rouge were important, but the transformation was really about descending that inner tunnel with something like a dinner bell and waking Lili. She always liked the sound of crystal tinkling. It was about climbing out with her dewy hand in Einar's, reassuring her that the bright clattering world was hers.

He sat on the bed. He closed his eyes. The street was full of rifle noises from motor cars. The wind was rattling the terrace doors. Behind his eyelids he watched coloured lights erupt against the black, like the fireworks shot the previous Saturday over Menton's harbour. He could hear his heart slow. He could feel the gooey tape strapped against his penis. A little flutter of air rose through Einar's throat. He gasped as goose pimples ran down his arms, down the knuckles of his spine.

With a shiver, he was Lili. Einar was away. Lili would sit for Greta through the morning. She would walk along the quay with Hans, her hand visoring out the August sun. Einar would be only a reference in conversation: 'He misses Bluetooth quite a bit,' Lili would say, the world would hear.

Once again there were two. The walnut halved, the oyster knifed open.

Lili returned to the living room. 'Thank you for coming so

quickly,' Greta said. She spoke to Lili softly, as if she might crack at the sound of a harsh voice. 'Sit here,' Greta said, plumping the pillows on the sofa. 'Drape one arm over the back of the sofa, and keep your head turned to the screen.'

The session lasted the rest of the morning and through the afternoon. Lili, in the corner of the sofa, staring at the scene of abalone shell – a fishing village, a poet in a pagoda by a willow tree – in the Chinese screen. She became hungry but told herself to ignore it. If Greta didn't stop, neither would she. She was doing this for Greta. It was her gift to Greta, the only thing Lili could give her. She'd have to be patient. She'd have to wait for Greta to tell her what to do.

Later that afternoon, Hans and Lili set out on a stroll through Menton's streets. They stopped at the stands that sold lemon soap and figurines carved from olive wood and packages of candied figs. They spoke of Jutland, of the slate sky and the hog-trampled earth, of the families who lived on the same land for four hundred years, their children marrying one another, their blood thickening to muck. With his father dead, Hans was now Baron Axgil, although he hated the title. 'It's why I left Denmark,' he said. 'The aristocracy was dead. If I'd had a sister, I'm sure my mother would have wanted me to marry her.'

'Are you married now?'

'I'm afraid not.'

'But don't you want to marry?'

'I did, once. There once was a girl I wanted to marry.'

'What happened to her?'

'She died. Drowned in a river.' And then, 'Right in front of me.' Hans paid an old woman for a tin of mandarin hand soaps. 'But that was quite a while ago. I was practically still a boy.'

Lili could think of nothing to say. There she was, in her housedress, on the street ripe with urine, with Hans.

'Why aren't you married?' he said. 'I would think a girl like you would be married and running a fishery.'

'I wouldn't want to run a fishery.' She looked up at the sky. How blank and flat it was, cloudless, less blue than Denmark's. Above Lili and Hans, the sun throbbed. 'It'll be a while before I'm ready to get married. But I want to some day.'

Hans stopped at an open-front store to buy Lili a bottle of orange oil. 'But you don't have for ever,' he said. 'How old are you?'

How old was Lili? She was younger than Einar, who was then nearly thirty-five. When Lili emerged and Einar withdrew, years were lost: years that had wrinkled the forehead and stooped the shoulders; years that had quietened Einar with resignation. Lili's posture was the first thing one might notice, its fresh resilience. The second was her soft-voiced curiosity. The third, as Greta reported it, her smell – that of a girl who hadn't yet soured.

'I really can't say.'

'You don't seem like the type of girl who's too coy to admit her age,' Hans said.

'I'm not,' Lili said. 'I'm twenty-four.'

Hans nodded. It was the first fact made up about Lili. As Lili said it, she assumed she'd feel guilty about lying. Instead she felt a bit freer, as if she'd finally admitted an uncomfortable truth. Lili *was* twenty-four; she certainly wasn't as old as Einar. Had she said so, Hans would have thought her a strange fraud.

Hans paid the clerk. The bottle was square and brown, its cork stopper no bigger than the tip of Lili's little finger. She tried to pull it out, but couldn't prise it loose. 'Help me?' Lili asked.

'You're not as helpless as all that,' Hans said. 'Give it another tug.'

And Lili did, and this time the little cork popped free and the scent of oranges rose to her nostrils. It made her think of Greta.

'Why don't I remember you from when I was a boy?' Hans asked.

'You left Bluetooth when I was very young.'

'I suppose that's right. But Einar never said he had such a beautiful baby cousin.'

When she returned to the apartment, Lili found Greta still in the living room. 'Thank God you're back,' she said. 'I want to work some more tonight.' Greta led Lili, who was still holding her packages of the soaps and orange oil, to the camelback sofa. She arranged Lili against the pillows and, with her fingers spread across Lili's skull like a many-pronged clamp, turned her head towards the Chinese screen.

'I'm tired,' Lili said.

'Then go to sleep,' Greta said, her smock smudged with oily pinks and silvers. 'Just lay your head against your arm. I'm going to keep painting a little more.'

The next afternoon, Hans met Lili at the gate of the apartment. Again they walked through the narrow streets that swirled around St-Michel's hill, then down to the harbour to watch two fishermen sort through their haul of sea urchins. In late August, Menton was hot, the air humid and still. So much warmer than the hottest summer day in Copenhagen, Lili thought. And because Lili had never known such heat – this, after all, was her first trip out of Denmark – she found the weather exhausting. She could feel the housedress sticking to her back as she stood next to Hans, watching the wet net bulging with urchins, Hans's body so close to her own that she thought perhaps she could feel his hand on her arm, which was burning in the sun. Was it his hand, or something else? Simply a hot breeze?

Two gypsy children, a boy and a girl, approached Lili and Hans, trying to sell them a little carved elephant. 'Real ivory,' they said, pointing at the elephant's tusk. 'A deal for you.' The kids were small and dark around the eyes, and they stared at Lili in a way that made her feel unsafe.

'Let's go,' she said to Hans, who laid his hand on the warm wet small of her back, steering her away. 'I think I need to lie down.'

But when Lili returned home, Greta was waiting for her.

She posed Lili in front of her easel, settling her on the sofa. 'Sit still,' Greta said. 'I'm not finished.'

The next day Hans drove Lili up the corniche to Ville-franche, his Targa Florio's spoked wheels shooting shellrocks down to the sea. 'Next time don't leave Einar up in Denmark!' he yelled, his voice as pebbly as it was when he was a boy. 'Even good old Einar should have a holiday!' The wind was warm in Lili's face, and by the late afternoon she was again feeling weak in the stomach. Hans had to rent a room at the Hôtel de l'Univers for Lili to rest in. 'I'll be just downstairs having a coffee and an anisette,' he said, tipping his hat. Later, when she emerged from the narrow room, Lili found Hans off the lobby in the Restaurant de la Régence. She was barely out of her dreamy state and only said, 'Sometimes I just don't know what's wrong with me.'

On another day-trip Hans and Lili drove to Nice to shop for paintings in the antique stalls. 'Why doesn't Greta ever want to come along with us?' Hans enquired. 'Too busy painting, I guess,' Lili said. 'She works harder than anyone I know. Harder than Einar. One day she's going to be famous. You'll see.' Lili could feel Hans's eyes on her as she said this, and she found it remarkable that such a man as Hans would pay any attention to her opinions at all. In one of the stalls, tended by a woman with soft white fuzz on her chin, Lili found an oval burial portrait of a young man, his cheeks oddly coloured and his eyes closed. She bought it for fifteen francs, and Hans promptly bought it from her for thirty. And he asked, 'Are you feeling all right today?'

Each day, before her outings with Hans, Lili would pose for Greta on the sofa. She'd hold a book about French birds, or Edvard IV, in her lap, because her hands when empty would twitch nervously. Except for noise from the street, the apartment was quiet and the mantel clock would tick so slowly that at least once each afternoon Lili would rise to make sure it was properly wound. Then she would stick her head over the rail of the terrace, waiting for the hour when Hans would call at the gate. He'd taken to yelling up from the street: 'Lili!

Hurry up and come down!' and she would run down the
seven flights of tiled stairs, too impatient to wait for the caged
lift.

But before he arrived, Greta would clap her hands together
and say, 'That's it! Hold your face just like that – that's what I
want. Lili waiting, waiting for Hans.'

One day Lili and Hans were at an outdoor café at the foot of
St-Michel's steps. Five or six gypsy children, their clothes
dirty, came to their table selling postcards, the photographs of
the Côte's beaches hand-tinted with colour pencils. Hans
bought a set for Lili.

The air was thick, the sun hot on Lili's neck. The beer in
her glass was turning brown. The week of afternoons with
Hans had begun to fill Lili with expectations, and she now
wondered what Hans thought of her. He had taken a stroll on
the promenade with Lili; he had linked her arm through the
curve of his elbow; Hans, with his dark chuckle and his
billowing linen shirts, with his brown skin deepening in the
August sun, with his long-lost nickname Valnød, had come to
know Lili, but not Einar. Hans hadn't seen Einar since they
were boys. It was Lili and not Einar who had felt the rough tips
of Hans's fingers on her skin.

'I'm very glad I've met you,' she said.

'So am I.'

'And that we're able to get to know each other, in this way.'

Hans nodded. He was looking through the set of postcards,
holding up his favourites – of the municipal casino, of a citrus
grove at the foot of a hill – for Lili to inspect. 'Yes, you're
a terrific girl, Lili. You'll make some lad very happy one
day.'

Then Hans must have realized what Lili was feeling, because
he set down his cigarette and the postcards and said, 'Oh, Lili?
Did you think that maybe . . . with us? Then I'm very sorry.
But it's just that I'm too old for you, Lili. I've become too
much of a grouch for someone like you.'

Hans began to tell Lili about the girl he loved and lost. He

said his mother had asked him never to return to Bluetooth
when Ingrid – it was years ago, all of this – became pregnant.
They settled in Paris, across from the Panthéon, in a
wallpapered flat. She was skinny, except for her growing
stomach, with long freckled arms. They went swimming on an
August afternoon, not unlike today, Hans added, nodding
towards the sky. At a river with a bed of white rocks and
sprinkled with yellowing leaves, Ingrid waded into the water,
her arms out for balance. Hans watched from the shore, eating
a piece of ham. And then Ingrid's ankle turned and she cried
out, and a current pulled her under. 'I couldn't get to her in
time,' Hans said.

Apart from that tragedy, his life had been good. 'Because I
left Denmark,' he said. 'Life there is too neat and orderly for
me. Too cosy.' Greta would sometimes say that as well, when
she couldn't paint and friends invited them to another
smorgasbord. 'Too cosy to work,' she'd say, her silver bracelets
shaking. 'Too cosy to be free.'

'And now I've been on my own so long I'm not sure I
could ever get married. Too stuck in my old ways, I am.'

'Don't you think marriage is the one single thing we should
all hope for most in life? Doesn't it make you more whole than
living all alone?'

'Not always.'

'I think it does. Marriage is like a third person,' Lili said. 'It
creates someone else, more than just the two of you.'

'Yes, but not always for the best,' Hans said. 'Anyway, how
would you know anything about all of this?'

Just then something told Lili to check her handbag. Her
hand felt the empty iron of the chair's back. 'It's gone,' she said
so softly that Hans's forehead lifted and he murmured, 'What?'
Again, 'My handbag is gone.'

'The gypsies,' Hans said, jumping to his feet. The café was
in a small square with six alleyways running into it. Hans ran a
few feet down one alley and realized the gypsies weren't there,
and then ran into the next, his face reddening.

'Let's go to the police,' he finally said, leaving francs on the table. He warned another woman whose drawstring satchel was hanging from her chair. He pulled Lili's hand. He must have seen the white in her cheek, because he kissed it, gently.

The only things in the handbag were a little wad of money and a lipstick. The bag was Greta's, a cream kid bag with loop handles. Other than the lipstick and a few dresses and two pairs of shoes and her camisoles and underwear, Lili owned nothing. She was free of possessions, and that was part of the appeal in those early days of Lili – that she came and went, and there was nothing more to concern her than the wind lifting her hem.

The police station was on a *place* with orange trees growing in a little central park. The evening sun reflected in the station's front windows, and Lili could hear the clatter of the shop owners closing their shutters. Lili realized her sunglasses were also in the bag, a funny pair with flip-up lenses Greta's father had sent from California. Greta would be angry that they were gone, that Lili had failed to pay attention to who or what was around her; and just then, just as Hans and Lili reached the steps of the police station, where a family of dingy white cats was rolling on its backs, just then Lili realized that she couldn't report the stolen handbag. She stopped on the steps.

Lili had no identification, she had no passport; why – and it had never occurred to her, nor had anyone ever bothered to ask – she didn't even have a family name.

'Let's not make a fuss about this,' she said. 'It's just a silly old bag.'

'Then you'll never get it back.'

'But it isn't worth the trouble,' she said. 'And Greta is waiting. I just realized I'm late. I'm sure she's waiting for me. She wanted to paint this evening.'

'She'll understand.'

'Something tells me she wants to see me right now,' Lili said. 'I just have this funny feeling.'

'Come on now. Let's go inside.' Hans took Lili's wrist. A pull up the first step. He was still being playful, in a fatherly sort of way. He tugged again, and this time the pressure on her wrist hurt a little more, although it was no more painful than an aggressive handshake.

And just then – why, she would never know – something told both Lili and Hans to look down at the front of her dress. Growing on the white housedress patterned with conch shells was a round stain of blood, a stain so red it was nearly black. It was seeping outward like the ringed wave of a pebble landing in a pond.

'Lili? Are you hurt?'

'No, no,' she said. 'I'm fine. I'll be fine. But I should be getting home. Back to Greta.' Lili could feel herself shrinking inward, retreating back down the tunnel, back to Lili's lair.

'Let me help you. How can I help you?'

As each second passed Hans felt further away; his voice sounded as if it were travelling through a dull iron pipe. It was like at the Rådhuset ball: the blood was heavy, but she felt nothing. Where it was coming from she had no idea. She was both alarmed and amazed, like a child who has accidentally killed an animal. A little voice in her head shouted, 'Hurry!' – a frantic little voice equally panicked and enjoying the small brief drama of an afternoon in Menton in August. Lili left Hans on the steps of the police station, turning three corners immediately, running away from him as the gypsy children had run off from her, the stain on her dress spreading as persistently, as appallingly, as a disease.

Ten

❧

Greta's new style was to paint with pastel-bright colours, especially yellows and candy pinks and ice blues. She still painted only portraits. She still used the paints that arrived in glass bottles with unreliable stoppers from the firm in Munich. But where her previous paintings were serious and straightforward and official, her new paintings, in their levity and colour, looked, as Lili once said, like sweets. The paintings were large and depicted their subject, by now almost always Lili, outdoors, in a field of poppies, in a lemon grove, or against the hills of Provence.

While she painted, Greta thought of nothing, or what felt to her like nothing: her brain, her thoughts, felt as light as the paints she mixed into her palette. It reminded her of driving into the sun, as if painting were about pressing on blindly but in good faith. On her best days, ecstasy would fill her as she pivoted from her paintbox to the canvas, and it was as if there were a white light blocking out everything but her imagination. When her painting was working, when the brush-strokes were capturing the exact curve of Lili's head, or the depth of her dark eyes, Greta would hear a rustling in her head that reminded her of the bamboo prodder knocking oranges from her father's orange trees. Painting well was like harvesting fruit: the beautiful dense *thud* of an orange hitting the California loam.

Even so, Greta was surprised by the reception the Lili paintings received in Copenhagen that autumn. Rasmussen offered to hang them in his gallery for two weeks in October.

Her original triptych, *Lili Thrice* sold outright, after a brief dispute between a Swede in purple pigskin gloves and a young professor from the Royal Academy. Her portrait of Lili sleeping on the camelback sofa fetched more than 250 kroner; it wasn't as much as Einar's paintings earned, but closer than ever before.

'I need to see Lili every day,' Greta said to him. She was beginning to miss Lili when she wasn't around. Greta had always been an early riser, up well before dawn, before the first ferry call or rattle from the street. That autumn, there were mornings when Greta woke even earlier than that, the apartment so black she couldn't see her hand before her. She would sit up in the bed. There next to her lay Einar, still sleeping, at his feet Edvard IV. She herself was still caught in the hazy hallway of sleep, and Greta would wonder, where was Lili? Greta would quickly climb out of bed and begin searching the apartment. Where had Lili gone to? Greta would ask herself, lifting the tarps in the front room, opening the cupboard of the pickled-ash wardrobe. And only as she unbolted the front door, her lips repeating the question nervously, would Greta fully emerge from the thick mist of sleep.

One morning that autumn, Greta and Einar were in their apartment. It was the first time since April that they had needed a fire. The stove was a triple-decker, three black iron boxes stacked up on four feet. Greta held a match to the peeling paper of the birch logs inside. The flame took, and began to burn away the bark.

'But Lili can't come every day,' Einar protested. 'I don't think you understand how hard it is, sending Einar away and asking Lili in. It's too much to ask every day.' He was dressing Edvard IV in the cable-knit sweater sent up from the fisherman's wife. 'I love it. I love her. But it's hard.'

'I need to paint Lili every day,' Greta said. 'I need your help.'

And then Einar did a strange thing: he crossed the studio and kissed Greta's neck. Einar had — as Greta thought of it — the

Danish chill in him; she couldn't think of the last time her husband had kissed her anywhere but on her mouth, late at night, when all was black and quiet except for the occasional rambling drunkard being dragged to Dr Møller's door across the street.

Einar's bleeding had returned. He had been fine since the incident in Menton, but then one day recently he pressed a handkerchief to his nose. Greta watched the stain seep through the cotton. It troubled her, and it reminded her of the final months with Teddy Cross.

But just as it suddenly began, the bleeding would stop, leaving no trace except Einar's red and raw nostrils.

Then one night just the week before, as the first frost was collecting on the windowsills, Greta and Einar were quietly eating their supper. She was sketching in her notebook as she brought forkfuls of herring to her mouth. Einar was sitting idly, stirring his coffee with a spoon – daydreaming, as far as Greta could tell. She looked up from her sketch, a study of a new painting of Lili at a maypole. Across the table the colour was draining from Einar's face. His spine became more erect. He excused himself, leaving a little red spot on the chair.

Over the next two days Greta tried to ask him about the bleeding, about its cause and source, but each time Einar turned away in shame. It was almost as if she were striking him, his cheek jolting from the blow of her question. It was clear to Greta that Einar hoped to hide it from her, cleaning himself with old paint rags he later threw into the canal. But she knew. There was the smell, fresh and peaty. There was his unsettled stomach. There were the bloody rags the next morning clinging to the stone pylon of the canal's bridge.

One morning Greta went to the post office to make a telephone call in privacy. When she returned to the studio, Lili was lying on a cherry-red chaise borrowed from the props department at the Royal Theatre. Her nightdress was also borrowed; a retiring soprano, whose throat was old and blue and all leaping tendons, had worn it singing Desdemona. It seemed to Greta that Lili never knew how she looked. If she did, she wouldn't be lying like this, with her legs open, each foot on the floor, ankles drunkenly turned. With her mouth open and her tongue on her lip, she looked as if she had passed out on morphine. Greta liked the image, although she hadn't planned it. Einar had been up the previous night with a cramp in his stomach and, Greta feared, the bleeding.

'I've made an appointment for you,' Greta now said to Lili.

'What kind of appointment?' Lili's breath began to quicken, her breasts lifting and falling.

'With a doctor.'

Lili sat up. She looked alarmed. It was one of the few times Greta could see Einar edging back into Lili's face: suddenly the dark blush of whiskers burst on to her upper lip. 'There's nothing wrong with me,' Lili said.

'I didn't say there was.' Greta moved towards the chaise. She tied the satin ribbons on Lili's sleeves. 'But you've been ill,' Greta continued, her hands tucking themselves into her smock's patch pockets, where she stored the gnawed pencils, the picture of Teddy Cross in the waves at Santa Monica beach, a little swatch of the bloody dress Lili had been wearing when she returned to the rented apartment in Menton, crying Hans's name. 'I'm concerned about the bleeding.'

Greta watched Lili's face: it seemed to be curling at the edges with shame. But Greta knew she was right to bring it up. 'We need to know why it's happening. If you're not hurting anything by—' she began. Greta shuddered, a chill crossing her back. What was happening to her marriage, she wondered, picking at the ribbons woven into the collar of the nightdress. She wanted a husband. She wanted Lili. 'Oh, Einar.'

'Einar isn't here,' Lili said.

'Please tell him to meet me at Central Station for the 11.04 train to Rungsted,' Greta said. 'I'm going to the art shop.'

She went to the wardrobe, looking for a scarf.

'What if Einar doesn't return in time?' Lili asked. 'What if I can't find him by then?'

'He will.' And then, 'Have you seen my scarf? The blue one with the gold fringe?'

Lili looked into her lap. 'I don't think so.'

'It was in my wardrobe. In my drawer. Did you borrow it?'

'I think I left it at the Café Axel,' Lili said. 'I'm sure they have it behind the counter. I'll go and get it now.' And then, 'Greta, I'm sorry. I didn't take anything else. I didn't touch anything else.'

Greta felt the pique bunching up in her shoulders. Something is very wrong, she told herself, and then shoved the thought aside. No, she wasn't going to let a borrowed scarf upset her marriage. Besides, hadn't Greta told Lili to take anything that she wanted? Didn't Greta want, more than anything, to please Lili? 'You stay here,' Greta said. 'But please make sure Einar makes his train.'

The walls of the Café Axel were yellow from tobacco. Students from the Royal Academy went there for *frikadeller* and *fadøl*, which were half-price between four and six. When Greta was a student she would take a table by the door and sketch, her pad propped in her lap. When a friend walked in and asked what she was drawing, she would firmly close her pad and say, 'Something for Professor Wegener.'

Greta asked the barman about the blue scarf. 'My cousin thinks she left it here,' she said.

'Who's your cousin?' The barman rolled his hands in a tea towel.

'A slight girl. Not as tall as me. Shy.' Greta paused. It was difficult to describe Lili, to think of her floating through the world on her own, with her fluttering white collar and her brown eyes lifting towards handsome strangers. Greta's nostrils flared.

'Do you mean Lili?' the barman asked.

Greta nodded.

'Nice girl. Comes in and sits over there, by the door. I'm sure you know this, but the boys fall over themselves trying to get her attention. She'll share a beer with one of them and then, when his head is turned, disappear. Yes, she left a scarf.'

He handed it to her, and Greta tied it around her head. There it was again, the faint smell of mint and milk.

Out on the street, the air was damp, its chill deep and salty. Already her summer tan had faded and her hands had chapped. She thought of how beautiful Pasadena was in October, with the burned-out San Gabriel Mountains plum-brown and the bougainvillaea climbing chimneys.

Central Station echoed with the efficient swish of moving feet. Pigeons murmured in the timber rafters above, their chalky dung lurching down the red-oak beams. Greta bought a roll of mints from a news-candy boy, whose customers were leaving trails of paper wrappers across the floor.

Einar arrived at the ticket kiosk looking lost. His cheeks were raw from scrubbing, his hair slick with tonic. He had been running, and he wiped his brow anxiously. Only when she saw him in a crowd did Greta think about how small he was, his head barely high enough to rest on another man's breast. That was how Greta saw him: she exaggerated his slightness; she told herself, she came to believe, that Einar, with his bony wrists and his backside small and curved, was practically a child.

Einar looked up at the pigeons, as if he were in Central Station for the first time. He shyly asked a young girl in a pinafore for the time.

Something in Greta settled down. She went to Einar and kissed him. She straightened his lapel. 'Here's your ticket,' she said. 'Inside is the address of the doctor I want you to see.'

'First I want you to tell me something,' Einar said. 'I want you to agree that there's nothing wrong with me.' He was rocking on his heels.

'Of course there's nothing wrong with you,' Greta said, swatting her hands through the air. 'But I still want you to see the doctor.'

'Why?'

'Because of Lili.'

'Poor little girl,' he said.

'If you want Lili to stay – with us, I mean – then I think a doctor should know about her.' Afternoon shoppers, mostly women, were nudging by them, their net bags bulky with cheese and herring.

Greta wondered why she continued to speak of Lili as if she were a third person. It would crush Einar – she could imagine his fine bones crumpling into a heap – were she to admit, aloud at least, that Lili was no more than her husband in a dress. Really, but it was the truth.

'Why are you doing this now?' Einar asked. The red rim of his eyelids nearly made Greta turn the other way.

'I love Lili as much as you do, more than—' but she stopped herself. 'The doctor can help her.'

'How? How can anyone but you and me help Lili?'

'Let's see what the doctor says.'

Einar tried one last time. 'I don't want to go. Lili wouldn't want me to go.'

Greta straightened her back, her head lifting. 'But I want you to go,' she said. 'I'm your wife, Einar.' She pointed him towards platform 8 and sent him on his way, her hand falling on the small of his back. 'Go on,' she said as he shuffled across the floor, past the news-candy boy, through the trail of paper wrappers, his body slipping into the crowd of shoppers, his head becoming one of a hundred, mostly women, who were busy with Copenhagen errands and fat with children, whose breasts were falling just as Einar's were lifting, who would one day – Greta knew even then – look at Einar in a crowd and see only themselves.

Eleven

❧

Einar sat by the window, the noon sun curled in his lap. The train was passing houses with red tiled roofs, laundry and children waving in the gardens. An old woman was opposite him, her hands around her bag handle. She offered a mint from a foil roll. 'Going to Helsingør?'

'To Rungsted,' he said.

'Me too.' A square of open-knit lace was holding up her white hair. Her eyes were snow-blue, her earlobes fatty and loose. 'You have a friend there?'

'An appointment.'

'A medical appointment?'

Einar nodded, and the old woman said, 'I see.' She tugged on her cardigan. 'At the radium institute?'

'I believe so,' he said. 'My wife made the appointment.' He opened the envelope Greta had given him. Inside was an ecru card with a note Lili had written to Greta last week: *Sometimes I feel trapped. Do you ever feel that way? Is it me? Is it Copenhagen? Kisses—*

'Your card says Dr Hexler,' the old woman said. 'On the back is Dr Hexler's address. It's on my way. I'll be happy to take you. Some say he runs the best radium institute in Denmark.' The woman hugged her bag against her breasts. 'Some say he can cure almost anything.'

Einar thanked the old woman and then sat back in his seat. Through the window the sun was warm. He had considered skipping the appointment. When she told him to meet her at Central Station, a furious flash of an image ran through his

his head: that of Greta, her chin high above the crowd, waiting at the station for him to arrive. He thought about defying her and never showing up. He thought about her chin slowly falling as the minutes and hours passed and it became more and more evident that he would not come. She would shuffle home. She would open the door to the apartment in the Widow House and find him waiting for her at the table. Einar would say, 'I don't want to see the doctor.' And she would pause, and then say, 'All right.'

'We're here,' the old woman on the train said. 'Get your things.'

Red waxy cones from the yew trees were lying along Rungsted's streets. It had rained in the morning, leaving a damp, evergreen smell. The old woman inhaled deeply. She walked quickly, her hips squirming in her skirt. 'Don't be nervous,' she said.

'I'm not nervous.'

'There's nothing wrong with being nervous.' They turned on to a street of houses behind low walls with white iron gates. An open-top motor car drove past them, its engine snapping. The driver, a man in a leather golf hat, waved at the old woman. 'Here we are,' the woman said at a corner across from the harbour, at a blue building so indistinguishable it could have been a bakery. She squeezed Einar's arm, just under the pit. Then she hooked up her collar and headed towards the sea.

Einar had to wait in Dr Hexler's examination room for almost an hour. Half the room looked like a parlour, with a carpet and a cabinet-sofa and bookshelves and a spider plant in a stand. The other half had a rubber floor, a padded table, glass jars of clear liquids, and an oversized lamp on casters.

Dr Hexler entered, saying, 'Didn't the nurse ask you to remove your clothes?' His chin was long and extended with a cleft deep enough to sink a slot. His hair was silver, and when he sat in the chair opposite Einar he revealed a pair of Argyle socks. The woman from the train had said he was equally known for his rose garden, which, outside the clinic's window, was cropped for the winter.

'Trouble in the marriage?' he said. 'Is that what I understand?'

'Not exactly trouble.'

'How long have you been married?'

'Six years,' Einar said. He recalled their wedding in St Alban's Church in the park; the young deacon was English and, that morning, nicked by his razor. He had said, in a voice as light as the air floating through the pink-glass windows and into the laps of their wedding guests, 'This is a special wedding. I see something special here. In ten years the two of you will be extraordinary people.'

'Any children?' Dr Hexler asked.

'No.'

'Why not?'

'I'm not really sure.'

'You do conduct intercourse, is that right?' Dr Hexler's face was stony, and Einar could imagine him in his rose garden with that same face, discovering with grave disappointment a petal-eating mite. 'There is regular copulation?'

By now Einar had stripped down to his underpants. The pile of clothes on the chair looked sad, the white shirtsleeves reaching limply from the waist of his trousers. Dr Hexler waved him to sit on the cabinet-sofa. Through a hose with a funnel on the end he ordered his nurse to bring in coffee and a dish of sugared almonds.

'Is there ejaculation?' he continued.

Around Einar bricks of indignity were being laid. Each insult, from Greta, and now from Dr Hexler, was a red brick of hurt stacking with the others to build a wall. 'Sometimes,' Einar answered.

'Good enough.' Dr Hexler flipped a page in his notepad. And then, 'Your wife tells me you like to dress as a woman.'

'Is that what she said?' Then the nurse entered, a woman with frizzy red hair. She set down the coffee and the almonds. 'Sugar?' she asked.

'Mrs Wegener told me about a girl,' Dr Hexler continued. 'A girl called Lili.'

'Excuse me, Mr Wegener?' the nurse asked. 'Sugar?'

'No. Nothing for me.' She poured the coffee for Dr Hexler and then left.

'Mr Wegener, I'm a specialist. There's virtually no trouble I haven't treated. If you are embarrassed, please remember that I'm not.'

Einar didn't know why, but he suddenly wanted to believe Dr Hexler would understand; that if he were to tell Hexler about the tunnel that led to Lili's lair, that if Einar were to admit Lili wasn't really him but someone else, Hexler would tap a pencil against his lips and say, 'Ah, yes. No need to worry. I've seen this before.'

Einar began, 'Sometimes I feel a need to go and find Lili.' He'd come to think of it as a hunger. Not like a hungry stomach an hour before dinner; it was more like when you've missed several meals, when you're hollow. When you're concerned about where your next plate of food will come from, if it will ever come. It could make Einar dizzy. 'Sometimes I lose my breath when I think about her,' Einar said.

'Where do you go to find her?' Dr Hexler asked. His thick glasses made his eyes look as huge as pickled eggs in a jar of oil.

'Inside me.'

'And is she always there?'

'Yes. Always.'

'What would you think if I were to tell you to stop dressing as her?' Dr Hexler leaned forward in his chair.

'Do you think I should, doctor? Do you think I'm hurting something by doing this?' Einar felt small in his underpants, the crack of the couch's cushions nearly swallowing him. Now Einar wanted some coffee, but he could barely reach to the table for the urn.

Dr Hexler switched on the examination lamp, its silver bowl whitening with light. 'Let's have a look,' he said. He briefly pressed his hand on Einar's shoulder as he stood.

'Please stand,' Dr Hexler said, wheeling over the lamp, its casters trembling. He aimed the light at Einar's stomach. The few freckles around his navel looked garishly brown, the few black hairs reminding Einar of the dust that gathers in a corner. 'Do you feel anything when I do this?' Dr Hexler asked, his palm against Einar's stomach.

'No.'

'And this?'

'No.'

'What about here?'

'No.'

'I see.' He was sitting in front of Einar on a steel stool. More than anything else Einar wanted Dr Hexler to declare that there was nothing wrong with Lili and Einar, that their shared body was no more a malnormality than a nailless toe, or even Dr Hexler's long chin with the cleft so deep it could nearly receive a key.

'How about down there?' he said, pointing a tongue depressor at Einar's crotch. 'May I have a look?'

When Einar lowered his underpants, Dr Hexler's face stopped, only his nostrils, with their pores jammed with dots of black, moving. 'Appears to be all there,' he said. 'You can pull them up again. You seem to be in quite good health. There's nothing else you want to tell me about?'

Only the day before Einar had crammed a rag into his underpants. Had Greta told the doctor about that as well? Einar felt cornered. 'There's something else I suppose I should mention,' he began.

When Einar told him about the bleeding, Dr Hexler's shoulders pressed together into a hump. 'Yes, your wife said something about this. Is there anything in the blood? Is it clotty?'

'I don't think so.' Another brick of indignity was mortared into place. The only relief Einar could find just then was from shutting his eyes.

'It's time for an X-ray,' Dr Hexler said. He seemed surprised when Einar said he'd never had one before. 'It will tell us if

there's something wrong,' Dr Hexler said. 'It may also drive
this desire out of you.' From the way his eyebrows lifted above
his spectacles, Einar could tell Dr Hexler was proud of his
clinic's technology. He went on to discuss gamma rays and
natural radium emanating from radium salts. 'Ionizing radiation
is turning out to be the miracle cure for all sorts of things. It
works on ulcers, dry scalp, and most certainly impotence,' he
said. 'It's become the treatment of choice.'

'What will it do to me?'

'It will look inside you.' And then, as if offended, 'It will
treat you.'

'Do I really need one?'

But Dr Hexler was already sending orders through the
funnel.

When they were ready for Einar, a skinny man with a sharp
Adam's apple led him out of Dr Hexler's office. This was
Vlademar, Hexler's assistant, and he led Einar to a room with
tiled walls and a floor sloped for run-off, a drain in the corner
covered with mesh. White canvas straps hung from the trolley
in the middle of the room, the buckles shiny under the lights.

'Let's strap you in,' Vlademar said. Einar asked if it was
necessary. Vlademar grunted his reply, his Adam's apple
jabbing up.

The X-ray machine was the shape of an inverted L, its metal
casing painted a muddy green. It extended over the trolley, a
large grey eye of a lens pointed at the stretch of skin between
Einar's navel and his groin. There was a black glass window in
the room, behind which, Einar imagined, Dr Hexler was
telling Vlademar which round-knobbed levers to pull. It
occurred to Einar, as the lights in the room dimmed and the
machine coughed and then whirred, its casing vibrating tinnily,
that this was only the beginning of doctors and tests. Somehow
Einar knew the X-rays would show nothing, and Dr Hexler
would either order more or send him to a second specialist, or
a third. And Einar didn't mind, not just then, because anything
seemed worth undertaking for the sake of Greta and Lili.

Einar had expected the X-ray's light to be gold and flecked, but it was invisible, and he felt nothing. At first Einar thought the machine wasn't working. He nearly sat up and asked, 'Is something wrong?'

Then the X-ray machine switched into a higher gear, its whirring lifting an octave. The dented green metal casing rattled more, sounding like a baking sheet shaking dry. Then Einar wondered if he felt something on his stomach, but he wasn't sure. He thought of a stomach alive with glow worms nested from the Bluetooth bog. He wondered if he felt a warm, fizzy feeling or if he was imagining it. He propped himself up on his elbows to look down, but there was nothing different about his stomach, grey in the dimmed room. 'Please be still,' Dr Hexler said through a funnel speaker. 'Lie back down.'

But nothing was happening, or what seemed to Einar like nothing. The machine was clattering, and a blank feeling spread across his abdomen: he couldn't tell if he felt something hot there or not. Then he thought he felt the pinch of a burn, but when he looked again, his stomach was just the same. 'Lie still, Mr Wegener,' Hexler's voice boomed again. 'This is serious.'

Einar couldn't tell how long the machine had been running. Had two minutes passed, or twenty? And when would it end? The room dimmed further, now nearly black, and a yellow ring of light rippled around the grey lens. Einar was bored, and then, suddenly, sleepy. He closed his eyes, and it felt as if his body was becoming densely heavy. He thought about looking down to his stomach one last time, but his arms wouldn't move to lift him. How had he become so tired? His head felt like a lead ball attached to his neck. In his throat Einar tasted his morning coffee.

'Try to go to sleep, Mr Wegener,' Hexler said. The machine roared even louder, and Einar felt something hot press against his stomach.

Then Einar knew something was wrong. He opened his eyes just long enough to see someone lean his forehead against the black glass window, then a second forehead pressing, smudging. If Greta were here, Einar thought dreamily, she would unstrap me and take me home. She would kick the green machine until it stopped. A crash of whipping metal shook the room, but Einar couldn't open his eyes to see what had happened. If Greta were here, she'd yell at Hexler to turn off the damn machine. If Greta were here ... but Einar couldn't finish the thought because he was asleep – no, beyond sleep.

Twelve

❧

As Dr Hexler's X-ray machine continued to clang, Greta pressed her forehead against the black glass window. Maybe she'd been wrong; maybe her husband didn't need to see a doctor. She wondered if she should have listened to his protests.

On the other side of the glass, Einar was lying strapped to the trolley. He looked beautiful, with his eyes closed, his skin a soft grey through the glass. The small mound of his nose rose up from his face. 'Are you sure he's comfortable?' she asked Dr Hexler.

'For the most part.'

She'd worried that Einar was slipping away from her. It sometimes bothered her that Einar never became jealous when a man on the street ran his eyes over her breasts; the only time he commented on it was when he was dressed as Lili, and then he'd say, 'How lucky you are.'

In her consultation with Dr Hexler the week before, he had said there was a possibility of a tumour in the pelvis that could be causing both infertility and Einar's confused state of masculinity. 'I've never seen it myself, but I've read about it. It can go undetected, with its only manifestations being odd behaviour.' Part of her wanted the theory to make sense. Part of her wanted to believe that a little scalpel curved like a scythe could slice free the tumour, its rind as blood-orange and tight as a persimmon, and Einar would return to their marriage.

On the other side of the window there was a crash of metal, but Dr Hexler said, 'Everything's fine.' Einar was writhing on

the trolley, his legs pressing against the straps. They were so
taut with tension that Greta thought the straps might snap and
Einar's body would fling itself across the room. 'When will
you be finished?' she asked Hexler. 'Are you sure everything is
going all right?' She fingered the ends of her hair, thinking at
once how she hated its coarseness and that if anything were
ever to happen to Einar, she wouldn't know what to do.

'An X-ray takes time,' Vlademar said.

'Is it hurting him? It looks like he's in pain.'

'Not really,' Dr Hexler said. 'There might be a small surface
burn or ulceration, but not much else.'

'He'll feel a bit sick in the stomach,' Vlademar added.

'It will do him good,' Dr Hexler said. He was calm-faced,
with stubby black lashes that beat around his eyes. He stuttered
the first syllable of every sentence, but his voice was dark with
authority. After all, the clinic drew the richest men in
Denmark, men with bellies loose over their belts who, in their
flurry to manufacture rubber shoes and mineral dyes and
superphosphates and Portland cement, lost control of all that
hung below their belts.

'And if it's the devil your husband's got in him,' Vlademar
added, 'I'll zap it out.'

'That's the beauty of the X-ray,' Hexler said. 'It burns away
the bad and keeps the good. It might not be an exaggeration to
call it a miracle.' Both men smiled, their teeth reflected in the
black glass, and Greta felt something small and regretful
beneath her breast.

When it was over, Vlademar moved Einar to a room with
two small windows and a folding screen on castors. He slept
for an hour while Greta sketched. She was drawing Lili, asleep
in the institute's bed. If the X-ray found a tumour and Dr
Hexler removed it, then what would happen? Would she
never again see Lili in Einar's face, in his lips, in the pale green
veins that ran on the underside of his wrists like rivers on a
map? She had contacted Dr Hexler in the first place in order to
ease Einar's mind – or had it been to ease her own? No, she
had first telephoned Hexler, from the little booth at the post

office, because she knew she had to do something for Einar. Wasn't it her responsibility to make sure he got the proper attention? If she'd ever promised herself anything, it was that she'd never let her husband simply slip away. Not after Teddy Cross. Greta thought of the blood bursting from Einar's nose, seeping through the lap of Lili's dress.

Einar turned in the bed, moaning. He was pale, his skin loose on his cheek. Greta placed a warm cloth across his forehead. Part of her hoped Hexler would instruct Einar to live freely as Lili, to take a job as a salesgirl behind the glass counter at Fonnesbech's department store. Part of Greta wanted to be married to the most scandalous man in the world. It had always annoyed her when people assumed that just because she had married she was now seeking a conventional life. 'I know you'll be as happy as your mother and father,' a cousin from Newport Beach had written after her marriage to Einar; it was all Greta could do to keep herself from burning the cousin from her memory. But I'm not like them, she told herself as she shredded the letter into the iron stove. *We're* not like them. That was long before Lili showed up, but even then Greta knew she had married a man who would take her somewhere unlike anywhere she'd ever been. It was what she had first seen in Teddy, although that turned out not to be the case with him. But Einar was different. He was strange. He almost didn't belong to this world. And on most days, Greta felt, neither did she.

Beneath the window, Dr Hexler's bare rose bushes were trembling in the wind. The other window overlooked the sea. There were black clouds, as dark and full as ink in water. A fishing boat was struggling to return to harbour. But how could she remain married to a man who sometimes wanted to live as a woman? I'm not going to let something like that stop me, she told herself, her sketchbook in her lap. Greta and Einar would do what they wanted. No one could keep her from doing as she pleased. Perhaps they would have to move somewhere where no one knew them. Where nothing spoke for them – no gossip, no family name, no previously established reputation. Nothing except their paintings and the little whisper of Lili's voice.

She was ready, Greta told herself. For whom or what or where, she wasn't sure, but she was always ready.

Einar stirred again in his bed, struggling to lift his head. The bulb overhead cast a yellow bell of light on his face, and his cheeks looked hollow. Hadn't he looked fine just this morning? But maybe she hadn't paid enough attention to Einar during the past few months. Maybe he had become ill in front of her eyes and she had failed to notice until now. How busy she'd become, painting and selling her work and writing to Hans in Paris about arranging a visit for Lili, about the availability of an apartment in the Marais, with two skylights, one for herself and one for Einar – what with all of that, Greta might have missed something grave fading into the face of her husband. She thought of Teddy Cross.

'Greta,' Einar said. 'Am I all right?'

'You will be. Rest some more.'

'What happened?'

'It was a strong X-ray. Nothing to worry about.' The skin beneath his navel had burned slightly.

Einar pressed the side of his face into the pillow. He fell asleep again. There he was, Greta's husband. With his fine skin, and his small head with the temples that dented softly, almost like a baby's. With his nose flaring with breath. With his smell of turpentine and talc. With the skin around his eyes red and nearly on fire.

Greta replaced the cloth across his forehead.

When Dr Hexler finally arrived, Greta said, 'At last.' They went into the corridor. 'Is he going to be all right?'

'He'll be better tomorrow, and even better the day after.' Greta thought she saw concern in the wrinkles around Dr Hexler's mouth. 'The X-ray didn't show anything.'

'No tumour?'

'Nothing.'

'Then what's wrong with him?' Greta asked.

'In terms of his physical health, nothing at all.'

'What about the bleeding?'

'It's hard to be sure, but probably nothing more than his diet. Be sure he avoids any stony fruit and fish bones.'

'Do you really think that's all there is to it? His diet?' Greta took one step back. 'Do you really believe he's a perfectly healthy man, Dr Hexler?'

'His health is normal. But is he a normal man? Not at all. Your husband isn't well.'

'What can I do?'

'Do you keep a lock on your wardrobe? To keep him out of your clothes?'

'Of course not.'

'You should do so immediately.'

'What good would that do? Besides, he has dresses of his own.'

'Get rid of them right away. You shouldn't be encouraging this, Mrs Wegener. If he thinks you approve of it, he might think it's all right for him to pretend he's Lili.' Dr Hexler paused. 'Then he'll have no hope. You haven't been encouraging this, have you? I hope for his sake that you've never told him that you approve.'

It was what Greta feared most, that somehow Lili would be blamed on her. That she had somehow harmed her husband. The corridor's walls were dull yellow and scratched. Next to Greta was a portrait of Dr Hexler, the type of portrait that she used to paint.

One day just a few weeks before, Greta received a telephone call from Rasmussen, saying that Lili had come into the gallery. 'Of course I recognized her from your paintings,' he said. 'But something might have been wrong. She seemed weak, or thirsty.' Rasmussen said he had given Lili a chair, and she quickly fell asleep, one silver bubble on her lips. Soon after, Baroness Haggard came to the gallery with her Egyptian chauffeur. The baroness liked to think of herself as the most current of the aristocracy, and she couldn't get over the irony – the 'modernism', as she put it – of coming across the paintings' subject sleeping before the paintings themselves. The gallery filled with the soft leather sound of the baroness's ostrich gloves applauding 'the whole moment'. Five paintings were hanging, paintings done in the heat of late August in southern France, each lit as if from behind by the slow, creeping Menton sun. They showed Lili just as she now was in the chair: tentative, inward, exotic in size and poise, with her large nose and bony knees, her lids oily, her face bright. 'The baroness bought all five,' Rasmussen had reported. 'And Lili slept through the whole transaction. Greta, is something wrong with her? I certainly hope not. You aren't keeping her out too late, are you? Take care of her, Greta. For your sake.'

'You're really not concerned about the bleeding?' Greta asked Dr Hexler. 'Not in the least?'

'Not as much as I am about his delusion that he is a woman,' the doctor said. 'Even an X-ray can't cure that. Would you like me to talk to Einar? I can tell him that he's injuring himself.'

'But is he?' Greta finally asked. 'I mean, is he really?'

'Well, of course. I trust you agree with me, Mrs Wegener. I trust you'd agree that if this doesn't stop, we'll have to take more drastic measures. That a man like your husband can't live much of a life. Of course Denmark is very open, but this isn't about openness. It's about sanity, wouldn't you agree with me, Mrs Wegener? Wouldn't you agree that there's something not quite sane about your husband's desires? That you and I, as responsible citizens, cannot let your husband free to roam as Lili? Not even in Copenhagen. Not even on occasion. Not even under your supervision. I trust you'll agree with me that we should do whatever it takes to get this demon out of him, because that is what it is, don't you agree with me, Mrs Wegener? A demon. Mrs Wegener, don't you agree?'

And just then, Greta, who was thirty and a Californian and who could count at least three instances when she had nearly killed herself by accident – the second, for example, was when she performed a handstand on the teak railing of the *Frederik VIII*, which first carried her family to Denmark when she was ten – realized that Dr Hexler knew very little, if anything at all.

She'd been wrong, and she heard Einar moan in his bed
behind the folding screen.

Part Two

Paris
1929

❧

Thirteen

Just off the boulevard de Sebastopol, north of Les Halles Centrales, there was a little street that ran for two blocks. Over the years the street's name had changed. It was once known as the rue du Poivre – a pepper warehouse had thrived and failed there. When it was known as the rue des Semaines, there was a hotel for returning soldiers. But now it was known – at least colloquially, because the blue-and-white street sign was missing – as the rue de la Nuit. The buildings on the street were black, with soot on the windowsills, on the abandoned gas lamps, in the trough of the *pissoir*, on the torn awning of the tobacco shop, which also peddled wheat, vodka and girls. The doors on the street were numbered but signless. No one aside from the tobacco-shop proprietor, who had a red moustache that caught the crumbs of his morning brioche, seemed to live on the street or conduct any sort of business, legitimate or otherwise. Number 22 was a door with a bubble-glass window, beyond that a hallway that smelled like the sooty *pissoir*. At the top of the stairs, another door, this one dented with kicks, and beyond that a counter with a woman named, or so she said, Madame Jasmin-Carton, and her Manx cat, Sophie.

Madame Jasmin-Carton was fat but still young. A thick brown fur grew on her forearms, in which her gold chain bracelets sometimes snagged. She once told Einar that one of her girls had gone off and married a Greek prince, leaving Madame Jasmin-Carton with the Manx cat. She also reported that over the years the visitors to her *salles de plaisir* included ambassadors, a prime minister and a good dozen counts.

For five francs Madame Jasmin-Carton would give Einar a key chained to a brass bulb. The key admitted him to Salle No. 3, a narrow room with an armchair covered in green wool, a wire wastepaper basket thoughtfully emptied, and two small windows with their black shades drawn. There was a bulb in the ceiling that cast light around the green chair. Behind a smell of ammonia was the trace of something salty and bitter and wet.

It was May now, two sunny, warm days for every cold one. The narrow room was always cold. In the winter Einar had sat in the green chair in his overcoat and watched the puffs of his breath. He hadn't been coming to Madame Jasmin-Carton's long enough to know, but he imagined that in August the dim walls – already yellow from tobacco, and streaked – would sweat on their own.

Today, Einar peeled off his jacket, which had panel pockets and a fashionable looped belt. Greta had bought the jacket for Einar, as she did nearly all his clothes; she trusted he knew nothing of how to dress for Paris. Except of course Lili's clothes: the drop-waist dresses with the matching silk headbands, the kid gloves that pulled past the elbow with pearly clasps, the shoes with the rhinestone ankle straps. Lili bought those herself. In a marmalade jar Einar would set aside Lili's weekly allowance, and she would spend her way through it in two or three days, her hand reaching into the jar's narrow mouth and snatching the centimes. The Lili money: that was the entry in Einar's budget. He would look for francs in the pockets of his gabardine trousers to give her more. If he found none, sometimes Lili would run to Greta, who with Lili only seemed to know the words 'yes' and 'more'.

Einar lifted one of the black shades in the little room. Behind the smudged glass was a girl in a leotard and black stockings, one foot on a bentwood chair. She was dancing, although there was no music. Peering out of another little window was the face of a man, his oily nose pressed white to the glass. His breath left a stain of fog. The girl seemed aware of Einar and the other man; before she yanked off a bit of clothing she would look around, although not directly at their flat-nosed faces, and dip her chin.

She peeled a pair of gloves similar to Lili's off the fleshy pipe of her arm. The girl was not pretty: black hair electric and dry, a horse's jaw, hips too wide and stomach too narrow. But there was something lovely in her modesty, Einar thought; in the way she neatly draped her gloves and then her leotard and finally her stockings over the back of the bentwood chair, as if she knew she would need them again.

Soon she was naked except for her shoes. She started to dance more energetically, her toes pointing, her hands held out. She threw her head back, exposing her white-blue trachea pressing against her skin.

For almost six months Einar had been visiting Madame Jasmin-Carton's, heading out in the afternoon when Greta was meeting with a collector or one of the magazine editors at *La Vie Parisienne* or *L'Illustration* who hired her to sketch their stories. But Einar didn't go to Madame Jasmin-Carton's for the same reason as the other men, who would press their pocked noses against the little windows, their tongues like sea urchins mashing up against a fishmonger's glass. He only wanted to watch the girls strip and dance, to study the curve and heft of their breasts, to watch the thighs, eerily white and tremulous like the skin on a bowl of steamed milk, flap open and closed — he could almost hear the knee bones slap together through the greasy glass window. He also liked the underside of their forearms, where their veins, hot with shame and resentment, would flow greenly; and the pad of flesh that swelled beneath the navel — that part of a woman made him think of the pillow carried by a ring bearer at a wedding. He visited Madame Jasmin-Carton's to examine women, to see how their bodies attached limb to trunk and produced a female. How the girl with the electric black hair would hold her chin down as she distractedly cupped each custardy breast. How the girl after her, a blonde with a wiry body, walked around the half-circle black room with her fists on her hips, which were all bone. Or how the girl from last Tuesday, whom Einar had never seen before, parted her freckled thighs and flashed her genitalia. The thighs closed quickly, and then she danced angrily, the sweat pouring down her neck, while the pink image of her sex burned in Einar's eyes, even when he shut them and tried to forget who he was or where he was; even later, when he lay down next to Greta and tried to sleep while her bedside lamp burned and her fat-tipped pencil scratched away at the leather-spined notebook that held drawing after drawing, a career's worth, of Lili.

Einar and Greta now lived in the Marais. They'd left Copenhagen over three years before. It was Greta's idea. One day a letter had arrived at the Widow House, and Einar could recall Greta reading it quickly and then lifting the lid of the iron stove and dropping it in. He could recall the brief yellow light that poured from the stove as it devoured the letter. Then she told Einar that Hans wanted them to move to Paris. 'He thinks, and so do I, it would be best,' she said. 'But why'd you burn his letter?' Einar asked. 'Because I didn't want Lili to see it. I don't want her to know that Hans wants to see her again.'

They rented an apartment in a cut-stone townhouse on the rue Vieille du Temple. The apartment was on the fourth floor, the top, with skylights cut into the steep roof and windows facing the street. The rear faced the courtyard, where during the summer geraniums grew in window boxes wired to the ledges and laundry stiffened on the line. The house was just down the street from the Hôtel de Rohan, with its entrance curving into the pavement and the two great black doors of its gate. The street was narrow but drained well in winter, and sliced through the Marais with its grand *hôtels* reconfigured as government offices or warehouses for dry-goods importers or simply abandoned, and its Jewish shops, where Einar and Greta would buy dried fruit and sandwiches on Sundays when everything else was closed.

The apartment had two workrooms. Einar's, with a few

landscapes of the bog perched on oversized easels. And Greta's, with her Lili paintings, sold before they dried, and the spot on the wall, perpetually wet and thick, where she dabbed out her colours until they were just right: the brown of Lili's hair, which turned to honey after one swim in an August sea; the purply red of the blush that clasped around the base of her throat; the silvery white of the inside of her elbows. Each workroom had a daybed covered with kilims. Sometimes at night Greta would sleep there when she was too tired to climb into the bed they shared in the little room at the back of the apartment, where there was a darkness that felt to Einar like a cocoon. In their bedroom, with the lamps turned off, it was too dark for Einar to see even his hand in front of his face, and this he liked, and he'd lie there until dawn, when the laundry pulley would squeak and one of their neighbours would get busy hanging out another load.

In the summer mornings Lili would rise and ride the omnibus down to the Bains du Pont-Solférino on the quai des Tuileries. The pool had a row of changing huts that were made of striped canvas, like tall, narrow tents. Inside Lili would change into her bathing dress, carefully arranging herself beneath the frilled skirt so that she could remain, as she thought of it, modest. Since they left Denmark her body had changed, and now her breasts were fleshy with muscle gone soft, enough to fill the little dented cups of her bathing dress. Her rubber bathing cap, with its pneumatic smell, would pull her hair back, tugging on her cheeks and giving her an exotic look with her eyes slanted and her mouth flattened out. Lili had learned to carry a hand mirror with her, and in the canvas cabin, in the summer mornings, she would look at herself, waving the mirror across each inch of her skin, until the pool attendant flapped the canvas and demanded whether Mademoiselle needed some assistance.

With that, Lili would slip into the pool, holding her head above the water. She would bathe for thirty minutes, her shoulders turning as each arm lifted over her head with the motion of a windmill, until the other women in the pool – for this pool, like the tea room where she sometimes took her coffee and croissant, was reserved for ladies – stopped and hung on to the lip of the pool to watch little Lili, so graceful, so long-armed, so, they would cluck, *puissante*.

It was what she liked most: her head gliding across the surface of the pool like a little duck; the other ladies in their wool bathing dresses watching her with their mixture of indifference and gossipy intrigue; the way she could pull herself from the pool, her fingertips pruned, and pat the towel down her arms as she dried in the glittering light that reflected off the Seine. She would watch the traffic across the river. And Lili would think that all of this was possible because she and Greta had left Denmark. She would think, in the summer mornings, on the lip of the pool filled with Seine water, that she was free. Paris had freed her. Greta had freed her. Einar, she would think, was slipping away. Einar was freeing her. A shiver would run up her damp spine; her shoulders would shudder.

In the hut, after returning the pink towel to the attendant, she would peel off the bathing dress, and if she was in a particularly strong trance about her life and the possibility of it all, she would let out a little gasp when she discovered that down there, between her white, goose-pimpled thighs, lay a certain shrivelled thing. It was so vile to her that she would snap closed her thighs, tucking it away, her knee bones smacking; she could hear the muffled smack, and the sound of it – like two felt-wrapped cymbals meeting in crescendo – would remind Lili, would remind Einar, of the girl at Madame Jasmin-Carton's who had danced resentfully and snapped her knees together in such a harsh manner that he could hear the smack of bone even through the smudged glass.

And so there Einar would be – a little Danish man in the changing hut of Paris's finest ladies' pool. At first he would be confused, his face blank in the hand mirror. He wouldn't know where he was, couldn't recognize the reverse stripes of the inside of the hut's canvas. Didn't recognize the slip and splash of the ladies swimming laps. The only clothing on the hanger was a simple brown dress with a belt. Black shoes with wedgy heels. A purse with a few coins and a lipstick. A chiffon scarf patterned with pears. He was a man, he would suddenly think, and yet he had no way back to the apartment unless he put on all these clothes. Then he'd see the double string of Danish amber beads; his grandmother had worn them her whole life, even when farming the sphagnum fields, the beads around her throat clickety-clacketing against her sternum as she stooped to fill in the hole of a red fox. She had given them to Greta, who hated amber, who gave them to Einar; and Einar – he recalled – gave them to a little girl named Lili.

It came to him like that: in pieces, slowly, triggered by the amber beads or the swat of the attendant's hand against the canvas door as she enquired once again whether Mademoiselle needed assistance. He would put on the brown dress and the wedgy shoes as best he could. He would burn with shame as he clasped the belt, although now it would seem to him that he knew nothing about the tricky snaps and clasps of a woman's dress. His purse held only a few francs; more weren't coming for another three days, he knew. But Einar would decide against walking and take a cab back to the apartment because the discomfort of the brown dress was too much to bear on the streets of Paris. The scarf hung over the back of the chair, nearly fluttering on its own, and Einar couldn't bear to tie it over his head and around his throat. It looked as if it might strangle him, the gauzy chiffon with the yellow pears. It belonged to someone else.

And so Einar would set out from the ladies' pool in Lili's clothes, with the rubber bathing cap still on his head, dropping a franc into the attendant's ever-extended hand, gliding like the little duck on the pool's surface, above the whispery gossip of the French ladies who would linger at the pool until it was time to return home and help their Polish maids prepare lunch for their pinafored children, while Einar, sloppy and red-eyed in Lili's clothes, would return to Greta, who, in the course of the morning, had set the props and sketched the study for another painting of Lili.

★

One day in early May, Einar was sitting in the place des
Vosges, on a bench beneath a hedge of trees. The wind kept
lifting the fountain's trickle, throwing it at his feet and staining
the sand-coloured gravel around him. In the morning Lili had
gone for a swim. In the afternoon, Einar had returned to
Madame Jasmin-Carton's and witnessed through the little
black glass a man and woman make love on the floor. It had
cost him three times the usual entry fee; Madame Jasmin-
Carton had been advertising the spectacle for a month on
notecards tacked above the peep windows. The notecards,
with the information of the public liaison neatly printed out,
reminded Einar of the notes Lili and Greta had used to
communicate with each other during the early days in
Denmark: as if there were something about the crisp, echoey
air of Copenhagen that couldn't support the secret words they
needed to say.

The boy was tall and stringy, not much more than an
adolescent with his bluish-white skin and sleepy blue eyes and
ribs that could be counted one, two, three. He quickly peeled
himself out of his cheap tweed suit, and then helped the
woman, who was older, out of her dress. Not counting
himself, Einar had never before seen a man sexually aroused,
the way it pointed up like a spear in the first inches of its
trajectory. The boy's was red-tipped and drippy and angry.
The woman took it in her easily, and then, at just that
moment, seemed grateful. They thrashed around on the floor
of the little dark half-circle room, while pressed to every
window was the face of a man old enough to be the boy's
grandfather. Quickly he finished up, his seed flying up in a
heavy arc into the woman's puckered face. He stood and
bowed. He left the room, his tweed suit a bundle under his
arm. Only then, when Einar looked down into his own lap,
did he discover the salty stain, as if a teacup of seawater had
overturned. Then he knew, although he supposed he had
always known: he wanted the boy to do that to Lili. To kiss
her just before the boy's chest flushed red and his mouth
twisted with pleasure.

After that, Einar found himself on the bench in the place des Vosges. He opened his coat to allow his lap, which he had rinsed out in Madame's handbasin, to dry. Children were splashing each other in the fountain and pushing hoops across the gravel paths, and one girl was flying a paper kite shaped like a bat. Italian governesses were talking loudly over their prams parked in a circle. Einar turned away from them, embarrassed by his stain. The sun had been warm at the pool that morning, but now it kept slipping behind streamers of clouds, the park suddenly turning grey, the children, it seemed, mere cut-outs of themselves. Einar's lap wouldn't dry. The wet wool reminded him of the dogs on the farm in Bluetooth, how they'd come home from a day hunting for frogs. They'd be crusty and dank, their fur hard, and they'd never really lose that wet smell.

The little girl with the kite let out a scream. The string had slipped out of her hand and now the kite was tumbling from the sky. She was following it with her finger as it fell. Then she began to run, the bow in her hair flopping against her ears. Her governess yelled for her to stop. The governess looked angry, her Italian face red and stormy. She told the little girl, Martine, to wait by the pram. The kite was hurtling towards the earth, its black paper fluttering in its frame. Then it crashed near Einar's foot.

The governess snatched the crumpled kite with a pretty hand and a hiss. Then she took Martine's wrist and led her back to the pram, pulling her close to her side. The other governesses were standing under the hedge of trees, their prams huddled together at the bumper. When Martine and her governess joined them, they all looked over their shoulders in suspicion. Then the pack wheeled away, the squeak of their wheels a cry.

This was when Einar knew something had to change. Einar had become a man governesses feared in a park. Einar was a man with suspicious stains on his clothes.

It was May 1929, and he would give himself exactly one year. The park was dim, the sun hidden by clouds. The hedge of trees, with their fresh leaves shaking, looked cold. Again, a wind lifted the trickling water from the fountain and sprayed it on to the gravel. If in exactly one year Lili and Einar weren't sorted out, he would come to the park and kill himself.

It made him straighten his back. He could no longer bear the chaos in his life. Greta owned a silver-plated pistol from her California days. She'd grown up with it tucked in her stocking. He would return to the park with it and, under the black May night, he would press it to his temple.

Einar heard footsteps running towards him, and he looked up from his lap. It was Martine in her yellow pinafore. She looked frightened but enthusiastic. She stopped running and inched closer. Her soft hand reached out. Between Einar and her lay the kite's tail, a row of rag-bows on a string. Martine wanted it, and from the little smile pushing through her frown, Einar could tell she wanted to be friendly with him. She grabbed the tail. Then she laughed, her face like gold. When she curtsied and said, '*Merci*,' everything Einar knew about himself pressed together as one: the cottongrass apron strings around his waist; his head held in Greta's young hands; Lili in the *sennep*-yellow shoes in the Widow House; Lili this morning swimming laps in the river pool. Einar and Lili were one, but it was time to split them in two. He had one year.

'Martine – Martine!' called the governess. Martine's buckled shoes ground through the gravel. One year, Einar told himself. And then again, from over her shoulder, Martine called cheerfully, '*Merci*.' She waved, and Einar and Lili as one waved in return.

Fourteen

After three years in Paris, Greta had never worked harder in her life. In the mornings, when Lili was out doing the shopping or bathing at the pool, Greta would complete her magazine assignments. There was an editor at *La Vie Parisienne* who called nearly every week, panic in his fussy voice, asking for a quick drawing of the opera's latest production of *Carmen*, or a sketch to accompany the story on the exhibition of dinosaur bones at the Grand Palais. Really, there was no need to accept such a job, Greta would tell herself. Her name had been appearing in the magazines for a couple of years; but on the telephone the editor would squeak about his need for artwork. As Greta, the receiver between her chin and shoulder, watched Lili slip out of the apartment, Greta would think to herself, Oh, why not? Yes, she would do the sketch. Yes, she could deliver it by the morning. But I really must be getting to it, Greta would say, replacing the receiver in its cradle and then going to the window to see Lili, quick in the daylight, off to the Marché Buci, her pink spring coat bright against the dull, rain-soaked street.

Not until Lili returned would Greta's real work begin. Then she would boil a cup of tea for Lili and say, 'Come and sit here,' posing her on a stool or next to a potted palm tree, placing the cup and saucer into Lili's hands. No matter what the weather, Lili would always return to the apartment cold, her hands trembling. Greta feared she didn't have enough flesh on her frame, but she could never get her to eat anything more. The bleeding returned every now and then, once every

few months, announced by a slow drop of blood inching across
Lili's upper lip. Then she would lie in bed for days, as if stored
in those few crimson drops was all her energy. Greta had taken
Einar to one or two French doctors, but as soon as they began
to probe with their questions ('Is there anything else I should
know about your husband?'), she would realize that none of
them would have any more answers than Dr Hexler. She
would worry as Lili lay in bed, sleeping through the day,
staining the sheets, which Greta would later have to shove into
the incinerator behind the apartment. But then, after a few
days, sometimes a week, just as quickly as it had begun, the
bleeding would cease. 'How dull it is to spend a week in bed,'
Lili would say, throwing the bolster pillow to the carpet.

If she were to count them up, Greta would discover that she
had more than one hundred paintings of Lili by now: Lili
bathing in the pool; Lili as a member of a wedding party; Lili
examining carrots at the market. But most were Lili set in
landscapes, on a heath, in an olive grove, against the blue line
of the Kattegat Sea. Always her eyes brown and huge, hooded;
the delicate curve of her plucked eyebrows, hair parted around
the ear to reveal an amber earring hanging against her neck.

Einar himself no longer painted. 'I'm having a hard time
imagining the bog,' he'd call from his studio, where his
canvases and his paints were kept tidy. Out of habit he
continued to order bottles of paint from Munich, even though
the best paints in the world were sold just across the river at
Sennelier, where the clerk kept a perpetually pregnant cat.
Greta hated the cat, whose bloated stomach sagged to the floor,
but she enjoyed chatting with the clerk, a man called Du Brul,
who often said, with his Van Dyck goatee twitching madly,
that she was his most important lady customer. 'And some
believe a lady cannot paint!' he'd say as she left the shop with a
box of paint bottles wrapped in newsprint, the cat hissing as if
she were about to give birth.

The apartment on the rue Vieille du Temple had a central
room big enough for a long table and two reading chairs by the
gas fireplace. There was a red velvet ottoman in the room,

large and round, with an upholstered column rising from its centre, like the kind in shoe shops. And an oak rocker, with a brown leather cushion, shipped over from Pasadena. She had begun to call the apartment the *casita*. It didn't look like a *casita*, with its split-beam ceilings and the *portes-fenêtres* with their copper lock-bolts separating the rooms. But for some reason it made her think of the *casita* on the rim of the Arroyo Seco she and Teddy Cross had moved into after they left Bakersfield. The sunlight that poured in from the mossy brick patio had helped Teddy rise every day with another idea for a pot to throw on his wheel, or two colours to combine for a glaze. He had worked quickly and freely when they lived there. There was an avocado tree in the back garden that produced more heavy green grenades of fruit than they could possibly eat or give away. 'I want to be like the avocado tree,' Teddy would say. 'Constantly producing.' Now in Paris, in the *casita*, Greta thought of herself as the avocado tree. From the branch of her filbert brush the Lili paintings continued to drop and drop and drop.

For a while she regretted Einar's abandoned career. Many of his landscapes hung in the apartment, from moulding to skirting board. They were a constant and sometimes sad reminder of their inverted lives. At least to Greta. Never did Einar admit that he missed his artist's life. But she sometimes missed it for him, finding it hard to understand how one who had spent his life creating could simply stop. She supposed his old drive – the need to turn to a blank canvas with a chestful of ideas and fear – was now transferred to Lili.

Within a year of their arrival in Paris, Hans had begun to sell the Lili paintings. With the magazines calling, Greta's name began to float around Paris, in the cafés along boulevard St-Germain, in the salons where artists and writers lay on zebra-skin rugs drinking distilled liqueurs made from yellow plums. So many Americans in Paris, too, each talking about the other, eyeing one another in that American way. Greta tried to stay clear of them, of the circle that gathered nightly at 27 rue de Fleurus. She remained suspicious of them, and they of her, she knew. Their nights of fireside gossip about who was or wasn't modern didn't interest Greta. And in those societies of wit and airs, Greta knew, there was no room for Lili or Einar.

But the demand for the Lili paintings continued, and just as Greta began to feel as if she couldn't keep up, she had an idea. She was painting Lili in a field of lucerne grass in rural Denmark. To do this she had Lili stand in her studio with her fists on her hips. The portrait of Lili Greta managed easily enough, although she had to imagine the flat Danish summer sunlight on Lili's face. But the background of the field, with the grass rising behind Lili, didn't interest Greta very much. To paint the grass properly, and the distant kettle-hole lakes, would take Greta several days; first the horizon would have to dry, then the lakes, then the first layer of grass, then a second and a third.

'Would you like to finish this one up for me?' Greta asked Einar one day. It was May 1929, and Einar had been out the whole afternoon. He returned to the apartment saying he'd spent the afternoon in the place des Vosges, 'Watching the children fly their kites'. He looked especially thin in his tweed suit, his coat over his arm. 'Is everything all right?' she asked as he loosened his tie and went to make himself a cup of tea. In his shoulders Greta saw a sadness, a new melancholy blacker than anything she had seen before; they hung like a frown. His hand sat cold and lifeless in hers. 'I'm having a hard time keeping up. Why don't you start doing some of my backgrounds? You know better than me what a field of lucerne grass should look like.'

With Edvard IV in his lap, Einar thought about this. His shirt was wrinkled, and next to him on the table was a plate of pears. 'Do you think I can?' he said.

She led him into her studio, showed him the half-finished portrait. 'I think there should be a kettle-hole lake on the horizon,' she said.

Einar stared at the half-finished painting. He looked at it blankly, as if he didn't recognize the girl. Then, slowly, an understanding filled his eyes, the lids pulling back, his brow smoothing out. 'A few things are missing,' he said. 'Yes, there should be a lake, and also a single willow growing from the bank of a stream. And perhaps a farmhouse. Too far off in the horizon to be sure what it is, just a pale brown blur of something. But there'd probably be a farmhouse.'

He stayed up most of the night with the painting, smudging his shirt and his trousers. Greta was happy to see him at work again, and she began to think of other paintings she could share with Einar. Even if it meant fewer afternoons with Lili, she wanted Einar to have his work. As she prepared for bed she heard him in her studio, the clink of the glass paint bottles. She couldn't wait to call Hans in the morning to tell him that Einar was painting again. That she'd found a way to produce even more Lili paintings. 'You'll never believe who's helping me out,' she'd say. The memory of Hans at the Gare du Nord over three years ago revisited her. It was when she and Einar first arrived in Paris, with only a handful of addresses in their notebooks. Hans was waiting at the station, his camelhair coat a still beige column in the crowd of black wool. 'You'll be fine,' he assured Greta, kissing her cheek. He clasped both his hands around Einar's neck, kissing his forehead. Hans chauffeured them to a hotel on the left bank a few blocks from the Ecole des Beaux-Arts. Then he kissed them goodbye. Greta remembered feeling crushed, that Hans would meet them with open arms and then disappear so quickly. She watched his Borreby head slip through the lobby door. Einar must have felt the same disappointment, or worse. 'Do you suppose Hans didn't want us to come?' he said. Greta was wondering that herself, but she reminded Einar how busy Hans was. In truth, she had sensed a grave reluctance from Hans, in his stance as straight and steely as one of the columns supporting the station's roof.

Einar said, 'Do you suppose we're too Danish for his taste? Too provincial?' And Greta, who looked at her husband with his bog-brown eyes and his shaking fingers and Edvard IV in his arms, replied, 'It's him, not us.'

At the hotel they let two rooms, trimmed in red, one with a curtained alcove. The hotel's factotum declared proudly that Oscar Wilde had lived his final weeks in these rooms. 'He passed on in the alcove,' the proprietress reported with a dip of her chin.

Greta took little note of this bit of history. It seemed too grey a fact for her to press on to Einar. They lived in the two rooms for several months while they hunted for an apartment. After only a few days the hotel became dreary, with its curling wallpaper and rust stain bleeding in the sink. But Einar insisted that he pay for their lodging, which ruled out the nicer apartments available at the Hôtel du Rhin or the Edouard VII. 'There's really no need to suffer,' Greta had said, proposing more luxurious surroundings, and perhaps a view and decent maid service for evening coffee. 'Are you really suffering?' Einar replied, causing Greta to drop the subject. She sensed the unease between them that happened when they travelled.

There was a little stove in the corner on which she would boil water for their coffee. They took to sleeping in the alcove, in the bed that sagged in the middle and placed them close to the wall that permitted every squeal from the next room to pass through. Einar set up his easel in the room with the alcove; Greta took the second room, feeling a sense of relief when its door latch caught and she was alone. The trouble was, she couldn't paint alone. She needed Lili.

They had been in Paris only a month when Greta said, 'I want to celebrate it with Lili.' Greta could see the terror in her husband's eyes, the way his pupils expanded and shrank. Lili hadn't yet appeared in Paris. It was one of the reasons they had left Copenhagen. After the visit to Dr Hexler's, a letter had arrived from him. Greta had opened the letter and read Hexler's threat of reporting Einar and Lili to the health authorities. 'He could become a danger to society.' Greta imagined Dr Hexler dictating the letter to the red-haired nurse through the hose with the funnel on the end. The shock of the letter – that anyone besides herself should try to control Lili's future – upset her deeply, and she wasn't thinking properly when Einar, home from a visit with Anna, entered the apartment. Before she could stop herself, Greta quickly dropped the letter into the iron stove. 'Hans has written,' she said. 'He thinks we should move to Paris.' And then, 'We're going to move at once.'

Lili arrived in Paris knocking on the door of Greta's hotel room. Lili's hair was longer now, a darker brown with the sheen of good furniture, combs studded with baby pearls holding it back. She was wearing a dress Greta had never seen before. It was purple silk with a scoop-neck collar that dipped towards a crack of cleavage. 'You bought a new dress?' Greta asked. For some reason this made Lili blush, a cloud of red appearing on her throat and her chest. Greta was curious about the cleavage Einar had managed to squeeze together. Was his chest doughy enough to push into a beginner's corset and offer up as a pair of breasts?

They went to the Palais Garnier to hear *Faust*. Immediately Greta became aware of the men noticing Lili as she floated up the gold-railed stairs. 'That man with the black hair is looking at you. If we're not careful, he might come over.'

Their seats were next to a couple who had just returned from California. 'Twelve months in Los Angeles,' the man said. 'My wife had to prise me away.' He mentioned visiting Pasadena on New Year's Day to watch the Tournament of Roses. 'Even the horses' manes were braided with flowers,' the wife reported. Then the opera began and Greta sat back. She found it difficult to concentrate on Dr Faust, who was regretful in his dark laboratory, while she had Lili on her right and on her left a man who had recently walked by her family home off Orange Grove Boulevard. Her leg jiggled; she mindlessly rolled the bone in her wrist. She knew something had begun to unfurl tonight. What was it Carlisle used to say about her? No stopping good old Greta once she gets going. No one can stop her at all.

At the intermission, both Lili and the man's wife excused

themselves. The man, who was middle-aged and wore a beard, leaned towards Greta and asked, 'Is there any way I could see your cousin later on?'

But Greta denied the man at the Opéra Lili. Just as she would later deny herself her own longings – denied because she hardly recognized them. While she and Einar were still at the Oscar Wilde hotel, Hans would pick Greta up in the dark lobby and walk her to his office on the rue de Rivoli. Hans had agreed to talk with her about her career. But at some point when they were crossing the Pont Neuf, Hans's hand would fall to the small of her back and he would say, 'I suppose I don't have to tell you how pretty you are.'

The first time this occurred she swatted his hand away, believing it must have fallen there by accident. Then it happened again, a week later. And again. The fourth time, Greta told herself that she couldn't allow him to touch her like this. How could she ever face Einar again? she would think when Hans's hand caressed her spine as they crossed the river. Still walking, Greta felt nothing, inside or out, only the hand on her back. It occurred to her that her husband hadn't touched her in a very long time.

They continued on to his office, into the windowless study behind the front room with the filing cabinets where Hans looked up names for Greta to contact. He opened a folder and ran his finger down a list of patrons and said, 'You should write to him . . . and him . . . but be sure to avoid *him*.' Standing next to Hans, Greta thought she felt a finger on her arm, but that was impossible because the file was open in both his hands. She thought she felt his touch again on the small of her back; but no, he hadn't set down the file.

'Do you suppose we'll be all right here?' she said.

A smile nearly cracked Hans's lips. 'What do you mean?'

'Einar and me? In Paris? Do you suppose we can get along here just fine?'

His smile disappeared. 'Yes, of course. You have each other.' And then, 'But don't forget about me.' His face was leaning almost imperceptibly towards her. There was something between them – not the file, but something else. They said nothing.

But Hans can't be for me, Greta thought. If anyone should have Hans, it should be Lili. Even though it was cool in the back office she suddenly felt warm and sticky, as if a moist film of dirt covered her. Had she done anything irreversibly wrong?

'I'd like you to become my dealer,' she said. 'I'd like you to handle my paintings.'

'But I only deal in old masters and nineteenth-century pictures.'

'Maybe it's time you took on a modern painter.'

'But that wouldn't make any sense.' And then, 'Listen, Greta, there's something I've been meaning to tell you.' He moved closer to her, the folder still in his hand. The light in the room was grey, and Hans looked like an adolescent not yet used to his new, larger body.

'Don't say another word until you agree to take me on.' She didn't want to, but she moved to the opposite side of the desk. In between Greta and Hans now lay a tabletop of paperwork. All at once she wanted both to let him hold her and to run back to the hotel room, across the Pont Neuf, where Einar was probably waiting, shivering by the stove.

'Let me put it this way,' she said. 'I'm giving you the chance to take me on right now. If you decide not to, I'm sure you'll regret it one day.' She was rubbing at the shallow scar in her cheek.

'How will I regret it?'

'You'll regret it because one day you'll say to yourself, I could have had her. That Greta Wegener could have been mine.'

'But I'm not turning you away,' Hans said. 'Don't you understand?'

But Greta did understand. Or at least she understood Hans's intentions. What she couldn't figure out was the hummingbird patter in her chest – why wasn't she scorning Hans for making such an untoward advance? Why wasn't she reminding him how much this would hurt Einar? Why couldn't she even bring herself to say his name?

'Is it a deal?' she said.

'What?'

'Are you going to represent me? Or am I going to have to leave now?'

'Greta, be reasonable.'

'I think I am. This is the most reasonable response I can think of.'

They both stood leaning on their opposite ends of the desk. The stacks of documents were held down by bronze paperweights shaped like frogs. Everywhere she read his name, on the papers, over and over. Hans Axgil. Hans Axgil. Hans Axgil. It reminded her of when she was little and she had practised her penmanship: Greta Greta Greta.

'I'll do it,' he said.

'What?'

'Represent you.'

She didn't know what to say. She thanked him and gathered her things. She offered her hand. 'I suppose a handshake is in order,' she said. He took her hand, and there it was, her hand lost in the mitt of his, nearly trapped; but then he released her.

'Bring me some paintings next week,' he said.

'Next week,' and Greta stepped into the front room of Hans's office, where the sunlight and the city noise poured through the windows, and a clerk's typewriter clacked and clacked.

Fifteen

The smell of blood woke Einar. He got out of bed, careful not to disturb Greta. She looked uneasy, her face caught in a bad dream. The blood was trickling down his inner thigh, one slow hot line. A bubble of blood was caught in his nostril. He had woken as Lili.

In the spare bedroom, dawn fell on the pickled-ash wardrobe. Greta had given the top section to Lili. The bottom drawers were still Greta's, shut with a hair lock. In the mirror, Lili saw her bloody nose, her nightshirt with the single stain of blood. She was unlike Greta. The blood never worried her, it came and went, and Lili would take to bed with it like a cold. To her, it was part of all this, she thought as she dressed shimmying the skirt over her hips, brushing the static out of her hair. It was June, and a month had passed since Einar had decided, on the bench in the park, that his and Lili's lives would have to part. Lili felt the threat of that, as if time were no longer endless.

At the Marché Buci the morning dew was drying. There were alleys and alleys of vendors, each with a stall protected by a zinc roof. The vendors were laying out their tables of cracked porcelain, their bureaus with the missing handles, their racks of clothes. One woman sold only ivory dice. A man had a collection of ballet slippers which he had a hard time parting with. There was a woman who sold fine skirts and blouses. She was in her forties, with short grey hair and chipped front teeth. Her name was Madame Le Bon, born in Algeria. Over the years she had come to know Lili's taste, and she would hunt the death sales in Passy for the felt skirts Lili liked and the white blouses with appliqué in the collar. Madame Le Bon knew Lili's shoe size, knew she wouldn't wear pairs that exposed her nailless toe. She bought camisoles for Lili that were small in the bust, and old-fashioned whalebone corsets that helped with that problem. She knew Lili liked crystal drop earrings, and, for the winter, a rabbit-fur muff.

Lili was thumbing through Madame Le Bon's rack when she noticed a young man with a high forehead looking at the picture books in the next stall. His topcoat was hanging over his arm, a canvas suitcase at his feet. He was standing at an odd angle, as if all his weight were on one foot. He seemed uninterested in the picture books, flipping through their pages and then looking up at Lili. Twice their eyes met; the second time he smiled.

Lili turned her back and held a tartan skirt up to her waist. 'That's a nice one,' Madame Le Bon said from her chair. She had created a little changing room by hanging sheets on a washing line. 'Try it on,' she said, holding back the sheet.

Inside the sun was bright through the sheets. The skirt fitted well, and outside Lili heard a foreigner's voice ask Madame Le Bon if she sold men's clothes.

'Nothing for you, I'm afraid,' she said. 'Only for your wife.'

The foreigner laughed. Lili then heard hangers being pushed along the pipe of a rack.

When she emerged from the stall, the man was folding and unfolding cardigans on a table. He fingered the pearly buttons and checked the cuffs for fray. 'You have nice things,' he said, smiling first at Madame Le Bon and then at Lili. His blue eyes were big on his face; in the hollow of each cheek were one or two pocks. He was tall, and on the breeze was his aftershave, and Lili, closing her eyes, could imagine him pouring the yellow tonic into the cup of his hand and then slapping his face and throat. It was as if she already knew him.

Madame Le Bon logged the tartan skirt into her register. The man set down the cardigan and approached Lili with a

gentle limp. 'Excuse me,' he said in slow French. 'Mademoiselle.' He shuffled towards Lili. 'I was just noticing—'

But Lili didn't want to talk to him; not just yet. She took the
sack with the skirt, quickly thanked Madame Le Bon, and
ducked behind the changing stall and into the next booth,
where a bald man sold damaged china dolls.

When Lili got home Greta was up, moving around the
apartment with a damp rag. Carlisle was arriving this morning
for a summer visit. The apartment needed cleaning, feathery
puffs of dust blowing about in the corners. Greta refused to
hire a maid. 'I don't need one,' she'd say, swatting dust with
her gloves. 'I'm not the type of woman who has a maid.' But
to tell the truth, she was.

'He'll be here within the hour,' Greta said. She was wearing
a brown wool dress that clung to her in a pretty way. 'Are you
going to stay dressed as Lili?' she asked.

'I thought I might.'

'But I don't think he should meet Lili right away. Not first.
Not before Einar.'

Greta was right, and yet part of Einar wanted Lili to be the
first to meet Carlisle, as if she were his better half. He hung the
plaid skirt in the wardrobe and undressed, down to the square-
cut silk underwear. The silk was an oyster grey. It was soft; it
made the tiniest swish when he walked. He didn't want to
replace the silk underwear with the wool shorts and vest that
itched, that trapped the heat and set him on fire on a warm
day. He didn't want Lili to be completely folded away in the
wardrobe. He hated tucking her away. When he shut his eyes,
Einar saw only her; he couldn't come up with a picture of
himself.

He pulled on his trousers. Then he left the apartment.
'Where are you going?' Greta asked. 'He'll be here any
minute.'

The sky was cloudless. Long, cool shadows cast themselves
from the buildings on to the street. Rubbish was wet in the
gutter. Einar felt lonely, and he wondered if anybody in the

world would ever know him. A wind hurled up the street, and it felt as if it were passing through his ribs.

He walked to the short street north of Les Halles. Not very many people were around, only the tobacco-shop owner leaning in his door frame, a fat woman waiting for a bus, a man walking quickly in a suit too tight for him, his bowler hat pulled down.

In the hallway of number 22 there was a wine-stained scarf lying on the stairs that led to Madame Jasmin-Carton's door. 'Early today,' she said, stroking her cat. She passed Einar the key to Salle No. 3. It had become his regular room. The armchair covered in green wool. The wire wastepaper basket always emptied – a weak illusion that no one else ever used the room. And the two windows on opposite ends of the room with their black shades drawn. Einar had always lifted the shade of the window on the right. Pulled its taut cord and let the blind roll up with a snap. He couldn't count the number of times he had sat in the green armchair with his breath fogging on the window while a girl, genitalia exposed, danced on the other side. It had become a habit, almost daily, like swimming at the *bains*, or his walk to the corner of the rue Etienne-Marcel to fetch the mail at the Hôtel des Postes, most of which was for Greta. And Madame Jasmin-Carton never charged him less than five francs, never offered a discount, although he wasn't sure he would have wanted one. She did, however, let him stay in Salle No. 3 as long as he wanted; sometimes he'd sit in the green wool chair for half a day. He had slept there. Once he brought a baguette and an apple and some Gruyère and ate his lunch while a woman with a belly that hung like a sandbag danced around a rocking horse.

But the other window shade Einar never touched. That was because he knew what was in there. He somehow knew that once he had pulled that shade he would never return to the window on the right.

Today, however, it felt as if there was only one window in Salle No. 3, the little black one on the left. And so he pulled on the left window's shade. It snapped open, and Einar peered through.

On the other side was a room painted black, with a wood-plank floor separating at the seams. There was a little box, also painted black, on which a young man had planted one foot. His legs were hairy, making Einar think of Madame Jasmin-Carton's arms. He was an average-sized boy, a bit soft in the middle and smooth-chested. His tongue was hanging from his mouth and his hands were on his hips. He was rolling them, which caused his half-hard penis to flop about with the weight of a smelt on a dock. From his smile, Einar could tell the boy was in love with himself.

He didn't know how long he watched the boy bouncing on the balls of his feet, his penis growing and shrinking like a lever going up and down. Einar didn't remember falling to his knees and pushing his nose to the glass, but that was how he found himself. He didn't recall unbuckling his pants, but they were bunched at his ankles. He didn't know when he had removed his coat and tie and his shirt, but there they were, in a pile on the green armchair.

There were other windows looking into the boy's room. And in one, just opposite Einar, was a man with a little grin on his face. Einar couldn't make out much other than the grin, which seemed lit by a lamp of its own. He seemed to like the boy as much as Einar did, from the way that grin burned. But after a few minutes of staring across the room to the face of the man, Einar began to see his eyes. They were blue, he thought, and seemed focused not on the boy, who now had his penis in his hand and his other hand fondling a nipple the size of a centime, but on Einar. The man peeled his lips further apart, and the grin seemed to burn even brighter.

Einar stepped out of his trousers, dropped them on the green armchair. He was part Einar, part Lili. A man in Lili's oyster-grey knickers and a matching camisole that hung delicately from her shoulders. Einar could see a faint reflection of himself in the window's glass. For some reason, he didn't feel garish. He felt − it was the first time he had ever used this word to describe Lili – pretty. Lili now felt relaxed, her bare white shoulders reflecting in the glass, the pretty little cove at the base of her throat. It was as if it were the most natural thing in the world for a man to be staring at her in her intimate underthings, the straps of the camisole across her shoulders. As if something inside Einar had snapped, like the canvas window blind, and told him, more plainly than ever before, that this was who he was: Einar was a guise. Peel away the trousers and the striped tie, which Greta had given him on his last birthday, and only Lili was left. He knew this; he had known this. Einar had eleven months. His year was slipping away. It was warm in the little room, and in the window's reflection he saw Lili's forehead damp with perspiration, glowing like a half-moon.

The dancer continued, seemingly unaware of Einar and the other man. The boy's eyes were closed, his hips rocking, a creep of black hair showing in the pits of his arms. The man across the room continued to stare, his smile widening even further. The light somehow shifted, and Einar could see his eyes nearly turn gold.

Standing at the window, Einar began to fondle his breasts through the camisole. His nipples were hard, aching. As he rubbed them, an underwater feeling rippled through Einar. His knees were becoming weak, damp at the back. Einar stood back from the window to give the man a full view, to let him see his hips wrapped in the silk, let him see his legs, which were as smooth as the boy's were hairy. Einar wanted the man to see Lili's body. Einar stepped back far enough so the man could see all of him, except from that position in Salle No. 3 Einar couldn't see the man. Not that it mattered. And so for several minutes Einar rubbed himself in the window, imitating the motions he'd seen the girls perform over the months through the window on the right.

When Einar moved closer to the window and peered across the room, both the boy and the man were gone. Suddenly Einar became embarrassed. How had he come to this – showing off his odd-shaped body, the camisole cupping his soft chest, his inner thighs pale and soft, silvery under the light, to a couple of strangers? He sat in the armchair on his pile of clothes, pulling his knees to his chest.

Then there was a light knock on the door, two taps. Then again.

'Yes?' Einar said.

'It's me.' It was a man's voice.

Einar said nothing, stayed still in the armchair. This was what he wanted more than anything in the world, but he couldn't bring himself to say it.

Then another two taps on the door. His mouth was dry; his heart was climbing his throat. Einar wanted the man to know that he was welcome. Silent in the armchair, Einar wanted the man to know it was all right.

But nothing happened, and Einar thought the chance for . . . for something had fallen away.

Then the man quickly pushed himself through the door. He stood with his back pressed against it, his chest filling with breath. He was about Einar's age, but white at the temples, whiskery. He had dark skin, a large nose. He was wearing a black overcoat, buttoned to the throat. Around him was a faint scent of salt. Einar remained seated, the man a foot or two away. He nodded. Einar brought his hand to his brow.

The man smiled. His teeth looked sharp, angled. He seemed to have more teeth than most men. The lower half of his face seemed to be all teeth. 'You're very pretty,' the man said.

Einar sank back in the chair. The man seemed to like what he saw. He unbuttoned his overcoat, split it open. Beneath he was wearing a businessman's suit with a wide stripe in the wool. With the knot of his tie diamond-shaped, he was well groomed except for one thing: his flies were open and through them poked the eye of his penis.

He stepped towards Einar. Then another step. The head of his penis was peeking from beyond the foreskin. It smelled salty, and Einar began to think of the beaches of Jutland, of Skagen, where his mother was laid to sea in the fishing net picked clean of gills, and then the man's penis was only inches from Einar's mouth, and Einar closed his eyes. A blur of images ran through his head: the inn with the seaweed roof, the bricks of peat stacked in the fields, the white boulder speckled with mica, Hans lifting Einar's imaginary hair to tie the apron.

Einar's mouth opened. He could almost taste something bitter and warm, and just as Einar's tongue emerged from his mouth and the man took one final step closer, just when Einar knew for sure that Lili was here to stay and very soon Einar would have to disappear, just then there was a heavy knock on the door, and then another, and it was Madame Jasmin-Carton, yelling for them to come out at once, yelling angrily, in disgust, with her Manx cat mewing as violently as her mistress, as if someone had just stepped on her long-lost tail.

It was early afternoon when Einar emerged from Madame Jasmin-Carton's. She had given him less than a minute to dress and leave her premises for ever. He was on the black street with his clothes rumpled and untucked and his tie in his hand. The tobacco-shop owner was standing in his door, picking at his moustache, eyeing Einar. There was no one else on the street. Einar had hoped that the man would be waiting outside Madame Jasmin-Carton's, that they would go to the little café around the corner for a coffee and, perhaps, a carafe of red wine. But he wasn't there, just the tobacco-shop owner and a little brown dog.

Einar entered the *pissoir*. Its metal walls smelled wet. Next to the basin Einar straightened his clothes and tied his tie. The little brown dog followed Einar in, and begged.

For months Einar had been thinking about visiting the Bibliothèque Nationale, and at last he set out. It occupied a block of buildings, bordered by the rue Vivienne, the rue Colbert, the rue de Richelieu and the rue des Petits-Champs. Hans had arranged for Einar's ticket of admittance, writing to the library's administration on his behalf. The Salle de Travail des Imprimés, with hundreds of seats, had a bureau in the middle of the room where Einar had to fill out a *bulletin personnel*, registering the purpose of his visit: *researching a lost girl*. There he also wrote on slips of paper the names of books he wanted. The librarian behind the bureau was girlish, with downy cheeks and a clip made from pink shell holding back her fringe. Her name was Anne-Marie, and she spoke so softly that Einar had to lean towards her face and smell her peanuty breath. When he handed her the slips of paper with the names of half a dozen scientific books on sexual problems, she blushed, but then set out to do her job.

Einar sat down at one of the long reading tables. A student a few chairs down looked up from his notebook, then returned to his work. The room was cold, motes of dust in the lamplight. The long table was scratched. The sound of a page turning filled the room. Einar was worried that he looked suspicious, coming in here at his age, his trousers wrinkled, a faint sweaty scent sticking to him. Should he go and find the toilet and look at himself in the mirror?

Anne-Marie delivered the books to his table. She said only, 'We will be closing today at four.'

Einar ran his hand over the books; three were in German, two in French, the last from America. He opened the most recent, called *Sexual Fluidity*, published in Vienna, written by Professor Johann Hoffmann. Professor Hoffmann had performed experiments on guinea pigs and rats. In one, he grew breast glands in a formerly male rat rich enough to feed a second litter. 'Pregnancy, however,' Professor Hoffmann wrote, 'remains elusive.'

Einar looked up from the book. The student had fallen asleep on his notebook. Anne-Marie was busy loading a trolley. He thought of himself as the formerly male rat. A rat on its wheel running through his head. Now the rat couldn't stop. It was too late. The experiment continued. What was it Greta was always saying? Worst thing in the world is to give up! Hands swatting through the air, silver bracelets jangling. She was always saying that, and: Come on now, Einar. When will you ever learn?

Professor Hoffmann described documented cases of red-breasted hens which had produced a nestful of chicks but then one day abandoned their roosts, altered their plumage over the course of a summer, and slowly turned into roosters. By the next season these roosters had begun to impregnate hens from their own coop. 'Miraculous but true,' Professor Hoffmann wrote.

Einar thought of the promise he'd made to himself in the park last month: something would have to change. May had slipped into June, just as the months had slipped into years. More than four years ago, Lili was born on the lacquer trunk.

At four o'clock Anne-Marie rang a brass handbell. 'Please leave your materials on the table,' she announced. She had to rock the shoulder of the student to wake him. To Einar, she pressed her lips together till they turned white and then nodded goodbye.

'Thank you,' he said. 'You'll never know how helpful this has been.'

She blushed again, and then said, a little smile emerging, 'Should I set aside these books? Will you need them tomorrow?' Her hand, which was pale and no larger than a baby starfish, fell softly on Einar's arm. 'I think I know of some others. I'll pull them for you in the morning. They might be what you're looking for.' She paused. 'I mean, if that's what you want.'

Sixteen

❦

Much to Greta's concern, Carlisle's foot dragged through the gravel of the Tuileries. Each night he soaked his leg up to the knee in a tub of Epsom salts and white table wine, a balm his room-mate at Stanford, who went on to become a surgeon in La Jolla, had first concocted. Carlisle had become an architect, building bungalows in Pasadena in orange groves that were being paved into neighbourhoods. They were small houses, built for teachers at Pasadena Poly and Westridge School for Girls, for policemen, for the migrants from Indiana and Illinois who ran the bakeries and the printing shops along Colorado Street. He sent Greta pictures, and sometimes she put her chin in her fist and dreamed of one of the bungalows, with a screened-in sleeping porch and windows shaded by Blood of China camellia trees; not that she really saw herself settling into one of the little houses, but sometimes she wanted to stop and wonder.

Carlisle's face was handsome and long, his hair less yellow-white than Greta's and with more kink in the strand. He had never married, spending his evenings at his drafting table or in his oak rocker with a green-glass lamp pulled near for reading. There were girls, he reported to Greta in his letters, girls who joined his table at the Valley Hunt Club or who worked as assistants on his jobs, but no one who meant much. 'I can wait,' he would write, and Greta would think, holding the letter in the sunlight at the window, So can I.

The spare bedroom in the *casita* had an iron bed and brocade wallpaper. There was a lamp with a fringed shade that Greta worried wouldn't provide enough light. The *charcuterie* on the corner had lent her a zinc tub for the Epsom-and-white-wine balm; typically geese lay dead in it, their necks curled over its rim.

In the mornings Carlisle would take his coffee and croissant at the long table in the *casita*'s front room, his bad leg a thin rail in his pyjamas. At first Einar would slip out of the apartment just as the knob on Carlisle's door began to turn. Einar was timid around Carlisle, Greta noticed. He would quieten his step whenever he passed Carlisle's door, as if to avoid a chance meeting in the hall, beneath the crystal-bowl lamp. At dinner, Einar's shoulders would bunch up, as if it pained him trying to think of something to say. Greta wondered if something had passed between them, a harsh word, perhaps an insult. Something invisible seemed to be hanging between them, a thread of will that she couldn't quite, at least not yet, understand.

Once, Carlisle invited Einar to a vapour bath on the rue des Mathurins. It wasn't like the Bains du Pont-Solférino, out in the sunlight along the Seine. Instead, it was a pool for men in a gymnasium with steamy air and yellow marble tiles and palm trees drooping in Chinese *cache-pots*. When Einar and Carlisle returned from the bath, Einar immediately locked himself in his room. 'What happened?' Greta asked her brother. And Carlisle, whose eyes were red from the water, said, 'Nothing. He just said he didn't want to swim. Said he didn't know you had to swim naked.' And then, 'He nearly fainted at the sight of it. But hasn't he ever been to a Turkish bath?'

'It's the Dane in him,' Greta said, knowing it wasn't true. Why, she thought, the Danes would look for any excuse to remove their clothes and prance around.

Shortly after Carlisle arrived, Hans stopped by one morning to look over Greta's latest paintings. There were two to show him: the first was Lili, large and flat, on the beach in Bornholm; the second was Lili standing next to a Blood of China camellia tree. Einar had painted the sea in the background of the first, working steadily and tidily on its pale blue summer tide. The camellia tree, however, he couldn't quite pull off, unfamiliar as he was with the puckering red blossoms and the buds as shiny and tight as acorns. She'd taken on an assignment from *Vogue* – illustrating next winter's fox-lined coats – and so the only time she had to finish the camellia portrait was in the middle of the night. For three nights she stayed up, delicately painting the bloom of petals in each flower, with the hint of sorbet yellow at its centre, while Einar and Carlisle slept, her studio silent except for Edvard IV's occasional sigh.

She finished the painting only hours before Hans arrived to see it. 'Still wet,' she said, serving him coffee, and a cup for Carlisle, another for Einar, his hair wet at the tips.

'It's a good one,' Hans was saying, looking at the camellia painting. 'Very Oriental. That's what they like these days. Maybe you should try painting her in an embroidered kimono?'

'I don't want to make her look cheap,' she said.

'Don't do that,' Einar said, so quietly Greta wasn't sure if the others had heard.

'That's not what I meant,' Hans said. He was in a pale summer suit, his legs crossed, his fingers drumming the long table. Carlisle was on the velvet ottoman, Einar in the rocker. It was the first time the three men had been together, and Greta kept moving her eyes from her brother, with his leg up on the velvet cushion, to her husband, with the wet tips of his hair against his thin throat, to Hans. She felt as if she were a different person with each of them. As if she rolled out a different repartee for each of them; and maybe she did. She wondered if they felt they knew her at all. Perhaps she could be wrong, but it was how she felt – as if each of them wanted something different from her.

Hans had respected her wishes, withdrawing his attention, remaining focused on selling her work. There were times, when they found themselves alone, in the back room of his office or in her studio while Lili was out, when Greta could feel his eyes on her. But when his back was turned she couldn't

help staring, at the spread of his shoulders, at the blond hair
creeping over his collar. She knew what she was longing for,
but she forced herself to shove it aside. 'Not while Einar's still
. . .' In her chest she could feel the clamps closing with a clang.
She expected those passions, such heartswell, from Lili. Not
from herself, not any more, not now, with a studio full of
unfinished portraits and assignments from the magazines
waiting to be drawn, and her light-stepped husband weak in
body, confused in mind, and her brother showing up in Paris
with his incomplete statement, 'I've come to help,' and Hans,
at her long workman's table, his long fingers drumming the
pine top, waiting for the paint of the camellias to dry, waiting
for a second cup of coffee, waiting for Greta to produce a
painting of Lili in a kimono, waiting, patiently, with a flat
brow, simply waiting for Greta to fall into his arms.

    This was the household, then, her *casita*, from which Greta
set out one afternoon that summer. It was hot, the black traffic
exhaust hanging heavily. The sun was dull in a hazy sky,
reducing the sparkle of the city. The beige front stone of the
buildings looked soft, like warm cheese. Women walked with
handkerchiefs, swabbing sweat from their throats.

    The Métro was even hotter, its handrail sticky. It was only
June, and she and Einar wouldn't take their holiday in Menton
for another several weeks. She wondered if she would make it
– something about the summer would have to change, Greta
told herself – but then the train scraped along its rails and
stopped.

    She emerged from the station in Passy, where the air felt
cooler. There was a breeze, and a scent of cut lawn, and the
trickle of a fountain. She heard the springy thud of a tennis ball
landing on red clay. She heard someone beating a rug.

    The apartment house was a former villa, built from yellow
granite and copperwork. It had a little half-circle drive that was
spotted with motor oil, and a sentry of rose trees clipped into
tight pompoms. The front door was made of glass and
ironwork. Above it was a balcony, its door open, a curtain
blowing. Greta heard a woman's laugh, followed by a man's.

Anna had rented the second-floor apartment. She was singing three nights of *Carmen* at the Palais Garnier; after her performance, she'd eat a midnight supper of cold crab claw at Prunier's. Lately she'd begun to swear she would never return to Copenhagen. 'It's just too orderly for me,' she'd say, a hand balled against her breast.

Anna answered the door. Her blond hair was tight in a bun at the nape of her neck. The skin in her throat seemed to be scarring into permanent brown lines where her folds of fat lay. She was wearing a large ruby cocktail ring, designed like an exploding star. She had made a name for herself in the opera world; skinny young men with deeply sunk eyes sent her unset gems, ginger-snap biscuits and nervously written cards.

The living room was small, arranged with a settee with gold legs and a tapestry pattern on the cushion. There was a slim vase of tiger lilies, the buds veined and green. A maid in black uniform was serving lemonade and anisette. A man, tall and oddly dressed in a dark blue overcoat, was standing behind the chair.

'This is Professor Bolk,' Anna said.

'I guessed that,' Greta said. 'But aren't you warm?'

'Professor Alfred Bolk.' He offered his hand. 'For some reason, I'm always a bit cold,' he said, shaking his shoulders slightly in his coat. His blue eyes were dark and flecked with gold. He had hair like the dark blond of good wood, oiled back over his head so that it curled up at his neck. He was wearing a blue silk tie with a large knot and a diamond pin. His calling cards he carried in a silver case. He was from Dresden, where he ran the Municipal Women's Clinic.

The maid served Professor Bolk coffee poured over ice. 'I can't take lemon,' he explained, lifting his glass. There was a breeze from the balcony door, and Greta sat next to the professor on the sofa. He smiled politely, his shoulders up. She supposed she should wait for him to ask questions, but she suddenly felt a need to tell someone about Lili and Einar. 'It's about my husband,' she began.

'Yes, I understand there's a certain little girl named Lili.'

So he knew. At first, Greta didn't know what to say. Yes, where to begin? Had it all started that day four years ago when she asked him to try on Anna's shoes? Or was there something else? 'He's convinced he's a woman inside,' she said.

Professor Bolk made a small noise of sucking air between his teeth. He nodded quickly.

'And to tell the truth,' Greta said, 'so am I.' She described the short-sleeved dresses and the *sennep*-yellow, shoes and the specially sewn camisole; she reported on Einar's outings to the Bains du Pont-Solférino and the shopping sprees at Bon Marché on the rue du Bac. She spoke of Henrik and Hans and the few other men over whom Lili's heart had swollen up and burst with a pinprick of frustration. She said. 'She's quite beautiful, Lili is.'

'These men . . . this Hans . . . is there anything else I should know?'

'Not really.' She thought of Hans, who probably that very minute was hanging the camellia portrait in his gallery. It didn't happen very often, but nothing disappointed her more than when Hans stopped by at the studio and, with his fingers rubbing his chin, rejected a painting. 'Not good enough,' he'd say two, three times a year, shocking Greta, leaving her incapable of moving, of seeing Hans to the door. Sometimes, when the world was quiet, she wondered if such crushing disappointment could be worth it.

It had been Anna who first mentioned a doctor. 'Should he maybe see someone?' she said one day. She and Greta were in a frame shop down the street from the Oscar Wilde hotel. There were bins of old frames, some that weighed over a hundred pounds. The frames were dusty, dirtying their skirts. Then she said, 'I'm worried about him.'

'I told you what happened with Hexler back in Denmark. I don't know if he could take another doctor. It might crush him.'

'Doesn't it concern you just a little? About how ill he looks? How thin he's become? It sometimes seems he's hardly there at all.'

Greta thought about this. Yes, Einar looked pale to her, with thin blue pads spreading beneath his eyes. A translucence had developed in his skin. Greta had seen this, but had it worried her, more than everything else? And the bleeding, returning irregularly for more than four years now. She'd learned to live with him, with his transformation. Yes, it was as if Einar were on a perpetual track of transformation, as if these changes – the mysterious blood, the hollow cheeks, the unfulfilled longing – would never cease, would lead to no end. And when she thought about it, who wasn't always changing? Wasn't everybody always turning into someone new? In a bin with a chained lid, Greta found the perfect frame, its lip painted gold, for her latest painting of Lili. 'But if you know someone,' she said to Anna, 'if you have a doctor in mind, maybe I should talk to him. It couldn't hurt, could it?'

Professor Bolk said, 'I'd like to examine your husband.' This made Greta think of Hexler and his clanging X-ray machine. She wondered if Einar would ever let her take him to another doctor. Professor Bolk sipped his coffee, and pulled a notepad from his pocket.

'I don't think your husband is insane,' the professor offered. 'I'm sure other doctors will tell you your husband's insane. But that's not what I think.' There was a painting of Lili in Anna's living room. It showed her on a bench in a park. Behind her two men were talking, their hats in their hands. The painting hung above a side table full of silver-framed photographs of Anna, in wig and costume, hugging friends after performances. Greta had painted the park scene the year before, when Lili would show up at the *casita* and stay for three weeks and then disappear for another six, and when Greta was learning to work and live more and more without her husband. For a while the year before, when he refused to speak to her except as Lili, she herself had thought he had gone insane. He'd taken on a look, which came and went, of trance: eyes so dark that all she could see in them was a reflection of herself.

'I've met another man like him,' Professor Bolk said. 'A tram conductor. A young man, handsome enough, pretty even, slender, pale of course, a bit light on his feet. Nervous man, but who could blame him for that, what with his situation? He came to see me, and the first thing I noticed – how could I not? – was that he had breasts bigger than many teenage girls. By the time he came to see me he'd started calling himself Sieglinde. It was peculiar. One day he arrived at the clinic begging to be admitted. The other doctors said we couldn't admit a man to the Municipal Women's Clinic. They refused to examine him. But I agreed to, and one afternoon – I'll never forget it – I discovered he was both male and female.'

Greta thought about what this might mean, about the horrible sight of what must have lain lifelessly, like the extra flesh on the very old, between the man's legs. 'What did you say to him?' she asked.

The breeze lifted the drapes, and there was the sound of boys playing tennis; then their mother calling them inside.

'I told him I could help him. I told him I could help him choose.'

There was a part of Greta that wanted to ask, 'Choose what?' At once, she knew and didn't know the answer. For even Greta, who recently had often thought to herself, Oh, if only Einar could choose who he wanted to be . . . for even Greta could not imagine that a real choice was possible. She sat on the gold-legged sofa and thought about Einar, who in some ways no longer existed at all. It was as if someone – yes, someone – had already chosen for him.

'What happened to the man?' asked Anna.

'He said he wanted to be a woman. He said all he wanted was to be loved by a man. He was willing to do anything for it. He came to me in my office, wearing a felt hat and a green dress. He carried a pocket watch like a man, I remember, because he pulled it out during our meeting and kept looking at it, saying he had to go because he had come to splitting his days in half, living the mornings as a woman and the afternoons as a man.

'This was many years ago, when I was still a young surgeon. Technically I knew exactly what I could do for him. But I had never performed such complicated surgery, not then. And so for a month I stayed up at night reading medical texts. I attended amputations, studied sutures. Any time a woman at the clinic had her uterus removed, I watched in the operating amphitheatre. Then I'd study the specimen in our laboratory. Finally one day, when I was ready, I told Sieglinde I wanted to schedule a surgery.

'He had lost a lot of weight by then. He was quite weak. He must have been too frightened to eat. But he agreed to let me attempt it on him. He cried when I told him I could do it. He said he was crying because he felt like he was killing somebody. "Sacrificing somebody", that's what he said.

'I set the surgery for a Thursday morning. It was going to be in the large amphitheatre; there were that many people who asked to come. A few doctors from the Pirna Clinic as well. I knew that if I succeeded I would have done something extraordinary, something no one had even dreamed of. Who could think it possible, going from man to woman? Who would risk his career to try something that sounds like something from a myth? Well, I would.'

Professor Bolk shook out his coat.

'But then early that Thursday morning, the nurse went to Sieglinde's room and discovered that he was gone. He'd left his belongings, his felt hat, his pocket watch, his green dress, everything. But he was gone.' Professor Bolk drained his remaining coffee.

And Greta finished her lemonade, and Anna rose to call the maid ('*Les boissons,*' in a snappy voice), and Greta studied the professor, his left knee angled over his right. This time she knew she was right; he was no Hexler. He understood. He was like her, she thought. He could see things, too. She wouldn't have to think it over; her decision came like a clean blow to the head, with a pop of light at the back of her eyes. It made her start, jumping slightly in the settee, and Greta, who once in the south of France had nearly killed herself and Einar too by accidentally losing control of their motor car and hurling it towards a cliff spotted with mimosas springing from the rocks, thought: I must take Lili to Dresden. She and I will have to go.

Seventeen

The next day, the girl behind the desk located more books for Einar. Books called *The Sexes*; *The Normal and Abnormal Man*; *A Scientific Study of Sexual Immorality*; and *Die sexuelle Krise*, published in Dresden twenty years earlier. Most were about theories of gender development based on hypothesis and casual experimentation on laboratory rats. In one Einar read about a man, a Bavarian aristocrat, who was born with both a penis and a vagina. There was something about his plight – the confusion as a child, the parental abandonment, his hopeless hunt for a place in the world – that made Einar close his eyes and think, Yes, I know. There was a chapter on the myth of Hermes and Aphrodite. The book explained sexual pathology, and something called sexual intermediacy. Somehow Einar knew he was reading about himself. He recognized the duality, the lack of complete identification with either sex. He read about the Bavarian, and a dull distant pang lay at rest in Einar's chest.

Some of the books were old, from the last century, dust on their spines. Their pages turned with such a brisk crinkling noise that Einar feared the students would look up from their work on the long reading table and, from the twist of fear and relief in Einar's face, learn who he really was.

Anne-Marie would place the books in front of Einar in a little tilted stand that held them at an angle. She lent him a string of lead beads wrapped in felt that held the page open while Einar copied sentences into his pewter-backed notebook.

The tables were wide and nicked, and they made Einar think of the worktables the Copenhagen fisherwomen used when chopping the chub heads at the Gammel Strand fish market. In front of Einar, there was enough room on the table to fan out several books around him, and with their sand-coloured pages open he began to think of them as his little shoal of protection. And that was how it felt to read them, during those mornings when he would slip out of the apartment: as if each sentence about the male and female would protect Einar over the next year, when everything, as he had promised himself, would change.

He eventually read enough to become convinced that he too possessed the female organs. Buried in the cavity of his body were Lili's organs, the bloody packets and folds of flesh that made her who she was. At first it was hard to believe, but then the notion of it – that this wasn't a mental problem, but a physical one – made more and more sense to him. He imagined a uterus shoved up behind his testicles. He imagined breasts somehow trapped by his ribcage.

Einar spent a week in the reading room, and there was a point each day when he would become so overwhelmed by what he was discovering that he'd rest his head on his arms and softly cry.

If he nodded off, Anne-Marie, with her small white hand, would nudge Einar back to work. 'It's noon,' she'd say, and for a second he would become confused: noon?

Oh, yes. Noon.

Carlisle had taken to asking Einar to join him in the afternoons. 'Meet me at noon?' Carlisle would say each morning as Einar was slipping out of the front door, nearly lost in a white heat of anticipation about what was waiting for him at the library.

'I'm not sure I can,' Einar would reply.

'But why not?' Greta would say.

Carlisle knew not to ask Greta to join them. He once told Einar that even when they were little, she would sigh with disappointment whenever Carlisle suggested they head down to the archery range in the Arroyo Seco. 'She was always too busy to explore,' Carlisle would say. 'Reading Dickens, writing poetry, painting scenes of the San Gabriels, painting pictures of me. But she never showed them to me. I'd ask to see one of her little watercolours and she would blush, and fold her arms against her chest.'

So Carlisle turned to Einar. He had to prod Einar at first. There was something about Carlisle's blue eyes, which were clearer than Greta's, that seemed capable of reading Einar's thoughts. He found it difficult to sit still next to Carlisle, shifting his weight from one hip to the other, sitting up and then retreating in the rope-bottom chair.

Carlisle bought a car, an Alfa Romeo Sport Spider. It was red with spoked wheels and a running board with a red toolbox bolted to it. He liked to drive with the canvas top pushed back. The dash was black with six dials and a little silver handlebar that Einar would cling to as Carlisle shot around a corner. The floors were made of dimpled steel, and as Carlisle drove the Spider around Paris, Einar could feel the heat from the engine through the soles of his shoes.

'You should really learn to trust people more,' Carlisle said one day in the car, his hand moving chummily from the gear lever with its black-ball knob to Einar's knee. He was driving Einar out to a tennis stadium in Auteuil. The stadium was next to the Bois de Boulogne, a concrete bowl rising up among the poplar trees. It was late morning, and the sun was high and blank in the blue-white sky. The flags around the rim of the stadium were hanging limply. There were iron gates around the tennis park, and men in green blazers and straw hats were taking tickets and ripping them in two.

A man led Einar and Carlisle to a little sloping box that was painted green. There were four wicker chairs in the box, each with a striped cushion. The box was at the baseline of the tennis court, which was made of crushed clay as red as the rouge Lili once purchased at the front counter of Fonnesbech's.

On the court, two women were warming up. One was

from Lyon; the sail of her long pleated skirt was white, and she cut across the court like a schooner. The other was an American, a girl from New York, the programme reported; she was tall and dark, her hair as short and shiny as an aviator's leather cap.

'Nobody expects her to win,' Carlisle said of the American. He was holding his hand to his forehead to block out the sun. His jaw was exactly the same as Greta's: square, a bit long, pegged with a mouthful of good teeth. Their skin was the same, too: brown after only an hour of sun, a bit coarse in the throat. It was a throat Einar used to kiss passionately in the night. It was what he had liked most about Greta, even more than kissing her mouth: bringing his lips to her long throat and sucking lightly, licking in a little swirling motion, nipping, drilling away at the spot on her throat that was open and veined.

'Sometime I'd like to visit California,' Einar said. The match had begun, the American serving. She tossed the ball high, and Einar could almost see the muscles in her shoulder turn as she brought her racquet through the air. Greta often said she thought of oranges hitting the ground when she heard a tennis ball; Einar thought of the rye-grass court behind the brick villa, the powdered-sugar lines blowing in the wind.

'Does Greta ever say anything about it?' Carlisle asked. 'About coming home?'

'I've heard her say a lot would have to change before she would go back.' Greta had once said that neither of them would fit in there, in Pasadena, where rumour crossed the valley as rapidly as a blue jay in the breeze. 'It's not a place for you and me,' she had said.

'I wonder what she means,' Carlisle said.

'You know Greta. She doesn't want people talking about her.'

'But in some ways she does.'

The American girl won the first game, her drop shot barely lifting over the net cord and then falling deceptively to the clay.

'Have you ever thought about coming out for a visit?'

Carlisle asked. 'To California? Maybe come out for the winter to paint?' He was fanning himself with the programme; he held his bad leg out, the knee locked. 'Come out and paint the eucalyptus and the cypress? Or one of the orange groves? You'd like it.'

'Not without Greta,' Einar said.

And Carlisle, who at the same time was and was not exactly like his sister, said, 'But why not?'

Einar crossed his legs, his foot shifting the wicker chair in front of him. The girl from Lyon sailed across the court, her skirt taut, to return a backhand from the sneaky American, hitting the dirty white ball up the line for a winner. The crowd, which was handsome and hatted and collectively smelled like lavender and lime, erupted into a cheer.

Carlisle turned to Einar. He was smiling and applauding, and his forehead was beginning to sweat; and then, when the stadium fell silent to allow the girl from Lyon the peace to serve, he said, 'I know about Lili.'

Einar could smell the clay, its rich dustiness, and the wind blowing through the poplars. 'I'm not sure I know what you're—'

But Carlisle stopped him. Carlisle placed his elbows on his knees and stared at the court and began to tell Einar about the letters Greta had been writing over the past year. They would arrive once a week, fat in the mailbox, a half-dozen sheets of blue tissuey paper covered with her cramped words; she wrote them in such a fury that she didn't use margins, the small tight writing crossing the page from edge to edge. 'There's someone called Lili,' she wrote for the first time maybe a year before. 'A girl from the bogs of Denmark whom I've taken in.' The letters would describe Lili making her way around Paris, kneeling to feed the pigeons in the park, her skirt bunching around her on the gravel path. They described Lili sitting for hours on the stool in Greta's studio on the rue Vieille du Temple, the light from the window on her face. The letters arrived almost weekly, a summary of the previous days with Lili. They never mentioned Einar, and when Carlisle would reply, 'How's Einar?' or 'My best to Einar,' and even once, 'Isn't this your tenth wedding anniversary?' Greta never acknowledged the enquiry.

One day, after about six months of the weekly letters, a slim envelope arrived in Carlisle's mailbox. He remembered the day, he told Einar, because the black January rains had been falling for a week, and his leg was aching as if it had been hit by the carriage only the previous afternoon. He went down his driveway to the mailbox, his bamboo cane in one hand and an umbrella in the other. The ink on the envelope smeared in the rain, and he opened it in his hall, which was dark with panelled Pasadena oak. He read the letter as the water dripped from his hair on to the single page. 'Einar is leaving me,' Greta's letter began. 'You are right. After ten years he is leaving me.' Immediately Carlisle considered driving over to the post office on Colorado Street and sending a telegram. He put on his mackintosh while reading the rest of the letter, and it was only then that Carlisle began to understand what Greta meant.

A second letter arrived the next day, and then another, the day after. What followed was an almost daily account of Lili. The pages were just as crammed with description as before, but now tiny sketches of a girl's face would interrupt the sentences: Lili in a hat pinned with dry violets; Lili reading *Le Monde*; Lili staring up, her eyes round, at the sky.

'Then Greta started sending me sketches from her notebook. Studies for her paintings of Lili. She sent me the one of Lili in the lemon grove. And Lili in the wedding party.' He stopped while the American girl served. 'They're beautiful. She's beautiful, Einar.'

'Then you know.'

'It didn't take me long to understand,' Carlisle said. 'Of course I don't know much about this,' he said. A small brown bird landed on the rail of the box. Its head revolved, looking for seed. 'But I'd like to help. I'd like to meet Lili. To see if there's anything I can do. You see, it's Greta's way of doing things, sending the letters and drawings. She'd never come out and ask for help. But I can tell she needs it. I can tell she thinks

you could stand some help, even more than she can give you.'
And then, 'It's hard on her. You can't forget that this is just as
hard on her.'

'She said that?'

'Greta would never say anything like that. But I can tell.'

Einar and Carlisle watched the tennis. The day was warm,
the girls towelling their faces. 'Have you seen a doctor?'
Carlisle asked.

Einar told him about Dr Hexler. Just saying his name
brought back the nausea; he could nearly feel a throb in his
gut.

'I don't see why you'd go to a medical doctor,' Carlisle said.
'Shouldn't you talk to someone about how you feel? About
what you're thinking? I'm going to take you to someone. I've
looked up some names, and I'm going to take you to talk to
someone who just might help. Help you resolve this once and
for all. Not to worry, Einar. I have an idea.'

And this was what Einar remembered most: the sight of
Carlisle's long legs out of the corner of his eyes, the bad leg
now at a hard angle. And the American girl on the court
becoming sweaty, a wet spot developing on her blouse just
beneath her breasts. And her face, which was dark and plain;
and how her head was large and her arms long, and there was
something about her that didn't seem right. Like the thin
tendril of a vein that pulsed up her forearm. Or the shadow
above her lip. And how the whole stadium was rooting against
her, more and more as she took a bigger lead against the
blonde girl from Lyon. It seemed the whole world was against
her – everyone except Carlisle, who leaned over and said,
'Don't you want her to win? Wouldn't it be more fun for her
to win?'

First Carlisle drove Einar to see Dr McBride. He was an
American psychiatrist connected to the embassy, his practice
on the rue de Tilsitt, down the street from the passport office.
Dr McBride had a wiry bush of hair and a moustache that was
black and grey. He was heavy in the throat and stomach, and

he wore white shirts starched as stiff as paper. He was from Boston, and during Einar's meeting with him he kept referring to himself as a 'black Irishman'. When he smiled, there was a flash of gold at the back of his mouth.

Dr McBride's office was more like a lawyer's than a doctor's. His desk was double-pillared and inlaid with a sheet of green leather. There was a wall of bookshelves, and a row of oak filing cabinets. By the window a medical dictionary was open on a stand. While Einar told Dr McBride about Lili, the doctor sat blank-faced, pushing his glasses up and down the bridge of his nose. When the telephone rang, Dr McBride ignored it and urged Einar to continue. 'What's the longest you've lived as Lili?' he asked.

'Over a month,' Einar said. 'Last winter she was here for a long time.' Einar thought about the past winter, when more often than not he would go to bed and have no idea who he would be when he woke in the morning. One night Lili and Greta found themselves held up at knifepoint after leaving the Opéra. The thief was a little man in a black pea coat, and his knife didn't look especially sharp in the winter moonlight. But he waved it at them and demanded their handbags. The man hadn't shaved for a few days, and he kept kicking the ground with one foot, saying, 'I'm serious, mesdemoiselles. Don't think I'm not serious.' When Lili moved to hand over her bag, Greta tried to take her wrist, saying, 'Lili, don't.' But the man snatched the bag, and then he was lunging for Greta's, who cried, 'Oh no you don't!' Greta began to run down the street, towards the Opéra, which was gold in the night. Lili remained against the wall, the thief in front of her. His foot struck the pavement again, and he seemed to be trying to think of what to do next. Greta was a block away when she turned around. Lili could only make out her silhouette: her fists on her hips, her feet apart. Then she started walking back towards Lili and the thief. The man smiled nervously. 'She's crazy,' he said, his foot kicking the pavement. He turned his wrist so that now his knife, which wasn't much more than a piece of cutlery, was pointing down. Then he began to run away from Greta.

'Do you think of Einar when you are Lili?' Dr McBride asked.

'Not at all.'

'But you think of Lili when you are Einar?'

'Yes.'

'What do you think about?' He removed the cap from his pen and placed the open instrument on a blank sheet of paper.

'Most of the time I just think her thoughts,' he said. Einar explained that if he were eating an apple tart sprinkled with cinnamon he'd wonder if he should save a slice for Lili. If he were arguing with the butcher, who tended to press his thumb against the scale, Einar would wonder if Lili would argue. He would convince himself that she wouldn't take on the butcher, who was skinny and handsome with spiky blond hair; and so, mid-sentence, Einar would apologize and ask the butcher to continue wrapping his lamb.

Dr McBride pushed up his glasses.

Across the street at the café, Carlisle was waiting. Einar now thought of him, reading his Baedeker, pulling the pencil from behind his ear and marking a recommended site. Just then he was probably finishing his coffee and checking his watch.

'And how do you feel about men?' Dr McBride asked. 'Do you hate them?'

'Hate men?'

'Yes.'

'Of course not.'

'But it would be natural for you to hate men.'

'But I don't.'

'And Lili? How does she feel about men?'

'She doesn't hate men.'

Dr McBride poured some water from a silver pitcher. 'Does she like men?'

'I'm not sure I know what you mean.'

The doctor took a sip. Einar could see the impression his lips left on the rim of the glass, and suddenly Einar realized he was thirsty.

'Has she ever kissed a man?'

Einar was trying to think of a way to ask for a glass of water, but it seemed impossible. He thought perhaps he should simply stand up and pour himself one, but that felt impossible too. And so Einar just sat there, and he felt like a child in Dr McBride's chair, which was covered in an itchy yellow wool.

'Mr Wegener, I'm only asking because—'

'Yes,' Einar said. 'Yes, she's kissed a man.'

'Did she like it?'

'You'll have to ask her.'

'I thought I was asking her.'

'Do I look like Lili?' Einar said. 'Do I look like a woman to you?'

'Not really.'

'Well, then—'

Dr McBride's telephone rang, and together they stared at its black receiver, which trembled with each ring. Finally it went silent.

'I'm afraid you are a homosexual,' Dr McBride eventually said. He capped his pen with a little click.

'I don't think you understand.'

'You're not the first person this has happened to,' Dr McBride said.

'But I'm not a homosexual. That isn't my problem. There's another person living inside me,' Einar said, rising from the chair. 'A girl named Lili.'

'And it breaks my heart,' Dr McBride continued, 'when I have to tell men like you that there's nothing I can do for them. As a black Irishman, I find it very sad.' He sipped from his water glass, his lips clamping on the rim. Then he stood, moving around to the front of his desk. His hand moved to Einar's shoulder, nudged him to the door. 'My only advice is that you restrain yourself. You're always going to have to fight your desires. Ignore them, Mr Wegener. If you don't . . . well, then, you'll always be alone.'

Einar met Carlisle at the café. He knew Dr McBride was wrong. Not so long ago Einar might have believed the doctor and sulked away in pity for himself. But Einar told Carlisle that it had been a waste of time. 'Nobody is going to understand me,' he said. 'I don't see the point of any of this.'

'But that's not true,' Carlisle protested. 'We need to find you the right doctor. That's all. So Dr McBride doesn't know what he's talking about. So what? That doesn't mean you should give up.'

'Why are you doing this?'

'Because you're unhappy.'

'Yes, but why?'

'Because of Greta.'

A few days later, Carlisle drove Einar to the Etablissement Hydrothérapique, a hospital known for its care of nervous maladies. The hospital was out towards Meudon, hidden from the road behind a grove of sycamore trees. There was an attendant at the gate, who pushed his face into the car and asked whom they were visiting. 'Dr Christophe Mai,' Carlisle said. The attendant eyed them, biting his lip. He passed them a clipboard to sign.

The hospital was a new building, a deep box of cement and glass. It was shaded by more sycamores, and plane trees scarred in the trunk. Steel grates covered the windows on the ground floor, their padlocks bright in the sun.

They had to sign another sheet of paper at the front entrance, and a third when they finally arrived at Dr Mai's office. A nurse, a woman with white curls, told them to wait in a little room that, once she closed the door behind her, felt securely sealed.

'I didn't tell Greta where we were going today,' Carlisle said. A few days earlier Einar had overheard them talking about him. 'He doesn't need to see a psychiatrist,' she had said, her voice travelling via the crack beneath the door. 'Besides, I think I know someone who can help him. And he isn't a psychiatrist. This is someone who can really do something.' Then her voice fell, and the rest Einar failed to hear.

Dr Mai's office was brown and smelled of cigarettes. Einar could hear feet shuffling outside in the hallway. There was something so unpleasant about the hospital that a little sensation rose up inside him, telling him that this was where he belonged. In the brown carpeting, there were tracks from trolleys, and Einar began to imagine himself strapped to a trolley that would wheel him into the deepest part of the hospital, from which he would never return.

'Do you really think Dr Mai can help me?'

'I hope so, but we'll have to see.' Carlisle was wearing a seersucker blazer and crisply pleated trousers and a yellow tie. Einar admired his optimism, the way he sat expectantly in his summer clothes. 'We've got to at least try.'

He knew Carlisle was right. He couldn't live much longer like this. Much of the muscle on his body had disappeared over the past six months; Dr McBride had weighed him, and when the little black weights slid over to the left, Einar realized he didn't weigh much more than when he was a boy. Einar had begun to notice a peculiar colour in his skin: a grey-blue like the sky at dawn, as if his blood were somehow running at a slower pace. And a weakness of breath that caused his eyesight to give out whenever he ran more than a few paces, or whenever a sharp sudden noise, like the *crack!* of a motor car, surprised him. And the bleeding, which Einar both dreaded and welcomed. When he felt the first spurt of it on his lip or between his legs, he would become dizzy. No one would tell him this, but Einar knew it was because he was female inside. He'd read about it: the buried female organs of the herma- phrodite haemorrhaging irregularly, as if in protest.

Dr Mai turned out to be a pleasant man. His hair was dark and he was wearing a yellow tie that was oddly similar to Carlisle's. They both laughed about it, and then Dr Mai led Einar into his examining room.

The room was tiled, with a window that looked through an iron grate into the park of sycamores and plane trees. Dr Mai dragged back a heavy green curtain to reveal the examining table. 'Please sit down,' he said, his hand falling on the table's pad. 'Tell me why you're here.'

He was leaning against a cabinet with glass doors. He was holding a clipboard to his chest, and he nodded as he listened to Einar explain Lili. Once or twice Dr Mai adjusted the knot of his tie. Occasionally he wrote something down.

'I don't really know what kind of help I'm looking for,' Einar was saying. 'I don't think I can keep living like this.'

'Like what?'

'Like I don't know who I really am.'

With that, Dr Mai ended the interview. He excused himself, leaving Einar on the padded table, his feet swaying. Outside in the park, a nurse was walking a young man in striped pyjamas, his dressing gown hanging open. The man had a beard, and there was a frailty to his step, as if the nurse, whose apron ran to her feet, were the only thing propping him up.

When Dr Mai returned he said, 'Thank you for visiting me.' He shook Einar's hand and led him to Carlisle.

On the drive back into Paris, they said nothing for a long time. Einar watched Carlisle's hand on the gear lever, and Carlisle looked down the road. Finally he said, 'The doctor wants to admit you to the hospital.'

'For what?'

'He suspects schizophrenia.'

'But that's impossible,' Einar said. He looked over to Carlisle, who kept his eyes on the traffic. In front of them was a truck, and each time it hit a rut, gravel would spill from its bed on to the Spider's hood. 'How could I be schizophrenic?' Einar said again.

'He wanted me to sign the papers to admit you right then.'

'But that's not right. I'm not schizophrenic.'

'I told him it wasn't that urgent.'

'But you don't think I'm schizophrenic, do you? That just doesn't make any sense.'

'No, I don't. But when you explain it . . . when you explain Lili, it does sound like you think there are two people. Two separate people.'

'Because there are.' It was evening, and the traffic had slowed because an Alsatian had been hit; it was lying in the middle of the road, and each car had to pick its way around it.

The dog was dead, but it appeared uninjured, its head resting up on the granite kerb of the *rond-point*.

'Do you think Greta thinks that? Do you think she believes I'm insane?'

'Not at all,' Carlisle said. 'She's the one who believes in Lili the most.'

They passed the Alsatian, and the traffic opened up. 'Should I listen to Dr Mai? Do you think maybe I should stay with him for a little while?'

'You'll have to think about it,' he said. Carlisle's hand was holding the black ball of the gear lever, and Einar felt there was something Carlisle wanted to say. With the wind, and the coughing exhaust of autobuses, it was difficult to talk. The city traffic was heavy, and Einar looked to Carlisle, as if to urge him to say what he wanted. Tell me what you're thinking, Einar wanted to say, but didn't. Something was hanging between them, and then they were in the Marais, in front of the apartment, and the something passed, gone as the Spider's engine went idle. Carlisle said, 'Don't tell her where we've been.'

Tired, Einar went to bed after supper, and Greta joined him even before he nodded off.

'So early for you,' he said.

'I'm tired tonight. I've worked through the past few nights. Delivered half a dozen sketches this week. To say nothing of Lili's portrait on the mudflat.' And then, 'You did a lovely job with the background. I couldn't be happier with it. Hans said the same. I've been meaning to tell you that.'

He felt her at his side, her long body warm beneath the summer sheet. Her knee was touching his leg, her hand curled at his chest. It was as much as they touched each other now, but somehow it seemed even more intimate than those nights early in their marriage when she would tug off his tie and loosen his belt: the curled hand like a little animal nuzzling his chest; the knee pressing reassuredly; the damp heat of her breath; her hair like a vine growing across his throat. 'Do you think I'm going insane?' he said.

She sat up. 'Insane? Who told you that?'

'No one. But do you?'

'That's the most ridiculous thing I've ever heard. Who's been telling you that? Did Carlisle say something to you?'

'No. It's just that I sometimes don't know what's going on with me.'

'But that's not true,' she said. 'We know exactly what's going on with you. Inside of you lives Lili. In your soul is a pretty young lady named Lili. It's as simple as that. It has nothing to do with being crazy.'

'I was just wondering what you thought of me.'

'I think you're the bravest man I know,' she said. 'Now go to sleep.' And her fist curled tighter, and the strand of hair crept across his throat, and her knee pulled away.

A week went by. He spent a day cleaning out his studio, rolling up his old canvases and storing them in the corner, glad to get them out of the way. He enjoyed painting Greta's backgrounds, but he didn't miss creating something on his own. Sometimes, when he thought about his abandoned career, he felt as if he were finished at last with a tedious chore. And when he thought of his many paintings – so many dark bogs, so many stormy heaths – he felt nothing. The thought of coming up with a new idea exhausted him, the thought of conjuring and then sketching a new scene. It was someone else who had done all those little landscapes, he told himself. What was it he used to tell his students at the Royal Academy? If you can live without painting, then go right ahead. It's a much simpler life.

Einar was sleeping late and rising tired. Each morning he'd promise himself that he would live the day as Einar, but when he went to the wardrobe to dress, it was like coming across the belongings of an ancestor in the attic.

More often than not, Lili would emerge from the bedroom and sit on the stool in Greta's studio. Her shoulders would hunch and she would play with her shawl in her lap; or she'd turn her back on Greta, who was painting another portrait, and look out of the window, down the street, for Hans or Carlisle.

Carlisle next suggested Dr Buson, a junior member of a psychiatric clinic in Auteuil. 'How did you hear of him?' Einar asked Carlisle, who had settled into Paris faster in six weeks than Einar had in three years. Already he was into his second box of calling cards, and hosted weekend trips to Versailles and St-Malo. There was a tailor on the rue de la Paix who knew from memory Carlisle's shirt size.

He was driving Einar to Dr Buson's clinic, and Einar could feel the heat of the engine through the metal floor.

'Hans gave me his name,' Carlisle said.

'Hans?'

'Yes. I called him up. Told him a friend of mine needed to see a doctor. I didn't say who.'

'But what if he—'

'He won't,' Carlisle said. And then, 'So what if he does? He's your oldest friend, isn't he?' Now, with his blond hair blowing around his face, Carlisle could have been no one in the world but Greta's twin; he pushed his hair over his ears.

'Hans asked about you,' Carlisle continued. 'He said he knows something's wrong. He said he saw you one day walking along the quai du Louvre, heading down to the Seine, and he almost didn't recognize you.'

Carlisle's hand was fiddling with the wiper gauge, and Einar kept expecting it to fall from the little knob to his knee again. 'He told me you walked right past him,' Carlisle said. 'Said he called your name but you just walked by.'

It sounded impossible. 'By Hans?' Einar said, and in the reflection of the car's window Einar could see the vaguest outline of himself, as if he were just barely there. He heard Carlisle suggest, 'Maybe you should tell him. He'd understand.'

Dr Buson, who was about Einar's age, was of Genevois origin. He had black hair that stood up at the crown, and his face was thin in the cheeks, his nose long. He had a way of turning his head to the left when he spoke, as if he wasn't sure whether or not he would make his next statement a question. Buson met Einar and Carlisle in a little white room with a reclining chair over which hung the silver bowl of an examination lamp. There was a cart on castors, its top covered with a green cloth. Lying on the cloth in a fan shape were a dozen pairs of scissors, each a different size. On the wall was a pull-down chart of the human brain.

This time Carlisle joined Einar in the interview. For some reason, Carlisle made Einar feel small, as if he were Einar's father and would both answer and ask the questions. Next to him, Einar hardly felt capable of speaking. The window looked into a courtyard, which was dark with rain, and Einar watched a couple of nurses trot across the paving stones.

Dr Buson was explaining how he treated people with confused states of identity. 'Usually they want some sense of peace in their lives,' he was saying. 'And that means choosing.'

Carlisle was taking notes, and Einar suddenly found it remarkable that he could travel from California and take Einar on as if he were his most important project. He didn't have to do it, Einar knew. Carlisle didn't have to try to understand. Outside in the courtyard, a nurse slipped on the wet stones, and when her colleague pulled her up, the nurse turned over her hand to reveal a bloody palm.

'In some ways I think people who come to see me are rather lucky,' Dr Buson was saying. He was sitting on a steel stool that could be raised and lowered with a spin. He was wearing black trousers beneath his laboratory coat, and black silk socks. 'They're lucky because I say to them: "Who do you want to be?" And they get to choose. It isn't easy. But wouldn't we all want to have someone ask us who'd we like to be? Maybe just a little?'

'Of course,' Carlisle said, nodding, jotting something in his notepad. Einar felt lucky to have Carlisle there, driving him to all the doctors, putting his hands on the steering wheel after each miserable appointment and saying, 'Don't worry. There's a doctor for you.' Something in Einar settled, and he felt his breath slow. He wished that Greta were the one trying to help.

'And that leads me to my procedure,' Dr Buson was saying.

'It's a rather new operation, one that I'm quite excited about because it's so full of promise.'

'What is it?' Einar said.

'Now I don't want you to get too excited when I tell you, because it sounds more complicated than it is. It sounds drastic but it really isn't. It's a rather simple surgery that is working on people with behaviour problems. The results so far are better than any other treatment I've ever seen.'

'Do you think it would work on someone like me?'

'I'm sure of it,' Dr Buson said. 'It's called a lobotomy.'

'What is that?' Einar asked.

'It's a simple surgical procedure for cutting nerve pathways in the front part of the brain.'

'Brain surgery?'

'Yes, but it isn't complicated. I don't have to cut open the cranium. No, that's the beauty of it. All I have to do is drill a few holes in your forehead, right about here . . . and here.' Dr Buson touched Einar's head, at his temples, and then at a spot just above his nose. 'Once I've put the holes in your head then I can go in and sever some of the nerve fibres, those that control your personality.'

'But how do you know which ones control my behaviour?'

'Well, that's what I've discovered recently. Haven't you read about me in the paper?'

'It was a friend who sent us here,' Carlisle said.

'Well, he must have seen the articles. There's been quite a bit of press.'

'But is it safe?' Carlisle finally asked.

'As safe as many other things. Listen, I know it sounds radical. But I've had a man come to me who believed he was five people, not just two, and I went into his brain and fixed him up.'

'How is he now?' Einar asked.

'He lives with his mother. He's very quiet, but happy. She was the one who brought him to me, his mother was.'

'But what would happen to me?'

'You would come to the hospital. I'd prepare you for

surgery. It's important that you're rested and that your body isn't weak. I'd have you come to the hospital and gain some strength before I took you into the operating theatre. It takes no time at all. And then you'd rest. The actual surgery, it takes only a few hours. And then in about two weeks you'd be ready to leave.'

'And from there where would I go?' Einar asked.

'Oh, but I thought you already knew that.' Dr Buson's foot stretched out, jiggling the cart on its castors. 'You'll have to sort out some things before you come in for the surgery. You won't be the same after it's over.'

'Is it really all that simple?' Carlisle said.

'Usually.'

'But who would I be after you did this?' asked Einar.

'That,' Dr Buson said, 'is something we still cannot predict. We'll just have to see.'

Einar could hear the clack of clogs against the paving stones in the courtyard. The rain was beginning to fall harder, now tapping the window. Dr Buson span a little on his stool. And Carlisle continued to take notes on his pad. Outside, the nurse with the injured hand re-emerged from a doorway with an oval window above it. Her hand was bound in gauze. She was laughing with her colleague, and the two girls – they were barely twenty, probably only auxiliaries – ran across the courtyard to the other side, where there was another door with an oval window just above, this one gold and bright with light and streaked with rain.

Eighteen

᠂ᢒᡒᢍᢀ᠂

When Greta met Professor Bolk for the second time, in the early autumn of 1929, she arrived with a list of questions written in a notepad with an aluminium spiral along the top. Paris was now grey, the trees shaking themselves free of their leaves. Women stepped out into the streets busy pulling gloves across their knuckles, and the shoulders of men were hunched up around their ears.

They met in a café on the rue St-Antoine, at a table in the window that allowed Greta a view of the men and women emerging from the depths of the Métro, their faces soured by the weather. Professor Bolk was waiting for her, his thimble of espresso drained. He seemed displeased with her for arriving late; Greta offered up her excuses – a painting she couldn't leave, the telephone ringing – while Professor Bolk sat stone-faced, scraping the underside of his thumbnail with a little stainless-steel knife.

He was handsome, Greta thought, with a long face and a chin that was dimpled like the bottom of an apple. His knees did not fit properly beneath the tabletop, which was round and stained, the marble scratched and rusted and as rough as slate. A little band of cut-out brass circled the piece of marble, and Greta found it uncomfortable to lean in to talk privately with Professor Bolk, the piece of brass pressing into the underside of her arm.

'I can help your husband,' Professor Bolk was saying. At his feet was a bag with a gold buckle and half-loop handles, and Greta wondered if it could be as simple as Professor Bolk arriving at the *casita*'s door with that black bag and spending a few hours alone with Einar. She told herself it wouldn't work out like that, but she wished it could, the way she sometimes wished Carlisle would rub enough spearmint oil into his bad leg and it would heal, or the way she had wished Teddy Cross would sit in the sun long enough to burn the illness from his bones.

'But he won't be your husband when I'm finished,' Professor Bolk continued, opening his bag. He pulled out a book covered in green marbled paper, the leather of the spine chipped and worn like the seat of an old reading chair.

Professor Bolk found the right page, and then he looked up, his eyes meeting Greta's, uncaging a wingbeat in her chest. On the page was a diagram of a man's body showing both the skeleton and the organs in a busy display of parallel and crossing lines that made Greta think of one of the Baedeker maps from *Paris and its Environs* Carlisle had used when he first arrived. The man in the diagram represented an average adult male, Professor Bolk explained; his arms were spread out, and his genitals were hanging like grapes on a vine. The page was dog-eared and smudged with pencil markings.

'As you can see,' Professor Bolk said, 'the male pelvis is a cavity. The sex organs hang outside. In the pelvis there's nothing much but the lines of intestine, all of which can be rearranged.'

Greta ordered a second coffee, and was suddenly struck with a desire for a dish of quartered oranges; something made her think of Pasadena.

'I'm curious about your husband's pelvis,' Professor Bolk said. It was a strange way of putting it, Greta thought, although she liked Professor Bolk, warming to him as he told her about his training. He had studied in Vienna and Berlin, at the Charité Hospital, where he was one of the few men ever to develop specialties in both surgery and psychology. During the war, when he was a young surgeon whose legs were still growing and whose voice hadn't dropped to its final basso timbre, he amputated more than five hundred limbs – if one

counted all the fingers he chopped off in an attempt to salvage
a hand half-destroyed by a grenade whose lead time was a little
shorter than the captain had promised. Bolk had operated in
tents whose flaps trembled in the wind of bombs; sacrificing a
leg but saving a man, all in the glow of matchlight. The
ambulance runners would serve up on wood-board stretchers
men with their abdomens blown apart, sliding the half-alive
soldiers on to Professor Bolk's operating table, which was still
wet from the previous man's blood. The first time Bolk
received a man like that, with the middle of his body reduced
to an open bowl of guts, Bolk couldn't think of what to do.
But the man was dying in front of him, the soldier's eyes
rolling in his head and begging Bolk for help. The gas tanks
were almost empty, and so there was no way to put the man
fully out. Instead, Bolk laid a sheet of gauze across the young
man's face and set to work.

It was winter, and hailstones were pelting the tent, and the
torches were blowing out, and the corpses were stacked like
firewood, and Bolk decided that if he could sort out enough of
the intestines – the liver and kidneys were OK, in fact – then
maybe the boy could live, although he would never shit
properly again. The blood seeped up Bolk's sleeves, and for an
hour he didn't lift the gauze from the boy's face because, even
though he was unconscious from the pain, Bolk knew he
couldn't bear to see the agony fluttering in the boy's eyelids.
Bolk sewed carefully, unable to see much. As a boy Bolk had
skinned pigs, and the inside of the soldier felt no different from
that of a hog: warm and slick and dense, like plunging your
arm into a pot of winter stew.

As the night deepened and the shelling lifted but the
freezing rain fell only harder, Bolk began to stretch what was
left of the soldier's skin over his wound. There was a nurse in a
bloodied apron, Fräulein Schäpers, and the patient she'd been
attending had just vomited his innards on her, and then
instantly died. She took half a minute to wipe her face and
then joined Bolk. Together they stretched the soldier's skin,
from just beneath his sternum to the flaps of it hanging over his

pelvis. Fräulein Schäpers held the flesh together as Bolk ran a
cord thicker than a bootlace through the soldier, pulling the
skin as tight as the canvas seats of the collapsing stools in the
tent with the stovepipe chimney that served as their canteen.

The young man lived, at least long enough to be loaded into
an ambulance truck racked with shelves for the patients,
shelves that would make Bolk think of the bakery trucks that
used to career around Gendarmenmarkt, delivering the daily
loaves on which he would dine when he was a medical student
and poor and determined to become a doctor all of Germany
would admire.

'Five hundred limbs and five hundred lives,' Professor Bolk
said to Greta at the café on the rue St-Antoine. 'They say I
saved five hundred lives, although I can't really be sure.'

Outside, leaves were stuck to the top step of the entrance of
the Métro, and people would arrive and slip, although
everyone managed to catch the green copper rail just in time.
But Greta watched, waiting for someone to fall and scrape his
hand, or worse, although Greta didn't want to see it, she just
knew it would happen.

'When can I meet your husband?' Professor Bolk asked.

Greta thought of Einar on the steps of the Royal Academy
of Fine Arts; even at that age – he was already a professor, for
heaven's sake – Einar looked like a boy just on the eve of
puberty, as if they both knew in the morning he would lift his
arm to wash and discover the first thread of gold-brown hair.
He had never been right physically, Greta knew. But now she
wondered if it had ever mattered. Perhaps she should send
Professor Bolk back to Dresden alone, she thought, playing
with the spoon in her coffee cup. She suddenly wondered
whom she loved more, Einar or Teddy Cross. She told herself
it didn't matter, although she didn't believe it. She wished she
could decide and settle down with the satisfaction of the
information, but she didn't know. And then she thought of
Lili: the pretty bone at the top of her spine; the delicate way
she held her hands as if she were about to land them on the
keys of a piano; her whispery voice like the breeze that floated

up through the papery petals of the Iceland poppies that filled
the planting beds of Pasadena in winter; her white ankles
crossed and quiet. Whom did she love more, Greta asked
herself – and then Professor Bolk cleared his throat, his Adam's
apple lifting, and said, as if there were no doubt, 'So. I will see
you and Lili in Dresden.'

But Greta couldn't take Einar to Dresden. At least not yet.
There were many reasons, including the private exhibition of
her latest paintings, all of which showed Lili lying on a table,
her hands folded over her stomach, her eyes sealed as if dead.
The paintings, which were small, the size of a good dictionary,
hung in the parqueted hall of a countess who lived within
calling distance of not only the best *atelier* in Paris, but also the
best apothecary, who knew everything about masks of
Normandy mud and female rinses mixed of lime juice and the
Pure Pasadena Extract Greta gave him in exchange for the
cosmetic appliances like the Dermaclean machine that Lili
required more and more.

The paintings – there were only eight – sold in an
afternoon, to people whose chauffeurs were waiting in the
open doors of Nürburg convertible limousines on the street
below, the walnut panelling reflecting the early autumn sun.
Hans had arranged the show, which he told more than one
newspaper editor was the first must-see of *la rentrée*. He was
wearing an opal pin in his suit's lapel. He squeezed Greta's
hand when each painting was pulled from the countess's walls,
which were trimmed with a picture-frame moulding clogged
with a century of paint. And Greta, despite the continuous
accumulation of her fortune in the main branch of Landmands-
banken, found her eyes glazing over as she watched the leather
hoods of chequebooks open and the pens scratch through the
carbon paper.

That was one reason she could not take Einar to Dresden
right away. A second reason was Carlisle, who was contem-
plating staying in Paris over Christmas. If she knew anything,
she knew Carlisle was quite like herself in at least one way: his

impulse to take on a project with an obsessive need to reach a solution. There had never been a painting Greta hadn't finished. True, even she could now admit, many – especially during her early years in Denmark – had never been any good. Oh, if she could only return to Copenhagen on the blackest night and pull from the walls of all those offices along Vesterbrogade and Nørre Farimagsgade the drably official paintings she had produced when she was so young, so unsure of what she wanted to, or could, achieve! She thought of a severe portrait of Herr I. Glückstadt, the financier behind the East Asiatic Company and the Copenhagen Free Harbour; she had applied straight silver paint to reproduce his cap of hair; and his right hand, clutching a pen, was no more than a square, a blurry block, of flesh-coloured paint.

And Greta knew that she and Carlisle shared this same need to continue working; inside their nearly identical-sized bodies hung an urge to achieve. One day, Carlisle had returned to the *casita* with a burst of news that had forced Greta to rest her brush in the cup of turpentine and sit on the daybed.

'Einar and I have met some doctors,' he began. Driving around in his convertible had given Carlisle some colour, and his face was even more handsome than Greta had recalled. When she closed her eyes and listened to her brother's voice, which was flat and precise, she nearly thought she was listening to a recording of herself.

Carlisle described the visits, the futility of them, the humiliation Einar had endured. 'He can bear more than most men,' Carlisle was saying, and Greta thought to herself, Yes, I already know.

'But there is one doctor,' Carlisle continued. 'Dr Buson. He thinks he can help him. He's dealt with this before. With people who think they're –' and here Carlisle's voice cracked, something which Greta's never did – 'who think they're more than one person.'

Carlisle explained the lobotomy, the sharp little drills that Dr Buson had set out on the cart with castors. He had made it sound no more complicated than swatting a fly.

'I think it's what Einar wants to do,' Carlisle said.

'That's too bad, because I've found a doctor myself,' Greta interrupted. She had pressed coffee grounds through a cylinder of steaming water, and now she was pouring it. When she went to look, there was no cream in the kitchen, and something inside her welled up — as if she were a little girl in the mansion in Pasadena and one of the Japanese maids had failed to set out the promised dish of candied dates — and she had to keep herself from stamping her foot. Even Greta hated it when she became petty, but sometimes she couldn't help herself.

'He thinks he can help Einar change,' she continued. She apologized for not having any cream; she thought of saying, 'I suppose I'm no good at managing both the house and my work, even if I like to think I am,' but decided it would sound insincere, or ungrateful, or something — oh, she didn't know what — and now she became hot beneath her long skirt and the blouse that was tight in the sleeves, and she wondered why she was discussing her husband with her brother, why Carlisle should have any say at all.

But she stopped herself.

'But Dr Buson thinks he can help Einar change,' Carlisle said. 'Is your doctor proposing the same thing? Did he say anything about the drills through the forehead?'

'Professor Bolk thinks he can change Einar into a woman,' Greta said. 'Not mentally, but physically.'

'But how?'

'Through surgery,' Greta said. 'There are three surgeries that the professor wants to try.'

'I don't think I understand.'

'Trust me.'

'Of course I trust you. But what kind of surgery?'

'Transforming surgery.'

'Have you told Einar?' Carlisle asked.

'Not yet,' she said.

'It sounds terribly risky.'

'No more than what you're proposing.'

Carlisle was on the velvet ottoman, his leg up. She liked having him stay with them, to fill the morning hours while Lili slept, to stay with Greta when Lili set out on errands and a bathe. She supposed in some ways she had silently asked for his help. 'I'm not going to let him go to see Buson,' she said. 'He could come back a child, an infant practically.'

'It has to be Einar's decision,' Carlisle said. 'He's an adult, he'll have to decide.' Always the reasonable one, her brother. Sometimes too pragmatic for Greta.

Greta sipped her coffee; how she hated black coffee! She said. 'It's up to Einar.' And then, 'Of course.'

And that was another reason why Greta couldn't take Einar to Dresden just yet. She would have to find the day, when she was free and Einar was happy because Lili had visited recently and her stay hadn't been painful but joyous: with a victorious game of badminton on the lawn behind Anna's apartment, or an evening of cinema at the Gaumont-Palace; after a day like this was when Greta could explain to Einar his options for what to do next with Lili. It wouldn't be easy. Greta imagined Carlisle had done a fine job convincing Einar about Dr Buson's skill, about the potential of the lobotomy, which to her sounded both gruesome and cruel. She would never let Einar go through with something like that. But Carlisle was right about one thing: Einar would have to decide for himself. Greta would have to make him believe, as she did, that Bolk could solve their problem, the problem that had both defined and ruined their marriage, more resolutely than any other man in the world. Bolk had already returned to Dresden, and so she would have to convince Einar on her own: take his hand in hers, push her hair over her ears, and explain the promise, the glittering promise, that lay in Dresden.

And yet there was one more reason why Greta hesitated over taking Einar to Dresden.

By March 1918 the winter rains had ended, and Pasadena was green, as green as the jade Buddha Akiko kept in her dormer room on the third floor of the Waud mansion. Greta and Teddy had buried baby Carlisle in the Bakersfield strawberry fields and resettled in Pasadena, saddened and, as Mrs Waud stressed by the way she anxiously played with her rings, a bit scarred.

But at least the rains had ended, and Pasadena was green, with its winter rye lawns like blankets of felt, its beds of snapdragons springing forth with pink and white blossoms, the Iceland poppies floating above the soil. In the orange groves, the white blossoms were like jackets of snow. To Greta, the roots of the orange trees looked like elbows pushing through the damp soil; they were the dull colour of flesh, and just as thick as a man's arm. The rains had softened the ground for the earthworms, which, in their blue-grey skins, reminded Greta of baby Carlisle's birth matter. She'd never forget the worm-like colour of the cord, twisted like a corkscrew. Nor the bluish mucus sealing the baby's eyes, or the sheen of her own fluids covering him, as if he were encased in a thin, greasy sheet of protection, one her own body, in its independent wisdom, had designed.

She thought of this that spring when she was managing the orange groves in her father's absence. She'd survey the land in the car with the flip-down windscreen that carried her through the mud. She was supervising the crews, mostly teenage boys from Tecate and Tucson, hired to pick the understock. Beneath a tree whose fruit was falling prematurely, she saw a nest of worms slide through a clod of dirt. And this, now, made Greta think of Teddy and his cough. For nearly a year the sputum had hurled from his lungs, and at night he would soak the sheets in a sweat so icy that at first Greta had thought he'd spilled a glass of water into their bed. At the sound of the first cough, which had crept ominously up his throat like a ball of broken glass, she had suggested a doctor. He would cough and she would lift the telephone receiver to call Dr Richard-son, an egg-shaped man originally from North Carolina. But Teddy would argue, 'There's nothing wrong with me. I'm not going to see any doctor.'

Greta would return the receiver to its cradle and say only, 'All right.' She'd have to wait until he was out of the house to make the phone call. Whenever he coughed and brought his handkerchief – which she herself had taken to pressing with a black iron – to his mouth, Greta would glance out of the corner of her eye to see if anything had come up with the cough. Sometimes it was dry, and she would silently sigh. But other times the cough would be phlegmy and a sluggy whitish fluid would swing from Teddy's mouth to his handkerchief. And then, more and more, he would hack up a thick clot of blood. Because Greta, and not Akiko, would rinse all of Teddy's laundry, including his handkerchiefs, she would see just how much blood he was coughing up. She would have to change the sheets nightly, and dip the handkerchiefs, and sometimes his shirts, into tubs of bleach, the bitter chlorine smell rising to her nostrils and stinging her eyes. The blood didn't come out easily, and she would rub her fingertips raw trying to rid the handkerchiefs of their stains, which reminded Greta of the dropcloths she used around her easel's back when she was painting, which now, settled in the *casita* in Pasadena, she wasn't doing at all. But still, whenever Greta lifted the receiver, Teddy would say, 'I'm not going to see any doctor, because I'm not sick, for Christ's sake.'

A couple of times she managed to summon Dr Richardson to the *casita*. Teddy would greet him in the sunroom, his hair falling into his eyes. 'You know how a wife can be,' Teddy would say. 'Always worrying over nothing. But honestly, doc, there's nothing wrong with me.'

'Then what about your cough?' Greta would interrupt.

'Nothing more than a farmer's hack. If you grew up in the fields you'd be coughing too,' he'd say, smiling, laughing, causing Dr Richardson and Greta both to laugh as well, even though Greta saw nothing funny in what Teddy was doing.

'It's probably nothing,' Richardson would say. 'But do you mind if I take a look?'

'As a matter of fact I would.' The sunroom had a floor paved with tiles Teddy had cast at his studio. They were the colour of amber and laid with a black grout. In the winter, the tiles were too cold to stand on even in socks.

'Then call me if it gets any worse,' Dr Richardson would say, clasping his bag in retreat.

And Greta, who more than anything else wanted to be a good wife, who didn't want her husband to snigger with his buddies over how possessive and sneaky and shrill she'd become, would push her hair back over her ears and say, 'All right then. If you're not going to see Richardson, you'd better damn well take good care of yourself.'

The reason she considered this spring, the spring of 1918, greener than any other she could recall was that Teddy's room in the sanatorium, where he was now settled, had a view of both the Arroyo Seco and the San Gabriel Mountains; she would sit in the chair at the window and study the green while Teddy slept. The sanatorium was a tan stucco building with a belltower that hung on the lip of a cliff over the *arroyo*. There was a path around the property that was lined with rose bushes. The rooms were diamond-shaped and had hand-crank windows with views both north and south. Teddy's bed was white iron, and every morning a nurse would come and get him into his rocking chair and then roll up the blue-striped mattress, where it would sit on the open springs at the foot of the bed like a huge roll of toffee.

Teddy had been in the sanatorium most of the winter, and rather than improving, he seemed only to worsen with each week. His cheeks were hollow, and his eyes clogged with something that looked like spoiled milk. Greta would arrive in the morning and immediately dab his eyes clean with the corner of her skirt. Then she would comb his hair, which had thinned to nothing more than a few colourless strands. On some mornings, his fever would be running so high that his forehead would be wet, and yet he was too weak to lift his own arm to wipe his brow. More than once she'd arrive and find him in his rocking chair like this: at the hand-crank window, in the sunlight, burning up from the fever and the flannel dressing gown that the nurse had tied around his hollow waist. From the way his face was twisted up, Greta could see he was trying to lift his arm to drag the flannel sleeve across his forehead; the sweat was dripping from his chin as if he'd been caught in a downpour. But this was March, and the winter rains were over, and all of Pasadena was jade green; instead of the clear blank sunlight burning the tuberculosis out of his lungs and his marrow, it was only setting Teddy on fire, so that before ten o'clock and the first arrival of his twice-a-day glass of kumquat juice, Teddy would have fainted beneath the weight of his fever.

By April, Teddy was sleeping more and more. Greta would sit in the rocker, the white padding on its arms worn threadbare, while he lay in bed on his side. Sometimes he would shift in his sleep, and the springs would creak, and it would sound to Greta like a groan from his bones, which were filled with tuberculosis, like an éclair stuffed with cream. His doctor, a man called Hightower, would come to the room, his white coat open over a cheap brown suit. Teddy continued to refuse treatment from Dr Richardson, who treated not only every Waud in Pasadena, but also the families of Henrietta and Margaret and Dottie Anne. 'Dr Hightower is fine for me,' he'd say. 'I don't need a fancy person's doctor.'

'What the hell is "a fancy person's doctor" anyway?' Greta would say, regretting her raised voice the moment it escaped her throat. She didn't want to contradict him, more than anything she didn't want to hurt Teddy by saying she knew more than he. That was how she felt about it, and so she politely tolerated Dr Hightower during his daily visits. The doctor was always in a rush, and he often did not have the proper paperwork in the manila file shoved up under his arm. He was a lanky man, with Norwegian-blond hair, like very light coffee. A transplant from Chicago, and there was something about the tips of his extremities – his nose, his ears, his nubby fingers – that looked frostbitten.

'How're you feeling today?' Dr Hightower would ask.

'A little better,' Teddy would say, honestly believing it, or unaware that it was possible to answer anything else. Dr Hightower would nod and check something off on a chart in his file. Greta would excuse herself to make a call over to the grove-house, where a load of orange pickers up from Tecate was expected any hour. And with the receiver at the nurse's station pressed against her ear, Greta would make a second call to Richardson, saying only, 'He's getting worse.'

Her mother visited, usually in the afternoons when Teddy would have his one good hour. Greta and Teddy sat silently while Mrs Waud rattled on about opening up the beach house in Del Mar, or about the telegram from Greta's father, who was reporting even more enthusiastically than the newspapers that the end of the war was near. Greta silently hoped her mother would intervene in that way only she could: throwing open the curtains and nudging Teddy out of bed and into a hot mineral bath, bringing a cup of tea laced with bourbon to his lips. 'Alrighty, now let's get you well!' Mrs Waud would say, rubbing her hands together and pushing the loose strands of hair back over her ears. 'Enough of this tuberculosis nonsense!' Mrs Waud would say – or at least Greta secretly hoped she would say. But Mrs Waud never did; she left Teddy to Greta. She would pull on her gloves at the end of the visit and then kiss Teddy's forehead through her surgical mask and simply say, 'I want you sitting up the next time I come.' She would then slit up her eyes and look over at Greta. In the corridor outside the room, Mrs Waud would remove her mask and say, 'Make sure he's getting the best care, Greta.'

'He won't see Richardson.'

'He simply must.'

And Greta would telephone Richardson again, giving Teddy's latest status.

'Yes, I know,' Dr Richardson would say. 'I've consulted with Dr Hightower. To be honest with you, I'm not sure there's anything more I could do for him. We'll just have to wait and see.'

When Carlisle drove down from Stanford to visit, he pulled Greta aside and said, 'I don't like this Hightower. Where'd he come from?' She explained that he was assigned by the sanatorium, but Carlisle interrupted her: 'Maybe it's time to bring Richardson in.'

'I've tried.'

'Is there anything I can do?'

She thought about this. She heard Teddy cough on the other side of the door. The wire springs of the bed trembled. There was a deep wheezing gasp for breath. 'I'll have to think about it. I'm sure there's something, yes. I'll just have to think about it.'

'You know how serious this is, don't you?' Carlisle said, taking her hand.

'But Teddy's strong,' she said.

Later that afternoon, when Carlisle had left, and the sun was sliding over the foothills, and the purply shadows were falling like blankets on the canyons of Pasadena, Greta took Teddy's cold hand. The pulse on the underside of his wrist was faint, and at first she didn't think it was there at all. But it tapped lightly, infrequently. 'Teddy?' she said. 'Teddy, can you hear me?'

'Yes,' he said.

'Does it hurt?'

'Yes.'

'Do you feel any better today?'

'No,' he said. 'I'm afraid I'm worse. Worse than I've ever been.'

'But you'll be getting better. Teddy? Do me a favour? I've called Richardson. He's coming by in the morning. Please let him take a look at you. That's all I'm asking. He's a good doctor. He saved me when I was little and had the chickenpox. I had a fever of a hundred and six, and everyone, including Carlisle, had written me off, and here I am today as strong as anyone, with nothing left of that damn disease except for this little scar.'

'Greta, dear?' Teddy said, the tendons in his throat leaping. 'I'm dying, dear. You know that, don't you? I'm not going to get any better.'

And to tell the truth, she didn't know that, not until just then. But of course he was dying; he was closer to dead than alive: his arms were thin and loose with yellowing flesh, his

eyes infected, his lungs sponges so heavily soaked with blood
and sputum that they would sink straight to the bottom of the
Pacific. And his bones, that was the cruellest part: his bones
were sopped; there was a wet living fire gnawing away at his
bones. She thought of the pain he must be bearing but about
which he never complained. It nearly killed her to have her
husband in pain. 'I'm sorry,' Teddy said.

'Whatever for?'

'For leaving you.'

'But you're not leaving me.'

'And I'm sorry for asking you to do this,' he said.

'Do what? What are you talking about?' She felt a panicky
film of sweat spread across her back. The room was warm with
the effluvia of malady. She should crank open the window, she
was thinking. Give poor Teddy some fresh air.

'Would you help me with it?'

'With what?' She didn't understand him, and she thought
about calling Richardson and reporting that Teddy was now
speaking nonsense. An ominous sign, she knew Richardson
would say, his drawl heavy on the phone line.

'Take that pillow . . . the rubber one. Put it over my face for
just a little bit. It won't take long.'

She stopped. Now she understood. A final request from her
husband, whom she wanted to please more than anyone in the
world. More than anything she wanted him to leave this world
still in love with her, gratitude his final memory. A rubber
pillow sat in the rocking chair; Teddy was trying to lift his
hand to point.

'Just hold it against my face for a minute or two,' he said.
'It'll be easier that way.'

'Oh, Teddy,' she said. 'I can't. Dr Richardson will be here
in the morning. Wait until then. Let him take a look at you.
He might know what's next for you. But just hold on till then.
Please stop talking about that pillow. Please stop pointing at
that pillow.' The sweat was collecting at the small of her back,
and on her blouse beneath her breasts. It was almost as if she

had a fever, her forehead slick, a drop of sweat slipping past her ear.

She turned the window crank and felt the cool air. The pillow was black, with thick edges, and smelled like a tyre. Teddy was still pointing at it. 'Yes,' he said. 'Bring it over here.' She touched it, its skin thick like a hot-water bottle. It was limp, only half filled with air. 'Greta, my dear . . . one last thing. Just press it against my face. I can't take this any longer.'

She picked up the pillow and held it to her chest, the rubbery smell filling her. She couldn't do it. Such a horrible way to die, beneath this smelly old thing, rubber the last scent of your life. Worse than what was going to kill him, she told herself, fingering the pillow's elastic edge. Worse than anything she'd ever imagined. No, she couldn't do it, and she threw the pillow out of the window, the black pad falling like an injured raven into the Arroyo Seco below.

Teddy parted his lips, his tongue appearing. He was trying to say something, but the effort overcame him and he fell asleep.

Greta moved to his side and held her palm in front of his mouth. The breath was no stronger than the wake of a butterfly. As evening fell all around, the halls of the sanatorium became silent. The blue jays made a last dash in the ponderosa outside Teddy's window, and Greta took his cold moist hand. She could no longer look at him, turning her head to the hand-crank window, watching the Arroyo Seco become a black pit. The San Gabriel Mountains turned into black silhouettes of something large, something black and faceless looming over the valley where the Wauds lived among the canyons and the orange groves, and where Greta was holding her breath until she thought she would pass out; and when she finally gasped for air and blotted the tears with her cuff, she dropped Teddy's hand. Again she placed her palm beneath his nose, and then, in the night, she knew, by his own will, Teddy Cross was gone.

Part Three

Dresden
1930

Nineteen

❧

Einar's train entered Germany. It stopped in a brown field, the turned soil silver with frost. Outside, the sun was weak in the January sky, and the birch trees edging the field huddled against the wind. All he could see was the flat of the fields and the reach of the grey sky. There was nothing else. Nothing but a diesel tractor abandoned in winter, its red metal seat trembling on its spring.

The border patrol checked passports on the train. Einar could hear the officers in the next compartments, their boots heavy on the carpet. They spoke rapidly but they sounded bored. There was the thin whine of a woman explaining her papers, and one of the officers saying, '*Nein, nein, nein.*'

Two officers arrived at Einar's compartment, and there was a flutter in his chest, as if indeed he were guilty of something. The officers were young and tall, their shoulders pressed tightly into their uniforms, which looked to Einar uncomfortably starched. Their faces were shiny beneath the peaks of their caps, as shiny as the brass buttons on their cuffs, and Einar suddenly thought that the officers, who were barely out of their youth, were made of brass themselves: all gold and shiny and cold. They had a metallic smell, too, probably a government-supplied shaving cream. One of the officers had chewed his nails to stubs, and his partner's knuckles were scraped.

Immediately Einar felt as if the officers were disappointed with him — as if, no matter what, he was incapable of causing any trouble. The one with the raw fingernails demanded

Einar's passport; when he saw it was Danish, he became even less interested. He opened it while looking at his partner. Neither of the officers, who were breathing through their mouths, checked the information in Einar's papers, or held up the photograph, taken so long ago in a musty-smelling photographer's studio steps from Rundetårn, to compare it to Einar's face. The officers said nothing. The first one threw the passport into Einar's lap. The second, whose eyes narrowed in on Einar, slapped his own stomach, the brass buttons on his cuff shaking, and Einar almost expected the *dang!* of a bell. Then the officers were gone.

Later, the train hauled itself into speed again, and the afternoon fluttered down over the fields of Germany, where in spring rows of rape would erupt with their violent yellow blossoms and their seductive scent of the nearly dead.

The rest of the ride Einar was cold. Greta had asked him if he wanted her to join him. Einar thought he had hurt her when he said no. 'But why not?' she had asked. They were in the front room of the *casita*, and Einar didn't answer. It was hard for him to say, but he thought that he might not have the courage to go through with it if Greta was with him; she would have reminded him too much of their previous life. They'd been happy, he kept telling himself. Einar and Greta had been in love. If she had come along, Einar feared, he wouldn't keep his appointment with Professor Bolk; Einar might have instead told Greta they should switch trains in Frankfurt and head south, back to Menton, where the blank sunlight and the sea could make everything seem simple. As he was saying 'No, I'll go alone,' he could almost smell the lemon trees in the park in front of the municipal casino. Or, Einar might have said he was returning to Bluetooth, where now another family lived in the farmhouse next to the sphagnum fields; he might have tried to run away, and taken Greta with him, to the room of his youth where the feather mattress had been crushed thin and needly, and the wall by his bed was scratched with line drawings of Hans and Einar asleep on a rock; where the paint on the legs of the kitchen table was picked away from when Einar would hide under there and listen to his father call to his grandmother, 'Bring me more tea before I die.'

Before Einar left Paris, Carlisle had asked him if he knew what he was getting into. 'Do you really know what Bolk wants to do to you?' In fact Einar didn't know the details. He knew Bolk would transform him, but even Einar had a hard time imagining just how. A series of surgeries, he knew. The removal of his sex, which more and more had come to feel parasitically worthless, the colour of a wart. 'I still think you might want to see Buson instead,' Carlisle had tried. But Einar had chosen Greta's plan; in the night, when no one was awake in the world but the two of them, when they lay quiet beneath the bedclothes, their pinkies clasped, still there was no one he trusted more.

'Let me come with you,' Greta had tried one last time, drawing his hand to her breast. 'You shouldn't have to go through this alone.'

'But I can only do it if I'm alone. Otherwise . . .' He paused. 'I'll be too ashamed.'

And so Einar travelled by himself. He could see his reflection in the window of the train. His face was pale and thin around the nose. It made him think of a hermit who hadn't lifted his face to the window of his hovel in many years.

Lying on the seat across from Einar was a *Frankfurter Zeitung*, left behind by a woman travelling with an infant. In the paper was an obituary of a man who had made a fortune in pavement. There was a photo, and the man looked sad in the mouth. There was something in his face – the baby fat filling his chin.

Einar sat back in the seat and watched his reflection in the window. As the evening moved in quickly, the reflection grew more shadowy and angled, so that by dusk he didn't recognize his face in the glass. Then the reflection disappeared, and outside lay nothing but the distant twinkle of a pork village, and Einar was sitting in the dark.

They wouldn't know where to begin with his obituary, he

thought. Greta would write a draft and deliver it to the newspaper's desk herself. Maybe that was where they would begin, the young reporters with the thinning blond hair from *Nationaltidende*. They would take Greta's draft and rewrite it, running the obituary and getting it wrong.

Einar felt the train rattle beneath him, and he thought of how his obituary should begin:

He was born on a bog. A little girl born as a boy on the bog. Einar Wegener never told anyone, but his first memory was of sunlight through the eyelet in his grandmother's summer solstice dress. The baggy sleeves with the eyelet holes reaching into the crib to hold him, and he could recall thinking – no, nor thinking, but feeling – that the white eyelet of summer would surround him forever, as if it were another necessary element: water, light, heat. He was in his christening gown. The lace, woven by his dead mother's tatting aunts, hung down around him. It hung past his feet, and it would later remind Einar of the lace drapes that hung in the homes of Danish aristocrats; the blued cotton would fall to the baseboard and then fan onto the black-oak planks of a floor polished with beeswax by a bony maid. In the villa where Hans had been born there were drapes like that, and Baroness Axgil would snap her tongue – which was the thinnest tongue Einar had ever seen, and nearly forked – against the roof of her mouth whenever he, the girl born as a boy on the bog, moved to touch them.

The obituary would leave out that part. It would also fail to mention Einar, drunk on Tuborg, pissing into the canal the night he sold his first painting. He was a young man in Copenhagen, his tweed pants bunching up on the waist, his belt pelted with a mallet and a nail to drill another notch. He was at the Royal Academy of Fine Arts on a scholarship for boys from the country; no one expected him to paint seriously, only to learn a trick or two about framing and foreground, and then return to the bogs, where he could paint the eaves of the town halls of northern Jutland with scenes depicting the Norse god Odin. But then, on that early spring afternoon when the air was still crystallizing in his lungs, a man in a cloak stopped by the academy. The students' paintings were hanging in the hallways, up and down the walls of the open stairwell with the white balustrade where, years later, Greta would take Einar's head into her hands and fall in love with him. Einar's little scene of the black bog was up, in a frame of faux gold leaf he paid for with the money he'd earned from submitting to medical experiments at the Kommunehospitalet.

The man in the cloak spoke softly, and word spread through the halls of the academy that he was a dealer from Paris. He was wearing a wide-brimmed hat trimmed with a strip of leather, and the students could barely see his eyes. There was a little blond mustache curling down around his mouth, and the faint smell of newsprint falling behind him like exhaust. The acting director of the academy, Herr Rump, who was the less talented descendant of Herr G. Rump, introduced himself to the stranger. Rump escorted the man through the academy halls, where the floors were grey and unvarnished and swept clean by orphan girls not old enough to conceive. Rump tried to halt the stranger in front of the canvases painted by his favourite pupils, the girls with the wavy hair and apple-perky breasts and the boys with the thighs like hams. But the man in the cloak, who was reported to say, although no one could ever confirm it, 'I have a tongue for talent,' refused to be swayed by Herr Rump's suggestions. The stranger nodded in front of the painting of the mouse and the cheese done by Gertrude Grubbe, a girl with eyebrows so yellow and fluffy it was as if a canary had shed two feathers across her face. He also paused by the scene depicting a woman selling a salmon painted by Sophus Brandes, a boy whose father had been murdered on a ferry to Russia, due to a single leer at the murderer's adolescent bride. And then the man in the cloak stopped in front of Einar's little painting of the black bog. In the painting it was night, the oaks and willows only shadows, the ground as dark and damp as oil. In the corner, next to the boulder speckled with mica, was a little white dog, asleep in the cold. Only the previous day Herr Rump had declared it 'too dark for the Danish school,' and thus had given it a less-than-ideal spot on the wall, next to the closet where the orphan girls stored their hay-brooms and changed into the sleeveless apron-dresses that Herr Rump insisted they wear.

'This one is good,' the man had said, and his hand reached into his cloak and pulled out a billfold made of – again, this was rumoured too – lizard leather. 'What's the artist's name?' he asked.

'Einar Wegener,' said Herr Rump, whose face was filling with the hot bright colour of choler. The stranger handed him one hundred kroner. The man in the cloak pulled the painting from the wall, and then everyone at the academy – Herr Rump and the students who had been watching from the cracks in classroom doors and the adminstratrices in their pinned-up blouses and the orphan girls who were secretly plotting a plan, which would later fail, to push Herr Rump from an academy window, and, last of all, Einar Wegener, who was standing on the stairs exactly where Greta would later kiss him – had to blink. For the whole incident was so remarkable that the entire academy blinked in concert, every last member, whether artist or not, and slightly shook its collective head. And when they all opened their eyes, the sun shifted around the spires of Copenhagen and filled the academy's paned windows and the man in the cloak was gone.

The obituary would miss that day as well. It would also miss that one afternoon in August with Greta. It was before they were married, just after the war had ended. Greta had been back in Copenhagen only a month. She arrived at his office door at the academy wearing a straw hat pinned with dahlias, and when he opened the door she said, 'Come on!' They hadn't seen each other since she'd left for California as the war was breaking out. Einar asked, 'What's new?' and she only shrugged her shoulders and said, 'Here or in California?'

She led him out of the academy, into Kongens Nytorv, where the traffic was swirling around the statue of Christian V on horseback. In front of the Royal Theatre was a German soldier missing a leg; his canvas cap was on the pavement, catching coins. Greta took Einar's arm. She said, 'Oh.' She left the man money, and asked his name, but the man was so shell-shocked he could not follow her.

'I didn't realize,' Greta said as she and Einar continued walking. 'It all seemed so far away in California.'

They cut through the corner of Kongens Have, where the box hedges needed a trim and children were running away from their mothers and on the lawn young couples were lying on blankets patterned with tartan and wishing the rest of the world would go away and give them the privacy of two. Greta didn't say where they were headed, and Einar knew not to ask. The day was bright and warm, and the windows along Kronprinsessegade were open, the summer eyelet curtains fluttering. A delivery wagon passed, and Greta took Einar's arm. She said, 'Don't say anything.'

But Einar's heart was pounding, because the young girl who had kissed him on the academy's stairs had floated back into his life as fast as she had departed five years earlier. And during those five years he'd thought of Greta off and on, the way he would recall a disturbing and fascinating dream. During the war he dreamed of her in California. But the image of her dashing through the academy's halls, her paintbrushes shoved up under her arm, the ferrules reflecting the light, had also stayed with him over the course of the war. She was the busiest student he'd ever known, off to balls and ballets but always ready to work, even if it meant late at night when most others needed an aquavit and sleep. When he thought of the ideal woman, more and more he'd come to think of Greta. Taller than the rest of the world, and faster. He could recall one day lifting his head from his desk in his office at the academy and from his window seeing her run through the honking traffic circling Kongens Nytorv, her blue-grey skirt like a plough through the grilles and bumpers of the carriages and the motor cars, whose drivers were squeezing the rubber bulbs of their horns. And how she would wave her hands through the air and say, 'Who cares?' For certainly Greta didn't care about anything but that which made sense to her, and as Einar became more and more silent in his adulthood and lonelier at his canvas and more convinced that he was a man who would never belong, he began to ponder over his ideal version of a woman. And that was Greta.

And then she turned up at his office on that warm August afternoon and now she was leading him through the streets of Copenhagen, beneath the open parlour windows along Kronprinsessegade, where they could hear the squeal of children ready for their summer holiday on the North Sea, and the yelp of lapdogs ready for a stretch of their tiny legs.

When they reached her street Greta said, 'Be sure to duck.' He didn't know what she meant, but she took his hand and they hid behind the parked motor cars as they moved down the street. It had rained the night before, and the kerbs were wet, and the sun on the wet pneumatic tyres brought the scent of warm rubber to his nose, a scent that he would later think of when he was driving around Paris with Carlisle the summer when they – all of them – were plotting Lili's future. Greta led them from car to car, as if they were dodging enemy fire. They worked their way down the block like this, down the block in Copenhagen that housed Herr Janssen, proprietor of the glove factory in which a fire had killed forty-seven women hunched at their foot-pedalled machines; down the block that housed Countess Haxen, who at eighty-eight had the largest collection of teacups in all northern Europe, a collection so vast that even *she* didn't mind when a tantrum overcame her and she hurled one of them at the wall; down the block where the Hansens lived with their twin daughters, girls who were so blonde and beautiful in duplicate that their parents were in constant fear of kidnapping; down towards the white house with the blue door and the window boxes planted with geraniums that were as red as hen's blood and that smelled, even from across the street, bitter and full and faintly obscene. It was the house where Greta's father had lived during the war, and now that it was over, he was returning to Pasadena.

From behind the bonnet of a Labourdette Skiff, Greta and Einar watched the removal men haul the shipping crates down the steps and into the cargo of their waiting lorry. Einar and Greta could smell the geraniums and the shipping straw, and the sweat of the men as they heaved the crate carrying Greta's canopy bed. 'My father's leaving,' Greta said.

'Are you?'

'Oh, no. I'm going to stay on my own. Don't you see?'

'See what?'

'At last I'm free.'

But Einar didn't see, not just then. He didn't see that Greta would need to be alone in Denmark, relationless in Europe, in order to become the woman she saw herself as. She needed to put an ocean and a continent between herself and her family in order to feel that at last she could breathe. What Einar didn't understand then was that it was another of Greta's brazenly American traits, that bubbling need to move away and reinvent. Never before had he imagined himself doing the same.

And this was another part of his life that the obituary written by *Nationaltidende* would miss. They wouldn't know where to look for it. And like most newspapermen, the young reporters with the thinning hair wouldn't be careful enough to check the source. Time was running out. Einar Wegener was slipping away. Only Greta would remember the life he had led.

The obituary that would never be written should have followed with this:

There was a day last summer when Lili woke up in her room in the *casita* and found herself unbearably hot. It was August. For the first time since they were married, Greta and Einar had decided not to holiday in Menton. Mostly because of his deteriorating health. The bleeding. The weight loss. The eyes sinking deeper into their sockets. And, sometimes, his inability to hold his head up at the table. No one knew what to do. No one knew what Einar wanted to be done. And Lili woke up on that hot morning, when the exhaust from the lorries delivering to the *charcuterie* on the corner was rising through the open window and dusting her face with grime. She was lying in her bed, wondering if she would rise at all today. And the morning passed, as she stared at the curled plaster in the ceiling, at the white petals in the centre around the base of the chandelier.

Then she heard voices in the front room. A man, and a second. Hans and Carlisle. She listened to them talking to Greta, although Greta couldn't be heard, so it was like hearing two men talk and talk. Their scratchy voices made Lili think of three-day growth on a throat. Lili must have fallen asleep, because the next thing she knew the sun was coming into the room from a different angle, now from over the green copper roofs across the street, where a hawk had built its nest, but Hans and Carlisle were still talking. And then they were at her door, and then inside the room, where Lili had thought more and more of installing a lock in the door but never came to doing so. She watched them enter, and it seemed more like a memory than something that was actually happening. They were saying, 'Come on. Get up.' And then, 'Little Lili.' She could feel them pull on her arms; again, the pull was more like memory than an actual tug. One of them brought a cup of milk to her mouth. A second pulled a dress over her head. They led her to the pickled-ash wardrobe to find a pair of shoes, and she stepped into a panel of sun and felt her skin ignite. And yet Hans and Carlisle sensed this, and so they found a parasol, a paper umbrella with bamboo ribs, and quickly opened it.

Somehow they got her to the Tuileries. And there they walked, Lili's elbows linked with each of theirs. They moved beneath the poplars, in the swaying shadows that, to Lili, looked like large fish about to break the surface of the sea. Hans pulled up three green folding chairs, and they sat together in the afternoon as the children passed and the young lovers strolled and the lonely men with the quick eyes headed over to their side of the park, near L'Orangerie. Lili thought of the last time she was alone in the park; a few weeks earlier she had been out for a walk, and two little boys passed her, and one of them had said, '*Lesbienne.*' The boys were probably ten or eleven, blond with down on their cheeks, and their shorts showed most of their hairless thighs, and yet these pretty little boys had managed to hurl something so cruel, and wrong.

Lili sat with Hans and Carlisle, and she was hot in the dress they had chosen for her: one of the capped-sleeved dresses printed with conch shells that had come from the rented apartment in Menton. She knew then that her life with Einar was over. The only question that remained was whether she would have a life as Lili. Or would it all be over, and she would rest? Would Einar and Lili exit, hand in hand? Bones buried in the bog.

And Einar knew that his obituary would miss that as well. It would report everything about him except the life he had lived. And then the rhythm of the train's speed slowed, and he opened his eyes and the conductor called down the passage-way: 'Dresden! Dresden!'

Twenty

Greta was sitting on the velvet ottoman. Her hair was falling in her face, and Edvard IV was in her lap, shaking. With Einar in Dresden, she suddenly felt incapable of settling down to work. She could think only of Einar in Germany, making his way to Professor Bolk's laboratory. She had an image of Lili lost on a street, and Einar frightened on the professor's examination table. Greta had wanted to travel with him, but he wouldn't let her; he said this was something he had to do on his own. She couldn't understand that. There was another train to Dresden only three hours after Einar's, and she'd bought a ticket. She would turn up at the Municipal Women's Clinic half a day after him, and there would be nothing Einar could do. Lili would want her there, Greta knew. But as she was packing her bags and making plans to leave Edvard IV with Anna, Greta stopped herself. Einar had asked her not to come: she heard his careful words over and over, the way they had caught in his throat.

Greta was older now. When she looked in the mirror there was a faint, handsome line on each side of her mouth, two lines that reminded her of the entrance to a cave – a bit of an exaggeration, she knew, but even so. She had promised herself she wouldn't care about lines and wrinkles or even the few stray grey hairs that had grown into her temples like fur caught in a broom. But she did, although she had a hard time admitting it. Instead, she let it pick at her, as the months and the years passed and she settled more into her role as American artist abroad, while California receded further and further, as if the calamitous earthquake predicted by a doctor of physics on the palm-shaded campus of Cal Tech had already erupted on the Golden State and launched the whole coast into the Pacific; Pasadena slipping further and further away, a lost ship, a lost island, now only memory.

Except of course for Carlisle. During the autumn he had shuffled around Paris, the cuffs of his trousers muddying in the rain. The ache in his shin came and went with the clouds that rolled in off the Atlantic; and he and Lili would set out from the *casita* beneath their umbrellas, Lili wrapped up in her pink mackintosh that looked so heavy Greta worried she might collapse. Greta and Carlisle had had words about Einar's choice of doctor. He told her plainly that he thought she was doing the wrong thing for Einar: 'He could end up regretting this,' Carlisle had said, conceding. It stung her, this criticism, and she continued to feel its blow through the autumn as he changed the compress on Lili's forehead, or as he sat on Lili's bed playing poker with her, or as they bundled themselves up to head out for a night at the opera. 'Sorry you can't join us,' Lili would call with her small voice. 'Don't work too much!'

Sometimes Greta would feel burdened by her work, as if she were the only one in the world labouring while the rest were off and out, enjoying themselves. As if everything had come to rest on her shoulders, and should she stop and put down her head, their small, intimate world would implode. She thought of Atlas, who held up the world; and yet that wasn't right, because not only did she hold it up, she had also created it. Or so she sometimes thought. On some days she was exhausted, and would wish she could tell someone this, but there was no one, and so she spoke to Edvard IV as he ate his bowl of chicken skin and gristle.

No one except Hans.

The day after Einar left for Germany, Hans came to see her. He had just visited his barber, and the hair on the back of his neck was bristly, the skin pink with irritation. He was telling her about a new idea for an exhibition: he wanted to approach the headmistress of a private girls' school to see about hanging

a series of Lili paintings in the halls. Hans was pleased with the
idea, from the way he was laughing into his coffee cup.

Over the past couple of years he had seen other women,
Greta knew: an actress from London; an heiress to a jam
fortune. Hans was careful not to tell Greta about them,
avoiding mentioning whom he'd spent the weekend with in
Normandy. But he would tell Einar, and the news would fly
back to Greta in Lili's breathless way: 'An actress whose name
is up in lights above Cambridge Circus!' Lili would report.
'Isn't it exciting for Hans?'

'That must be very nice,' Greta would reply, 'for him.'

'Where's Einar got to?' Hans now said.

'He's gone to Germany to look after his health.'

'To Dresden?'

'Did he mention it to you?' She looked around the
apartment, at her easels and her paintings leaning against the
wall and the rocker. 'Lili went with him as well. It's quiet here
without them.'

'Of course she went with him,' Hans said. Down on one
knee, he began to lay out on the floor the most recent
paintings of Lili. 'He told me about it.'

'About what?'

'About Lili. About the doctor in Dresden.'

'What are you talking about?'

'Come on, Greta. Do you really think I don't know by
now?' He lifted his face to hers. 'Why have you been afraid to
tell me?'

She leaned against the window. Outside the rain was frozen,
and it was tapping lightly on the glass. There were a half-dozen
new pictures of Lili, a series of her at her toilette, the add-a-
pearl necklace Greta had given her around her throat. The
paintings showed the pink in Lili's cheek and the reds in her
make-up tray, bright in contrast to the silvery white of her
flesh. In the paintings Lili was wearing a sleeveless dress with a
scoop neck, and her hair was curled up under. 'Can you really
see Einar in them?'

'I do now,' Hans said. 'He told me this past autumn. He was

having a hard time deciding what to do, whether to have Dr
Buson treat him or Professor Bolk. He just turned up at the
gallery one day, just walked into the back office. It was raining
and he was wet, so at first I didn't see that he'd been crying.
He was white, even whiter than Lili in the paintings. I thought
he might collapse right then. It seemed he was having trouble
breathing, and I could see his pulse throbbing in his throat. All
I had to do was ask what was wrong, and he began to tell me
everything.'

'What did you say to him?'

'I said it explained a lot of things.'

'Like what?'

'About Einar and you.'

'About me?' Greta said.

'Yes, about why you've been so defensive all these years, so
very private. In some ways you took it on as your secret, not
just his.'

'He's my husband.'

'I'm sure it's been difficult for you.' Hans stood. The barber
had also given him a shave but missed a spot on his cheek.

'Not as hard as it's been on him.' Greta felt a wave of relief
pass through her; at last Hans knew. The subterfuge with Hans
could end; she could feel its tide receding. 'So what do you
think of our secret?'

'It's who he is, right? How can I blame him for who he is?'
He moved to her, took her in his arms. She could smell the
menthol of aftershave, and the hair on the back of his neck
tickled her wrist.

'Do you think I've done the right thing sending him to
Bolk?' she said. 'You don't think I've made a mistake, do you?'

'No,' he said. 'It's probably his only chance.'

He held Greta at the window, as the traffic sloshed quietly in
the wet street below. But she couldn't let him hold her much
longer, she told herself; she was still married to Einar, after all.
She'd have to pull away soon, she'd have to send Hans back to
the gallery with the pictures. His hand was at the small of her
back, the other on her hip. Her head was against his breast, the

menthol coming with every breath. Every time she tried to free herself, she felt inert. If she couldn't be with Einar, then she wanted Hans, and she shut her eyes and nuzzled her nose into his neck, and just as she felt herself relax and sigh and feel the years of loneliness fall away, she heard the scratch of Carlisle's key turning in the front door.

Twenty-one

❦

Einar paid the driver five reichsmarks, and then the taxi pulled away. Its headlamps swept past the winter skeleton of an azalea and sloped into the street. Then the circular drive was dark, except for the glow of the lantern lamp hanging above the door. Einar could see his breath, and he felt the cold seeping into his feet. There was a black rubber button beside the door, and Einar waited before pressing it. Moisture was collecting along the letters of the brass plaque. DRESDEN MUNICIPAL WOMEN'S CLINIC. A second plaque listed the clinic's doctors: Dr Jürgen Wilder, Dr Peter Scheunemann, Dr Karl Scherres, Prof. Dr Alfred Bolk.

Einar rang the bell and waited. He heard nothing inside. As far as he could tell, the clinic looked more like a villa, set in a neighbourhood of linden and birch trees and iron fences with spindles like spears. There was the sound of an animal in the underbrush, a cat or a rat digging against the cold. A curtain of fog was descending, and Einar nearly forgot where he was. He rested his forehead against the brass plaque and closed his eyes.

He rang again. This time he heard a door inside, and a voice, as buried as the animal sound in the shrub.

At last the door opened, and a woman in an efficiently grey skirt, braces pressing against her breasts, stared at him. Her hair was silver and cut sharp along the jaw, her eyes also grey. She looked as if she never slept much, as if the pillow of skin in her throat kept her head upright while all the world rested.

'Yes?' she said.

'I'm Einar Wegener.'

'Who?'

'I'm here to see Professor Bolk,' Einar said.

The woman pressed her hands against the pleats in her skirt. 'Professor Bolk?' she said.

'Is he here?'

'You'll have to telephone tomorrow.'

'Tomorrow?' He felt something close in around him.

'Do you think your girl is here?' the woman asked. 'Is that why you've come?'

'I'm not sure I know what you mean,' Einar said. He could feel the woman's eyes on him, on his bag holding Lili's clothes.

'Do you have a room where I could stay?' Einar heard himself asking.

'But this is a women's clinic.'

'Yes, I know.'

He turned away and headed into the dark street, where he waited at a corner lit by a cone-shaped lamp hanging above the intersection on a wire. Eventually a taxi stopped, and it was closer to dawn than dusk by the time he settled into the Höritzisch Hotel near the Hauptbahnhof in the Altstadt. The Höritzisch's walls were papered with a trellis pattern and were thin enough to pass along the transactional rates of the prostitute in the room next door. In the night, Einar lay in his clothes on the eiderdown. He listened to a train pull into the station, its wheels screaming along the track. In the station, a few hours before, beneath the canopy of blackened glass, a woman in a coat with rabbit-fur trim had asked him to take her home, and just thinking of her now made his face burn with shame. Her voice, and the voice of the whore next door, began to fill Einar's head, and the image of their painted mouths and the slits in their flimsy skirts, and Einar closed his eyes and became frightened for Lili.

When he returned to the clinic the next day, Professor Bolk was unable to see him. 'He will call you,' said Frau Krebs, in the same grey skirt. When he heard this, Einar, on the clinic's portico beneath the lantern lamp, began to cry. The day was no warmer than the previous night, and he began to shiver as he heard the gravel of the driveway crunch beneath his feet. He had no other business to attend to, so he wandered around the city, both hungry and nauseous.

Altmarkt and its stores were busy in the wind, the aisle of the Hermann Roche pharmacy filled with bank clerks on their lunch hour. The buildings were covered with soot that was darker than the sky, and the awnings were painted with the names of the shops whose bronze-case cash registers were sitting more and more idle with each passing month of recession: CARL SCHNEIDER, MARIEN APOTHEKE, SEIDENHAUS, RENNER KAUFHAUS and HERMANN ROCHE DROGERIE. Motor cars were parked in the centre of the square, and there were two boys in tweed hats and breeches, their shins blue and chapped, parking the cars. A woman with her curls pinned up climbed out of her half-door sedan; she was crammed into a blue stretch dress, the wedge of her stomach testing the strength of the threads holding the buttons to her blouse. The two boys steered her car into a narrow space, and then they began to laugh and waddle, mocking the woman, who was applying lipstick obliviously.

The smaller boy looked up and saw Einar and laughed again. The boys looked like brothers, with sharp-tipped noses and cruel matching laughs. Einar realized the boys were no longer laughing at the fat woman, who was picking her way through the traffic and over the tram tracks to make her way into Hermann Roche, which was having a half-price sale on Odol mouthwash and Schuppen pomade. They were laughing at Einar, whose face was hollow and whose topcoat was flapping against the poles of his legs. Einar watched the fat woman through the plate-glass window fingering the cans of Odol. He wished he could be her, examining the prices on the pyramid of cans, tossing a tin of Schuppen into her basket. Einar imagined the woman driving her sedan home to Loschwitz and placing the toiletries in the cabinet above her husband's sink.

He continued to walk around the city looking in shop windows. A milliner was having a sale, and there was a line of women stretching out of the door. A grocer was setting out a crate of cabbages. And Einar stopped at the window of a kite shop. Inside, a man with glasses on the tip of his nose was bending wooden rods at a workbench. All around him were different types of kites. A kite like a butterfly, like a pinwheel. Dragon kites and ones with foil in their wings like flying fish. There was an eagle kite, and a small black kite with bulging yellow eyes like a bat's.

Einar went to the box office of the Semperoper and bought a ticket to *Fidelio*. He knew that homosexuals gathered at the opera, and he feared that the woman behind the glass, which was smudged with breath, might think he was one of them. She was young and pretty, with green eyes, and refused to look at Einar, cautiously pulling his money through the bowled slot in the window as if she wasn't sure whether or not she wanted it. And once again Einar became exhausted by the world failing to know who he was.

And then Einar climbed the forty-one steps of the Brühlsche Terrace, which overlooked the Elbe and the right bank. The terrace was planted with square-cut trees and bordered by an iron rail against which strollers leaned to examine the endless arc of the Elbe. The wind was running with the river, and Einar turned up his collar. A hunchbacked man with a cart was selling bratwurst in a bun and little glasses of wine. He handed Einar his food and then poured the apple wine. It was the Nordic burial drink, Einar knew, and Einar balanced the wine on his knee as he took a bite of the steaming bratwurst, its skin tight and crisp on the end. Then he took a sip of wine and closed his eyes. 'You know what they call this?' the peddler said.

'What?'

'The Brühlsche Terrace. You know they call it the balcony of Europe.' The man smiled, a few teeth missing. He was waiting for Einar to finish the wine so he could take back the glass. The terrace looked out across the river to the concave towers of the Japanese Palace and beyond that to the ox-eyed roofs of Neustadt and the villas with their well-wooded

gardens and then to all of open-fielded Saxony. From the
terrace, it seemed as if the rest of the world lay beneath Einar,
waiting.

'Ever rub a hump?' the peddler said.

'Excuse me?'

'You've never rubbed a hump?' The man turned, thrusting
his hunchback at Einar. 'Supposed to bring you good luck,
rubbing a man's hump. You never heard that before?' he said,
looking over his shoulder. 'Lots of people pay me to rub it for
luck.'

'But why?'

'Old saying. Rub the hump of a hunchback and luck will
come your way. People cross the street to come over and
touch me.'

'How much?' Einar asked.

'Fifty pfennig.' The river was grey and choppy, and Einar
handed the man the aluminium-bronze coin. Beneath the
rough wool coat the man's back felt dense, like a rock wrapped
in a blanket. Then, although he wasn't sure, Einar thought he
felt the tap of a pulse.

He finished his wine and returned the glass to the peddler,
who wiped it clean with the tail of his shirt. 'Good luck to you
then, sir,' the peddler called, pushing his cart. Einar watched
him, the yellow-stone façades and green-copper roofs of
Dresden behind him, the great rococo buildings that made it
one of the most beautiful cities Einar had ever seen – the
Albertinum, the domed Frauenkirche, the Grünes Gewölbe,
the elegant plaza in front of the opera house – a handsome
backdrop to the little man and his bratwurst cart. Above the
city, the sky was pewter and hammered with storm. Einar was
cold and tired, and, standing to leave the Brühlsche Terrace, he
nearly felt his past shift beneath him.

Two more days passed before Professor Bolk sent word that
he could meet Einar, who returned to the Municipal Women's
Clinic on a bright morning, the pavements wet and shining. In
daylight the clinic looked larger, a cream-coloured villa with

evenly arched windows and a clock in the eaves. It was set in a small park of oak and birch and willow trees and holly bushes.

Frau Krebs admitted him, escorting him down a hall with a mahogany floor black and dull with wax. The hall was lined with doors, and Einar lifted his eyes and felt embarrassed by his curiosity as he looked into each room. On one side of the hall each room was filled with a panel of sunlight, and there were twin beds by the windows, their eiderdowns plumped like sacks of flour.

'The girls are in the *Wintergarten* right now,' Frau Krebs was saying. On the nape of her neck, just beneath her hairline, was a birthmark that looked like the ghost of spilled raspberry jam.

The clinic had thirty-six beds, reported Frau Krebs, one pace ahead of Einar. Upstairs were the departments of surgery, internal medicine and gynaecology. Across a courtyard, she pointed out, was a building with a sign above the door that said PATHOLOGY.

'The pathology building is our latest addition,' Frau Krebs said proudly. 'It's where Professor Bolk keeps his laboratory.' The building was square and built from yellow stucco that made Einar think – and he felt ashamed for doing so – of Greta's chickenpox scar.

Einar's first meeting with Professor Bolk was brief. 'I've met your wife,' he began.

Einar, who was hot beneath his suit and the starched butterfly-collar shirt that was grabbing at his throat, settled on to the examination table. Frau Krebs entered the room, her black shoes squeaking, and handed the professor a file. He was wearing gold-wire glasses that reflected the overhead light and hid the colour of his eyes. He was tall and younger than Einar expected, handsome in the jaw. Einar understood why Greta liked him: he had hands so quick, and an Adam's apple so light, that when he spoke Einar became almost hypnotized by his bird-like hands moving through the air, landing on the corner of his desk where three wood boxes organized his papers, or by the point of his Adam's apple punctuating his sentences like the persistent beak of a woodpecker.

Professor Bolk requested Einar to strip and stand on the scale. The stethoscope pressed coldly against his chest. 'I understand you're a painter,' Professor Bolk said, but continued, 'You're awfully thin, Mr Wegener.'

'I don't have much of an appetite any more.'

'Why not?' The professor pulled a pencil from behind his ear and made a note in the file.

'I don't know.'

'Do you try to eat? Even when you aren't hungry?'

'Sometimes it's difficult,' Einar said. He thought of the nausea during the last year; waking in the sunlight of the apartment with a stomach that felt as if it had just the night before succumbed to Hexler's X-ray. And the pail with the bent handle he had begun keeping at the side of his bed, which Greta would empty in the morning with never a word of complaint or pity, only a long hand gently on his forehead.

The examination room had green tiles running halfway up the walls; in the mirror above the handbasin Einar could see the green reflecting in his face, and he suddenly thought he must be the sickest person at the Dresden Municipal Women's Clinic, because most of the women who came there were not ill, but rather burdened with the results of a single night with a handsome young man whom they would never see again.

'Tell me what you paint,' Professor Bolk said.

'Not much these days.'

'Why is that?'

'Because of Lili,' Einar ventured. Little Lili hadn't yet worked her way into the conversation, and he wondered what Professor Bolk knew of her; had he heard about the pretty girl with the stem-like throat trying to break out of the dry, sick skin of old Einar?

'Has your wife told you about my plans?' Professor Bolk asked. The green tiles and the harsh overhead light left no olive pall in Professor Bolk's face; his skin was the fresh colour of baking dough. Was it only Einar whose face had turned dimly green? Einar brought his fingertips to his cheeks and felt the sweat.

'Did she tell you how I want to proceed?'

Einar nodded. 'She told me you were going to turn me into Lili once and for all.' That wasn't all Greta had told him. She had also said, 'This is it, Einar. This is our only chance.'

'Can you join me tonight for dinner at the Belvedere?' Professor Bolk said. 'Do you know where it is? On the other side of the Elbe? By the Brühlsche Terrace?'

'I know where it is.'

Professor Bolk's hand, the palm of which was surprisingly damp, fell on Einar's shoulder as he was saying, 'Einar, I want you to listen to me. I understand. I understand what you want.'

They met for dinner at the Belvedere. The hall of the restaurant was white and gold, and through the colonnade, outside, the evening fog was deepening to a rich blue on the Elbe and the distant heights of Loschwitz. There were potted palms in *cache-pots* at each of the waiter stands. On a stage an orchestra was playing the overtures of Wagner.

A waiter in tails brought a bottle of French champagne in a silver ice bucket. 'This isn't a celebration,' Professor Bolk said as the waiter pushed the mushroom cork from the bottle. A *pop!* filled their circle of the dining room, and women at neighbouring tables turned their necks, buried in winter velvet, to see.

'Maybe it should be,' Einar said, his voice mixing with the light *clang* of the flat-bladed fish knives the waiter was placing on the table. Einar thought of Lili, whom he had considered sending to dinner at the Belvedere in his place.

With his fish knife Professor Bolk picked apart his trout. Einar watched the blade, hooked at the tip, peel away the flimsy skin, baring the pink flesh. 'To tell the truth,' Professor Bolk was saying, 'the first time I met someone like you, I was a little unsure of what to say. At first I didn't think anything could be done.'

Einar nearly gasped. 'You mean you've met someone else like me?'

'Didn't Greta tell you about my experience with another

man —' and here he leaned in over his plate — 'in your position?'

'No,' Einar said. 'She told me nothing of it.'

'There was one man I wanted to help,' Professor Bolk said. 'But he ran away just before I was to begin. Too scared to go through with it. Which I understand.'

And Einar sat in his chair and thought, To go through with what? Einar could tell that Professor Bolk believed Einar knew more than he actually did. Professor Bolk talked about the previous patient. The man was so convinced he was a woman that he had taken to calling himself Sieglinde Tannenhaus, even when he was dressed as a man. He was a conductor on a tram route between Wölfnitz and Klotzsche and insisted everyone call him fräulein. Not one of the passengers understood what he meant. They'd only stare blankly at him in his blue uniform and black tie.

'But then on the morning of the first surgery, the man disappeared,' Professor Bolk explained. 'He slipped out of his room in the clinic, somehow getting by Frau Krebs. Then he was gone. Eventually he returned to his job on the tram, now wearing the female version of the conductor's uniform, a dark blue skirt with a canvas belt.'

The waiter returned to pour wine. Einar could guess what the professor was promising. The hooked blade of the fish knife winked with light from the candelabrum on the banquette behind them. Einar supposed it would be a swapping of sorts. He would exchange the spongy flesh that hung between his legs for something else.

Outside, the Elbe was flowing blackly, and a paddle-ship bright with lights passed beneath the Augustusbrücke. Professor Bolk said, 'I'd like to begin next week.'

'Next week? Can't you start any sooner?'

'It'll have to be next week. I want you to move into the clinic and rest there, gain some weight. I'll need you to be as rested as possible. We can't risk an infection.'

'An infection of what?' Einar asked, but then the waiter arrived at their table and his vein-backed hands cleared the dishes and the fish knives and then swept away the bread-crumbs with a little silver brush.

Einar returned in a cab to the Höritzisch. The prostitute next door was out, and so he slept soundly, only turning on to his side when a train screeched into the Hauptbahnhof. When he rose at dawn, he bathed down the hall in the unheated closet with the slatted door. Then he put on a brown skirt and the white blouse with the needlepoint collar and a coarse-wool cardigan and a little hat that sat on his head at an angle. His breath was visible in the mirror, his face pale. He would enter the clinic as Lili, and it was she who would exit the clinic later in the spring. It wasn't a decision, just a natural progression of events. In the bathroom of the Höritzisch Hotel, with the shrill scrape of arriving trains screaming through the slats in the door, Einar Wegener closed his eyes, and when he opened them, he was Lili.

When she arrived at the clinic Frau Krebs admitted her, ordering Lili into one of the clinic's white gowns that tied around the waist with a twisted cord.

Frau Krebs, whose face was rosy with blooms of burst capillaries, led Lili to the room at the back of the clinic where she would rest for the week. There was a bed with a steel-pipe footrest. Frau Krebs pulled back the window's yellow curtain. The room looked out over a little park sloping down to a field at the edge of the Elbe. The river was steely blue in winter, and Lili could see sailors on the deck of a freighter huddling in their coats. 'You'll be happy here,' Frau Krebs said. There were shifting clouds in the sky, and one pulled away from the others, and a hole opened up. A column of light fell upon the Elbe, hammering a circle of water in front of the freighter as gold as the necklace around Lili's throat.

Frau Krebs cleared her throat. 'Professor Bolk told me you'd be coming,' she said. 'But he failed to give me your name. So typical of him.'

'It's Lili.'

'Lili what?'

And outside another cloud shifted, opening a larger pale-blue hole in the sky, and the river brightened and the sailors in their coats looked heavenward, and Lili thought and held her breath and then said, 'Elbe. Lili Elbe.'

That afternoon she went downstairs to take her tea in the clinic's *Wintergarten*. She found a metal chair off by itself, and soon Lili felt the sun on her face through the glass. The day had opened up, and now the sky was blue. The sun had warmed the solarium enough to fill the air with the showery smell of the curling-arm ferns and the ivy climbing strings tacked to the walls. The *Wintergarten* looked down to the Elbe, and the wind that had swept away all the clouds was whitecapping the river. The whitecaps reminded Lili of the Kattegat in Denmark, and the paintings that Einar had done of the winter sea. Years ago, Lili used to sit in the rope-bottom chair in the Widow House and stare at Einar's paintings; she would look at them with a sense of detachment, as if they had been painted by an ancestor of whom she was vaguely proud. And as she now looked out over the brown field and then down to the river she marvelled that anyone at all could recreate the sight with oil paint and a brush. How had Einar done that? She asked herself.

During that week, Lili slept late in the mornings; it was as if the more rest she got, the more tired she became. In the afternoons she'd take her tea and torte in the *Wintergarten*. She would sit there in the metal chair, her teacup balanced on her knee, nodding shyly at the other girls who came down for gossip. Occasionally one of them would laugh so loudly that she would draw Lili's eye: a circle of girls, young girls, with longish hair and healthy throats, each swelling at her own pace beneath the regulation gown with the twisted cord-belt. Most of the residents were at the clinic for that reason, Lili knew; and out of the corner of her eye she would watch them not with scorn or pity but with interest and longing, for the girls all seemed to know one another and none of them – from the way their high-pitched laughs would shoot around the *Wintergarten* at such a force that Lili thought for sure those silver-ball peals would shatter the glass walls – seemed to care in the least that they were living in the Dresden Municipal Women's Clinic for the next several months. The clinic seemed like a society, one that had not yet inducted her. Maybe one day, she told herself, feeling the sun on her knees and on her wrists, which she overturned so that the undersides could feel the warmth that had begun to seep into the rest of her.

She knew that Professor Bolk wanted her to gain weight. Frau Krebs would bring her a dish of rice pudding in the afternoons, thoughtfully hiding an almond in it in the Danish way. The first time Lili spooned the clumpy pudding into her mouth and tasted the hard, ribbed seed of the almond, she lifted her eyes and said, in Danish, forgetting where she was, '*Tak, tak.*'

On her third day at the clinic, Lili was sitting in the *Wintergarten* when she noticed the green shoots of crocuses on the other side of the glass wall. They were bright and trough-shaped, and they were huddling in the breeze. They looked bold against the patchy brown lawn, which Lili imagined unfurling into a carpet of green over the next several weeks. The river was flowing the colour of oil today, the current slow and carrying a low-sitting freighter whose deck was covered by black tarps pulled tightly with rope.

'Do you think spring will come early?'

'I'm sorry?' Lili said.

'I noticed you were looking at the crocuses.' A girl had somehow taken the metal chair next to Lili, pulling it at an angle so that they could look at each other across the white cast-iron table.

'They seem early to me,' Lili said.

'It's what I would expect for this year,' said the girl, whose woody blond hair fell past her shoulders, whose nose turned up at the end. Her name would turn out to be Ursula, an orphan from Berlin, not yet twenty and landed in Dresden because of the simplest of mistakes. 'I thought I loved him,' she would later say.

The day after they met, the sun was even stronger. Lili and Ursula, wrapped in roll-neck sweaters and fur hats with earflaps borrowed from Frau Krebs, headed into the park. They walked down the path that led through the field of crocus shoots, which had now spread like a rash. Out there, overlooking the Elbe, in a breeze that was more ferocious than Lili could ever have guessed from inside the *Wintergarten*, Ursula asked, 'And you, Lili? Why are you here?'

Lili thought about the question, biting her lip and burying her wrists inside her sleeves, and finally said, 'I'm ill inside.'

Ursula, whose mouth naturally pouted up, said, 'I see.'

From then on the two girls took their tea and torte together each afternoon. They would choose chocolates from one of the many boxes Ursula had smuggled out of her last place of employment. 'It's these chocolates that caused all my trouble,' Ursula said, holding up one shaped like a seashell and then pushing it into her mouth. Ursula told Lili about the chocolate shop on Unter den Linden where she had worked, where the richest men in Berlin hurried in at lunch or at five o'clock, their topcoats hanging over their arms, to buy three-layered boxes of chocolates wrapped in gold foil, the packages tied up in a satin ribbon. 'You probably think it was one of them who I loved.' Ursula told Lili, setting her teacup into its saucer. 'But it wasn't. It was the mixing boy in the back, the boy who dumped the sacks of walnuts and the tubs of butter and the buckets of milk and the ground cocoa beans into the vats.' Vats big enough for two young lovers to curl up into. His name was Jochen, and he had freckles from head to toe. He was from Cottbus, near the Polish border, in Berlin to make his fortune but now indentured to the stainless-steel vats and the mixing arm whose blade, were he not careful, could catch his bony hand and turn it around a hundred times in less than a minute. It was four months before Ursula and Jochen spoke, the girls in front in their pink button-up uniforms forbidden to speak to the mixers in the back, where the air was hot and smelled of sweat and bittersweet chocolate and filled with language that mostly revolved around the private parts of the girls stationed

behind the glass cases at the front of the shop. Then one day
Ursula had to go into the back to ask when the next batch of
nougat would emerge, and Jochen, who was then just
seventeen, pushed his cap back on his head and said, 'No more
nougat today. Tell the jerk to go home and apologize to his
wife instead.' That was when Ursula's heart filled up.

The rest Lili could imagine: the first kiss in the back room;
the gentle tumble into the bowl of the stainless-steel vat; the
passion in the middle of the night when the chocolate house
lay still, when all the mixing arms hung motionless; the sobs of
love.

How very sad, Lili thought, sitting in her metal chair as the
afternoon sun hit the Elbe. In five fast days she and Ursula had
become friends. And despite Ursula's current predicament, Lili
longed for something similar to happen to her. Yes, she told
herself. It will be like that with me: instant love; helpless,
regrettable passion.

The next morning Professor Bolk appeared in the door of
her room. 'Please don't eat anything today,' he said. 'Not even
milk with your tea. Nothing at all.' Then he added,
'Tomorrow's the day.'

'Are you sure?' Lili asked. 'You won't change your mind?'

'The amphitheatre is scheduled. The nurses' shifts have been
assigned. You've gained some weight. Yes, I'm sure. Tomorrow is your day, Lili.' Then he was gone.

She went to breakfast in the hall with the arched windows
and the pine-plank floor and the side table laid with plates of
rolled meats and baskets of caraway-seed rolls and an urn of
coffee. Lili took her coffee to a table in the corner and sat
alone. She ran a butter knife under the seal of a tissuey blue
envelope and opened a letter from Greta.

Dear Lili,
I wonder how you're liking Dresden? And Professor
Bolk, whom I assume you have met by now. His
reputation is very impressive. He is nearly famous, and
maybe after all of this he most certainly will be.

No real news from Paris. My work has slowed down since you left. You are the perfect subject to paint, and when you're gone it is difficult to find anyone quite as beautiful. Hans visited yesterday. He's worried about the art market. He says the money is drying up, not just here but all over Europe. But that doesn't concern me. It never has, but you know that. I told him this, and he said it was easy for me to say because between Einar and me we would always have something to sell. I'm not sure why he said this, but I suppose it would be true if Einar still painted. Lili, have you ever thought of painting? Maybe you could buy yourself a little tin of watercolours and a sketchpad to help pass the time, which must move slowly there. Despite what they say, Dresden isn't Paris, I am sure.

I hope you are comfortable. That's what worries me the most. I wish you had let me come with you but I understand. Some things you must do alone. Lili, don't you just sometimes stop and think about what it will be like when it's all over? The freedom! That's how I think of it. Is that how you think of it? I hope so. I hope you think of it that way because that is what it should feel like to you. It does to me, at least.

Send word as soon as you can. Edvard IV and I miss you terribly. He's sleeping on your daybed. Me, I'm hardly sleeping at all.

If you want me, just send word. I can arrive overnight.

With love,

Greta

Lili thought of her life in the casita: Einar's former workroom, tidy and untouched; the morning light that poured into Greta's studio; the ottoman quilted with velvet and dented beneath the handsome weight of Carlisle; Greta in her smock, hardened with a dozen smears of paint, her hair running like ice-water down her back; Hans honking his horn from the streets below, calling Lili's name. Lili wanted to go back, but that would have been impossible now.

In the afternoon she met Ursula again, who was red in the cheeks from running down the stairs. 'There's a letter from him!' she said, waving an envelope. 'It's from Jochen.'

'How'd he know where to find you?'

'I wrote to him. I couldn't help it, Lili. I broke down and wrote to him and told him how much I loved him and it wasn't too late.' Her hair was pulled into a pony-tail, and she looked even younger today, with cheeks that were full and dimpled twice. 'What do you think he wants to say?'

'Find out,' said Lili. Ursula opened the envelope and her eyes began to move across the letter. Her smile started to fall almost imperceptibly, and by the time she turned over the page her mouth was a tight little frown. Then she ran the back of her hand beneath her nose and said, 'He might come to visit me. If he can save enough money and get time off from the chocolate shop.'

'Do you want him to come?'

'I suppose so.' And then, 'I mustn't get my hopes up, though. It might be hard for him to get the time off from the shop. But he says he'll come if he has the time.'

They said nothing for several minutes. Then Ursula cleared her throat. 'I understand there's going to be an operation.'

Lili said yes; she picked at the lint in her lap.

'What are they going to do to you? Are you going to be all right? Will you be just the same when they're through?'

'I'll be better,' Lili said. 'Professor Bolk is going to make me better.'

'Oh, creepy old Bolk. I hope he doesn't do anything wrong to you. Bolk the Blade – that's what they call him, you know. Always ready to open a girl up with his knife.'

For a second Lili became frightened.

'I'm sorry,' Ursula said. 'I didn't mean anything by that. You know how girls can talk. They don't know anything.'

'It's all right,' Lili said.

She and Ursula remained in the *Wintergarten* until the Elbe was gold with dusk and Frau Krebs's hand reached up like a rat climbing a schooner's line to pull the rope attached to the nickel dinner bell that hung in the clinic's eaves.

Later, in her room, Lili prepared for bed. Frau Krebs had given her a small chalky pill. 'To help you sleep,' Frau Krebs had said, biting her lip. And Lili washed her face at the sink with the rose-coloured flannel. The make-up – the muted orange of her powder, the pink of her lipstick, the brown of the wax she used on her eyebrows – ran down the sink with the water. When she held the eyebrow pencil with the waxy tip, her fingers poised to draw, a strange feeling would fill her chest, as if she were reliving something. Einar had been an artist, and she wondered if that feeling, the tight flutter just beneath the ribs, was what he experienced as the slick tip of his brush moved into the rough blank expanse of a new canvas. Lili shuddered, and a taste of something not unlike regret rose in her throat, and she had to swallow hard to hold down the sleeping pill.

The next morning she felt dreamy and dull. A knock on the door. A nurse with upturned hair shifting Lili out from beneath the sheets. A trolley, smelling like alcohol and steel, waiting at the side of her bed to take her away. The distant sight of Professor Bolk's face, asking, 'Is she all right? Let's make sure she's all right.' But not much else registered with Lili. She knew it was still early, and she was wheeled down the hall of the clinic before the sun lifted over the rape fields east of Dresden; she knew the swinging doors with the porthole windows closed on her before the dawn light hit the cornerstones of the Brühlsche Terrace, where she had looked out over the Elbe and the city and all of Europe and where she had convinced herself she would never again look back.

When she woke up, she saw a yellow felt curtain pulled against a window. Opposite sat a single-door wardrobe with a mirror and a key laced with a blue-thread tassel; at first she thought it was the pickled-ash wardrobe, and then she recalled, although it had happened to someone else, the afternoon when Einar's father found him in the cupboard of his mother's wardrobe.

She was lying in a bed with a steel-pipe footrest; she was looking at the room through the footrest, and it was like staring out of a barred window. The room was wallpapered in a pink-and-red pattern of nosegays. In the corner there was a chair draped with a blanket. Beside the bed a mahogany table covered with a piece of lace and a cup of violets. The table had a single drawer, and she wondered if her belongings were in it. On the floor was a dust-coloured carpet, the nap worn bald in spots.

She tried to lift herself, but a heavy pain spread through the middle of her body, and she fell back on to the pillow, which was hard and spiny with feathers. Her eyes rolled up into her head until the room went black. She thought of Greta, and she wondered if Greta was now in this room, in the corner opposite the window where Lili didn't have the strength to turn her head to peer. Lili didn't know what had happened to her, not just then, not with the chloroform still swirling in her nostrils. She knew she was ill, and at first she thought she was a child with a ruptured appendix in the provincial Jutland hospital with its rubber-floored halls; she was ten years old, Hans would soon arrive at the door with a fistful of Queen Anne's lace. But this couldn't make sense, because Lili was also thinking about Greta, who was Einar's wife. It caused her to ask herself, nearly aloud: Where is Einar?

She thought of them all: Greta and Hans and then Carlisle, whose flat, persistent voice was good at sorting things out; she thought of frightened Einar, lost in his baggy suit, separated from the rest of them, somehow away – permanently away. She lifted her eyelids. On the ceiling was a light bulb set in a box of reflecting silver. There was a long string attached, and she saw that the string ran down to her bedside, its tail capped with a little brown bead. The bead was lying on the green blanket, and for a very long time she thought about releasing her hand from beneath the clamp of the blanket and pulling the brown bead and turning off the light. She focused on it, the brown bead a piece of carved wood like the ones that ran along the wire of an abacus. Finally, when she moved to free her hand, the effort and the pain of shifting her body exploded in her like a crash of hot light. Her head pushed back into the pillow – the feathers matting against her skull – and she closed her eyes. Only hours before, in the black of morning, at the hands of Professor Alfred Bolk, Einar Wegener had passed from man into woman, two testicles scooped from the pruned hammock of his scrotum, and now Lili Elbe slipped into unconsciousness for three days and nights.

Twenty-two

❦

Greta couldn't stand it. She would button up her smock and clip her hair back with the tortoiseshell comb and mix her paints in the Knabstrup bowls and stand in front of a half-finished portrait of Lili and fail to understand how to complete it. The painting – with Lili's upper body complete and the lower half only a pencil outline – looked to Greta as if it were someone else's work. She would stare at the canvas, the edges taut from the nails she hammered in herself, only to find it impossible to concentrate. Anything at all could disrupt her. There was a solicitation at the door for a subscription library. There was Edvard IV lapping sloppily in his water bowl. There was the open door to Einar's studio, revealing his daybed tidy with the pink-and-red kilim laid across, and the neatness and emptiness of a room where no one lived any more. A dresser with empty drawers; a wardrobe with nothing inside but a single hanger on the lead pipe. She felt a throb in her chest, and the only thing she could think of was Einar rattling across Europe in a railway carriage, arriving in Dresden, at night, an icy dew dampening the tips of his hair, the clinic's address tight in his fist.

There was another exhibition of her paintings in Hans's gallery, and for the first time she didn't attend the opening. Something in her felt sick of it all, though she was careful not to repeat such a sentiment to Hans. How ungrateful it would sound. How petulant. Greta, who five years ago didn't have a reputation and who just this morning sat for an interview with a handsome journalist from Nice with hooded eyes who would interrupt her and say, 'When did you first know you were great?' Yes, all of that, and more, in five years; but even so Greta would sit back and think, Yes, I've done something with myself – but what did it matter? She was alone, and her husband and Lili were in Dresden, alone.

More than a week after Einar left for Dresden, on a day slick with rain and screechy with skidding motor cars, Greta had met Hans at his gallery. He was in his back office, and there was a clerk at a desk making entries into an account book. 'They didn't all sell,' Hans said of the paintings at the exhibition. One of Greta's paintings – Lili in a hut at the Bains du Pont-Solférino – was on the floor, leaning against the desk where the clerk was pushing his pencil against his lined paper. 'I wish you had come to the opening,' Hans was saying. 'Is something wrong?' And then, 'Have you met my new assistant? This is Monsieur Le Gal.'

The clerk was narrow-faced, and there was something in his soft brown eyes that made Greta think of Einar. She thought of him – Einar cautiously boarding a tram in Dresden, his eyes lowered and his hands folded shyly in his lap – and shuddered. She thought to herself, although not in so many words, What have I done to my husband?

'Is there anything I can do?' Hans asked. He moved towards Greta. The clerk was keeping his glasses and his pencil close to his task. And Hans came to Greta's side. They did not touch, but Greta could feel him there, as she stared down at the painting: Lili's smile stretched back from the pull of her tight bathing cap; Lili's eyes, dark and alive – bottomless, they seemed. Greta felt something on her arm, but when she looked there was nothing, and Hans was now standing by the clerk's desk, his hands in his pockets. Did he want to tell her something?

Carlisle had found them in their embrace, that afternoon with the freezing rain, when Hans's neck was pink from the barber. She hadn't heard the scratch of his key until it was too late, and there was an awkwardly long instant when both Greta and Carlisle froze – she with her head against Hans's chest,

Carlisle, a scarf around his throat, with his hand dangling back to the doorknob. 'I didn't know anyone was—' he began. She pulled away from Hans, who held up his hands and started to say, 'It's not what you're thinking . . .' 'I can come back,' Carlisle had said. 'I'll be back in a bit.' He was gone before Greta could say anything else.

Later that night, she had sat at the foot of his bed and rubbed his leg through the blankets, and said, 'Sometimes I think Hans is my only friend.' And Carlisle, with his nightshirt split open at the collar, said, 'I can understand that.' And then, 'Greta. No one's blaming you for any of this, if that's what you're thinking.'

Now, in Hans's office, with the clerk busy with his pencil and his ruler, Greta said, 'No word from Einar yet.'

'Are you worried?'

'I shouldn't be, but I am.'

'Why didn't you go with him?'

'He didn't want me to.'

Hans stopped, and Greta saw his lips press together; was he feeling sorry for her? How she'd hate it if things had come to that.

'Not that it upset me,' she said. 'Not that I don't understand why he had to go alone.'

'Greta,' Hans said.

'Yes?'

'Why don't you go and see him?'

'He doesn't want me there.'

'He was probably too embarrassed to ask for your help.'

'No, not Einar. He isn't like that. And besides, why would he be embarrassed? After all this, why would he be embarrassed now?'

'Think about what he's going through. This isn't like anything before.'

'But then why wouldn't he have let me go with him? He didn't want me there. He was clear about that.'

'He was probably too afraid.'

She stopped. 'Do you think?'

The clerk lit a cigarette, the match rough on the sandpaper strip along the box. Once again she wanted Hans to hold her, but she wouldn't let herself move towards his arms. She straightened her back and ran her fingers down the pleats of her skirt. She knew it was old-fashioned, but Greta couldn't bring herself to slip into his embrace while she was still Einar's wife.

'You should go and see him,' Hans said. 'If you want, I'll go with you. I'd be happy to go with you.'

'I can't go.'

'Of course you can.'

'What about my work?'

'It can wait. Or even better, pack your easel. Take your paints with you.'

'Do you really think I should?'

'I'll go with you,' he said again.

'No,' she said. 'That wouldn't be any good.'

'Why not?'

On the clerk's desk was a copy of *L'Echo de Paris*, folded open to a review of her latest exhibition. She hadn't read it yet, and there was a paragraph that leapt out at her as if underlined: 'After so many pictures of the same subject – this strange girl called Lili – Greta Wegener has become tedious. I wish upon her a new model and a new colour scheme. Coming from California, why hasn't she ever turned her eye to the golds and blues of her native land? Paint me a picture of the Pacific and the arroyos!'

'If I go I'll have to go by myself,' Greta said.

'Now you're sounding like Einar.'

'I am like him,' she said.

They were silent for a few minutes, studying the painting and listening to the rain mix with the traffic. Paris was cold, each morning the wet seeping deep beneath her skin, and Greta imagined that the only place damper and greyer was Dresden. Going there would be like slipping further into the cave of winter.

Again Hans said, 'If there's anything I can do . . .'

Once again he moved to her side, and then there was that sensation on Greta's arm, like a feather on her skin. She could feel him there, through his herringbone suit – his soft pulse of heat. 'Greta,' he said.

'I have to go.'

'Do you suppose it's time—'

'I really must be off,' Greta said.

'All right then,' Hans said. He helped her with her raincoat, tugging out the shoulders. 'I'm sorry.'

Then the clerk said, his voice hoarse, 'Will you be delivering any new paintings, Mrs Wegener? Should I expect anything sometime soon?'

'Not for a while,' she said, and when she stepped on to the street, with the motor cars swishing through the sleet and the shove of umbrellas on the pavement, she knew she'd have to fold up her easel and pack her paints and book a compartment on the next train to Dresden.

What surprised Greta most about Dresden was the way the people on the street failed to look up from their feet. She wasn't used to that, eyes refusing to lift to roam her long frame and to greet her. On her first day there she felt as if she had disappeared – deeply tucked into the folds of Europe, hidden from the world. And this caused a little panic in her, as she felt the gravel crunch beneath her feet, stepping towards the front door of the Dresden Municipal Women's Clinic; a panic because she suddenly feared that, if no one could find her, maybe she wouldn't be able to find Einar after all.

At first there was confusion. 'I'm looking for Miss Wegener,' Greta enquired at the front desk, where Frau Krebs was smoking a Hacifa cigarette.

The name Wegener meant nothing to Frau Krebs. She pursed her lips and shook her head, her exact line of hair slashing against her jaw. Greta tried again. 'She's slim and dark-eyed. Frightfully shy. A little Danish girl?'

'Do you mean Lili Elbe?'

Greta, who just then had a vision of Einar's face lifting with the sunlight as his train crossed the Elbe on the Marienstrasse Bridge, said, 'Yes. Is she here?'

In her room a portable gas stove was flickering. The yellow curtain was drawn, and the blue flames of the little stove were casting a wavy shadow across the bed. Greta was holding the steel piping of the bed's footrest. Tucked beneath the blanket was Lili, her arms lying flat along her sides. She was sleeping, breath in her nostrils. 'Please don't disturb her,' Frau Krebs whispered from the door. 'The operation was hard.'

'When was it?'

'Three days ago.'

'How is she?'

'That's not easy to say,' Frau Krebs said, folding her arms across her breasts. The room was warm with the effluvia of sleep, and its silence felt unnatural to Greta. She sat in the chair in the corner, pulling a blanket over her lap. She was cold, and tired from the train, and Frau Krebs left her alone with Lili.

They slept, Greta and Lili. A few hours later, when Greta woke, at first she thought she was waking from a nap on one of the sleeping porches in Pasadena. Then she saw Lili, whose head was rolling on the pillow. Her papery eyelids began to flutter.

'Please don't worry about me,' Lili said.

At last Greta could see Lili's eyes, the lids blinking heavily to swat away the dreamy sleep. Still as brown and slick as pelts. The only thing left of her husband, eyes through which Greta could recall his entire life.

She moved to the bed and began to stroke Lili's leg through the rough horsehair blanket. Something in the calf muscle felt softer to Greta; or maybe she was just imagining it — the way she thought maybe she was also imagining the swell of breasts beneath the blanket's sash.

'Do you know what they've done to me?' Lili asked. Her face seemed fuller in the cheek and throat, so full that the blade of her Adam's apple had disappeared into a little scarf of flesh. Was Greta imagining this, too?

'Nothing more than we talked about.'

'Am I now Lili? Have I become Lili Elbe?'

'You've always been Lili.'

'Yes, but if I were to look down there, what would I see?'

'Don't think about it like that,' Greta said. 'That's not the only thing that makes you Lili.'

'Was it successful, the operation?'

'Frau Krebs said so.'

'How do I look? Tell me, Greta – how do I look?'

'Very pretty.'

'Am I really a woman now?'

Part of Greta was numbing over with shock. Her husband was no longer alive. It, the tingling shock of it, felt like his soul passing through her. Once again Greta Waud was a widow, and she thought of Teddy's coffin, stalks of bird of paradise across its lid, sinking into the earth. But she wouldn't have to bury Einar. She had settled him into a felt-panelled compartment on a train bound for Germany, and now he was gone – as if his train had simply charged ahead into the icy January fog and disappeared for ever. She imagined that if she were to call his name it would echo, again and again, for the rest of her life.

She moved even closer to Lili. Once again, Greta was filled with a need to hold her, and she took Lili's head between her hands. The veins in her temples were throbbing lightly, and Greta sat on the edge of the hospital bed with Lili's dewy head in her palms. There was a crack in the curtain, and Greta could see through it across a lawn brightening with spring towards the Elbe. The river was running like clouds dashing along the sky. On the other side two boys in sweaters were launching a canoe.

'Oh, hello,' a voice said from the door. It was a young girl, with a little upturned nose. 'You must be Greta.'

Greta nodded, and the girl entered lightly. She was in her hospital gown and robe, her feet in slippers. Lili had fallen asleep again, and the room was grey. In the corner the gas heater was ticking, *click-click-click*. 'I'm Ursula,' the girl said. 'We've become friends.' With her chin she pointed to Lili. 'Is she going to be all right?'

'I think so. But Frau Krebs was telling me how hard it's been on her.'

'She's been sleeping most of the time, but the time I saw her awake she looked happy,' Ursula said.

'How was she before the operation? Was she frightened?'

'Not really. She adores Professor Bolk. She'd do anything for him.'

'He's a good doctor,' Greta heard herself saying.

Ursula was carrying a little box wrapped in foil printed with UNTER DEN LINDEN in fancy scroll. She handed it to Greta, saying, 'Will you give it to her when she wakes up?'

Greta thanked Ursula, noticing the swelling of her stomach. It distended unusually, high in her abdomen, lumpily. 'And how are you?' Greta asked.

'Oh, me? I'm fine,' Ursula said. 'More and more tired every day. But what can I expect?'

'Are they good to you here?'

'Frau Krebs is nice. She seems so strict at first, but she's nice. And the other girls, too. But Lili is my favourite. So very sweet. Concerned about everyone but herself.' And then, 'She told me about you. She missed you.'

For a moment Greta wondered what Ursula meant, but then let it pass. It didn't matter.

'You'll tell her I looked in?' Ursula said. 'You'll give her the chocolates?'

Greta took a room at the Bellevue. At night, after she had left Lili at the Municipal Women's Clinic, she would try to paint. Light from the flat-bottomed coal freighters would reach up to her windows. Greta would sometimes open them, and she could hear the chug and swish of a tourist boat's paddle and the deep grind of the freighters and the clang of a tram out in Theater-Platz.

She began a painting of Professor Bolk; it was on a large canvas she bought at a shop on Alunstrasse. She had carried the rolled-up canvas under her arm back to the Bellevue, crossing the Augustusbrücke. From the bridge with its half-circle look-out balconies she could see nearly all of Dresden: the

240 DAVID EBERSHOFF

Brühlsche Terrace with its benches freshly painted green; the bulbous sandstone dome of the Frauenkirche blackened with soot from the motor cars and the smelting works in Plauenscher Grund; the long line of silvery windows of the Zwinger Palace. A wind from the river came along and knocked the rolled-up canvas from beneath Greta's arm, and she caught it just as it unfurled like a sail on the bridge. It was flapping over the grooved-stone half-wall, and Greta was struggling to roll it back up when a hand landed on her shoulder and a familiar voice said, 'May I help?'

'I was just on my way back to the hotel,' Greta said as Professor Bolk took one end of the canvas and rolled it up like a window shade.

'You must be planning quite a large painting,' he said.

But that wasn't the case. At that moment Greta didn't know what she wanted to paint next; it didn't seem the right time to paint Lili.

'Can you walk me back to my hotel?' Greta said, pointing to the park of chestnut trees in front of the Bellevue, which sat like a squarely built lifeguard in his stilted chair cockily surveying the beach of the Elbe. 'I'd like to hear about the operation,' she said. 'About Lili's prospects.' Over the past few days she'd begun to sense that Professor Bolk had been avoiding her; two days she'd been in Dresden, and he still hadn't replied to the enquiries she left at Frau Krebs's desk. She even mentioned to Ursula that she wanted Professor Bolk to phone. But he never came to see her. Now she led him to her suite at the Bellevue. They settled into the chairs by the window, drinking coffee brought by a maid with a strip of lace pinned to her hair.

'The first operation was a success,' Professor Bolk began. 'It was rather simple. The incision is healing as it should.' He told Greta about the surgery in the operating amphitheatre, where before dawn one morning Einar had become Lili. He explained that the systematic tests – the blood counts and the urinalysis and the hourly monitoring of Lili's temperature – were all showing signs of proper healing. The Listerian antisepsis was protecting Lili from infection. 'The biggest concern right now is the pain,' Professor Bolk said.

'What are you doing about that?'

'A daily morphia injection.'

'Is there any risk to that?'

'Very little,' he said. 'We'll wean her off it over the next several weeks. But right now she needs it.'

'I see.' Now that she had Bolk at her side, her concern about him faded. He was no different from most busy, important men: impossible to track down, but once you had him his full attention was yours.

'I was concerned about her bleeding,' Professor Bolk continued. 'She shouldn't have been haemorrhaging like that. It made me think something was wrong with one of her abdominal organs.'

'Like what?'

'I didn't know. A crushed spleen. A hole in the lining of the intestine. Anything was possible.' He crossed his legs. Greta could feel her heart quicken as she became frightened for Lili.

'She's all right, isn't she? I shouldn't be worried about her, should I?'

'I opened her up,' Bolk said.

'What do you mean?'

'I opened up her abdomen. I knew something was wrong. I'd been in enough abdominal cavities to know something was wrong.'

For an instant Greta shut her eyes, and she saw, on the backs of her lids, a scalpel drawing a line of blood across Lili's belly. She had to stop herself from imagining Professor Bolk's hands, with the help of Frau Krebs, pulling apart the incision.

'It's true that Einar was indeed female. Or at least part female.'

'But I already knew that,' Greta said.

'No. I don't think you understand.' He snatched a star-shaped sugar biscuit from the tray brought by the maid. 'It's something else. Something rather remarkable.' His eyes were bright with interest, and Greta could tell he was the type of doctor who wanted something – a disease, a surgical procedure – named after him.

'In his abdomen,' Bolk continued, 'tangled in with his intestine, I found something.' Professor Bolk folded his hands together and cracked his knuckles. 'I found a pair of ovaries. Underdeveloped, of course. Small, of course. But they were there.'

Greta decided at that moment that she should paint Professor Bolk: the square line of his shoulders; his hanging arms; the long neck emerging from a starched collar; the skin around his eyes crinkled and tender. She sat back in her chair. An opera singer was staying in the suite next door, and Greta could hear her singing Erda from *Siegfried*: the rolling middle register; the voice swooping through the air like a hunting hawk. The voice sounded like Anna's, but that was impossible, because Anna was in Copenhagen, singing at the Royal Theatre again for the first time in years. When Lili was feeling better, Greta thought she would like to take her to the opera, and she imagined them holding hands in the dark of the Semperoper while Siegfried made his way to Brünnhilde's fire-rimmed mountaintop.

'What does it mean for her?' Greta finally asked. 'Are these ovaries real?'

'It means I'm even more certain that this will work.' And then, 'We're doing the right thing.'

'You really think this explains the haemorrhaging, then?'

'Probably,' he said, his voice rising. 'It explains almost everything.'

No, Greta thought; she knew the ovaries couldn't explain everything.

'There's a grafting process I want to try,' Professor Bolk went on. 'From a healthy pair of ovaries. It's been done with testicles but never with the female organs. But there have been results.

'I'd like to harvest some tissue from a healthy pair of ovaries and layer it over Lili's,' he said. 'But it's a matter of timing. A matter of finding the right pair.'

'How long will that take?' And then, 'Are you sure you can do this?'

'Not so long. I have a girl in mind.'

'From the clinic?'

'There's a young girl from Berlin. We thought she was pregnant when she arrived. But it turns out a tumour has taken over her stomach.' He stood to leave. 'She doesn't know, of course. What would be the point of telling her now? But she might be the one. It might be only a month or so.' He shook Greta's hand. When he was gone, Greta opened her double-lid paintbox and began to set out the bottles and lay down a tarp, and then, through the walls, came the opera singer's voice, slow and dark and climbing the notes alone.

Several weeks later Greta and Lili were sitting in the clinic's garden. The birch trees and the willows were shiny with buds. The hedges were still patchy, but dandelions had sprung up in the brick path. Two gardeners were digging holes for a row of cherry trees, burlap bags bundling their roots. The gooseberry shrubs were beginning to leaf.

A circle of pregnant girls was on the lawn, on a tartan blanket, weaving blades of grass. Their white hospital gowns, loose in the shoulders, were trembling in the wind. The clock in the clinic's eaves was striking noon.

A cloud shifted, and the lawn turned nearly black beneath the shadow. The cherry trees bent over in the wind, and a figure emerged from the clinic's glass door. Greta couldn't tell who it was. He was wearing a white lab coat, which was flapping like the pennants strung along the tourist cruiser that was plying the Elbe.

'Look,' Lili said. 'It's the professor.'

He moved in their direction, and the cloud shifted again, and Professor Bolk's face lit up, the sun on his spectacles. When he reached them he knelt down and said, 'It's going to be tomorrow.'

'What is?' Lili asked.

'Your next operation.'

'But why all of a sudden?' Lili asked.

'Because we're ready with the graft tissue. We should operate tomorrow.' Greta had told Lili about the next procedure, about the ovarian tissue that Professor Bolk would lay into her abdomen.

'I expect everything to go as planned,' the professor said. In the sunlight the skin in Bolk's face was thin, the sea-colour of his veins showing through. Greta wished Hans had travelled to Dresden with her. She'd talk it over with him; she'd like his counsel — the way he'd tent his fingers together in front of his mouth as he thought through a situation. Greta suddenly felt exhausted.

'What if it doesn't go as planned?' she asked.

'We'll wait. I want to work with tissue from a young girl.'

'All of this is hard to believe,' Lili said. She wasn't looking at Greta or Bolk. Her face was turned to the circle of girls, who were lying on their sides.

When Professor Bolk was gone, Lili shook her head. 'I still can't believe it,' she said, her eyes still on the girls. 'He's doing it, Greta. Just as you said he would. He's turning me into a little girl.' Lili's face was still, the tip of her nose red. She was whispering. 'I think he might be a man capable of miracles.'

A breeze pushed Greta's hair over her shoulder, and she looked to the shaded windows of Professor Bolk's laboratory — the stucco walls, the glassed-in corridor connecting it to the rest of the clinic. It was off limits to her, but Greta imagined the tiered operating amphitheatre and the steel trolleys cold to the touch and a shelf of jars filled with formaldehyde. One of the window shades was lifted, and for a minute Greta could see the silhouette of someone working in the laboratory, his head bent over his task; and then a second person — all black shadow — drew the shade again, and the stucco building was yellow in the sunlight and as lifeless as before.

'So,' she said. 'Tomorrow it is,' and she lowered Lili's head into her lap, and they closed their eyes and received the weak heat of the sun. They listened to the muted squeals of the girls on the lawn, and the faraway splash of a paddlewheel on the

Elbe. Greta thought of Teddy Cross, whom she had also once thought of as capable of miracles. There was that time with Carlisle's leg. Greta and Teddy had been married only a few months, and they were living in the Spanish house in Bakersfield, and the first hot winds were beginning to blow through the eucalyptus groves.

Greta was pregnant with baby Carlisle and sick on the sofa from Gump's. One day Carlisle drove over the Ridge Route in his yellow-fendered Detroiter to visit them and to investigate potential oilfields.

The strawberry fields were a carpet of green that spring, edged by the buttery gold of the poppies in the foothills. Men from Los Angeles and San Francisco had begun descending on Bakersfield as word got out that there might be oil beneath the land. The farmer to the south of Teddy Cross's parents had sunk a well with his hoe-axe and struck oil. Teddy was sure his parents could hit oil too, and Greta secretly wondered if Teddy felt the need to become rich in a strange effort to match her wealth. In the late afternoons, after tending to Greta, he would drive out on the rutted road to the Cross land and drill in the long shadow of an old oak. He used a tool with a gyre blade that could be extended with attachments; and with the sun glinting off the silvery underside of the strawberry leaves, Teddy would grind the drill through the loam.

And then Carlisle drove into Bakersfield. He was still lame then, on a pair of hand-cast crutches that came to his elbows, their grooved handles made of carved ivory. He had a second pair cast in sterling silver, which Mrs Waud requested him to use on formal occasions. On his first night at the Spanish house, while Greta was sleeping, she would later learn, Teddy drove Carlisle out to the Cross land and showed him his well. 'I'm worried about disappointing them,' Teddy said of his parents, who were huddled in their little house, the wall planks separated with gaps wide enough for the wind. The hole in the ground was about as wide around as a thigh and surrounded by a wooden platform. Teddy pulled up a sample of dirt with a cup attached to the rope. They examined it, the mouths of both young men open. Teddy looked to Carlisle, as if he expected him, just because he was up at Stanford, to be able to discern something from the cup of black soil. 'Do you think there's oil down there?' Teddy asked.

Looking over to the knotted oak at the edge of the strawberry field and then up to the purpling sky, Carlisle said, 'I'm not really sure.'

They were out there for half an hour, standing in the sunset, as the wind kicked up the dust and hurled it at their ankles. The bowl of the sky was dimming, and the stars were beginning to glitter. 'Let's get going,' Teddy said, and Carlisle, who never once blamed Teddy Cross for all that had happened to Greta, said, 'All right.'

Teddy moved to the truck, and Carlisle followed, except the cap of his crutch caught between the boards of the platform, and the next thing he knew his leg, the bad one, slipped down the well like a snake. He would have laughed at how quickly he found himself splayed on the platform, except that his leg had come back to life with pain. Teddy heard his cry and ran back to the dry well, saying, 'Are you OK? Can you get up?'

Carlisle couldn't get up, his leg jammed into the hole. Teddy began to peel away the planks with a crowbar, the boards coming loose with a creak that howled across the fields. The coyotes in the foothills were howling too, and the still black of the Bakersfield night was brought to life with Carlisle crying softly into his own shoulder. An hour passed before he was prised free, exposing the leg broken in the shin. There was no blood, but the skin was turning darker than a plum. Teddy helped Carlisle into the truck, and then drove him west through the night, across the width of the valley, the fields changing from strawberry to red-leaf lettuce to vineyards and finally to pecan orchards, and then over the mountains and into Santa Barbara. It was nearly midnight when a doctor with a monocle set Carlisle's leg, while a night nurse with a rusty red bob dipped strips of gauze into a tub of plaster. Then, much later, almost at dawn, Teddy and Carlisle pulled into the bamboo-shaded drive of the Spanish house. They were exhausted and, finally, home.

Greta was still sleeping. 'Asleep since you left,' said Akiko, whose eyes were as black as the bruised skin on Carlisle's shin. And when Greta woke, she was too drowsy with nausea to notice the plaster cast on Carlisle's leg; the cast was so chalky that it left little patches of dust wherever Carlisle dragged it. The dust Greta noticed, wondering with half-interest – as she always did with housework – where it had come from, swiping it from the cushion of the ottoman. She knew Carlisle had been injured, but it hardly registered with her at all. 'Oh, I'm fine,' Carlisle reported, and Greta left it at that, because the only way to describe how she felt was as if she had been poisoned. She looked at the cast and rolled her eyes back into her head. And when the summer descended and the mercury in the thermometers capped out at 110 degrees and Greta finally gave birth, the cast was sawn off Carlisle's leg. The baby was dead, but Carlisle's leg was healthier than it had ever been since that day when Greta and he were six. There was still a bit of a drag in the foot, but Carlisle no longer needed the crutches, and he could stride right into the Spanish house's step-down living room without holding the rail.

'The only thing good to come of Bakersfield,' Greta would sometimes say.

Then, for the rest of their marriage, she thought of Teddy Cross as a man capable of miracles – once, when one saw his lips pressed together in concentration, it seemed to Greta that he could do anything at all. But when Lili said the same of Professor Bolk, Greta looked down to the Elbe and counted the boats and then counted the girls on the lawn, and said, 'We will see.'

Twenty-three

❧❀❧

Lili woke herself up screaming. She didn't know how long she'd been sleeping, but she could feel the cap of morphine laced across her brain, her eyelids too heavy to lift.

Her shrieks were high and glassy and, even Lili knew, sliced through the corridors of the Municipal Women's Clinic, erupting a pimpling chill on the spines of the nurses and on the skin stretched across the bellies of the pregnant girls. There was an inflamed pain in the lower half of her body. If she'd had the strength, Lili would have lifted her head and looked down to her own middle to see if a bonfire burned there, baking the bones in her pelvis.

She dreamily felt as if she'd risen above her bed and was now looking down: little Lili, her body carved into existence by Professor Bolk, lay strapped beneath the blanket, her arms spread out, the underside of her wrists pale green and exposed. Ropes braided from Italian hemp crossed her legs, sandbags hanging from them, dangling heavily next to the bed. There were four on each side, each bag hooked to a thick rope that ran over Lili's shins, holding them down against the spasms.

A nurse Lili didn't recognize ran into the room. She was full-breasted and moustached, and cried, 'What can I get you?' She pushed Lili back against the stack of pillows.

It was as if the screaming belonged to someone else. For a moment Lili thought maybe it was Einar who was screaming: perhaps his ghost was rising inside her. It was a terrible thought, and she sank her head into the pillows and sealed her eyes. But she was still screaming – she couldn't help herself –

her lips chapped and crusted in the corner and her tongue a thin dry strip.

'What's wrong?' the nurse kept asking. She seemed only partially concerned, as if she had seen this before. She was young, with a glass-bead necklace that cut into her throat. Lili looked at the nurse, at the throat so padded with flesh that it nearly hid the necklace, and thought maybe she had seen the nurse before. The line of fine hairs above her lip – that was familiar – and the breasts stretching the bib of her apron. 'You mustn't move,' the nurse was saying. 'It'll only make it worse. Try to be very still.'

The nurse brought a green rubber mask to Lili's face; out of the corner of her eye Lili could see the nurse turn the nozzle of the tank and release the ether. And this was when Lili realized she had met the nurse before. She had a weak memory of waking herself up by screaming; and then the nurse rushing in, her breasts, caught in the apron's bib, swinging over Lili as she took Lili's temperature. There was the readjustment of the ropes across Lili's shins, and the glass stick of the thermometer slipped beneath her tongue. All this had happened before. Especially the cone of the green rubber mask, which fitted snugly over Lili's mouth and nose, as if one of the factories up the Elbe whose flame-rimmed smokestacks belched the black effluvium of poured plastic and rubber had moulded it especially for her.

It was several weeks before Lili began to emerge from the pain, but eventually Professor Bolk eliminated the doses of ether. The nurse, whose name was Hannah, unhooked the sandbags, freeing Lili's legs. They were too thin and blue for her to be able to walk down the corridor, but she could sit up again, for an hour or two each morning, before the daily morphia injection that sank into her arm with the deep sting of a wasp.

Nurse Hannah would wheel Lili down to the *Wintergarten*. There she would leave Lili to rest, parking the wheelchair next to a window and a potted fern. It was May, and outside the rhododendrons were puckered and full. Along the wall of

Bolk's laboratory, in the bed of soil and compost, tulips were reaching towards the sun.

On the lawn, with its litter of dandelions, Lili watched the pregnant girls gossip. The sun was bright against their white necks. Since the end of winter, there were new girls. There would always be new girls, Lili thought, sipping her tea, pulling the blanket over her lap, which beneath the blue hospital gown and the pads of gauze and the iodine dressing was open and weepy and raw. Ursula was no longer at the clinic, and this confused Lili. But she was too tired and too softened with drug to consider it further. She had once asked Frau Krebs about Ursula, and she had rearranged Lili's pillows and said, 'Don't worry about her. Everything is fine now.'

Greta could visit for only a few hours each afternoon. A rule, instituted by Professor Bolk and enforced by the metallic voice of Frau Krebs, banned visitors in the mornings and evenings. These were the times when the girls of the clinic were to be alone but together, as if their condition and trouble were a seal of camaraderie that outsiders couldn't share. And so each day Greta would visit from just after lunch, when Lili's lip would still hold a spot of potato soup, until late afternoon, when the shadows grew long and Lili's head would loll into her chest.

Lili looked forward to the sight of Greta entering the glassed-in *Wintergarten*. Often a large bouquet of flowers – first jonquils, then, as the spring progressed, waxy tulips, and finally pink peonies – would hide Greta's face as she appeared in the doorway. Lili would wait patiently in her wicker wheelchair, listening to the clack of Greta's shoes on the tiled floor. Often the other girls would whisper about Greta ('*Who's the tall American with the gorgeous long hair?*'), and that talk – the airy voices of the girls whose breasts were filling daily with milk – pleased Lili.

'As soon as we get you out of here,' Greta would say, settling into a recliner, her legs up on the long white cushion,

'I'm going to take you straight back to Copenhagen and let you have a look around.'

Greta had been promising this since she arrived from Paris: the train and ferry back to Denmark; reopening the apartment in the Widow House, which had remained shuttered for years; a spree in the private dressing room of Fonnesbech's department store.

'But why can't we go now?' Lili would ask. Not once in five years had she or Greta returned to Copenhagen. Lili had a vague memory of Einar instructing the shippers, their sleeves rolled to their elbows, to handle the crate that held his unframed canvases carefully. She remembered watching Greta empty the drawers of the pickled-ash wardrobe into a little trunk with leather hinges that Lili never saw again.

'You're not quite finished here,' Greta would remind Lili.

'Why not?'

'Only a little more time. Then we can go home.' How pretty Greta was, in her panelled skirt and her high-heeled boots, resting next to Lili. Greta had never loved anyone more than her, Lili knew. Now – now that even her government papers claimed she was Lili Elbe – she felt certain Greta wouldn't change. It was what got Lili through it, through the lonely nights in the hospital room beneath the heavy blanket, through the bouts of pain that sneaked up and mugged her like a thief. Lili was always changing, but not Greta, never Greta.

Professor Bolk would sometimes join Lili and Greta, standing over them, Greta's legs stretched out on the recliner, Lili in her chair. 'Won't you sit with us?' Greta would ask, repeating her request three or four times, but the professor never stopped long enough to take the cup of tea that Lili always poured for him.

'It seems to be working,' Professor Bolk said one day.

'Why do you say that?' Greta asked.

'Take a look at her. Doesn't she look well to you?'

'She does, but she's getting anxious to be done with this,' said Greta, standing to meet Professor Bolk.

'She's becoming quite a pretty young lady,' he said.

Lili watched them, their legs near her face, making her feel like a child.

'She's been here over three months,' Greta said. 'She's beginning to think about life outside the clinic. She's anxious to head out into the—'

'Stop talking about me like I'm not here,' Lili interrupted. It spilled from her mouth, the angry little interruption, as her food had done during the first druggy days after the operations.

'We weren't,' Greta said, kneeling. And then, 'No, you're right. How do you feel, Lili? Tell me. How do you feel today?'

'I feel fine except for the pain, but that's getting better. Frau Krebs and Nurse Hannah both say it'll ease up and then I can go home.' Lili now sat forward in her wicker wheelchair. She steadied her hands and tried to pull herself up.

'Don't stand,' Greta said. 'Not unless you're ready.'

Lili tried again, but her arms couldn't manage. She'd become so hollow, a nearly weightless girl emptied out by both illness and her surgeon's knife. 'I'll be ready soon,' Lili finally said. 'Maybe next week. We're moving back to Copenhagen, Professor Bolk. Has Greta told you we're returning to Copenhagen?'

'That's what I understand.'

'And we're moving into our old apartment in the Widow House. You'll have to come and visit us. Do you know Copenhagen? We have a marvellous view of the Royal Theatre's dome, and if you open the window you can smell the harbour.'

'But Lili,' Greta said, 'you won't be ready to leave next week.'

'If I keep on improving like this, then why not? Tomorrow I'll take my first steps again. Tomorrow let's try to walk a little in the park.'

'Don't you remember, Lili?' the professor said, holding his papers against his chest. 'There's another operation.'

'Another operation?'

'Just one more,' Greta said.

'Whatever for? Haven't you done everything already?' Lili

couldn't say the words, but she was thinking: But haven't you already restored my ovaries and carved out the canula I should have been born with? No, she could never say it. How humiliating it was, even with Greta.

'Just one last procedure,' Professor Bolk said. 'To remove your—'

And Lili – who was no older and no younger than her present mood, who was the ghost of a girl, both ageless and unageing, with adolescent naïveté erasing the decades of another man's experience who each morning cupped her swelling breasts like an over-anxious girl praying for her first menstruation – closed her eyes against the shame. Professor Bolk was informing her that down there, beneath the gauze and the brown iodine dressing that looked like the watered-down gravy Einar had endured during the war, just up from her fresh, still-healing wound, lay one last roll of skin that belonged to Einar.

'All I need to do is remove it and refold the—' Lili couldn't bear the details, and so instead she looked to Greta, whose lap was filled with an open notebook. Greta was sketching Lili at this moment, looking from her to the notebook and back, and when Greta's eyes met Lili's, Greta set down her pencil and said, 'She's right. Can't you hurry up the next operation, Professor Bolk? What's the wait?'

'I don't think she's ready. She isn't strong enough yet.'

'I think she is,' Greta said.

They continued to argue, while Lili shut her eyes and imagined Einar as a boy on the lichen rock watching Hans return a shot with his tennis racquet. She thought of Henrik's moist hand in hers at the Artists Ball. And the heat of Carlisle's eyes on her early that damp morning at the market. And Greta, her eyes narrowing into concentration, as Lili posed on the lacquer trunk. 'Do it now,' she said softly.

Professor Bolk and Greta stopped. 'What did you say?' he asked.

'Did you say something?' Greta said.

'Please just do it now.'

Outside in the back-park the new girls, whom Lili didn't recognize, were gathering their books and their blankets and were re-entering the clinic for the evening. The willows were sweeping the lawn of the Municipal Women's Clinic, and beyond the girls a rabbit dashed into a gooseberry bush. The current of the Elbe held the flat-bottomed freighters, and, across the river, the sun hit the copper roofs of Dresden and the great, almost silver dome of the Frauenkirche.

She shut her eyes and dreamed, somewhere in her future, of crossing the square of Kongens Nytorv, in the shadow of the statue of King Christian V, and the only person in the world who would stop and stare would be the handsome stranger, whose heartswell would force him to touch Lili's hand and profess his love.

When Lili opened her eyes, she saw that Greta and the professor were looking down towards the end of the *Winter-garten*. A tall man was standing in the door frame. He moved towards them, a silhouette, his coat over his arm. Lili watched Greta watch the man. Greta pushed her hair back over her ears. Her finger brushed at the scar on her cheek. Her hands rubbed together, the bracelets tinkling, and she said, her voice a soft gasp, 'Look.' And then, 'It's Hans.'

Part Four

Copenhagen
1931

❧

Twenty-four

❦

They returned to the Widow House, but over the years the building had declined. While in Paris, Greta had hired a man named Poulsen to manage the upkeep. Once a month she posted a cheque, enclosed with a note of instruction. 'I suppose the gutters need clearing by now,' she'd write. Or, 'Please rchinge the shutters.' But Poulsen followed none of the orders, and tended to little beyond sweeping the entrance hall and burning the rubbish. When Greta and Hans motored into Copenhagen on a morning when the snow was flinging itself against the city's sills, Poulsen disappeared.

The façade had faded to a pale pink. On the upper floors, gull droppings caked the window frames. A pane of glass was missing in an apartment where a fidgety woman in her nineties had died in the night, strangled by the twist of her bedsheet. And a fine black grime streaked the walls of the stairwell that led to the top floor.

It took Greta a few weeks to ready the apartment for Lili. Hans helped, hiring the crew to paint and the waxer to polish the floors. 'Has she ever thought about living on her own?' he asked one day, and Greta, startled, replied, 'What? Without me?'

Slowly she eased Lili into the sea of life in Copenhagen. On slushy afternoons, Greta held Lili's hand and strolled her through the box hedges, leafless in late winter, of Kongens Have. Lili would shuffle her feet and sink her mouth into the woolly wrap of her muffler; the operations had left her with a steady pain that flared up as her morphine wore off. Greta would say, feeling the tap of pulse in Lili's wrist, 'Take your time. Just let me know when you're ready.' She supposed the day would come when Lili would want to set out into the world by herself. She saw it in Lili's face, in the way she studied the young women, packages of butter rolls from the bakery in their hands, walking busily across Kongens Nytorv each morning, women young enough for hope still to flicker in their eyes. Greta heard it in Lili's voice when she read aloud from the wedding announcements in the newspaper. How Greta dreaded the day; she sometimes wondered whether she would have gone along with everything if she had realized, at the outset, that it would end with Lili leaving the Widow House, a slim suitcase in her hand. There were days during their first few months back in Copenhagen when Greta sometimes believed that she and Lili could create a life for themselves on the top floor of the Widow House and neither of them would leave for any longer than an afternoon. Sometimes, when she and Lili were sitting next to the iron stove, she came to think that the past years of upheaval and evolution had come to a close, and now she and Lili could paint and live peacefully, alone but together. And wasn't that the inexhaustible struggle for Greta? Her perpetual need to be alone but always loved, and in love. 'Do you ever think I'll fall in love?' Lili had begun to ask, as spring returned and the grey seeped out of the harbour, replaced by the blue. 'Do you think something like that could happen even to me?'

With the spring of 1931 came the contracting markets and the plummeting currencies and a general black cloud of ruin, economic and otherwise. Americans began to sail away from Europe, Greta read in the newspapers; she saw one booking air-and-sea passage at the Deutscher Aero-Lloyd office, a woman with a beaver collar and a child on her hip. A painting, even a good one, could hang on the wall of a gallery and remain unsold. It was a drab world for Lili to emerge into; it wasn't the same world.

Each morning Greta would nudge Lili, who sometimes couldn't wake on her own. Greta would pull a skirt from the hanger, and a blouse with wooden buttons, and a sweater with wrists patterned with snowflakes. She would help Lili dress, and serve her coffee and black bread and smoked salmon sprinkled with dill. Only by mid-morning would Lili become fully alert, her eyes blinking back the morphine, her mouth dry. 'I must have been tired,' she would say apologetically, and Greta would nod and answer, 'There's nothing wrong with that.'

When Lili was out on her own – either shopping at the Gammel Strand fish market or at the pottery class Greta enrolled her in – Greta would try to paint. Only six years had passed, but it seemed longer since she had last lived in the apartment with its ghostly smell of herring. Some things were the same: there were the horns of the ferries bound for Sweden and Bornholm, and the afternoon light, which sliced through the windows just before the sun dipped beyond the city, silhouetting the needles of the church spires. Standing at her easel, Greta would think about Einar then and Lili today, and Greta would shut her eyes and hear a tinkling bell of memory in her head but then recognize it as the *ping!* of the Cantonese laundress who was still calling from the street. She regretted nothing, Greta believed.

The King granted their divorce with a speed that alarmed her. Of course they could no longer live as man and wife, now that they were both women and Einar lay in memory's coffin. Even so, the officials, who wore black bow ties and whose fingers shook nervously, surprised Greta when they filed the paperwork with an uncharacteristic alacrity. She had expected – even counted on – a bureaucratic delay; she nearly imagined the request lost in an accordion file. Although she didn't like to admit it, she was like many young women from Pasadena who thought of divorce as a sign of moral flaccidity; or, more specifically, Greta thought of it as a sign of lacking a western spine. She found herself unusually concerned about what others might think and say about her – as if she were so frivolous and weak-minded that she had simply married the wrong man. No, Greta didn't like to think of herself that way.

She pressed for a death certificate for Einar Wegener, which no one in any position of authority agreed to, although everyone in the bureau knew of the nature of her case. There was one official, whose nose was long and wore the twitch of a white moustache just beneath it, who conceded that it was closest to the truth. 'I'm afraid I can't rewrite the law,' he said, a stack of papers nearly reaching his moustache. 'But my husband is dead,' Greta tried, her fists landing on the counters that separated her from the room of bureaucrats, with their sleeve bands and their abacuses and their yellow smell of tobacco and pencil shavings. 'He should be declared dead,' she tried on her last visit to the government office, her voice softening. Above the room of bureaucrats, watching them, was one of her early paintings: Herr Ole Skram in a black suit, vice-minister in the King's government for less than a month, noted only for his remarkable and well-witnessed death in the tangled tether of a hot-air balloon. But Greta's pleas failed. And so Einar Wegener officially disappeared, graveless and gone.

'She needs to lead her own life,' Hans said one day. 'She should get out on her own and make her own friends.'

'I'm not stopping her from doing that.' Greta had run into him at the entrance of the Royal Academy of Arts, under the arch. It was April, and the wind was easterly, chilled and salted from the Baltic. Greta turned up her collar against the wind. Students in sawn-off gloves were passing by. 'And you, too,' he said.

Greta said nothing, the chill creeping down her spine. She could see out into Kongens Nytorv. In front of the statue of King Christian V, a boy with a blue scarf dangling to his knees was kissing a girl. The thing about Hans was this: he always reminded her of what she didn't have; of what she'd convinced herself – when she sat in her reading chair waiting for Lili to return, her heart quickening at every false sound in the stairwell – she could go without. What was she afraid of?

'How about driving up to Helsingør with me tomorrow?' he proposed.

'I don't think I can get away,' she said. The wind picked up, hurtling through the academy's portico, where the walls were scraped from lorries too wide to pass. Greta and Hans went inside, into one of the side halls, where the floorboards were unvarnished and the walls painted a soft soap-green and the banister running up the staircase was white.

'When will you realize she's no longer yours?'

'I never said she was.' And then, 'I was talking about my work. It isn't easy to take even a day off from my work.'

'How would you know?'

She felt a sudden loss, as if the cruelty of progress and time had just then grabbed from her her days as a student at the academy; as if her past had remained hers until today. 'Einar's dead,' she heard herself say.

'But Lili isn't.' He was right. After all, there was Lili, probably this very minute sweeping the apartment, her face caught in a window pane of sun. Lili with her pretty bony wrists and her eyes nearly black. Just yesterday she had said, 'I was thinking about taking a job.'

'Don't you see I'm a little sad?' Greta said.

'Don't you see that I want you to tell me that?'

'Hans,' she said. 'Maybe I should go.' It was then that Greta realized they were at the foot of the steps where she and Einar had first kissed, and fell in love. The white balustrades and the plank steps worn from decades of tardy students with incomplete assignments shoved up beneath their arms. The paned windows were hooked against the cold. The hall was quiet; no one was around. Where had all the students gone? Greta heard a door somewhere catch in its latch. Then everything fell silent again, and something imperceptible passed from Hans to her, and outside the window, in the courtyard, in the long shadow of the academy, the boy with the blue scarf kissed his girl, again and again, and yet again.

Twenty-five

꧁✦꧂

Lili was sitting in the rope-bottom chair, wondering if now was the right time to tell Greta. Through the window Lili could see the masts of the herring boats on the canal. Behind her, Greta was painting a portrait of Lili's back. Greta said nothing as she outlined the painting, and Lili heard only Greta's bracelets tinkling. Smouldering in the pit of her groin was the leftover pain, so steady that more and more Lili had taught herself to ignore it; the inside of her lip was shredded from biting down. Professor Bolk had promised it would eventually go away.

She thought of the girls at the clinic. The day before Professor Bolk released Lili, they threw her a party in the garden. Two girls pulled a white cast-iron table on to the lawn, a third carried from her room a primrose in a *cache-pot* painted with bunnies. The girls tried to spread a yellow cloth across the table, but the wind was keeping it aloft. Lili sat at the head of the table, on a cold metal chair, watching the cloth fluttering as the girls tried to tie down its corners. The sunlight poured through the yellow cloth, filling Lili's eyes, the *cache-pot* in her lap.

Frau Krebs gave Lili a box tied with a ribbon. 'From the professor,' she said. 'He wanted you to have it. He had to go up to Berlin. To St Norbert Hospital, to attend a surgery. He said to tell you goodbye.' The ribbon was tight, and Lili couldn't pick it open, and so Frau Krebs produced an army knife from her apron and quickly cut through it, which disappointed the girls, because they wanted to weave it through Lili's hair, which had grown beyond her shoulders during her stay.

The box was large and packed with tissue, and inside Lili found a double-oval silver frame. In one oval was a photograph of Lili lying in the tall grass on the bank of the Elbe; the photo must have come from Greta, because Lili had never walked down to the river with Professor Bolk. And peering through the second oval was the face of a small man beneath a hat; his eyes were dark and shadowy and his skin so white it was almost glowing, and his neck looked thin in his collar.

From the rope-bottom chair Lili could see the double-portrait frame on the bookshelf. She could hear the scratch of Greta's pencil against the canvas. Lili's hair was parted down the middle and fell to both sides of her neck. The amber beads hung around her throat, and she could feel the cold gold of the clasp. Lili had a vision of a stocky woman with hammy legs and callused thumbs who had once worn the beads; Lili of course did not know the woman, but she could see her in rubber and canvas boots in a sphagnum field, the beads slithering down the crevice of her breasts.

It didn't bother Lili, what she remembered and what she didn't. She knew that most of her life, her previous life, was like a book she had read as a small child: it was both familiar and forgotten. She could recall a sphagnum field, muddy in spring and pocked with holes belonging to a family of foxes. She could recall the rusty, flat blade of a hoe slapping into the peat. And the hollow *clack!* of amber beads swinging around a throat. Lili could remember the silhouette of a tall boy with a large head walking along the ridge of the sphagnum field. She didn't know who it was, but Lili knew that there had been a time when she was a small frightened child watching that silhouette, black and flat, on the horizon of the field. Something in her chest would swell as the silhouette moved closer, as his silhouette arm pulled on the brim of his hat; this Lili knew. She could recall telling herself that, yes, she was in love.

'You're blushing,' Greta said from her easel.

'Am I?' Lili felt the heat in her neck, and the quick collection of sweat around the rim of her face. 'I don't know why,' she said.

But that wasn't true. A few weeks earlier, she had been on her way to Landmandsbanken to lock away in the safe-deposit box the pearl-and-diamond brooch Greta had given her. But before heading to the bank, Lili had stopped in a basement store to buy two bristle brushes for Greta. The clerk, an old man with knuckles that were pink and soft, was reaching up to a shelf of turpentine. He was assisting a customer, a man with corkscrew hair growing past his ears. Lili couldn't see the customer's face, and she felt annoyed with him for having asked for the largest tin of turpentine on the highest shelf. 'I'm going to fetch a pair of gloves. I'll be right back,' the customer said to the clerk, who was still balancing on the ladder. The man turned around and passed Lili, saying, 'Excuse me, *frøken.*'

As the man slipped by her, Lili pressed herself against the shelf and held her breath. His hair brushed her cheek, and she smelled a faint scent of grain. 'Excuse me,' he said again.

Then Lili knew. She sank her chin into her chest, unsure of what she wanted to happen next. She worried about how she looked, her face probably raw from the wind. On the bottom shelf she stared at children's sets of watercolours in hinged metal boxes. She knelt to check the price of a red one with a dozen dry pads of colour. She began to pull her hair around her face.

Then Henrik saw her. His hand fell to her shoulder: 'Lili? Is it you?'

They stepped outside, the sack holding the tin of turpentine swinging on Henrik's arm. He was older now, the skin around his eyes thinner and faintly blue. His hair was darker, like stained oak, without much shine. And his throat had thickened, and his wrists. He was no longer pretty; he had become a handsome man.

They went for a coffee around the corner, settling around a table at a café. Henrik told Lili about himself; about his paintings of the sea that sold better in New York than in

Denmark; about the automobile accident on Long Island that nearly killed him, the spoked wheel of his Kissel Gold Bug flying off the running board and into his forehead; about his high-cheeked fiancée from Sutton Place who left him for nothing and no one else, simply because she didn't love him any more.

'I forgot,' Lili said suddenly at the café. 'I forgot to buy Greta's brushes.'

He walked her back to the shop, only to find it closed. Lili and Henrik were on the street, the store's sign swaying on its iron arm. 'I have some extra ones in my studio,' he said. 'We can go and get them if you like.' His eyes were tear-shaped, and she had forgotten how short and stubby his eyelashes were. Again there was the scent of grain, like the shuck of wheat.

'It all makes me a little worried,' Lili said, as Henrik's face moved closer to hers.

'Stop,' Henrik said. 'Please don't worry about me.' The shop's sign continued to rattle on its arm, and Henrik and Lili set out for his studio on the other side of the Inderhavn, where, later, after Henrik had poured her red wine and fed her strawberries and showed her his paintings of the sea, they kissed.

'You're blushing even more,' Greta now said. She turned on a lamp and began to rinse her brushes in a jar. 'Do you need a pill?' Greta asked. 'Are you feeling all right?'

Lili didn't know how to tell Greta. When they'd moved back to Copenhagen, Lili had said, 'Do you really think we should go on living together? Two women in this apartment?'

'Are you worried about what people might say?' Greta said. 'Is that it?'

And Lili, who wasn't entirely sure why she had said it, answered, 'No. Not at all. It's just that . . . I was thinking of you.'

No, Lili couldn't tell Greta about Henrik, at least not yet. After all, where would she begin? The kiss in the dim light of his studio? The wrap of Henrik's arm around Lili's shoulders as he walked her into Kongens Have at dusk just as the

governesses were wheeling their prams home for the evening?
His hand, which was backed with thick black hair, holding her
throat, and then the soft cushion of her breast? The letter from
Henrik slipped to Lili the next day via the Cantonese
laundress, the folded square of paper smudged with ink
professing love and regret. Yes, where would Lili begin? Only
three weeks had passed since the meeting at the art shop, but it
felt to Lili as if during that time her life had begun anew. How
could she tell Greta that?

'I feel like going out for a walk,' Lili said, standing.

'I'm not done yet,' Greta said. 'Sit for just a few more
minutes?'

'I feel like going now, before it gets dark.'

'Do you want me to come with you?'

'I'll be fine.'

'All alone?'

Lili nodded, an inexhaustible doubleness welling up inside
her: she both loved and resented Greta for caring so much. It
was as simple as that.

She opened the wardrobe for her coat and scarf. Greta began
to tidy her paints and her brushes and her easel. Edvard IV
started barking at Lili's ankles. The last angled sunlight shot
into the apartment. The horn of the Bornholm ferry called,
and while she pulled on a blue felt coat with bamboo-hook
buttons, Lili thought about walking to the dock and climbing
the gangway and taking a seat in the cabin that looked across
the bow towards that little island in the sea.

But she wouldn't set sail, at least not yet. 'I'll be back,' she
heard herself saying.

'Yes, well . . . good.' And then, 'You're sure you don't want
company?'

'Not tonight.'

'All right then.' Greta hoisted Edvard IV into her arms and
stood in the centre of the apartment, in a sinking pane of light,
as Lili prepared to leave her. Lili felt the need to escape.
Henrik had told her he'd be working late in his studio. 'Look

for the light,' he wrote in a note smuggled into the apartment in the folded laundry.

'Will you be gone long?'

Lili shook her head. 'I'm not really sure.' She was ready, buttoned into her coat. She would have to tell Greta about Henrik, but not tonight. 'Good-night,' she said, feeling something, and when she opened the door she found Hans, his knuckle raised and about to knock.

He came in. Lili remained at the door. He looked tired, his tie loose. He asked them to join him for dinner. Lili said, 'I was just on my way out.' Greta said that Lili had become quite busy lately. She sounded angry about it, from the way she told Hans about Lili's new job at Fonnesbech's department store, standing behind the perfume counter. 'They hired me because I speak French,' Lili explained, still in her coat. The manager at Fonnesbech's, a woman whose black blouse flattened out her breasts, asked Lili to speak to the customers with an accent. 'Speak like a Frenchwoman. Pretend you're someone else. The store is a stage!' Each day Lili arranged the cut-glass bottles on a silver tray and held her eyes low and quietly asked the passing shoppers if they'd like a dab to the wrist.

'I should be going,' Lili said. She moved to kiss Hans goodbye.

He said he'd like to join her walk, but then Greta said that Lili wanted to be alone. 'I'll come just for a bit,' he said. 'Then I'll be back, Greta, and we'll have some supper.'

On the street, the night was damp. Across the way a woman was knocking on Dr Møller's door. Lili and Hans hesitated outside the Widow House's door. 'Where to?' he said.

'I was headed to Christianshavn. But you don't have to come with me,' she said. 'It's too far.'

'How's Greta been lately?'

'You know Greta. Always the same.'

'That's not true. Is she settling back all right?'

Lili stopped and wondered what he meant. Wasn't that the frustratingly wonderful thing about Greta? That she was always the same – always painting, always planning, always pulling back her hair?

'She's fine.' And then, 'I think she's angry with me.'

'Why?'

'Sometimes I wonder why she let me go through with all of this in the first place. If she thought everything was going to be the same afterwards.'

'She never thought that,' Hans said. 'She always knew what it meant.'

The woman, whose arm was in a sling, was admitted to Dr Møller's house. Lili heard a shout from the sailor's window above.

Then Hans asked, 'Where are you going, Lili?' He took her hands between his and began rubbing away the cold. Sometimes Lili was surprised that she didn't simply crumble beneath the touch of a man. She could hardly believe that her flesh and bone could withstand the scrutiny of a man's fingertips. She felt this even more with Henrik, whose hands had pressed every knuckle of her spine. His hands had cupped her shoulders and she had expected herself to fold up like a piece of paper, but it didn't happen, and Henrik had continued touching her, kissing her.

'We've known each other a long time,' Hans said.

'I think I've fallen in love,' Lili began. She told Hans about Henrik, about how they would kiss in his studio in the evening and all Lili could think of was never again returning to the Widow House.

'I thought that might be the case,' Hans said. 'Why haven't you told Greta?'

'She'd be jealous. She'd try to stop it.'

'How do you know?'

'She tried to stop it once before.'

'Wasn't that a long time ago?'

Lili thought about this. He was right, of course. Even so, he didn't know Greta the way she did. He hadn't endured the slanting glare every time she set out from the apartment, or when she returned late at night. What was it Greta once said to

Lili? 'Obviously I'm not your mother, but just the same I'd like to know where you're keeping yourself these days.'

'Doesn't she have a right to know?' Hans asked.

'Greta?' She wasn't always like that, Lili had to admit. Wasn't there the time just last week when Greta met Lili at the employees' entrance of Fonnesbech's and said, 'Sorry to change our plans, but Hans and I are going to have dinner. I'm sure you won't mind fending for yourself'? Hadn't Greta said, the other day when they were waking from a nap, 'I had a dream about you getting married'?

'Can I walk you to the bridge?' Hans said.

'I'll be fine,' she said. 'Go back up and see Greta.' Then it occurred to her how close he and Greta had become: the shared meals at the long table; the quiet evenings in the Widow House, playing poker until Lili returned; the way Greta had uncharacteristically begun to rely on him, saying more and more often, 'Let me check with Hans.'

'Do you want to marry her?' Lili said.

'I haven't asked her.'

'But you will?'

'If she lets me.'

Lili wasn't jealous; why should she be? She felt relief, although at the same time she felt the pull of a rushing memory: Hans and Einar playing outside the farmhouse; the apron hanging next to the stovepipe; Greta nearly chasing Einar through the halls of the Royal Academy; Greta trotting down the aisle of St Alban's Church on their wedding day, always in a hurry. Lili's life had flipped itself over, and she was grateful.

'She won't marry me until she knows that you are settled and living well.'

'She said that?'

'She didn't have to.'

There was another shout from the sailor above, and the slam of a window. Lili and Hans smiled. In the streetlight Hans looked as young as a boy. His cowlick stood up, his cheeks pink on the point. Lili could see his breath, could see her own breath mixing with his. 'You're a whore!' the sailor yelled, as he always did.

'Have I done anything wrong?' Lili asked.

'No,' Hans said, releasing her hands, kissing her goodbye on the forehead. 'But neither has Greta.'

Twenty-six

❧

After thinking about it, Greta abandoned her latest portrait of Lili. The nape of the neck was wrong, too fat at the stump; and Greta had painted her back too wide, the stretch from one shoulder to the other nearly filling the canvas. It was ugly, and Greta folded it up and burned it in the iron-footed stove in the corner, the paint fumes burning her throat.

It wasn't the first painting that had failed, or the last. She had tried to complete the first group of portraits since returning to Copenhagen, but they continued to turn out misconceived. Lili was either oversized or strangely coloured, or the dreamy white light Greta liked to paint into Lili's cheeks came off as curdy. While Lili was at Fonnesbech's perfume counter, Greta once tried hiring a model from the Royal Academy. She picked out the smallest boy in the class, a reedy blond with heavy lashes who tucked his sweaters into his trousers. She set out the lacquer trunk in front of the window and asked the boy to stand on it with his hands clasped at the small of his back. 'Look at your feet,' Greta instructed, settling behind her easel. The canvas was blank, and its bumpy grain suddenly seemed impossible to sketch over. She pencilled in the curve of his head and the line of his flank. But after an hour the portrait began to look cartoonish, with huge, watery eyes and an hourglass waist. She handed the boy ten kroner and sent him home.

There were other models: a handsome woman who was a cook at the Palace Hotel, and a man with a waxed moustache who, when asked to strip to his vest, revealed a chest that was a black carpet of hair.

'The market is tightening,' Hans said the night he came to visit, when he returned to the flat after seeing Lili out. The gallery on Krystalgade was closed, its windows smudged with whitewash. The proprietor had disappeared; some said he fled to Poland with bad debts; others said he was now loading crates of curry on the Asiatic Company's docks. And he was just one of many. The Henningsen porcelain factory, which had ordered another twenty kilns to produce soup bowls for America, collapsed. Herr Petzholdt's cement churners went idle. Rumour mixed with the burnt-butter scent spewing out of the Otto Mønsted margarine factory. And the aerodrome, which once had buzzed like a beehive, sat blank and quiet, sending off the few emigrants and receiving only the occasional air freighter on its clean white strip.

'Nobody's buying anything,' Hans said, holding his chin in his hand, studying the paintings Greta had arranged around the room. 'I'd like to wait for things to get better before we take these out. Now's not the time. Perhaps next year.'

'Next year?' Greta stood back and looked at her work. None was beautiful; none had the glow of light for which she had become known. She'd forgotten how to create it, the backlight that brought Lili's face to life. The only painting that seemed to have any merit was her portrait of Professor Bolk: tall and large-handed and sturdy in his wool suit with the windowpane plaid. The others didn't compare, Greta saw; and she saw Hans, with his wrinkled brow, trying to find a way to tell her.

'I was thinking of travelling to America,' Hans said. 'To see if there's any business left there.'

'To New York?'

'And to California.'

'To California?' Greta leaned against the wall, amid her paintings, and thought of Hans removing his felt-brimmed hat for the first time beneath the Pasadena sun.

Carlisle was on his way over to Copenhagen, booking

passage via Hamburg. He had written that the winter had been dry in Pasadena, the poppy beds burned out by March. This was in response to Greta's one-sentence note: 'Einar is dead.' And Carlisle wrote in return: 'Pasadena is dry, and the Los Angeles River isn't running, and why don't you and Lili come for a visit?' And then, 'How is Lili? Is she happy?' Greta buttoned his letter away in the pocket of her smock.

On some afternoons, Greta would slip into Fonnesbech's and watch Lili, across the counters displaying the kid gloves and silk scarves folded into triangles: Lili behind the glass case, her amber beads against the collar of her uniform and her hair falling into her eyes. A customer would pass and Lili would hold up a finger, and the lady would stop and bring a bottle of perfume to her nose. A smile and a sale, and Greta would watch it from across the floor, behind a rack of half-priced umbrellas. Greta spied like this a few times, but the last time was when she left Fonnesbech's and came home to a cable from Carlisle: 'I'm sailing on Saturday.'

And here was Hans, saying he was thinking of travelling to California himself. 'I don't suppose you'd want to go with me?' he said.

'To California?'

'Well, sure,' he said. 'And don't tell me you can't.'

'I can't.'

'Why not?'

And Greta didn't say it, for even she knew it would sound absurd. But who *would* look after Lili? She thought of Carlisle right then, sunning his leg on a canvas chaise on the deck of the *Estonia*.

'Greta, I could use your help,' Hans said.

'My help?'

'In America.'

She took a step back from Hans; he seemed so much taller than she: had she never noticed how high he stood? It was getting late, and they hadn't eaten. Edvard IV was lapping at the water in his bowl. Her husband's boyhood friend, that was who he was. But Hans didn't seem like that any more; as if that part of him — those memories of him — had vanished with Einar.

'Give it some thought,' Hans said.

'I could give you names to look up. I could write letters of introduction, if that's what you need. It wouldn't be any trouble at all,' she was saying.

'That's not it. Don't you see?'

'See what?'

His hand fell to the small of her back.

'But what about Lili?' she said.

'She'll be fine on her own,' Hans said.

'I couldn't leave her,' Greta said. His hand was caressing her hip. It was a spring night and the shutters were shaking in the wind, and Greta thought of the house on the hill in Pasadena where in the summer the Santa Anas flung eucalyptus branches against the screens.

'You'll have to,' Hans said. He wrapped his arms around her. She could feel his heart beating beneath his shirt, and she could feel her own in her throat.

When he arrived, Carlisle didn't stay in the spare bedroom. Instead, he took a room at the Palace Hotel, with a view out over Rådhuspladsen and the three-dragon fountain. He said he liked the sound in the square of the trams crossing lines, and the call of the man selling spice biscuits from his cart. Carlisle said he liked looking at the long brick wall of Tivoli, which was reopening for the season, the seats of the Ferris wheel shaking in the sky. He said he liked visiting Lili at the counter at Fonnesbech's, where she had earned a little lapel pin for being the month's number-one salesgirl. He said he liked seeing her busy and walking down Strøget, chatting with the other salesgirls as they emerged from the employee entrance in their matching blue suits. Carlisle said to Greta that he thought Lili should live on her own.

'What makes you say that?' Greta answered.

'She's a grown woman.'

'I'm not so sure about that,' she said. 'Anyway, it's up to her.'

'Do you mean that?' he said.

'Of course I mean that,' said Greta, who never saw a mirror-image of herself when she looked at her twin.

One night the previous week Greta had been standing in the doorway of a building opposite Fonnesbech's employee entrance. It was early evening, and she had hurried out of the Widow House so quickly that she'd forgotten to change out of her smock. She held her hands in the pockets, fingering the photographs of Teddy and Einar, the letters from them, their wedding bands. She was pressing herself against the portico of an apartment house with a horsehair doormat.

She waited only a few minutes until the metal door swung open, filling the tiny street with light and the chatter of girls. Their shoes began to clack against the grate in the pavement. Greta waited for Lili to join up with three or four girls headed to the Turkish coffee house where young people lounged on the floor propped up by pillows embroidered with silk thread and little mirrors. 'See you tomorrow,' two girls called to the rest. 'Good-night,' another said. 'Have fun,' a fourth said over her shoulder, with a wave. The girls' cheeks were downy and curved with baby fat, and their pony-tails swayed as they walked down the little street and then turned on to Strøget. Lili was still talking with other girls, one with a bag of groceries, another with some sort of brace around her hand. Greta couldn't hear what they were saying, but then the rest of the girls said, 'So long.' And at last Lili was alone in the street. She checked her watch and looked to the low, damp sky.

A woman on a bicycle pedalled by, jittering as she rode over the slick cobblestones. Then Lili tied a scarf over her head and headed down the street. Greta watched her glide away, and very soon Lili was only a blue coat supported by two thin ankles and shoes clickety-clacking in the drizzle.

Greta followed. Lili apparently wasn't in a hurry, moving out of the way of other people in the street, stopping to look in the window of a shop that sold mops and other cleaning supplies. In the window was a pyramid display of black-and-white Zebralin cans, and a photograph of a woman scouring her stovetop. Lili turned and looked at her watch again; and then her ankles, which from a distance looked no thicker than a child's, began to step quickly away from Greta. Down Snaregade with its half-timber building and a burned-out streetlamp and towards Gammel Strand. Soon she was walking along Slotsholms Canal, its curved railing tied with the lines of one-man dories. There was a white life buoy looped to the rail, and an abandoned sturgeon hanging heavily on a hook. Light from the Børsen on the other side of the canal fell on to the water, and the Børsen's twisted-copper spire was bright in the night. Lili continued to walk, looking at the fishing boats secured on the other side of the canal, their black masts creaking.

Lili stopped, unclasped her handbag. It was too dark for Greta to see Lili's eyes as she rifled through it, pulling out a handkerchief and a coin case and then the little enamel box that held her pills. Lili clicked it open. She put one on her tongue, and Greta thought she could make out Lili cringing as she swallowed the chalky tablet.

Greta thought about calling out to Lili, but then stopped herself. She watched Lili walk further into the night towards the Knippelsbro. It was April, and the winds were blowing in from the Baltic. As Lili reached the second bridge, the wind fluttered the tail of her scarf. She stopped to fix the knot at her throat. She stopped to look for traffic, but there was none. The Inderhavnen was choppy. Greta could hear the icy water sloshing against the bridge's double bascule. She heard the Swedish ferry setting out to make its last crossing of the evening.

Greta didn't know exactly where Lili was headed in Christianshavn, but she could imagine: an assignation probably, a rendezvous. Into her head popped a piece of an old song: *There once was an old man who lived on a bog.* She held the cold metal rail of Slotsholms Canal. The rail was bubbling with rust, and it smelled of salt, and Greta wrapped both hands around it as she watched Lili slip across the bridge, across the Inderhavnen, the tail of her scarf fluttering like a child's hand, waving goodbye.

Twenty-seven

❧

By late spring the shiny green buds of the willow trees in Ørstedsparken had split open, and the rose beds around Rosenborg Slot were reddening with early leaf. The sky's long winter canopy had lifted, and the evening began to stretch itself towards midsummer.

Lili, who had gained even more strength, accepted – the way a child accepts a mother's kiss – Henrik's offer of marriage. He proposed the night before sailing to New York on the *Albert Herring*. He had packed his trunks, with their chipped-leather handles, and crated up his paints and brushes. 'To New York!' Henrik kept saying. 'To New York!' Lili, who had told the other salesgirls at Fonnesbech's about Henrik's imminent departure, lifted her head and said, 'Without me?'

They were in Henrik's studio in Christianshavn, the scent of the canal coming through the window. The studio was empty except for the trunks and the crate marked with red letters: HENRIK SANDAHL, NEW YORK. The furniture's removal had shoved snarls of dust and feathers into the corners, the little puffs undulating with the breeze from the window. Henrik, his hair recently sheared down to a fine cap of curls, said, 'Of course not.' And then, 'I've asked you before, and I'll ask you again. Marry me?'

Lili had always wanted this. She knew one day she would marry; sometimes, when she thought about it, she felt she could play no greater role in this world than as a man's wife, Henrik's wife. Silly thought, even Lili knew, something she would never repeat to Greta, who didn't think like that at all. But that was how Lili felt. She imagined shopping on the second floor of Fonnesbech's, where the men's clothing hung on racks, and fingering the material of French-cuff shirts until she found the right one for Henrik. She imagined a net shopping bag bulging with groceries – the slab of salmon, the potatoes, the bouquet of parsley – that would become their dinner. She imagined the dark that would fall across their bed, and the way the mattress would dent as Henrik moved towards her.

'I want you to know one thing about me,' Lili said. She thought about the evening in Orstedsparken years ago, when she left him crying her name. 'Before we marry.'

'Tell me anything.'

'My name wasn't Lili Elbe when I was born.'

'I know that already,' he said. 'I already told you that I know. I know who you are.'

'No,' Lili said. 'You know who I was.' She told him about Professor Bolk, about the stucco clinic along the Elbe, about Frau Krebs nursing her back to health. She'd never told anyone. Lili's small circle – Greta, Hans, Carlisle, Anna – already knew about her, but she had never handed over the details of her nearly impossible transformation to anyone else. She had never asked anyone to enter that intimate circle, which sometimes felt too cramped to welcome another soul.

'I thought something like this had happened,' Henrik said. Lili could detect no horror in his face. Even now, it was what she sometimes expected: upon hearing the news, the world would turn away in disgust. 'I'm not surprised.'

She asked him what he thought of her; do you think I'm a freak of some sort, she asked. For Lili's notion of herself could flip-flop nearly by the minute: sometimes she looked in the mirror and exhaled and felt the settling peace of gratitude; other times she saw a man-woman, its head peering out of the collar of a dress. Greta and Hans told her not to think like that. But when she was alone, the self-doubt could creep back into her chest.

Henrik told her he didn't know what else he could say except that he was in love with her. 'I'm in love with an extraordinary woman,' he said. Lili used to think she couldn't return the love of a man who saw her for who she was. She once told herself that she would push away anyone who recognized her as anything less than female. It was why she had first turned her back on Henrik, that evening in the park. Now, she took his hand.

'You can still love me like this?' she said.

'Oh, Lili,' he said, rocking her shoulder. And then, 'When will you ever understand?'

'That's why I can't go to New York with you right away,' she said. 'I need to return to Dresden. One last time.' She told him that Professor Bolk wanted her to return. He wanted to attempt a final metamorphosis. She didn't want to explain the details to Henrik. He would worry, she thought. He might try to talk her out of it. He might believe it wasn't possible.

Last year, before she'd left Dresden, Professor Bolk had promised he could do something else for Lili, something that would make her even more of a woman than she already was. Something that Greta said was 'crazy even to think about'. Something so magnificent it was like an all-white dream, but was, Professor Bolk promised in his basso voice, more than possible. As she was preparing to leave the clinic, Bolk had told Lili that the ovarian transplants had succeeded. He eventually wanted to try a uterine transplant to make her fruitful. 'You mean I could become a mother?' Lili had asked. 'Haven't I done everything I've ever promised? And I can do this too,' Bolk had said. But Greta dissuaded her. 'Why would you want to do that?' Greta had said, swatting her hands. 'And besides, that's utterly impossible. How on earth could he ever do that?'

In the year since then, Lili had written to Professor Bolk often, telling him of her recovery and her afternoons at the perfume counter and Greta's difficulties painting and of Henrik. Less frequently than Lili wrote, Professor Bolk would reply, on a thin sheet of paper typed by Frau Krebs. 'That's wonderful news,' he'd answer. 'If you ever think you'd like to proceed with the last operation, the one we discussed, please let me know right away. I'm even more confident about it than before.'

Now she would go. She hadn't yet told Greta. But Lili knew more than anything else that she had to return to Dresden to finish what Bolk had started. To prove to the world – no, not the world but to herself – that indeed she was a woman, and that all her previous life, the little man known as Einar, was simply nature's gravest mishap, corrected once and for all.

'Then meet me in New York at the end of the summer,' Henrik now said, sitting on his trunk that the next day a deckhand would load on to the ship bound for New York via Hamburg. 'It's settled at last. We'll marry there.'

A few weeks later, on an early-summer morning, Lili was sitting for Greta. She was wearing a white dress with a V collar and an eyelet hem, her hair pinned back. Greta had given Lili a small bouquet of white roses to hold in her lap. She asked Lili to cross her ankles and to lift her chin.

There was so much to tell Greta now – the news of Henrik, and Lili's determination to return to Dresden. How had she allowed so much to remain unsaid between them? A little secret had grown into a second world that Greta knew nothing about. Lili felt the regret sinking in her bowels: their long intimate life reduced to this.

Greta had been working on the portrait for nearly a week, and it was going well: the light in Lili's face was alive, and correct; so were her deep-set eyes, and the thin trace of blue in her temples, and the red heat self-consciously burning in Lili's throat. As she stood at her easel, Greta was telling all this to Lili – how she looked, how the painting was turning out. 'This one's going to be beautiful,' Greta was saying. 'At last I'm getting you right. It's been a while, Lili. I was beginning to wonder.'

Over the past year Lili had watched Greta turn out paintings that looked hurried and poorly planned. One portrait of Lili

made her look grotesque, with black oily pupils and hair frizzy
with static and swollen shiny lips and the veins in her temples
bright and green. Others were weak in resemblance, or bland
in colour and conception. Not all were bad, but some, and Lili
knew that Greta was struggling. It wasn't like the years in Paris,
when everything Greta painted had a shimmering quality,
when strangers would look at the portraits of Lili and stroke
their chins and say, 'Who is this girl?' But even more surprising
was Greta's loss of desire to work. She let more and more days
pass when she didn't paint, strings of days that together would
leave Lili wondering, while she was down at Fonnesbech's,
what Greta did to pass the time. 'I'm still getting used to being
back in Copenhagen,' Greta would sometimes say. 'I thought
we had left it for good.' Other times she'd say she simply
wasn't in the mood to paint – a sentiment so unlike Greta that
Lili would reply, 'Is everything all right?'

But on this morning in early summer the most recent
portrait looked beautiful. Greta was chatting freely, as she'd
done each morning during the week. She was saying, 'I don't
suppose I ever told you about the time I asked my mother to
sit for a painting. It was when I went back to Pasadena during
the war. She was imperious then, managing the household and
the garden, searching the grounds for an untrimmed hedge.
God save the gardener who left a leaf on the lawn. One day I
asked her if I could paint her. She thought about it, and then
made me schedule the time with our butler, Mr Ito. And so I
made five appointments to meet her in the breakfast room,
where the morning light was good. Teddy Cross and I were
seeing each other then, and Mother knew it, but she didn't
want to hear about it. I was eighteen, and about to burst over
with love, and all I could think about, let alone talk about, was
Teddy. How he spoke about things in his long, slow voice.
How his shoulders curved down. How his hair felt to my
hand. But my mother didn't want to hear a single word about
Teddy. She'd hold up her hand the moment I began. And so
for five mornings I painted her as she sat in the chair at the
head of the breakfast-room table, her back to a window with a

bougainvillaea just outside. It was during an autumn heatwave, and I watched the sweat bubble up on her lip. And all I could do was bite my tongue and say nothing about how I felt.'

'How'd it turn out?' Lili asked.

'The painting? Oh, she hated it. She said it made her look mean. But that isn't true. It makes her look like a mother who wants to keep her daughter from stepping into something painful but knows she can't. She knew nothing was going to keep me from Teddy. She knew it, and she pressed her lips together and sat as still as a corpse for five mornings in a row.'

'Where is it?'

'The painting? In Pasadena. In the upstairs hall.'

Then Lili decided it was time to tell Greta. She could no longer keep anything from her. There was a terrible stretch of time in Einar's life – from the time Hans left Bluetooth until the day he met Greta at the academy – when he lived without anyone to reveal his secrets to. Lili could remember that, the feeling of biting down on one's thoughts and feelings and storing them up for no one. Then Greta had changed Einar's life. Lili could remember the feeling of that, too, of realizing, gratefully, that at last the loneliness would fall away. How could she be less than honest with Greta for another minute? 'There's something I've been meaning to tell you.'

Greta murmured. Her eyes focused on the canvas; she tightened the tortoiseshell comb holding back her hair. Her hand was moving quickly, dabbing at the canvas and then circling through the paints poured into the Knabstrup bowls, and then returning to the nearly finished portrait of Lili.

But where to begin? What news should Lili deliver first: Henrik a few weeks ago about to board the *Albert Herring*, his hand fishing in his coat pocket for the diamond ring; the odd, sweet embarrassment they shared when the ring failed to slip past Lili's knuckle; the telegram from New York, describing the apartment on East Thirty-seventh Street with the limestone front where they would live; and the most recent letter from Professor Bolk asking Lili when he should expect her, he was anxious to see her again. Yes, where to begin?

'This is very hard for me,' Lili was saying. Lili imagined the shock that would flush into Greta's face; and the anger curling her fists. Lili wished there was another way. Another way for her and Greta. 'I'm not sure where to start,' Lili said.

Greta set down her brush. 'Are you in love?'

In the apartment below, there was a slam of the door. A few heavy footsteps. A window flinging open.

Lili sat back in the rope-bottom chair. She couldn't believe that Greta had guessed. She couldn't believe Greta had known – for Lili was sure that if Greta had known Lili was in love Greta would have tried to stop it. And it was then that Lili realized how wrong she was about Greta. Once again, Lili had been wrong.

'I am,' Lili said.

'Are you sure?' Greta asked.

'Yes, very.'

'Does he love you?'

'I can't really believe it, but he does.'

'Well, then, not much else matters, does it?' Sunlight was on her, and Lili thought about all the evenings Greta had brushed out Lili's hair, Greta's breasts against Lili's back. She thought about the bed they shared, and how their little fingers would curl around each other in the night. And how the morning light would fall on Greta's rested face, and Lili would kiss her cheek thinking, Oh, if only I could be as beautiful as you!

'Are you happy for me?'

Greta said she was. Then she asked who he was, and Lili held her breath and then told Greta it was Henrik.

'Henrik,' Greta said. Lili studied Greta's face for a reaction. She wondered if Greta would remember him; or if the fact that it was he would make it even harder on Greta. But her face held still, nothing moving except an almost imperceptible puff on her lips.

'He always loved you, didn't he?'

Lili nodded. She almost felt ashamed. She thought of the scar on Henrik's forehead, from the accident, and she welled up with relief that very soon she would begin a life in which she could kiss that crosshatched line every night. 'We're getting married at the end of the summer.'

Greta said softly, 'Married.'

'It's what I've always wanted.'

Greta was corking her bottles of paint. 'It's all good news,' she said. She wasn't looking at Lili as she wiped the lip of each bottle with the hem of her smock and then pushed in the cork. She moved across the room and knelt to roll a blank canvas. 'There are still times when I see you and I think to myself, Not so long ago we were married. You and me, we were married and we lived in that small dark space between two people where a marriage exists.'

'It was you and Einar.'

'I know it was Einar. But really, it was you and me.'

Lili understood. She could remember what it felt like to fall in love with Greta. She could recall what it was like to wonder idly about when Greta would next show up at the door. She could remember the small delicate weight of a photograph of Greta in the breast pocket of Einar's shirt.

'I'm doing my best to get used to everything,' Greta said. She was speaking so quietly that Lili could barely hear her. The horn of a motorcar blared from the street, and then there was the screech of brakes, then a silence. An accident must have been avoided, a near miss on the street outside the Widow House, two chrome bumpers shining at each other beneath the Copenhagen sun, which was rising and rising and would hold itself aloft until late in the night.

'Where will you marry?' Greta asked.

'In New York.'

'New York?' Greta was at the sink, scrubbing the paint from her fingernails with a little wire brush. She said, 'I see.'

Downstairs, the sailor began calling for his wife. 'I'm home!' he yelled.

'But there's something I want to do first,' Lili said. As the morning moved on, the heat was rising in the apartment. The bun of her hair was beginning to feel heavy, the V collar of the white dress sticking to her chest. *Nationaltidende* had predicted record heat, and something in Lili both welcomed it and despised it at the same time.

'I want to return to Dresden,' Lili said.

'What for?'

'For the last operation.'

Now she could see it in Greta's face: the fast flaring of the nostrils, the eyelids sealing with pique, the anger flushing her cheeks and nearly boiling over. 'You know I don't think that's a good idea.'

'But I do.'

'But Lili . . . Professor Bolk, he's . . . yes, he's a good doctor, but even he can't do *that*. Nobody can do that. I thought we settled this last year.'

'I've made up my mind,' Lili said. 'Greta, can't you understand? I want to have children with my husband.'

The sun was now reflecting off the Royal Theatre's dome. Lili Elbe and Greta Waud, as she had begun calling herself again, alone in the apartment. Their dog, Edvard IV, asleep at the foot of the wardrobe, his body arthritic and unreliable. Recently Lili had suggested that maybe it was time to put old Edvard down, but Greta had nearly cried in protest.

'Professor Bolk knows what he's doing,' Lili said.

'I don't believe him.'

'But I do.'

'Nobody can make a man pregnant. That's what he's promising to do. It'll never happen. Not to you or to anyone. Something like that was never meant to be.'

It stung, Greta's protest, and Lili's eyes became moist. 'Nobody believed a man could be turned into a woman. Isn't that right? Who would've believed that? No one but you and me. We believed it, and now look at me. It happened because we knew it could.' Lili was crying. More than anything else, she hated Greta for taking the other side.

'Will you think it over, Lili? For a little bit?'

'I already have.'

'No, take some time. Think it through.'

Lili said nothing, her face at the window. Downstairs, more boot-stomping, then the screech of a phonograph.

'It worries me,' Greta said. 'I'm worried about you.'

As the sunlight moved across the floorboards, and another horn from the street blared, and the sailor below shouted at his wife, Lili felt something in her shift. Greta could no longer tell her what to do.

The painting was complete, and Greta now turned it to show Lili. The eyelet hem was gauzy against her legs, and the bouquet of roses looked like something mysterious blossoming from her lap. If only I were half as beautiful as that, Lili thought to herself. And then she thought she should send the painting to Henrik as a wedding gift.

'He's expecting me next week,' Lili said. 'Professor Bolk.'

The pain was returning, and Lili looked at her watch. Had it been eight hours since she swallowed her last pill? She began to check her handbag for the enamel pillbox. 'He and Frau Krebs already know I'm coming. They have my room waiting,' she said, opening drawers in the kitchen, hunting for the little case. It frightened her how quickly the pain could return; from nothing to violent ache in only a few minutes. Like the return of an evil spirit, it was.

'Have you seen my pillbox?' Lili asked. 'I think it was in my bag. Or maybe on the windowsill. Have you seen it, Greta?' With the heat and the pain, Lili's breath quickened. She said, 'Do you know where it is?' And then, tacked on like a gentle touch to the wrist, 'I'd like you to come to Dresden with me. To help me recover. The professor said you should probably come. He said I'll need someone there afterwards. You wouldn't mind, Greta, would you? You'll come with me, won't you, Greta? This one last time?'

'You realize, don't you,' Greta said, 'that this is it?'

'What do you mean? The pain was opening so quickly that Lili was having trouble seeing. She sat down, bending over. As soon as she found the pills the relief would come in a few minutes, less than five. But right now it felt as if a knife were cutting through her abdomen. She thought of her ovaries –

alive, Professor Bolk had promised. It was as if she could feel them inside her, swollen and throbbing, still healing nearly a year after the operation. Where had she left her pill case, and what did Greta mean: This is it? She looked across the room, to where Greta was unbuttoning her smock, hanging it on the hook next to the slatted door to the kitchen.

'I'm sorry,' Greta said. 'I can't.'

'You can't find my pills?' Lili said, blinking back the tears. 'Try the wardrobe. Maybe I put them in there.' All at once Lili felt as if she was about to pass out: the heat and the missing pills and the fiery anguish inside and Greta walking around the apartment saying I can't. I won't.

Then Greta's hand sank deep into the bottom drawer of the pickled-ash wardrobe. She pulled out the little enamel box and brought it to Lili and said, her own voice shaky with tears, 'I'm sorry, but I can't take you. I don't want you to go, and I'm not going to take you.' Her shrug turned into a shiver. 'You'll have to go to Dresden alone.'

'If Greta won't take you,' Carlisle said, 'then I will.' He had come to Copenhagen for the summer, and in the evenings, after her shift at Fonnesbech's, Lili would sometimes visit him at the Palace Hotel. They would sit at the open window and watch the shadows creep across the bricks of Rådhuspladsen, and the young men and women in their thin summer clothes meeting up on their way to the jazz clubs in Nørrevold. 'Greta always did what she wanted,' Carlisle would say. Lili would correct him and say, 'Not always. She's changed.'

They began to prepare for the trip. They booked passage on the ferry to Danzig, and Lili, one day in her lunch break, bought two new dressing robes in the ladies' department of Fonnesbech's. She told her boss, whose arms folded up the moment Lili began to speak, that she'd be leaving in a week. 'Will you be back?' demanded the woman, whose black blouse made her look like a lump of coal.

'No,' Lili said. 'From there, I'm leaving for New York.'

And that was what added to the difficulty of the trip to

Dresden. Professor Bolk told her she should expect to stay a month. 'We'll operate right away,' he cabled. 'But your recovery will take time.' Lili showed the telegrams to Carlisle, who read them much as his sister had read them – with the paper pushed away from his face, his head tilted. But Carlisle didn't argue; he didn't advise otherwise. He read through the correspondence and said, when he was done, 'What exactly is Bolk going to do?'

'He knows I want to become a mother,' Lili said.

Carlisle nodded, made a little frown. 'But how?'

Lili looked at him, and suddenly feared that he might try to interfere. 'The same way he made me out of Einar.'

His glance ran up and down Lili; she could feel his eyes on her ankles, which were crossed, to her lap, to her small breasts, to her throat, which rose like a stem from the ring of amber beads. Carlisle stood: 'It's all very exciting for you. It's what I suppose you've always wanted.'

'Since I was little.'

'Yes,' Carlisle said. 'What little girl doesn't want that?' It was true, and Lili was relieved that Carlisle had agreed to travel with her. For a few days she had begged Greta to change her mind. Greta had held Lili in her arms, Lili's face in Greta's shoulder, and said, 'I think it's a mistake. I'm not going to help you make a mistake.' Lili packed her suitcase and picked up the ferry tickets with a light sense of dread, and she wrapped her sheer summer shawl around her shoulders as if fighting a chill.

She told herself to think of it as an adventure: the ferry to Danzig, the night train to Dresden, the month-long stay at the Municipal Women's Clinic. From there she would travel to New York. She had sent word to Henrik that she would arrive by the 1st of September. She began to think of herself as a voyager, embarking for a world only she could imagine. When she shut her eyes, she could see it: the living room of a New York apartment, with a police whistle rising from the street, and a baby bouncing in her lap. She imagined a little table with a doily across its surface and the silver double-oval frame holding two photographs, one of Henrik and her on their wedding day, the second of their first child in his long, eyelet-hemmed christening gown.

Lili needed to sort through her belongings to make sure everything was crated up so that when she sent for them, all would be ready. There were the clothes: the capped-sleeve dresses from that summer in Menton; and the dresses with the beaded embroidery from her days in Paris, before she became sick; and the rabbit-fur coat with the hood. Most of it, she realized, she wouldn't want in New York. They now seemed cheap, as if someone else had bought them, as if another woman's body had worn them thin.

Late one afternoon, as Lili was packing up the crates and sinking nails through their lids, Greta said, 'What about Einar's paintings?'

'His paintings?'

'Some are left. Stacked in my studio,' Greta said. 'I thought you might want them.'

Lili didn't know what to think. His paintings no longer hung in the apartment, and now for some reason she couldn't quite imagine what they looked like: small gold frames, scenes of the frozen earth, but what else?

'Can I see them?'

Greta brought her the canvases, rolled up inside-out, their edges fringed with a heavy waxy thread. She opened them across the floorboards, and it felt to Lili as if she had never seen them before. Most were of a bog: one was in winter, with hoarfrost and a dingy sky; one was in summer, with peat moss and a late-night sun; another was simply of the soil, blue-grey from the morainic clays mixed with lime. They were small and beautiful, and Greta continued to unroll them across the floor, ten, then twenty, then more, like a carpet of wild flowers blossoming beneath the eye. 'Did he really paint them all?'

'He once was a very busy man,' she said.

'Where is it?'

'You don't recognize the bog?'

'I don't think so.' It troubled her, for she knew she should know the place: it had the familiarity of a face lost in the past.

'You don't remember it at all?'

'Only vaguely.' Downstairs, the phonograph came on, an accordion polka, mixed with horn.

'The Bluetooth bog,' Greta said.

'Where Einar was born?'

'Yes. Einar and Hans.'

'Have you ever been there?' Lili asked.

'No, but I've seen so many paintings and heard so much about it that when I shut my eyes it's as if I can see it.'

Lili studied the paintings, the bog surrounded by hazel bushes and linden trees, and a great oak seemingly growing around a boulder. She had a memory, although it wasn't her own, of following Hans down a trail, the muck sucking her boots as she stepped. She remembered throwing things stolen from her grandmother's kitchen into the bog and watching them sink for ever: a dinner plate, a pewter bowl, an apron with cottongrass strings. There was the work of cutting the peat into bricks, and the hoeing in the sphagnum field. And Edvard I, a runt of a dog, one day slipping off a lichen rock and drowning in the black water.

Greta continued to lay out the paintings, holding down their corners with her bottles of paint and saucers from the kitchen. 'It's where he was from,' she said, on her hands and knees, her hair falling into her face. Methodically she unrolled each painting and anchored its corners and then aligned it into the grid she was creating of dozens and dozens of the little pictures that made up much of Einar's work.

Lili watched her, the way Greta's eyes focused in on the tip of her nose. Her bracelets rattled around her wrists as she worked. The front room of the Widow House, with its windows facing north, south and west, filled with the quiet colours of Einar's paintings: the greys and the whites and the muted yellows and the brown of mud and the deep black of a bog at night. 'He used to work and work, through the day, and the next day again,' Greta said, her voice soft and careful and unfamiliar.

'Can you sell them?' Lili said.

Greta stopped. The floor was nearly covered, and she stood and looked for a place to step. She had cornered herself against the wall, by the iron-footed stove. 'You mean you don't want them?'

Something in Lili knew she was making a mistake, but she said it anyway: 'I don't know how much room we'll have,' she said. 'I'm not sure Henrik would like them. What with his own paintings. He prefers things more modern. After all,' Lili said, 'it's New York.'

Greta said, 'It's just that I thought you might want them. At least some of them?'

When Lili shut her eyes, she too saw the bog, and the family of white dogs, and a grandmother guarding her stove, and Hans, sprawled over the curve of a mica-flecked rock, and then, strangely, young Greta in the soap-green hallway of the Royal Academy of Art, a fresh pack of red-sable brushes in her fist. 'I found the art shop,' Greta was saying, in that lost memory.

'It's not that I don't want them,' Lili heard herself saying, this day, one of her last in the Widow House, already slipping away into memory. But whose memory? 'I just can't take them with me,' and she shuddered, for suddenly it felt as if everything around her belonged to someone else.

Twenty-eight

❧

The day after Lili and Carlisle left for Dresden, there was a summer storm. Greta was in the flat, in the front room, watering the ivy in the pot on the Empire side table. The room was grey without the sun, and Edvard IV was asleep next to her trunk. The sailor below was out at sea, probably caught in the roll of the storm that very minute, and there was a clap of thunder, and then the giggle of the sailor's wife.

It was funny, Greta thought. How the years had passed, the endless repetition of the flat sunrises over Denmark and, across the globe, the sunset crashing against the Arroyo Seco and the San Gabriel Mountains. Years in California and Copenhagen, years in Paris, years married and not, and now here she was, in the emptied Widow House, trunks loaded and locked. Lili and Carlisle would arrive in Dresden later that day, if the rain hadn't delayed them. Yesterday she and Lili had said goodbye at the ferry dock. People around them, heaving luggage, dogs in arms, a team wheeling their bicycles up the plank. Hans was there, and Carlisle, and Greta and Lili, and hundreds of others, all saying *au revoir*. A pack of schoolchildren herded by their headmistress. Thin young men, hunting employment. A countess headed for a month of mineral baths in Baden-Baden. And Greta and Lili, next to each other, holding hands and forgetting about the rest of the world around them. One last time Greta shoved away the rest of the world, and everything she knew and felt shrunk down to the tiny circle of intimacy where Greta and Lili stood, her arm now around Lili's waist. They promised to write to each other. Lili promised she would take care of herself. Lili said, her voice nearly inaudible, they would see each other in America. Yes, Greta said, having trouble imagining it. But she said, 'Yes, indeed.' When she thought about it, a horrible shiver ran up her spine, her western spine, because it felt – this departure at the dock – as if she had somehow failed.

Greta was now waiting for Hans's horn from the street. Outside, the spires and the gables and the slate roofs were black in the storm, the Royal Theatre's dome as dull as old pewter. Then came Hans's call, and Greta scooped Edvard IV into her arms and shut out the lights, the bolt of the lock turning heavily.

The storm continued, and the drive out of the city was slippery. The apartment houses were stained with rain. Puddles were swallowing the kerbs. Greta and Hans witnessed a plump woman on a bicycle, her body battened down in a raincoat, crash into the rear ramp of a mason's lorry. Greta pressed her hands to her mouth as she watched the woman's eyes shut with fear.

Once they were beyond the city limits, the gold Horch, with its white cabriolet top buckled closed, began to roll across the fields. Meadows of Italian rye grass and timothy and fescue and cocksfoot were damp and dented in the rain. Red and white clover, lucerne-grass and trefoil lined the road, bent and dripping. And beyond the fields the kettle-hole lakes, dimpled and deep.

The ferry ride to Århus was choppy, and Hans and Greta sat in the front seat of the Horch during the crossing. The car smelled of Edvard's wet coat, curled by the damp. Hans and Greta didn't speak, and she could feel the churn of the ferry's engines when she set her hand on the dash. Hans asked her if she needed a coffee, and she said yes. He took Edvard IV with him, and when she was alone in the car she thought of the journey Lili and Carlisle were on; in a few hours they'd probably be settling into the room at the clinic with the view over the willows in the back-park down to the Elbe. Greta thought of Professor Bolk, whose likeness she had captured in a painting that never sold; it sat rolled up behind the wardrobe. And when she returned to Copenhagen in a few days, when she finished sorting through her furniture and her clothes and her paintings, she would send it on to him, Greta told herself. It could hang behind Frau Krebs's reception desk, in a grey wood frame. Or in his office, above the sofa, where, in a few years, other desperate women like Lili would surely come in pilgrimage.

It was night when they arrived in Bluetooth. The brick villa was dark, the baroness already retired to her apartment on the third floor. A butler with a few tufts of white hair and a snub nose led Greta to a room with a bed covered in a slip of lace. He turned on the lamps, his snub-nosed face bent forward, and lifted the windows. 'Not afraid of frogs?' he said. Already she could hear them croaking in the bog. When the butler left, Greta opened the windows some more. The night was clear, with a half-cut moon low in the sky, and Greta could see the bog through an opening in the ash and elm trees. It looked almost like a damp field, or a great lawn in Pasadena soaked after a January rain. She thought of the earthworms that were driven from the ground after a winter downpour, the way they writhed on the flagstone paths, trying to save themselves from drowning. Had she really been the type of child who would cut them in two with a butter knife stolen from her mother's pantry and then present them to Carlisle on a plate, beneath a silver warming bell?

The curtains were made of a blued eyelet and they hung down and across the floorboards, fanning themselves out like wedding trains. Hans knocked and said, through the door, 'I'm down the hall, Greta. If you need anything.' There was something in his voice. Greta could sense his curled knuckle pressed against the panelled door, his other hand gently on the knob. She could imagine him in the hall, lit by a single wall sconce at the top of the stairs. She imagined the point of his forehead pressing the door.

'Nothing now,' she said. And there was a silence, only the frogs chorusing on their patches of peat, and the owls in the elms. 'All right then,' Hans said, and Greta couldn't quite hear him retreat to his room, his stockinged feet padding across the runner. Their time would come, she told herself. All in time.

The next day Greta met Baroness Axgil in the breakfast room. The room looked out towards the bog, which sparkled through the trees. Around the room potted ferns balanced in iron stands, and a collection of blue-and-white porcelain plates was secured to the wall. Baroness Axgil was gaunt and long-limbed, her hands backed with rubbery veins. Her head, also Borreby in size and shape, was held up by a throat tight with tendons. Her silver hair was pulled back snugly, slanting her eyes. The baroness sat at the head of the table, Hans opposite her, Greta in the middle. The butler served smoked salmon and hard-boiled eggs and triangles of buttered bread. Baroness Axgil said only, 'I'm afraid I don't remember an Einar Wegener. W-E-G, did you say? So many boys came through the house. Did he have red hair?'

'No, it was brown,' Hans said.

'Yes. Brown,' said the baroness, who had invited Edvard IV into her lap and was feeding him strips of salmon. 'A nice boy, I'm sure. Dead how long?'

'About a year,' Greta replied, and she looked to one end of the breakfast-room table and then to the other and was reminded of another breakfast room on the other side of the world where a woman not unlike the baroness still reigned.

Later in the day Hans led her down a path alongside a sphagnum field to a farmhouse. It had a thatched roof and timber eaves, and a puff of smoke was rising from the chimney. Hans and Greta didn't approach the yard, where there were hens in a coop and three small children scratching the mud with sticks. A woman with yellow hair was in the door, squinting against the sun, watching her children, two boys and a girl. A pony in its pen sneezed, and the children laughed, and old Edvard IV trembled at Greta's leg. 'I'm not sure who they are,' Hans said. 'Been there a while.'

'Do you suppose she'll let us in if we ask? To have a look around?'

'Let's not,' Hans said, his hand falling to the small of her back, where it remained as they returned across the field. The long blades of grass swiped at her shins. And Edvard IV chugged behind.

In the graveyard, there was a wooden cross marked WEGENER. 'His father,' Hans said. A grassy grave in the shade of a red alder. The graveyard was next to a whitewashed church, and the ground was uneven, and flinty, and the sun burning the dew off the rye grass made the air smell sweet.

'I have his paintings,' she said.

'Keep them,' Hans said, his hand still on her.

'What was he like then?'

'A little boy with a secret. That's all. No different from the rest of us.'

The sky was high and cloudless, and the wind ran through the red alder's leaves. Greta stopped herself from thinking about the past and thinking about the future. Summer in Jutland, no different from the summer days of his youth, the days when Einar was certainly both happy and sad at once. She had returned home without him. Greta Waud, tall in the grass, her shadow lowering itself across the graves, would return home without him.

On the drive back to Copenhagen, Hans said, 'What about California? Are we still going?'

The Horch's twelve cylinders were running powerfully, the vibration shaking her skin. The sun was bright, and the top was down, and there was a strip of paper swirling about Greta's ankles. 'What did you say?' she yelled, holding her hair in her fist.

'Are we going to California together?' And just as the wind was rushing around her, sending her hair and the lap of her dress and the strip of paper whirling, her thoughts began to pass chaotically through her head: her little room in Pasadena with the arched window overlooking the roses; the *casita* on the lip of the Arroyo Seco, now let to tenants, a family with a baby boy; the blank windows of Teddy Cross's old ceramics studio on Colorado Street, transformed after the fire into a

printer's press; the members of the Pasadena Arts & Crafts
Society in their felt berets. How could Greta return to that?
But there was more in her head, and then Greta thought of the
mossy courtyard of the *casita*, where in the light filtering
through the avocado tree she painted her first portrait of Teddy
Cross; and the little bungalows Carlisle was building on the
streets off California Boulevard, where newlyweds from
Illinois were settling; and the acres of orange groves. Greta
looked to the sky, to the pale blue that reminded her of the
antique plates on the walls of the baroness's breakfast room. It
was June, and in Pasadena the rye grass would have burned out
by now, and the palm fronds would be brittle, and by now the
maids would have pulled the beds on to the sleeping porches.
There was a sleeping porch at the rear of the house; its screens
were on hinges, and as a girl she would open them up and stare
out, across the Arroyo Seco to the Linda Vista hills, and she
would sketch the rolling dry-green sight of Pasadena. She
imagined unpacking her paints and screwing together her easel
on the sleeping porch and painting that vista now: the grey-
brown of the blur of the eucalyptus, the dusty green of the
stalks of cypress, the flash of pink stucco of an Italianate
mansion peeking through the oleander, the grey of a cement
balustrade overlooking the expanse of it all.

'I'm ready to go,' Greta said.

'What's that?' Hans called, through the wind.

'You'll love it out there. It will make the rest of the world
seem very far away.' She reached over and stroked Hans's
thigh. It had all come to this: she and Hans would return to
Pasadena, and she realized that no one out there would ever
fully understand what had happened to her. The girls from the
Valley Hunt Club, now married certainly, with children taking
tennis lessons on the club's courts, would know nothing about
her except for the fact that she had returned with a Danish
baron. Already Greta could hear the gossip: 'Poor Greta
Waud. Widowed again. Something mysterious happened to
the latest. A painter of some sort. Some sort of mysterious
death. In Germany, I think I heard. But not to worry – now

she's back, and this time with a baron. That's right, little Miss
Radical has returned to Pasadena, and as soon as she marries
this fellow she, of all people, will become a baroness.'

That was part of what lay ahead for Greta, but she took
comfort in the thought of going home. Her hand was on
Hans's thigh and he smiled at her, his knuckles white around
the Horch's wheel as he steered them back to Copenhagen.

A letter from Carlisle waited for her. After she read it, she
slipped it into the side pocket of one of the trunks she was
packing. So many things to ship home: her brushes and her
paints and dozens of notebooks and sketches of Lili. It was just
like Carlisle not to send enough news: the operation took
longer than Bolk had thought, almost a full day. Lili was
resting, sleeping from the morphia injections she still received.
I'll have to stay in Dresden longer than I planned, Carlisle
wrote. Another several weeks. Her recovery will take longer
than any of us guessed. Progress has been slow so far. The
professor is a kind man. He sends his regards. He says he's not
worried about her. If he's not worried about her, then I
suppose we shouldn't be either, wouldn't you agree?'

A week later Greta Waud and Hans Axgil boarded the
Deutscher Aero-Lloyd for the first leg of their trip to Pasadena.
They would fly to Berlin, and then to Southampton; from
there they'd sail. The aeroplane, reflecting the fine summer
day, was on the tarmac of the Amager Aerodrome. Greta stood
with Hans and watched the skinny boys load their trunks and
crates into the silver belly of the aeroplane. Further down the
tarmac was a cluster of people around a platform, where a man
in a top hat was giving a speech. He had a beard, and a little
Danish flag on the corner of his lectern was flapping in the
wind. Behind him was the *Graf Zeppelin*, long and stormy
grey, like an enormous ribbed bullet. The people in the crowd
began to wave little Danish flags. She had read in *Politiken* that
the *Graf Zepp* was setting out on a polar flight. Greta watched
the crowd cheer, as the zeppelin hovered above the tarmac.
'Do you think they'll make it?' she asked Hans.

He was reaching for his calfskin valise. The aeroplane was ready for them. 'Why shouldn't they?'

The man making the speech was a politician she didn't recognize. Probably running for Parliament. And behind him was the *Graf Zepp*'s captain, Franz Josef Land, in a sealskin cap. He wasn't smiling. His eyebrows were bunched together over his glasses and he looked concerned.

'It's time,' Hans said.

She took his elbow, and they found their seats in the aeroplane. She could see the zeppelin through her window, and the crowd, which was moving away from the aircraft. Men in shirtsleeves and braces were beginning the untethering. The captain was standing in the doorway of his little cabin, waving farewell.

'He looks as if he wonders if he'll ever come back,' Greta said, as the aeroplane's porthole door locked with the turn of a wheel.

The voyage out on the *Empress of Britannia* was smooth, and the passengers sat in their striped loungers on the teak deck, and Greta thought of the handstand she performed when she was ten. She screwed together her easel, twisting its butterfly bolts through the holes in its legs. She pulled a blank canvas from one of her trunks, nailing it to a frame. And on the ship's deck, she began to paint from memory: the hills of Pasadena rising out of the Arroyo Seco, dry and brown in early summer, the jacaranda trees having shed their blossoms, and the last day-lily folding in the heat. With her eyes closed, she could see it all.

In the mornings Hans kept to himself in his stateroom, going through his papers and preparing for his arrival in California, where they would marry in the garden of the Waud house. In the late afternoons he would move a deck chair to her side. 'We're off at last,' he would say.

'Homeward bound,' she would say. 'I never thought I wanted to go home.'

It had come to this, Greta would think over and over, the

moist tip of her brush dipping into the paint. The shift of the past, the sprawl of the future; all of it she had navigated both rashly and cautiously, and it had come to this. Hans was handsome with his legs stretched out on the chaise. He was half in the sun, half out, Edvard IV at his feet. The ship's engines churned on and on. Its bow prised the ocean in two, splitting the endless dimpled water into halves, cutting what had once seemed interminably one into two. Greta and Hans each continued to work in the slanting light, in the air heavy with salt, through the dusk falling red and flat over the blank, shrinking sea, until the moon rose and the white party lights strung along the ship's rail came on and the chill of evening would send them to their stateroom, where they would be together at last.

Twenty-nine

❧

It was late July before Lili was awake long enough during the day to remember anything. For nearly six weeks she had lolled in and out of consciousness, vomiting in her sleep, haemorrhaging between her legs and in her abdomen. Every morning and night Frau Krebs would replace the bandages taped over her pelvis, pulling away the old ones that looked like scraps of royal velvet, so red and bright they were. Lili was aware of Frau Krebs changing the dressing and the gauze, and the welcoming sting of the morphia needle, and, on many days, the pressure of the rubber ether mask. Lili knew that someone was there laying a damp rag across her forehead, changing it when it warmed.

On some nights she would wake and recognize Carlisle asleep in the chair in the corner, his head back against the cushion, his mouth open. She didn't want to wake him – so kind he was to spend the night at her side. She'd tell herself to let him rest; she'd turn her head on the pillow and look at Carlisle, his face oiled with sleep, and his fingers curled around the loop holding the cushion to the chair's back. She wanted him to sleep through the night: and she'd watch his chest rise and fall, and think of the day they spent together before this last operation. Carlisle took her to a beach on the Elbe, where they swam in the current, and then sunned themselves on a blanket. 'You'll make quite a mother,' Carlisle said. Lili wondered why it was so easy for him to imagine it, but not Greta. When she closed her eyes Lili sometimes thought she could smell the powdery scent of a bundled infant. She could nearly feel the little dense weight of a child in her arms. She told this to Carlisle, who said, 'I can see it too.'

On the riverbank he ran his hand over his arm, pushing off the water. His wet hair was matted around his face, and then he said, 'It's hard for Greta, this part is.'

A tourist steamer was coughing up black exhaust, and Lili plaited the fringe of the blanket, weaving in blades of grass. 'I'm sure in some ways she misses Einar,' Carlisle said.

'I can understand that.' She filled with that strange feeling she got when Einar was mentioned: like a ghost passing through her, it was. 'Do you think she'd come and visit me?'

'Here, in Dresden? She might. I don't see why not.'

Lili turned on her side and watched the black column of exhaust rise and shift. 'You'll write to her, then? After the operation?'

A few days after the surgery, when Lili's fever stabilized, he wrote to Greta. But she didn't reply. He wrote again, and again there was no answer. He telephoned but heard through the static only a tinny, endless ring. A telegram couldn't be delivered. It took a cable to Landmandsbanken to discover that Greta had returned to California.

Now, in the middle of the night, Lili didn't want to disturb Carlisle's sleep, but she could barely remain silent. The pain was returning, and she was gripping the sash of the blanket, shredding it in fear. She concentrated on the bulb in the ceiling, biting her lip, but soon the pain had spread through her body, and she was screaming, begging for a morphia injection. She cried for ether. She whimpered for her pills laced with cocaine. Carlisle began to stir, his face lifting; for an instant he stared at her, his eyelids fluttering, and Lili knew he was trying to figure out where he was. But then he was awake and went to find the night nurse, who herself was asleep at her station. Within a minute the ether mask clamped down around Lili's nose and mouth and she slipped away for the rest of the night.

'Feeling any better today?' Professor Bolk asked on his morning rounds.

'Maybe a little,' Lili would try.

'The pain down at all?'

'A bit,' Lili would reply, even though it wasn't true. She'd try to push herself up in her bed. When the professor entered her room she would worry about how she looked; if only he would knock and give her a chance to apply her coral lipstick and her Rouge Fin de Théâtre, which was sitting on the table in its red tin the size of a biscuit, just beyond her reach. She must be quite a sight, she'd think as the professor, so handsome in his crisp lab coat, scanned down the paperwork on his clipboard.

'Tomorrow we should try to get you to walk,' the professor would say.

'Well, if I'm not ready tomorrow, then I'll surely be ready the day after,' Lili would say. 'Most likely the day after tomorrow I'll be up to it.'

'Is there anything I can do for you?'

'You've already done so much,' Lili would say.

Professor Bolk would turn to leave, but then Lili would force herself to ask what she most wanted to know: 'Henrik is waiting for me in New York. Do you think I'll make it to New York by September?'

'Without a doubt.'

The professor's voice, when he reassured her this way, was like a hand on her shoulder. She would then nod off to sleep, dreaming of nothing in particular but knowing, vaguely, that all would work out.

Sometimes she'd hear the professor and Carlisle talking outside her door. 'What can you tell me?' Carlisle would say.

'Not much. She seems pretty much the same today. I'm trying to get her more and more stable.'

'Is there anything we should be doing for her?'

'Just let her sleep. She needs her rest.'

Lili would turn on her side and nod off, wanting more than anything to obey the professor's orders. If she knew anything at all, she knew he was always right.

One day a voice in the hall woke her up. It was familiar, a

woman's voice from long ago, coppery and large. 'What's he doing for her?' Lili heard Anna ask. 'Hasn't he got any other ideas?'

'Only in the last couple of days did he begin to worry,' Carlisle said. 'Only yesterday did he admit that the infection should have cleared up by now.'

'What can we do?'

'I've been asking that myself. Bolk says there's nothing to do.'

'Is she taking anything?'

Then in the hall there was a crash of two trolleys, and Lili couldn't hear the voices, just Frau Krebs telling a nurse to be more careful.

'The transplant isn't working,' Carlisle said. 'He's going to have to remove the uterus.' And then, 'How long are you here for?'

'A week. I have two Carmens at the Opernhaus.'

'Yes, I know. Before the operation, Lili and I were out and she saw the poster. She knew you would be coming at the end of the summer. She's had that to look forward to.'

'And her marriage.'

'You've heard from Greta?' Carlisle said.

'She wrote to me. She's probably in Pasadena by now. Settled. You know about her and Hans?'

'I was supposed to be returning now myself,' Carlisle said.

Lili couldn't hear what Anna said next. She wondered why Anna hadn't come into the room yet. She could picture Anna bursting through the door and throwing back the yellow curtain. She'd be wearing a green silk tunic beaded in the collar, a matching turban swirling up from her head. Her lips would be as bright as blood, and Lili could imagine the mark they'd leave on her cheek. Lili thought about calling out, 'Anna!' Crying, 'Anna, are you going to come in and say hello?' But Lili's throat was dry, and she felt incapable of prising her mouth open to say anything at all. It was all she could do to turn her head to look to the door.

'Is it grave?' Anna said in the hall.

'I'm afraid Bolk hasn't really let on about what's likely to come next.'

Then they said nothing, and Lili was left to lie in her bed, motionless, except for the slow dull thump of her heart. Where had Carlisle and Anna gone?

'Is she sleeping now?' Anna finally said.

'Yes. She's in between morphia shots in the early afternoons. Can you come by tomorrow after lunch?' Carlisle said. 'But poke your head in now and have a look. So I can tell her you've been here.'

Lili heard the door crack open. She could feel another person enter the room – that subtle reshifting of air, the nearly imperceptible change in temperature. Anna's perfume drifted to Lili's bed. She recognized it from the counter at Fonnesbech's. It came in a short little bottle with a gold-mesh tassel, but Lili couldn't think of the name. Eau-de-Provence, or something like that. Or was it La Fille de Provence? She didn't know, and she couldn't open her eyes to greet Anna. She couldn't speak, and she couldn't see anything, and she couldn't raise her hand to wave hello. And Lili then knew that Carlisle and Anna were standing at the side of her bed and there was nothing she could do to tell them that she knew they were there.

The next day, after lunch, Carlisle and Anna bundled Lili into her wicker wheelchair. 'It's too beautiful not to be outside,' he was saying as he tucked the blanket around her. Anna wrapped Lili's head in a long magenta scarf, building a turban on her head that matched her own. Then they pushed Lili into the clinic's park, settling her against a gooseberry shrub. 'Do you like the sun, Lili?' Anna asked. 'Do you like it out here?'

Other girls were on the lawn. It was Sunday, and some had visitors who brought them magazines and boxes of chocolate. There was a woman in a pleated polka-dot dress who gave a girl chocolates wrapped in the gold foil from the shop on Unter den Linden.

Lili could see Frau Krebs in the *Wintergarten*, surveying the lawn and the girls and the curve of the Elbe below. She looked small from this far, as small as a child. Then she disappeared. It was her afternoon off, and all the girls liked to gossip about what Frau Krebs did in her spare time, even though the truth was that she headed into her garden with a hoe.

'Should we go for a walk?' Carlisle said, releasing the handbrake and pushing Lili across the stony grass. There were rabbit holes in which the wheels bounced, and although the rocking rattled her with pain, Lili couldn't help thinking how glad she was to be outside the clinic with Carlisle and Anna. 'Are we going down to the Elbe?' Lili asked when she saw that Carlisle was steering her away from the dirt path that led to the river.

'We'll get there,' Anna said, and they pushed Lili through a curtain of willows. They were moving fast, and Lili held the chair's arms as it hit tree roots and rocks. 'I thought I'd take you out for a bit,' Carlisle said.

'But I'm not allowed,' Lili said. 'It's against the rules. What would Frau Krebs say?'

'No one will know,' Anna said. 'Besides, you're a grown woman. Why shouldn't you leave if you want to?' Soon they were beyond the clinic's gate and out in the street. Carlisle and Anna pushed her through the neighbourhood, past the villas set back behind brick walls spiked with iron cupolas. The sun was warm but a breeze was running up the street, revealing the underside of the elm leaves. In the distance Lili heard the bell of a tram.

'Do you think they'll miss me?' she said.

'So what if they do,' said Carlisle; the way his face was tight with focus, the way he swatted his hand through the air again reminded Lili of Greta. It was almost as if Lili could hear the tinkle of silver jewellery. She had a memory – as if it were a story once told to her – of Greta sneaking down Kronprinses-segade with Einar in tow. Lili could remember the heat of Greta's hand in her own, the brush of a silver bangle against her fingers.

Soon Lili and Carlisle and Anna were crossing the Augustus-
brücke. In front of Lili lay all of Dresden: the Opernhaus, the
Catholic Hofkirche, the Italian-styled Academy of Art, and the
seemingly floating dome of the Frauenkirche. They came to
Schlossplatz and the foot of the Brühlsche Terrace. A
hunchback with a cart was selling bratwurst in a bun and
pouring glasses of apple wine. Business was good for him, a
queue of eight or ten people waiting, their faces growing pink
in the sun. 'Doesn't that smell good, Lili?' Carlisle said, as he
pushed her to the stairs.

Forty-one steps led to the terrace, where Sunday strollers
were out, leaning against the rail. The steps were adorned by
the Schilling bronzes of Morning, Noon, Evening and Night.
There was a fine grit on the steps, and from the base Lili
watched the long yellow skirt of a woman and the disc of her
straw hat climb the stairs, her arm looped through a man's.
'But how will we get up?' Lili asked.

'Not to worry,' Carlisle said, turning her chair around. He
gave it a pull up the first step.

'But your leg,' Lili said.

'I'll be all right,' Carlisle said.

'And what about your back?'

'Didn't Greta ever tell you about our famous western
spines?'

And with that, Carlisle, who never once, as far as Lili knew,
blamed Greta for his dented leg, began to lug Lili up the stairs.
With each bounce came a horrible jolt of pain, and Anna gave
Lili her hand to squeeze.

The terrace looked out across the Elbe to the Japanese
Palace and the right bank. Traffic in the river was heavy, with
the paddle-boats and the coal freighters and the dragon-fronted
gondolas and the rent-a-day rowing boats. Carlisle locked the
brake of Lili's chair in the space between two benches, beneath
one of the square-trimmed poplars, at the terrace's rail. Carlisle
stood next to her, Anna on her other side. Lili could sense
their hands on the back of her chair. Young couples were on
the terrace, holding hands, boys buying girls sacks of grape-

flavoured candy from a vendor with a cart. On the grassy beach on the other side of the Elbe, four little boys were flying a white rag-tail kite.

'Look how high their kite is!' Anna pointed to the boys. 'Higher than the city, it seems.'

'Do you think they'll lose it?' Lili said.

'Would you like a kite, Lili?' Anna said. 'Tomorrow we'll get you one if you like.'

'What do they call this place?' Carlisle said. 'The balcony of Europe?'

They said nothing for a while, and then Carlisle said, 'I think I'll go and buy a bratwurst from that little man. Are you hungry, Lili? Can I get you anything?'

She wasn't; she no longer ate much at all, which of course Carlisle knew. Lili tried to say, 'No, thank you,' but couldn't form the words.

'Do you mind if we go off for a few minutes to find that man?' Anna said. 'We won't be gone more than a minute or two.'

Lili nodded, and Carlisle's and Anna's shoes ground through the gravel, drifting away. Lili shut her eyes. The balcony of the whole world, she thought. Of my whole world. She could feel the sun on her eyelids. She heard a couple one bench over crunching on their sweets. And beyond that the slap of water on the side of a boat. A tram called, and then the bell of the cathedral. And for once Lili stopped thinking about the misty, double-sided past and the promise of the future. It didn't matter who she once was, or who she'd become. She was Fräulein Lili Elbe. A Danish girl in Dresden. A young woman out in the afternoon with a pair of friends. A young woman whose dearest friend was off in California, leaving Lili, it suddenly felt, alone. She thought of each of them – Henrik, Anna, Carlisle, Hans, Greta. Each, in his own way, partially responsible for the birth of Lili Elbe. Now she knew what Greta had meant: the rest Lili would have to undergo alone.

When she opened her eyes, Lili saw that Carlisle and Anna hadn't yet returned. She wasn't worried; they'd come back for her. They would find her in her chair. Across the river the boys were running and pointing to the sky. Their kite was lifting higher than the willows, higher than even the Augustus-brücke. It was flying up over the Elbe, a white diamond of bedlinen reaching, bright from the sun, tugging on the boys' spool-rolled string. Then the line snapped, and the kite sailed free. Lili thought she heard the over-excited shrieks of little boys buried in the breeze, but that would have been impossible; they were too far away. But she had heard a muffled shriek somewhere; where had it come from? The boys were jumping up and down in the grass. The boy with the spool received a punch from one of his pals. And above them, the kite was trembling in the wind, swooping like an albino bat, like a ghost, up and up, and then down, rising again, crossing the Elbe, coming for her.

Author's Note

This is a work of fiction loosely inspired by the story of Lili Elbe and her wife, Gerda. I wrote the novel in order to explore the intimate space that defined their unique marriage, and that space could only come to life through conjecture and speculation and the running of imagination. Some important facts about Lili's actual transition lie in these pages, but the story, as recounted here with its details of place and time and language and interior life, is an invention of my imagination. In early 1931, when Lili first came out publicly as a trans woman in a series of interviews with a Danish journalist, newspapers around the world ran accounts of her remarkable life. Many of those articles were helpful in writing this novel, especially those in *Politiken* and other Danish newspapers, as were the obituaries published by the Danish press. Another indispensable source were Lili Elbe's diaries and correspondence, which Niels Hoyer edited and published after Lili's death as a semi-fictional, hybrid biography *Man Into Woman*. Those journal entries and letters provided critical factual details of Lili's transition, especially regarding the events in Chapter One, the mysterious bleeding and physical decline, and Lili's journey to and stay at the Dresden Municipal Women's Clinic. The passages in my book that deal with these incidents are especially indebted to Hoyer's assemblage of Lili Elbe's original words. Nonetheless, I have changed so many elements of the story that the characters in these pages are entirely fictional. The reader should not look to this novel for very many biographical details of Lili Elbe's life, and no other character in the novel has any relation to an actual person, living or dead.

Reading Group Notes

Afterword

When *Vanity Fair* released its first photo of Caitlyn Jenner earlier this summer, it made me think of another trans woman who introduced herself to the world through a portrait roughly a hundred years before: Lili Elbe. In 1930 Lili traveled from the Paris studio she shared with her wife, Gerda, to Germany, for a series of surgeries at the Dresden Municipal Women's Clinic to complete her transition. While there she liked to sit on the sunny banks of the Elbe River pondering her past, when she lived as a man – her assigned gender at birth – named Einar Wegener, and her future as herself. (The Elbe would inspire her new last name.) After departing the clinic, Lili tried to maintain her privacy, but news of her surgeries began to leak to the European press, so she took the bold step of telling her own story. In a series of interviews with a Danish journalist, Lili came out as a trans woman, describing her journey, the role of her wife in her transition, and how art – the couple were both painters – had influenced and shaped her vision of herself. For a brief period in the early 1930s, Lili Elbe was international news, recognised as one of the first recipients of gender affirmation surgery, her name printed in newspapers around the world. Now, with Eddie Redmayne portraying her in the film *The Danish Girl*, many more people recognise her for what she's always been – a trans pioneer.

Almost twenty years ago, when I was a young writer, I first read about Lili. Many elements of her story resonated with me – her courage to be herself; that she had transitioned while in a marriage; the evocative settings of Europe between the world wars; and her important place in LGBTIQ history. One detail in particular lit my imagination: Lili's wife, Gerda, had painted several oil portraits of Lili, depicting a beautiful woman with enormous black eyes and lips like two valentines. These portraits, begun early in her transition, were the first public images of Lili. They showed Lili lying on a divan, her arms behind her head; Lili playing cards with a leg up on her chair; Lili looking over her shoulder with hooded eyes and a gaze that can mean many things. The Lili paintings became a sensation in the art worlds of Copenhagen and Paris – viewers were drawn to the portraits of a woman whose expression had nearly as many interpretations as the Mona Lisa's. In the same way, Lili Elbe herself has many interpretations. She can mean many things to many people. This is in part what makes her legacy so rich and inspiring. For me, the more I thought about Lili I began to think of her life as a story of art, love, and identity.

An artist sees that which does not yet exist. He or she imagines a future others cannot perceive. The artist interprets reality, making it even more vivid and lasting. The story of Lili Elbe is a story of art, of creating, of imagining what is to be. It is about artists who interpreted the world, and themselves, through their art. Curiously, Lili insisted she was not an artist, despite the successful career she had as a painter before she transitioned. She said art and painting belonged to Einar (one of those paintings hangs beside me in my office as I type these words; it is of a French chateau, signed Einar Wegener). But I disagree with her protests. Lili was an artist – her greatest creation was herself. She imagined a future life and did everything she could to create it. I spent many long hours looking at Gerda's paintings of Lili. They are not literal depictions of Lili (just as Monet's haystacks are not literal); they are interpretations, highly stylised, symbolic, and alive in colour (lots of pinks, greens, and yellows). Yet they capture Lili's essence and spirit more vibrantly than any photographs I have seen of her. The world first met Lili through these portraits and through these portraits I first came to understand some of the colours, contours, and shadows of her soul.

The story of Lili Elbe is also a story of love. We articulate and express many of our emotions through our relationships, and I came to believe that a key to understanding Lili was through

Gerda. In their marriage they created a cove of intimacy where their love could be its most authentic and most vulnerable. It was in this private space that Lili first emerged. I was curious about how and why Gerda accepted Lili into their marriage and Gerda's role in Lili's transition. Was it out of love and devotion, nurturing and protecting, or were Gerda's motivations more complicated? Lili would become Gerda's greatest muse and some of her most celebrated paintings − now worth thousands of dollars − are those of Lili. With Lili, Gerda saw some of her ambitions as an artist fulfilled.

And the story of Lili Elbe is of course a story of identity. Lili is now recognised as an icon in the trans movement. Her life, both as she lived it and as she described it by coming out in interviews and in *Man into Woman*, the partially fictional biography she helped write before her death, expanded the public's understanding of gender identity at the time. Since then she has inspired many of us, both trans and cis, to be ourselves. Lili knew that a false life is no life at all. Who are we? Whom do we want to become? How do we perceive ourselves? How do we want to be perceived? − these questions of identity are often at the core of our internal struggles. Resolve them and you are closer to being free. Almost a century ago Lili Elbe conquered these questions for herself. She posed for a portrait in an artist's studio and said to the world, This is me.

David Ebershoff
September, 2015

A conversation with David Ebershoff

❧

How did you first hear about Lili Elbe?

Many years ago I read a brief mention of her. It described Lili as the first successful recipient of gender affirmation surgery (a claim that would turn out to be not correct; Lili was one of the first but not *the* first). I had always thought that Christine Jorgensen, a World War II vet from the Bronx, was the first, and so I wondered who this was and why her name was not more widely known. And I was curious that the story involved art, artists, and marriage.

This was so long ago that I did what a writer used to do before Google: I went to the New York Public Library and began to search for references to her. That led me to some of the news reports about Lili from the early 1930s when she first told her story to a Danish journalist. Other references, brief and often contradictory, ultimately led me to *Man into Woman*, which was published in 1933, not long after her death, as a semi-fictional biography. This is where my true research began. *Man into Woman* is an important source for anyone who wants to know more about Lili Elbe, but, for me at least, it raised nearly as many questions as it answered. This early research also led me to some images of Gerda's paintings, which opened an important window onto the story.

**What challenges were involved in creating a character
who is a transgender woman, and yet lived in an era that
long preceded the contemporary trans rights movement?**

One of the challenges of imagining Lili was thinking about past
and present. She was very specific about how she thought of
her past when she lived as a man: she spoke of Einar as another
soul. This probably does not reflect how many trans men and
women today describe their own experiences, but it is how Lili
described hers. So a fundamental question for me was how to
depict the past for a character who was very clear about making
a break from her past. Whose childhood is remembered, which
memories, both physical and emotional, belonged to whom?
Lili thought of, and talked about, Einar as someone else, often
describing him as her brother or a family member. I had to
navigate this in order to tell the story with both authenticity
and depth. Some of the language in *The Danish Girl* might strike
today's reader as out of sync with how trans men and women
talk about their experiences, but it is authentic to how Lili talked
about herself and how she saw herself. I love fiction that takes a
reader deep inside a character's heart; fiction that allows me to
know a character more deeply than we can know most human
beings, perhaps even ourselves. This is, and always has been, one
of the roles of historical fiction – imagination inspired by facts
can lead the reader to an intimacy that the facts do not permit.
So, with Lili, I decided I wanted the reader to understand a
version of her life as she perceived it, not as we perceive her from
today. I was more interested in knowing her as she knew (or did
not know) herself.

How did you research the facts that are left to us?

In some ways writing a novel, especially a novel set in the past
and about characters who once lived, is about amassing enough
details and arranging them properly in order to offer the reader
a verisimilitude that satisfies his or her curiosity about the story

at hand. Yet all of this must be done in a voice and style that makes the story the novelist's own. *The Danish Girl* was written with the assistance of five libraries, each of which provided me invaluable sources about the novel's subjects, themes, and places: the Royal Library and the Royal Academy of Arts Library, both in Copenhagen; the library at the Dresden Hygiene Museum; the New York Public Library; and the Pasadena Public Library.

Some of the most important references for the novel include the news reports on Lili's transition that appeared in the Danish press in 1930 and 1931, especially those in *Politiken* and *Nationaltidende*. In 1931, after news of her transition began to leak to the European press, Lili Elbe set out to describe her life to the public, co-operating on a series of stories in *Politiken*. These pieces told the world about her transition, describing her emotional journey as well as the doctors in Germany who evaluated her and performed her surgeries. Months after these pieces ran, in a final gesture to Lili Elbe's courageous and groundbreaking story, *Politiken* published a detailed obituary under the byline of Fru Loulou. There's reason to believe Lili played a role in preparing the obituary (just as she played a role in writing *Man into Woman*, even though it was published posthumously); hence, Lili, in characteristic fashion, helped script how the world would perceive her after she was gone.

Shortly after Lili Elbe died in 1931, her friend, Niels Hoyer, edited and shaped her diaries and correspondence and published them in a book under the title *Fra Mand til Kvinde* (*Man into Woman*). This was an invaluable source for me, especially about Lili's transition, her stay at the Dresden Municipal Women's Clinic, and the medical examinations and procedures. Lili anticipated the book's publication and worked hard on the manuscript in the final year of her life. She was keen to tell her story, but she was also conscious of creating a sort of myth about herself. Just as Gerda's highly stylised portraits depict an interpreted version of Lili, Lili's efforts in telling her story – the news accounts, her writings that would become *Man into Woman* – are a stylised, interpretive version of her life. They are crucial sources, but they are not entirely factual, which, as a fiction writer, I found freeing. After all, this is a story about artists who lived with an ethos of creating and envisioning and forming their own reality.

How much of *The Danish Girl* is based on fact? Why did you choose at times to stray from the facts – especially with regard to Greta, whose name in real life is Gerda Gottlieb?

Some of the basic events of Lili's transition are based on fact, including the dress in the studio, the mysterious bleeding, and the stay at the Dresden Municipal Women's Clinic. These events are based on the sources I describe above. But much of my novel is invented. Why? When I made my first research trip to Denmark and began amassing the outline of Lili's life, I was struggling with how to interpret the story. Without a doubt, Lili is a pioneer of the transgender movement; from our perspective today we can look back and understand her place in history and see her life as one of tremendous courage and self-acceptance. She deserves to be remembered and celebrated as one of the first recipients of gender affirmation surgery and one of the first to publicly come out, placing her at the forefront of a powerful and unfinished movement seeking civil rights and human dignity for all trans people. But even in my early days of working on the book, I realised that our perspective from the future was not the same as her perspective at the time. I was more interested in how she thought of herself and her life as she lived it than how history thinks of her now. I understand and welcome the impulse to lionise her and define her story within the context of our own understanding of what it means to be trans today; but *The Danish Girl* tries to bring the reader into her interior life, which is fundamentally different from trying to place her in history. (Of course I'm always happy to see journalists and scholars writing about her and putting her into that historical context, it's eminently useful and interesting. Since *The Danish Girl* was first published in 2000, some scholars and writers have done important and much-needed work expanding our knowledge of Lili and Gerda. Sabine Meyer, Pamela Caughie, and Nikolaj Pors have all done important work and Pors is writing what will be the definitive biography of Lili Elbe.)

One day while in Denmark, I took the train up the coast to Kronborg Castle in Elsinore, once home, or so I thought, to the prince of Denmark who inspired Shakespeare's *Hamlet*. While touring the castle, with its views over the Øresund to nearby Sweden, I learned how far from the facts Shakespeare had strayed to write one of the greatest works of literature in human history. Before anyone accuses me of comparing myself to Shakespeare, let me be clear that that's not what I mean by telling this story. But writers do learn from the masters. One lesson I took from Shakespeare that autumn day inside the cold yellow-grey stone walls of Kronborg Castle was that writers throughout history have simultaneously turned to and away from facts to reach the emotional core of a story. I wanted to convey the emotional essence of Lili's life as she herself perceived it. She had left some of that self-perception in the historical record, via interviews and letters, *Man into Woman*, and through her legacy as Gerda's greatest muse, but I believed there were vast blanks – unpainted canvases, so to speak – in need of filling in order to truly understand her heart. Those blank canvases in history are where I am drawn as a fiction writer.

So, back to your question about Greta. The more I thought about this story I realised that Lili's wife was not a supporting character but an equal, and that the space between them, the private cave of their marriage, as I describe it in the novel, was where I wanted to take the reader. Some of this was documented, but some wasn't, for the intimacies of a marriage, or any romantic relationship, often aren't recorded for history. To write a love story, the story of a marriage, would require imagination and speculation – creating some of the details of how they lived, how they worked, how they fought, how they loved and cared for one another, turned to and away from one another. I decided to invent a character, Greta, who is both like the historical figure Gerda, and not like her. Greta is inspired by the real Gerda, who was a painter and found success through Lili, but many of the details of her life in the book are invented by me. I changed her name and nationality (Gerda was Danish) as a way of saying this character conveys the emotional truth of the story while straying from some of the facts. If you read *The Danish Girl*, you will not learn all the biographical facts about the actual Gerda, and yet I believe you will have a portrait of who, at her essence, she really was.

One more thing about fact and fiction: in an interview with Terry Gross of *Fresh Air* the great novelist E.L. Doctorow laid out some principles of writing historical fiction. Doctorow has long been a hero of mine. *The Book of Daniel* is one of my favorite novels and he's been something of a model for me personally because he had a successful career as a book editor while also writing novels inspired by the past. In this interview he talks about the question of fact and fiction. He talks sceptically about 'a strict demarcation' between fiction and non-fiction. In talking about the historical characters he wrote about he says, 'I'm dealing with the fictions they themselves made of their lives' and says he was drawn to characters who 'promulgated a myth about themselves.' Doctorow explains he always began 'with the fictions people create about themselves' and then went from there.

This resonates with me profoundly and has been an important part of my writing life, not only in *The Danish Girl* but also in my last book *The 19th Wife* and to a certain extent the book I'm writing now. 'We all compose our lives every day,' Doctorow says. Every rendering is an interpretation. Every construction has elements of invention. We can see that in the paintings depicting Lili and in the way Lili tried to shape her narrative before she died.

Greta is a fascinating character. Why does Greta suggest the dress in the book's opening scene? What motivates her, and how does she reconcile these motives with the pain it also causes her?

Greta possesses an unusual combination of independence and fidelity. She is self-driven and fiercely individual, yet at the same time she holds a profound sense of dedication to her spouse. Even at the beginning of the novel she knows her spouse at the deepest levels (or thinks she does). Greta encourages Lili to be herself because she knows this is who she is – and truth is always enough of a reason for Greta. Except nothing is ever that simple. Greta's career takes off with her paintings of Lili. She needs Lili as much as Lili needs Lili. And I believe Greta is never fully honest with herself or Lili about how Lili affected her as an artist. Greta could not have become the artist of her ambitions without Lili. Their motives and actions are snarled and inextricable.

Why do you think the story of Lili Elbe was all but forgotten until recently?

One could speculate forever why Lili faded from public understanding for so many decades. Lili underwent her surgeries in the early 1930s, a time of great anxiety in the world, especially the parts of Western Europe where she lived – Copenhagen, Paris, Dresden. The dark cloud of economic disaster, Fascism, and, eventually, Nazism and war was already rolling over the Continent. It does not surprise me that this story was lost in the horrible events of the subsequent fifteen years. That is one reason. Yet, of course, another reason is the very nature of Lili's story. Even today, transgender men and women routinely face bigotry, ignorance, and often horrific violence. But in the 1930s, Lili's story was unimaginable to most of the world: with Lili Elbe, many were learning for the first time about what we now call gender affirmation surgery. Around the world newspapers reported Lili's story with a mixture of awe and judgment. It was a big story at the time, but when Lili Elbe died in 1931, even the most sympathetic newspapers in Copenhagen reported on her as more of a one-of-a-kind than the beginning of a movement. Few saw her as a pioneer of anything or representing anything more than herself. And yet her legacy refused to be drowned by the closing waters of history. Her courage was too immense to be forgotten.

What inspired you about this story to make it the subject of your first novel?

Marriage fascinates me: how we negotiate its span, how we change within it, how it changes itself, and why some relationships survive and others do not. There isn't a single marriage that couldn't provide enough narrative arc for a novel. As I see it, the heart of this story lies in the intimate space that made up this marriage. It was in that space, protected by love, where Lili could first express herself freely, could first know herself truthfully. I was very curious about a marriage that could welcome Lili into it. Put simply, it is the question that we perpetually ask ourselves: What is love? What is love capable of?

Something else I came to understand when I began to read about Lili Elbe is that we all, in some ways, struggle throughout our lives to learn who we are and accept ourselves. I believe everyone has at least once looked in the mirror and thought, 'The world cannot see me as I really am.' There is universality to Lili's question of identity. We all want to be accepted for who we are.

Discussion Points

- What is the true nature of the marriage depicted in *The Danish Girl*? What does this story say about love and intimacy?

- Both Lili and Greta must change, for the sake of their marriage and for themselves. Discuss each woman's evolution.

- What role does Greta play in Lili's transition? What motivated her to help Lili?

- How does the city of Copenhagen influence the lives of the characters?

- Greta loves the people in her life in different ways. How do her expressions of love change over the course of the novel?

- When Henrik says to Lili, 'I already know. Don't worry about anything but I already know', what does he mean? Why does Lili tell Henrik she can't see him anymore?

- What does art and painting symbolise for Greta and Lili?

- Why does Lili put so much faith in her final operation? What does it mean to her?

- Discuss how Lili views her life before her transition. What has she said goodbye to? What will she always carry with her?

- Why doesn't Lili tell Greta about remeeting Henrik?

❧ Should Greta have done more to stop Lili's last operation? Why or why not?

❧ Lili is a pioneer in the movement for civil rights for trans men and women. Discuss how much and how little has changed since her time. What makes Lili a hero?

❧ Discuss the people Lili feels are responsible for her life – Henrik, Anna, Carlisle, Hans, Greta.

You can visit David at www.ebershoff.com

W&N

THE BOOKSELLER INDUSTRY AWARDS

IMPRINT OF THE YEAR 2015

For literary discussion, author insight,
book news, exclusive content,
recipes and giveaways, visit the
Weidenfeld & Nicolson blog and
sign up for the newsletter at:

www.wnblog.co.uk

For breaking news, reviews and exclusive competitions
Follow us 🐦 @wnbooks